The Sex Scandal
That Rocked the
Porn Industry

Amberee

The Millionaire's Best Asset

Kaycee Quinn

Amberee, The Millionaire's Best Asset

First published in 2018
© 2018 Kaycee Quinn

CME Books
Penrith, Australia
http://amberee.blogspot.com.au

ISBN: 978-0-9942137-7-8

National Library of Australia
Cataloguing-in-Publication entry:
Quinn, Kaycee
Amberee, The Millionaire's Best Asset

10 9 8 7 6 5 4 3 2 1

WARNING:

ADULT CONTENT 18+

(Violence, Abuse, Sexually Explicit content, Socially Tabooed Topics, Disturbing Scenes)

This book is not Erotica.

But, the story contains graphical descriptions including or pertaining to sexually-explicit, socially unaccepted and tabooed subject-matters that may offend and or be sensitive to some people.

Therefore:

- **Potential Purchasers** are advised: do not purchase this book if you are easily offended by possibly offensive content.

- **Readers** are advised: you should only read this book on the full understanding that you may read scenarios and or specific details you wish you hadn't.

PART 1

THE OFFICIAL AMBEREE STORY

$\mathscr{C}$HAPTER 1

The story we, the general public, were fed (and for the most part fully and whole-heartedly believed) can be condensed to:

Amber Ebony, a young Australian girl, was raised by a loving single-parent father following the death of her mother in a car accident when she was nine years old. When Amber neared her sixteenth birthday, she had sex with a boy from school and enjoyed the sensation so much she undertook increasing risks so she experienced sex at every opportunity available to her.

Once her father discovered her mid-act with the young man (who couldn't believe his luck and had become legendary amongst his social group), he took a serious and hard-parenting line to force her to not see the boy or have sex again until she was old enough. But Amber had caught the 'sucking and fucking cock' bug; she brazenly and defiantly had sex with other boys from her school and when she was caught out once more and verbally threatened with consequences, she ran away from home.

Amber hitched a ride to Sydney with a truck driver who happily paid to have sex with the gorgeous young girl offering her 'puss for payment'. She headed straight for Kings Cross where she spent a couple of months working as a prostitute while she saved the money to get a passport and head over to America to sight-see.

The young girl easily found men prepared to pay handsomely to have her wrap her naturally rosy lips or puss around their hard on, and she spent a few months touring the country well able to afford her travels. But Amber had become so hooked on having sex, by the time she landed in Hollywood where she immediately secured a live action porn feed gig, after attending a porn flick as a means to discover new tricks on how to satisfy the men she happily serviced, she aspired and set out to become a porn star.

At first, she found the competition fierce. So the business-savvy Amber gave herself the porn name 'Amber E, porn starlet (later changing it to Amberee, porn princess) and snuck into a party where it was rumoured some of the best directors of the porn industry would attend; with the help of Amber's enthusiastic and brazen personality teamed up with one of the wealthy young men infatuated by her looks, they provided the party entertainment, informally 'auditioning' for all those in attendance.

Her gamble and ingenuity worked. Within days Amber had signed on to star in her first two porn flicks: *Ride Her High*, and *The Millionaire's Best Asset* which rocketed the young starlet to fame and fortune.

Amberee continued to do live action feeds for *The Porn Shack* in between her other films and photo shoots, which led to the unexpected offer for her to play the lead character in the non-porn film *The Sexhouse Slave* in which she played the incredibly convincing role of a sex trafficked girl who died at the hands of the abuse afflicted upon her, and which triggered a lot of controversy with the media questioning if Amberee porn princess was herself the victim of sex trafficking or an out of control nymphomaniac in serious need of society's help. Loyal and admiring fans of Amberee were thrilled at the opportunity she gave them to secretly star alongside her for the film's real sex scenes; and after the release of the movie, to wide critical acclaim, Amberee received even more offers to appear in men's magazines and advertise a range of products valued from as little as ten dollars to luxury items only the wealthy can afford to indulge in.

It emerged Amberee could put 'neither pretty feet wrong' until her fourteenth year in the industry when she foolishly misjudged public perception and regrettably signed on to star in the porn flick, *Absexlution*, the advanced news of which had many people in the general public outraged, incensed at the very idea of her playing a church priestess who absolves constituents sins through the acts of debauchery, and ultimately ended the life and success she had long worked so hard for.

A colourful background befitting the exuberant, playful, promiscuous starlet.

That's the fake story of *Amberee, porn princess* we've been fed through magazine articles and rare interviews.

Now let's hear the real story behind all the lies and misperceptions Amber Entacott has slowly revealed to me, about what really went on behind the scenes.

PART 2

CHOICELESS & VOICELESS

d

$\mathcal{C}$HAPTER 2

Hello, I'm the girl you may know as *Amberee, porn princess.*

This exposé is written in the hopes one day the guilty parties will be arrested, tried and jailed for their crimes. In books and movies, for legal reasons, names and places are often changed to protect the rights and identities of the guilty. I've chosen to provide their real names and places - why shouldn't they lose their reputations and standing within the community? Why should they be protected?

This book is my account of how my life was stolen away from me and how I was turned into one of the richest, most profitable and recognised porn princesses known in modern times.

Here's the truth you'd never otherwise have learned.

Oh, and if you find any of my story hard to read, then please bear with me as you can only imagine how difficult it was for me to actually live through those parts.

ℭHAPTER 3

Mum and I didn't know it yet, but the day she met Murk Walters was the real day misfortunate, heartache, fear and violence crept into our lives.

Until meeting Murk near the local playground outside our school, it had only been Mum and me, so I will start by telling you a little bit about the Just Mum and Me years first:

I had never known who my father was, and Mum didn't like to talk about him or the circumstances of why they were no longer still together. But, she did say, with stronger bitterness than the coffee I had once sneakily tasted, it was because she had got pregnant with me, "sinfully out of wedlock at only eighteen years of age" to a man her parents had long voiced as "un-befitting" for their daughter to date was the reason why I didn't have any grandparents in my life either.

Although Mum and I only had each other, our life was great.

I never became aware it was financially tough for Mum while I was a baby, toddler and preschooler, that she constantly barely scraped by on the single parent pittance the government paid her; and that she regularly went to local charity organisations pop-up food stalls to get a fortnights worth of staples at a token price for us to live on, or our clothes and furniture were always someone else's discards. I was too young to be aware of things like that. I learned this via the many, many newspaper and television stories in the days, weeks and months following her death.

Including seeing my grandparents for the first time ever. Crying and explaining on camera to reporters Mum had been held captive and gang-raped for a week until the police busted in and she was freed, and resultantly became pregnant with me. The reason for their falling out: they couldn't understand why Marilyn refused to terminate the pregnancy and was too scared to press charges despite the pressure from police for her to do so, or why she wanted to always live with the reminder of the horrific event that had happened to her. And no, they wouldn't seek custody of her child - they didn't ever even want to meet her (me) due to them still finding it hard to deal with, especially now the manner in which their beautiful daughter had died. "Amber will have a better life living with her step-father than us," they stated boldly to the media.

My memories were of having a Mum who loved and enjoyed being with me, who laid on the floor playing with toys with me, who teased me, tickled me and sometimes chased me around our teeny-tiny townhouse backyard (if you could even call it that) and squealed as loudly as I did before her laughing infectiously whenever she caught up with me. A laughter I can still vaguely remember and, on the rare times I laugh, sometimes is replicated in me.

I never went hungry or had my needs unmet. Mum gave me kisses and cuddles daily, and told me I was beautiful and she was so glad I had come into her life. I was her little blessing; the whole reason she lived and breathed. She read to me every night, until I was old enough and learning to read on my own, when she then listened to me read instead.

When I started school Mum gained a casual job at the local fruit and vege shop, where she only had to work during school hours and not on weekends or during school holidays. Before long, Mum had an old secondhand car for us to get around in, so during the summer school holidays, when she didn't work, she asked if I wanted to go camping on the beach - which I always did - and so we packed our swimming costumes, towels and some clothes in a bag, along with sunscreen and hats, and sandwiches, fruits and drinks in a cooler, and we'd go for the very long drive to our favourite beach down the coast. The car didn't have air-conditioning or electronic windows, so we rolled the stiff windows down to let in the breeze, often causing my hair to whip around my face and go in my mouth and poke my eyes. But I didn't mind; I loved beach camping with Mum. It was the thing we both loved doing most in the world, escaping the city to camp in the dunes.

During the day time we visited the crowded, patrolled beaches, which often had a caravan park nearby, where we swam in the surf (really merely wading to my just-above-knee level) or an inlet or rocky pool (where I'd sit on the edge with my feet dangling in), and I made friends with other kids my age while Mum sat under the shade of our light blue beach igloo with all the belongings we had brought from the car to the sands with us, including food and drinks in the soft cooler. Mum keeping a keen eye on me, calling me whenever I drifted too far away.

Once it turned night though, and we'd had our dinner of hot chips with salt and vinegar or hamburgers with beetroot from the nearest fish and chip shop right around the time the sun was setting, instead of returning to our tent or caravan like other holidayer's we'd spent the day with, Mum bundled me into the car again, after making sure we had everything we'd brought with us, and had dusted ourselves completely off of sand to drive further down the coast to a remote area Mum told me not many holidaymakers learned about. Because of how remote and isolated the spot was, we'd only have the occasional local fishermen there to beach-fish at night that might catch us out, if we were unlucky.

Mum parked near the beach-access path, and we'd carry the stuff we needed for the night along the narrow sandy path lined with decaying slats of wood, trying not to get snagged by any of the overhanging branches of the dense bushland on both sides of us dividing the car park from the beach, or stub our toes on those slats, and then head left along the sand with the bushland parallel on one side, the surf not far in the distance on the other until Mum found a clearing in a valley part of the bushy, sandy dune areas, where Mum, once again, set up the beach igloo under the darkening sky, lined the ground with two of the sheet-sized towels which we used specifically for sleeping on purpose; meanwhile I was tasked with blowing up our inflatable travel pillows, with Mum reminding me, "but don't blow them too hard so they stay comfortable to rest our heads on".

"Shh," Mum said too, often holding her finger to her mouth while we scouted for a site or as we set up. "We're not supposed to camp on the beach or step into the dunes, so you can't tell your teachers or friends about this part of our holiday, okay, pumpkin? And if any Ranger comes, you have to say we are not camping, we are here for the sole purpose of doing some night-fishing but needed a catnap, okay." We had old fishing gear we had never used with us to make it convincing.

If I had to toilet-time, Mum got me to move a little bit away from our campsite, close enough so she could still see me, but not close enough my piddle might trickle down to our towels; and our number two's, which Mum told me to dig a hole to do it in and then bury with sand afterwards, didn't stink us out either. If Mum needed to toilet-time (she went further into the bushes than I went) or get something from the car, I was not allowed to leave the igloo without her first knowing about it. If anyone came along and asked what I was doing there during her absence, I had to say, "I'm not allowed to talk to strangers." even if it was a ranger. Mum was diligent, also, about reminding me if I removed food or drink from the cooler, I had to ensure I closed it properly again, too, so we didn't attract any unwanted nightlife into our little igloo cover - which is what we used instead of a tent so Mum had the opportunity to talk her way out of getting a fine if the Rangers ever did come across us.

We wouldn't have been able to have had our beach holidays without doing it this way. But I appreciated right from the start Mum still took me away despite her limited finances like most of my classmates at school; though, they all appeared to go to caravan parks where their family either had caravans with annexes or they pitched large family tents in the designated camp grounds; hardly any of the kids from my district ever had parents with the financial means to take them to holiday homes, resorts or hotels though. I fitted right in as being a kid whose parent was holidaying on a tight budget.

We slept with our heads under the igloo (which was really more like a small open dome than an igloo shape which, to an outsider should convince them we were only having our claimed catnaps) and our feet pointing out. I loved the waves crashing and whooshing, the ever-present breeze and the twinkling of the stars. The moonlight was bright enough we never needed a torch or lamp, so between the time it had become dark but it was before time to go to sleep, Mum and I often went for a stroll near the surf once we were set up; sometimes the complete distance of the kilometre or more long beach, even though strolling end to end took over an hour. One, it was a pleasant activity to do: we had no television or radio or anything else to entertain us, and we simply talked; and two, Mum was able to scope out how alone we really were. The emptier the beach, the more Mum relaxed. Most fishermen preferred to night-fish on the beach on the other side of the rocky points on the left hand end, accessed by a rough dirt track through the bushland; there was a great shallow inlet where they caught prawns and fished for flathead, usually with great success. (Mum had taken me there only once (by car), and we never went down that track again due to how potholed the track had been and the toll it took on the car's suspension. Most people accessing that beach owned 4WD's. Besides, Mum said, "Our beach is prettier, and strangely less popular." Though we did twice visit those beaches and inlets by going around the rocks at low tide. But it was rather dangerous, so we only did it those two times from memory). Occasionally, you found fishermen who preferred beach-fishing, and teenage surfers who had wild parties on the long stretches of isolated beaches in out of the way places like this one.

Mum didn't like staying when surfers had beach-parties. Once or twice she made us urgently pack everything again and sneak our own rough path through the bushes to reach the car once they arrived after I had fallen asleep; those parties meant easy discoverability and our being harassed and we wouldn't have people to turn to for help. Other times it started down pouring and Mum didn't want either of us getting sick, so we drove somewhere else - usually returning to one of the popular beach's car parks and slept in the car, parked as inconspicuously as we could be - me sleeping on the rear seat and Mum in the driver's seat with the seat reclined as far as it went.

In non-school holiday periods, we tended to stay at home. Mum didn't like going out much, especially not to parties where the adults drank alcohol. On weekends, Mum was usually too busy cleaning the townhouse so we'd pass inspections no matter how little notice they gave her. Sometimes, when she wanted a break, we'd go to our local river - if we found parking, which most times we couldn't, it was well-complained amongst locals the council hadn't put in enough parking spots for how popular our only cooling off spot could get. Mum had bought an old computer from the school when they were replacing the ones in the library for newer, faster working models, so we had everything we needed, even if the stuff we owned was all old and unwanted by the original owners. We were happy owning it.

I miss visiting the beach, and often dream of one day being able to go again.

CHAPTER 4

But then Murk entered our lives.

Like I said at the start of me telling you my story, I was eight when Mum met Murk.

School finished at 3.15 p.m., and Mum's shift ended at 3 p.m. Because it was a 10 to 15 minute drive from work to the school, it depended on the traffic as to whether Mum was already there waiting for me and chatting to the Mum's group, or I had to wait with one of the Mum's who took it in turns to stay back the few minutes until she arrived so I wasn't left alone.

Ever since school had restarted at the beginning of the year, Mum (when she arrived early) and the small group of other single Mums who all waited with each other for school to finish, often 'perved' on a particular man about their age who walked by with his dog each day, starting this year.

The path he took meant he had to walk past the council playground, past all their parked cars, and then past the rear gates of my school.

Mum, from what I was able to tell, wasn't interested in him, but the other Mum's often said things which us kids weren't supposed to hear, causing all the other mum's to laugh, and whisper conspiratorially, and there was one woman I saw (Katie's Mum) who made cheeky 'pinching' actions towards the man's bottom once he had passed, as they all stood watching him continue on past the locked school gates and over the crest until he inevitably disappeared from sight as he descended into the reserve area beyond. Over time, the mum's had plucked the courage to say hello to him, and were delighted when he smiled and said hello back, until it became a normal part of his walk by. Them all giggling delightedly once he couldn't hear them; my friends all found their Mum's embarrassing and thought my Mum was cool - she wasn't as silly as their Mums. Katie, especially, was embarrassed over how flirty her Mum was being with the man.

This had been going on all first term.

Then, one day the man walked into the fruit shop while Mum was on cashiering duty. Mum loved chatting with customers, especially the regulars, most of who were elderly. Mum didn't recognise him; he didn't have his dog and wasn't wearing his usual dark sunglasses or earphones. But he recognised Mum. She came to pick me up straight from work on the days she was rostered, still wearing her fruit shop uniform and smelling fruity sweet.

Mum was quick to tell the others in the group about the exchange, only after he had passed them for that day and once again said hello to everyone in the group, but then said a special hello to Mum only, right as I arrived to throw my arms around her leg and receive her daily kiss on the head. Mum had reddened in the face slightly, and said, 'Hi, Murk,' back. He had added with a wink, 'See ya later, Marilyn' and Mum replied, 'Yeah, you too.'

Due to my age, I didn't really understand what was going on, but as soon as he and his dog were out of hearing range, the other mothers, instead of bundling their kids into their cars and rushing to get home like they did every other day, all became instantly happy to stay and chat as though they had the rest of the afternoon to casually hang around and let the kids play together on the councils swings and slides for as long as they wanted, and rounded on Mum and asked how she had learned his name. I heard parts of the story as I played with the other kids within hearing and watching distance of Mum while we waited for them all to finally tell us it was time to hop in our respective cars.

"He fancies you," Mrs Ryleland said, excitedly.

Mum got a little flustered. "Oh, no. Do you think so?"

I think Mum was trying to be considerate of Katie's Mum's feelings; even us kids were aware Katie's Mum liked him and was hoping he'd ask her out.

The conversation then steered to whether Mum liked him in return.

Mum said something I didn't hear and soon all the other mums started trying to encourage her to like him and to hope for him to ask her out. And Mum smiled awkwardly, so I knew she wasn't comfortable. She wasn't interested in dating; she had told me she liked it only being us two girls and never wanted to change this.

After that, it soon became clear amongst the group Murk fancied Mum. He continued to do his fruit and vegetable shopping at the small fruit shop where Mum worked, quickly becoming one of her regulars, and they were starting to have conversations as she served him.

Finally, about a month or two after she had first spoken to him, Murk asked Mum out. I heard her telling Mrs Ryleland (who although she was still a Mrs, was actually a single mother like my Mum) and the other mums nervously, "I don't know what I was thinking. I said 'yes' without even thinking about it. What am I going to do? How do I get out of it? I really don't want to date anyone."

Some of the other single mums were envious he'd asked her out; and had no hesitation in telling her she should consider herself lucky. I remember Katie's mum saying, quite frustrated, "Marilyn, of course he must be a decent person … look how dedicated he is to taking his dog for a daily walk. You can tell a lot about a man through how he treats his pets, you know. I'll go out with him if you don't want to. I mean, we all thought he liked me at first, didn't we. I'd jump his bones any day."

Mum must have given in to their pressure; she later asked Mrs Ryleland if she would be able to look after me on Friday night, and promised to return the favour any time Mrs Ryleland wanted to go out on a date, too.

So on the Friday night, halfway through the school year, before dinnertime, Mum had clarified to me, "You're staying at Sarah's, I mean, Mrs Ryleland's overnight. I'll return to pick you up in the morning, around ten a.m."

I didn't want Mum to leave me at someone's house; she'd never done this before. Despite Mum's constant assurances I'd be alright, I was really nervous and soon after reluctantly watched my Mum leave. Mrs Ryleland was pleasant, and encouraged me to go outside and play with her son, Chad, who was the same age as me but in the other class for my age group (the dum-dum's group as we (Sally, Katie, Susie and I) meanly called it), until dinner is ready, with her added parting words said in a sing song voice, "I hope you like fish fingers and chips!"

All I wanted to do was sit in front of the Ryleland's front window, crying quietly and wait until Mum returned. Instead, I nodded my head thinking, "Yuck, fish fingers, could my day get any worse?" and went out the rear door, where Chad promptly drenched me with a water bomb, which painfully exploded on my face causing me to cry. Mrs Ryleland scolded her son and checked to ensure he hadn't injured my eye, and then got me an ice pack to help take the redness and stinging away.

Chad had two other brothers, and no sisters. And Mrs Ryleland yelled a lot at her sons and repeatedly threatened to smack them (which she never did), of which Chad was the middle boy and naughtiest. Her yelling made the boys get louder and more troublesome as the evening continued on.

"They're showing off because you're here," she told me as I sat quietly at the dinner table trying not to gag on eating the first of six fish fingers on my plate, watching silently as the boys poked and swiped at each other. I didn't get upset at all when the oldest boy stole one of my fish fingers at the encouragement of Chad while their mother wasn't looking. The brother didn't get upset when I stole a couple of his chips in return to let him know I didn't care if he took my fish fingers but he wasn't going to leave me hungry. Soon Chad and his younger brother had both stolen my other fish fingers, and replaced them with chips too, so I was relieved not to have to eat fish fingers after all (except that first one, I'd half eaten but Chad finished). But, they didn't steal them as a favour to me; they stole them because, well, they were simply naughty and selfish.

After dinner, Mrs Ryleland did her best to get her three sons to have a bath and get ready for bed, after I had. It took them ages to get them into the bath, and then even longer to get them out and get them each dried and dressed. I merely sat on the lounge chair quietly reading the book I had brought with me, as Chad streaked past me naked wagging his willy about (that's what Mrs Ryleland screeched at him to stop doing), which I was glad to read; Mrs Ryleland was punishing her sons for something they had done a few days ago by not letting them watch TV for a week and they were still tearing around the house, not doing as their mother asked and pleaded. Twice Chad re-entered the room and waved his boy part at me laughing with his brothers egging him on, who all found themselves hilarious.

I was exhausted from all the chaotic energy and noise of Chad and his brothers by the time Mrs Ryleland said it was time for us to go to bed (much later than what my Mum let me stay up to, even on weekends). And I wasn't mentally prepared to be woken up at six o'clock the following morning by how loud Chad and his two brothers were as they raced into the lounge room where I was sleeping. The morning dragged by, and I found myself looking up at the clock on the wall between the kitchen and dining room, sleepily counting down to ten o'clock when my Mum finally rescued me from all this bedlam.

I had imagined Mum would arrive, and after a few pleasantries, I'd thankfully be on my way home again. But no, Mrs Ryleland invited Mum in for a coffee, and said eagerly, 'Come in, come in. I want to hear all about your date with Murk!"

By the time we left it was past our usual lunchtime. Mrs Ryleland had told Mum it was 'lovely' having a girl in the house, and I was welcome to stay with them again 'any time.' Mum said she hoped I had behaved myself, and Mrs Ryleland assured her not only did I have beautiful manners, and was well behaved; I was a 'refreshing change' and 'easy to look after', which pleased my Mum. She gave me a huge cuddle and kissed me on top of my head, proud of me. I couldn't wait to get home so I had the chance to rave to Mum about how full on, noisy and extremely naughty Mrs Ryleland's boys were.

I was still miffed with Mum for her leaving me at the Ryleland's, so I deliberately didn't ask Mum how her night was, as punishment. But Mum hadn't noticed this, and told me the man she had gone out on a date with was really nice, nicer than she had originally imagined him to be, and she had agreed to see him again.

I was filled with dread when she said that. Did it mean Mum was going to leave me at the Ryleland's again? I really hadn't enjoyed my time at the Ryleland's in the slightest. It was not an experience I wanted to repeat any time soon or even ever again.

Mum never left me at the Ryleland's again. Mum didn't want to 'wear out my favours', but I soon had to get used to Murk (his real first name was Murdock, but he preferred people calling him by his nickname, Murk, and at a pinch, Murkie) coming over to our house, which quickly became a frequent occurrence. And I was dragged out on dates with them too.

I didn't like him the first time I properly met him. Yet Mum appeared to really like him the more she got to know him, and he spoiled her with little treats and compliments Mum admitted she wasn't used to receiving before. So I did my best to avoid his company, if I could manage it.

I suspected Murk knew I didn't like him. I sensed and caught him watching me a lot. And made me feel even more uncomfortable around him. I didn't know why I didn't like or trust him; I just didn't. He gave me the creeps.

Murk was all smiles, fake-sweet voice when he spoke to me, and doted his full attention on Mum; all the while keeping one eye secretly watching, scrutinising me. Mum never caught him doing that either. And I wondered if I should say anything to her or not.

Nearing the end of the year, I was now nine years old, Mum devastated me: she sat me on my bed and told me, "Murk and I have decided to get married. I know its quick and all, but … well, he asked, and I said yes. He's so different to any man I've ever dated before you came along. He hasn't pressured me to sleep with him; he's saving himself for the woman he marries!" (I didn't know what she meant back then. He had slept over in bed with her plenty of times.)

Great, now Murk was going to be my step dad. I couldn't be more unpleased.

I didn't want Mum to marry him. I still didn't know why I didn't like him. And the more I attempted staying away, to keep my distance from him, the more Mum endeavoured getting us to interact with each other more; one day coming and sitting on my bed as she came to tuck me in and pleading, "I know you feel like he has stolen me away from you, I understand that, sweetheart, I really do. But please, at least be nice to Murk, pumpkin. I love both of you. It's my deepest wish for you to both get on. Me loving him doesn't mean I'll ever stop loving you, I wanted you to know that, okay, pumpkin?"

I felt bad I was making Mum unhappy, so I promised to try and get on with Murk. To try to see why Mum liked him.

I was reluctant to admit he was always saying nice things about her, to her. Telling her the meals she had cooked tasted delicious, and it's clear she had put in a lot of effort; she kept a beautiful home and really looked after herself, and me; she was super-pretty and didn't even know it. He was always surprising her with little gifts and unexpected surprises - a chocolate bar here, an ice-cream there, a bunch of flowers, "for being the most beautiful person I've ever met." and an unexpected outing for Mum and me. I heard Mum telling the mum's group, "He doesn't just see me for my looks, like all the other men I've met. He remarkably seems to enjoy my company and wants to spoil me rotten for the privilege of letting him spend time with me and Amber." Those things always made Katie's mum really envious resulting from how close she had to being in Mum's place.

I still didn't like Murk, but I did a better job of hiding this from Mum, and him.

One day, right before school was about to break for the summer holidays and only days before their wedding was to take place, as Mum was giving me a bath, she had me standing and was washing my underarms and then pouring an ice-cream bucket of bath water to rinse off the suds, and my feelings of disliking Murk instantly intensified when I looked up to see him leaning against the bathroom entrance, staring intensely at me. Something about me stiffening and being uncomfortable about being naked in front of him must have prompted Mum to look up at me, and then turn to see what I was looking at. Murk was still gawking at me.

I don't remember what Mum said now, but I saw the instant alarm in her face. After her saying his name three times, Murk stopped staring and 'returned from his private thoughts', then looked at Mum, and said, "Oh, darling. I came in to ask if you'd like a cup of tea, but I got distracted watching you. You are such a great Mum. I was admiring how beautiful you are, and it hit me so suddenly and powerfully how great a Mum you are, and how lucky I am to soon be your husband."

He was no longer looking at me; he was looking Mum in the eyes and taking a step towards her. His voice lowered, and he said in a whisper, looking her deep in the eyes, "And it hit me, I can't wait to marry you and I hope we have a child of our own together, too, one day." Mum suddenly un-tensed, and said she'd love to have another child one day too. And then they were in each other's arms, kissing (Murk started it). He even pinched her bottom and said, "Gawd I love you." Murk asked Mum if she'd like that cup of tea and when she said she would, left the bathroom so Mum could finish getting me washed and ready for bed "in peace, before Amber catches a cold" and the moment was forgotten.

Or so I'd thought.

The next night, when Murk wasn't over, as Mum put me into bed, she asked a very strange question. She asked if Murk had ever done anything for me to dislike him. I had to be honest and say he hadn't; I thought it would sound stupid to say, "He's always looking at me," so I kept it to myself. And Mum asked a few more questions, and each time I answered as honestly as my nine year old self could. No, Murk had never touched me, or attempted to do anything to me without her knowing. Yes, of course I'd tell her if he ever wanted to force me to do anything I didn't feel comfortable doing. Yes, I knew I could tell her anything, even if it was something I thought she wouldn't want to hear. I didn't know what the questions meant, or why she was asking them, but she looked relieved when I said Murk hadn't ever done anything for me to dislike him. Had never hurt me, or said anything to cause me to feel scared.

When I asked her why she was asking me her questions, Mum had suddenly gone all light and said she was simply checking to ensure everything was okay with me. And she guessed she was a little bit scared of marrying him - mainly due to her relationship with my dad not having worked out. And then she reluctantly confessed, some men who are not a child's real father secretly say and do things to hurt the child - and she was making sure Murk wasn't one of them due to his unexpected appearance in the bathroom yesterday. She thought he had been staring at me, but it was a misunderstanding on her part, he hadn't realised he had been doing that, if that's what she thought he had been doing, he'd been 'millions of miles away thinking'.

I had considered lying to Mum, to get her to stop seeing him. But, Mum and I never lied to each other; so I stuck with telling her the truth. (You have no idea how much I regret that decision now.)

I guess my answers had satisfied her on top of his, and a week later they married as planned.

I was the flower-girl at their Registry Office ceremony. Mrs Ryleland, who had asked her parents to mind her boys so she was free to attend, was a witness. And some male photography colleague of Murk's who Mum and I had never met, but who had clapped Murk on the shoulder and said jovially, "Murkie, mate. You've hit the jackpot, here, old man." was the other witness they needed. After the ceremony, Mum and the man had chatted, and Mum had asked him, "How did you and Murk meet?" The guy had taken a little time to answer, before saying, "I was a customer of his photography business … and eventually became a partner. I am a great fan of his work."

After that, he had asked Mum questions about where they were going for their honeymoon, and Mum had been pressured into telling him everything about their arrangements, including the secret camping out in the sand dunes. He had laughed aloud and with his booming voice said, "So, you're turning my mate Murkie, here, into a criminal. Most women try to straighten wayward men up; I'm in awe you're turning a straightened man wayward."

I could tell Mum didn't like Alister very much. Just like me; I had instantly dislike him also - even more than I disliked Murk. He stared at me a lot, too, constantly licking his lips as he did so; but only when Mum and Mrs Ryleland weren't looking. Only Mrs Ryleland fancied him because she'd gone all flirty; but was deflated when she realised the interest was only one-sided.

The wedding and honeymoon coincided with school holidays, of course, which meant Mum didn't have to work. The three of us went on our next beach holiday, with Murk joining us now in our illegally camping in the dunes.

"I'm sorry I don't have the money yet to afford to take you on a decent holiday, my love.' I heard him tell her, after they had setup a tent-for-one for me and a two-man tent for them next to it, as they stood with Murk behind Mum, his hands around her waist hugging her belly as they looked toward the ocean. "But, I'm kind of glad to be a holiday rebel with you, my darling." Mum chuckled over those words.

Now, with the benefit of hindsight and the loss of my precious Mum, I can now see all this had been a big set up on the part of Murk Walters to marry and kill Marilyn Entacott, so he'd freely gain access to her kid. From his walks with the dog past the primary school which miraculously disappeared once they were dating, which disguised his covert scouting for a suitable victim-pair mission; to his sudden shopping at Mum's fruit and vege shop, which was a ploy to win her affections so he had the opportunities to set up the remainder of his deadly plan; to his marriage to Marilyn Entacott, which was simply a convenient way to ensure he became entrusted to raise his late wife's kid because no other family or relation existed or volunteered to raise her or else the poor kid tragically ended up in foster care; to his abrupt uprooting his step daughter from her former home and life, to ensure she had no one to share her dark secret with and had no means of possible escape. We hadn't been the original target, but the moment Murk had seen me, he had abandoned his plans to win over Katie's mum. They'll never know how close they came to Katie and her mum taking our places.

Oh yes. Along with his mates, they had secretly schemed the plan to acquire 'a prize' they would all benefit from. Each of them (except Uncle Jack) had gone to different towns far from home, to subtly try to acquire a prize or few; Murk was simply the first to succeed and the others had been summoned to help see Murk's through to completion because they only really wanted one prize at a time. It was safer for them this way.

℘HAPTER 5

On the last day of our beach holiday, I was exhausted after a day of swimming in the surf, playing with other kids out in the blazing sun, and going for a walk on the rocks with Mum and Murk, so was catnapping in my tent. Murk was still beach-fishing like he had been since we'd returned to our secret camping site, trying to catch our last night's dinner. With no luck.

Mum had left the dune area where we were safely hidden in the 'no entry - protected bushland' area from view of passing beach-goers, to wander to the beach edge to talk about what they should do about dinner with her husband of less than one week. I know the finer details, months later I couldn't help but hear Murk laughing about them with his mates one night while they were all heavily drinking - they loved reminiscing about their mission whenever they could, and bragging about how clever Murk and themselves had been. Uncle Spud laughing loudly, "You have no idea how glad I am I didn't have to continue dating my Sheila - one ugly fucker, mum and kid, compared to our little Amber beauty." And how easy it had been to get away with it. And he was glad he found the prettier mum and kid than the original 'ugly fucker, but who had all the other qualities we were looking for - no other family to worry about', Murk had found too.

Mum left Murk in charge of keeping an eye out to ensure I was okay. She headed into town to buy us hamburgers and chips for dinner. "Make sure you go to the fish and chip shop on Beach Road, not the one in town, my love. I swear my stomach pain the night before last was because we got burgers from that shop. I'd rather you go a little further and out of the way and get us food from the shop we know sells decent tucker."

Mum and I had had upset stomachs after getting our dinner from the town fish and chip shop too, (or so we thought at the time, but it was really resulting from Murk adding something to our food but, "not my own, I rightly faked the pains they had," or so he bragged too, to get out of having sex with Marilyn again, which "I only got through by imagining I was with her precious daughter in the tent next to ours.") so Mum was keen to avoid another physically uncomfortable night like that again by agreeing to buy from the little shop directly opposite the town's main beach.

""Are you sure it will still be open?" she asked me," Murk had bragged to my uncles. "And I go, I'm sure love. I saw their sign; they're open until nine pm every night except for Sundays when they close at eight. So off she goes never knowing that I was sending her to where the guys you hired could snatch her without witnesses, and I messaged you guys to let you know she was on her way so you could let them know. I knew it was still too soon to reward myself with our prize - I couldn't risk blowing things right when we were so close to completing the main part - and everything was all set with you guys. So all I had to do was be patient, play the role of unaware husband, stuck on the beach because his bride never returned with their dinner."

The seven other men sitting around the table, drinking beer, smoking cigarettes and 'weed', and playing cards had roared with laughter. I was nearing ten years old by the time I heard them sharing their story the very first time, but it became clear to me instantly, Mum's murder hadn't been a random act by unknown rapist murderers like the police and papers believed. It had been coldly planned and carried out by her new husband with the help of his friends long before he'd ever said the first word to her. And the purpose was so the eight of them had ample time to take turns at spending each night with their secret prize: me (the original intention being Katie, or one of the uncles handpicked selections).

I had woken from my nap in the tent to find it was now night time. Mum and Murk were both not in their tent, so I crawled out and wandered out from the dunes and along the beach where I saw the dark outline of a man fishing - the only other person on this isolated beach. The man of course was my new step dad, Murk, and I asked him where Mum was and he replied, "Gone into town to get us dinner. She should be back any time soon."

Thinking I'd wait for her back at the tent, I took a step when Murk grabbed my arm painfully and said in a mean voice, "No, you're to stay here with me. Sit!" He had already swiftly picked me up, bent me over his knees and smacked me on my backside three times really hard claiming I wasn't cooperating with Mum the day before, and Murk had hastily decided he needed to support my Mum in her parenting, and said to an upset Mum afterwards he thought if he stepped in and helped I wouldn't challenge her the next time.

His spanking me so harshly - way harder than the crime I had supposedly committed - had really hurt and I had cried for over an hour, so I wasn't going to take any risk of it happening again, especially as I didn't have Mum here to yell at him to stop it like the previous day. Even though Mum had eventually calmed down and forgiven Murk for his way of disciplining me, I suspected Murk had secretly enjoyed every moment of forcing me over his legs, pulling down my bikini bottoms and smacking my naked bottom until Mum screeched at him to stop, and demanded to know why he was doing this as she pulled me into her arms, cuddling and protecting me as they argued it out.

So I had no choice but to sit my still mildly tender butt onto the sand and watch Murk sitting on his collapsible camp stool, holding on to his fishing rod, one finger touching the fishing line so he would feel it when he got a nibble to try hooking whatever fish had taken the bait.

We sat in this way forever. Me being bored out of my brain drawing in the wet sand to give myself something to do, Murk fishing and quietly acknowledging the two other men, locals from the looks of them, who separately came to do a spot of beach-fishing their own selves. Eventually, to break my boredom, I also started asking Murk, "What time is it?" and "How much longer until Mum gets back?" until he grunted if I didn't want him to punish me in the exact same manner as yesterday, I'd best shut the fuck up and stop scaring the fish away.

By the time eight thirty p.m. came and went, only minutes after Murk received a text message on a different mobile phone to Murk's usual one, Murk rose from his camp stool and said with a faked concern not fooling me in the slightest, "I'm starting to get worried about your mother. She should have been back ages ago."

I had already been silently cursing Mum for her taking so long; and regretting my having come to ask Murk where she was in the first place. I have lived with the guilt of being annoyed with her ever since. But I try not to think about that, or even about Mum, it just makes me overwhelmingly sad. I miss her so much.

Mum had taken Murk's car (we'd left ours at home and used Murk's - it was the larger and more reliable vehicle), so we had no way of driving to town to go looking for what she was up to.

"Come on," Murk snapped at me, and leaving our things behind, me sulkily trailing behind Murk, we headed not towards the path leading to the car park, not even back to our secret campsite, but further along the beach towards where the first of the two fishermen had set himself on a similar collapsible stool Murk used, holding a larger fishing rod, with a bucket on the ground at his side which must have had fish he'd caught or bait in it, because I heard some splashing around and got a strong whiff of that horrible fishy guts smell.

We'd seen this old man the last two nights.

"Hey mate," Murk said as he approached. "You didn't happen to see my wife or our car when you arrived, did you? Blonde, shit hot attractive, driving a navy-blue hatchback."

"Nah, mate. The only person I seen when I came in is the other bloke further along. Everything alright?"

"My wife left slightly over two and a half hours ago to go into town and buy us some burgers and chips for tea. We all got upset stomachs after we ate from the fish and chip shop in town, so she said she was going to swing by some place she saw opposite a beach a little further along —"

"Barry's Burgers?"

"I think so. I'm not sure. Well, anyway, like I said, that was a little more than two and a half hours ago, and I'm starting to get really worried about her not being back. I'm hoping she's run into a friend or something and hasn't realised how much time has passed; but, we occasionally have car troubles, so I'm worried she might've broken down. You're sure you didn't see any cars on the road coming in, parked off to the side. It's not like there's many others headed out this way tonight for her to ask them to let me know what's causing her delay, she doesn't have a mobile so I can't try contacting her."

I had no idea why Murk told the man we occasionally had car trouble - that was Mum's car, not his we all came here in.

"No mate. Didn't pass anyone leaving here or broken down, or I'd have stopped to offer a hand."

"Oh, okay. Thanks. Come on, Amber, we'll try the other fisherman. He arrived after our friend here, I think. Hey, do me a favour mate, if you happen to see her arrive while we're going to ask this other guy, please let her know where we've gone?"

"Yeah, sure mate."

So, we continued on along the long beach towards the rocky cliff at the end where the other fisherman had walked all the way to and set himself up for fishing. But of course the second fisherman hadn't seen Mum either. I was the only one who had detected Murk lying about not knowing the fish and chip shop was called Barry's Burgers, but I'd observed enough now about how secretly mean Murk got I didn't dare question him in front of either of the two strangers. Murk looked at his watch again, and then said to me, "Come on, Amber. I think we'll have to walk to town. I'm starting to get even more worried, we're in for a long walk to get to town, but I don't see what other choice we have. We'll stop back at the tent so you can get some shoes on."

"Hey, look, I was about to pack up and call it a night. I can drive you into town if you like."

"Oh, mate, that'd be great. Thanks."

Murk helped the man pack up, and we walked along the beach, heading towards the access path. As we passed the first fisherman, he wished us luck and Murk told him Derrick had offered to drive us into town to look around. The first fisherman told Murk he was here for an overnighter, his wife had dropped him off and wouldn't be back to collect him until sun rise so he'd keep an eye on our belongings too. And would let Mum know where we had gone if she returned while we are gone. Murk thanked the guy and we all continued on towards the second fisherman's car. We didn't stop in at the tent first.

I sat in the rear seat of Derrick's late model 4WD. Murk sat in the front passenger seat. It was dark outside. Eerily so. And was getting close to ten pm. The trees and bushland on either side of the road was thick and densely packed. The 4WD's headlights made the trees on both sides of the road look like they crossed over each other in the middle, so we were travelling through an eerie tunnel made from trees. There was only two or three dark dirt lanes off this single road in and out surfers and fishermen used to gain access the north and south stretches of beaches adjacent to where we were camped at - ours was at the tip of the point in the weird landscape of things. I fleetingly saw the red tail lights of a distant vehicle as it headed along one of the dirt side roads on the right. My first thought was it looked like a police car. But it was more likely the local ranger paying a visit, to move people on after issuing them with a fine if he caught them camping on the beach. It meant he'd check the beach where we were staying next; so I needed to tell Mum as soon as we found her.

We drove for close to quarter of an hour before we reached the edge of town. As we approached a point where we were able to turn right to drive along Beach Road, which took us the long, curving way around three or four beach suburbs until we reached where Mum had gone to get our burgers, Derrick asked Murk, "Would your wife have gone straight ahead, or turned right here to go there this away?"

Murk shook his head, and replied, "I don't know. I think she'd have gone straight."

"Okay," Derrick replied. "How about we go this way to get there, and if we don't find her, we'll go that scenic route on the way back?"

"Okay," Murk said, and nodded.

Although I hadn't said it aloud, I was scared about what had happened to Mum, it not at all like her to not come straight back, but I hadn't yet started crying. I was getting close to it, though, sitting there in the back not making a sound.

We passed the local police station, and ambulance station. Derrick slowed the car's speed slightly as he passed each and craned his neck to look behind once he had passed, which were a few blocks apart from each other in the centre of the beach-side town. He commented the, "Cop car isn't parked outside the station," and instantly said also, "Ambo's gone as well. Must be an incident somewhere," but was quick to add, "most likely up over on the highway. Accidents always increase this time of year."

I didn't hear what Murk said in reply to Derrick. I was still wondering why Derrick had taken a quick glance at me both times before speaking to tell Murk those two details. And I was still keeping my eye out trying to spot Mum driving Murk's car in case she passed us heading in the opposite direction. I wanted to be the one who spotted her first.

Barry's Burgers was closed and shut up by the time we rolled up outside. Even though it was clear no one was still cleaning up, Murk asked, "Do you mind if I see if someone is still there?"

Derrick nodded. He lifted the handbrake but kept the motor running. Murk exited the car, ran across to the shop window, peered in through the dark and then returned shaking his head. "Definitely no one still there."

"Look, I know where Barry lives. We're close mates. I wouldn't ordinarily do this, but … look, I'll drive you there, so you can see if she came in and ordered the burgers; it might help us … figure things out where your wife is."

I suspected Derrick was intentionally careful with how he worded things because of me. Only I didn't know why he was doing that.

So, we headed back, not along the Beach Road Derrick had said we'd go along, but did a U-turn and headed back into town. We passed the local hospital as we drove by. All appeared quiet and peaceful from our vantage point. Five minutes later, in the heights where the houses gained magnificent unobstructed ocean views, we pulled into the driveway of a rundown old house. Murk ordered me to stay in the vehicle and Murk and Derrick headed towards the front door.

Derrick knocked in the darkness and after a pause the front porch light came on; and then the front door opened. A man with a huge beer-belly dressed in short pyjamas and a nightgown and wearing slippers became partly visible. He talked with Derrick and Murk for a few minutes, and then, the obese man retreated inside the house, closing the front door behind him, but he left the porch light on while Murk and Derrick returned to where I was waiting in the 4WD.

"Did he see Mum?" I couldn't help but ask as they took their seats; and Derrick started the car up and swung around to look past me so he could reverse out of the drive.

"No, sweetie," Murk said, in a falsely sweet voice, as though he held great affection for me. A concerned father saying to a beloved offspring.

Instantly a hard lump appeared in my throat, making it difficult for me to swallow. And my eyes stung so hard, they started watering. But I was determined I wouldn't cry. I'd be brave.

"Where are we going now, then?" I asked. I sounded like I was crying, even though I wasn't. Well, I don't think I was, anyway.

"We're going to go and stop in at the hospital, see if there's been any car accidents." Derrick said, eyeing Murk as though getting silent approval to tell me what they have planned.

Once again Murk instructed me to stay in the car, and the two men headed into the Emergency room entrance. Soon, they were inside the building, and I was left wondering where abouts they had gone and who they might talk to, and what was being said as I continued to worry about what had happened to Mum, and used the rear of my hand to dry my eyes - they were leaking even though I wasn't properly crying yet.

Did they think Mum had had a car accident, because as far as I knew, Mum was a really good driver, but I guessed accidents could happen to anyone? But wouldn't we have passed her damaged car if that had been the case?

My stomach was grumbling and I was starting to feel really tired despite my nap. It was now way past my bedtime and I was what I now know as 'emotionally exhausted'. I must have fallen asleep for a few moments waiting for Derrick and Murk to return, but I startled awake when the driver and passenger doors opened, causing the little light to come on, so I pushed myself into a sitting position once more and asked sleepily, "Did you find out anything about Mum?"

"We're going to head back via Beach Road, like we said we'd do," Murk told me. "It's okay, you can go back to sleep sweetie. I'll wake you as soon as we find Mummy."

Luckily for Murk and Derrick they closed their doors causing the indoor car light to go out again, so they didn't witness me get annoyed Murk had called Mum, Mummy. Mum had told me when I was little "Mummy is for little kids", and she thought I was grown up enough to call her Mum. When Murk had arrived on the scene, he had mistakenly told me one day to, "say thank you to Mummy, Amber," when I had failed to thank Mum for the glass of milk she handed me. Mum had needed to explain to Murk she doesn't want me being raised to use childish words, and preferred me to use the correct or acceptable adult version of English words for things, and "none of the baby-talk" as she called it. So Murk breaking the rule had irritated me over Mum once having made him aware of this particular rule. But once again, I was also irritated by his false closeness to me, as though he was my dad rather than step dad. I was quite understanding of the difference and was happy to keep the emotional distance, despite his now being in Mum and my lives permanently. I deduced he was faking it - due to him being in the company of a stranger. As a child, I'd get into big trouble if I did things like that.

$\mathscr{C}$HAPTER 6

Once again, I sat in silence looking out the side window hoping to spot Murk's car and point it out to them. But, we drove for ages and soon we were at a T-intersection and Derrick said to Murk, "I think we should turn right, and head into town to see if Stan's back at the station. What do you reckon?"

Murk agreed. So, Derrick turned right, and I noticed we were on the road that took us from our beach into the town. Not far along the road on the right hand side was the Police station again. We'd done a big circle. And still, the police car wasn't there.

"I think we should return to Platypus Beach," Murk said, "in case Marilyn has returned, and we didn't cross paths trying to find her. Is that alright mate?"

"Yeah, not a problem, mate. Happy to help, considering the circumstances."

So once again Derrick did a U-turn, and soon we were back travelling through the tree canopied road. And once again, I had fallen asleep before we arrived at our destination. Somewhere in my sleep, I saw what looked like the blue and red flashing lights of a police car, but I didn't hear a siren so thought I must have dreamt that.

I vaguely became aware of the driver's door opening and closing again, so I sat upright again and forced myself to reawaken properly. We weren't back at our beach; the car park didn't look the same. We looked like we were parked in the middle of a dirt track. We were surrounded by the thick bushland on both sides of the sole road to our beach point.

"Where's Murk?" I asked Derrick sleepily, realising he hadn't hopped into the vehicle with Derrick.

"Umm, your dad's staying, sweetie. I'm taking you to my place, so my wife can look after you."

"Did you find Mum?" I asked, hoping the answer'd be yes.

Derrick looked highly uncomfortable for a moment, and then said, "Yes, We found her. She's been involved in an accident. I - I can't tell you any more than that."

"Is Mum hurt?" I asked, panic starting to rise in me. "Can I go and see her first?"

Derrick started the engine and muttered, "Umm, yes. I think she might of been hurt, sweetie. But, no, you can't go and see her right now. Your dad is going to stay with her, and he'll fill you in when I take you to him in the morning."

The 4WD bounced a bit over the rough dirt road as Derrick navigated his way towards the tarred road (but not as badly as that time Mum had brought me along this road - I had figured out where we were now), and at one point I realised I hadn't dreamt about the police flashing lights at all. When we arrived at his place some fifteen to twenty minutes later, it was nearing midnight according to the little clock on his dashboard. He encouraged me, nicely, to get out of the vehicle and follow him.

Obviously Derrick's wife hadn't been expecting him to come home with a child, so her questions of, "Where have you been? You were due home ages ago. I was starting to get worried—" instantly changed to, "Who's this? What's going on?"

Derrick said, "Mumsie, this is Amber, and I need you to take care of her. There's been an ... accident ... on Wombat Trail, and Amber's mother has ... been hurt. Stan's asked me to bring her here for you to look after her; he wants me to head back out... to assist, until other officers ... from the city ... arrive to help out."

I suspected once again Derrick was being super careful with how he worded things by the way he was looking at his wife and paused before and after the words 'accident', 'been hurt' and 'from the city'.

My first thought was there was something he wasn't telling me about Mum's accident. Adults didn't seem to understand Mum preferred telling me the truth, even if that truth wasn't always what a person wanted to hear; but, I had long ago realised other parents didn't share the same philosophy as Mum, and kept what they thought was 'adult stuff' to only other adults and never their kids. Sally's Mum and Dad had tried keeping they were splitting up and getting a divorce from Sally for a long time before Sally had cried asking when daddy will be home having not seen him the full school term before her mum had decided she needed to finally tell Sally the truth.

Derrick's wife, Anne-Marie, immediately turned to me and said sweetly, "Aren't you a pretty little thing. Are you hungry or thirsty, sweetie-pie?"

I was nervous about talking to strangers again - Mum had always impressed upon me to only speak to people I know, and to never accept food or drink from a stranger, because you can never tell if they are a good or bad person or not. But I guessed Mum, and even Murk who'd learned Mum's rules, must have had good reason to trust Derrick and Anne-Marie to take good care of me, and I figured if Mum was hurt and was trusting strangers (and the policeman Stan knew where I had been taken) to sleep the night at Derrick and Anne-Marie's house, then it must be okay for me to accept any food and drink they offered me too. As I slowly decided to nod my head, Derrick told Anne-Marie, "Amber missed out on her dinner. Her Mum had her … accident … before getting to buy them their meals."

The two adults shared a brief, meaningful look between them again. Anne-Marie looking at her husband curiously, like she understood he couldn't say it in front of me, and wondering, like me, what the missing details were.

"Well, then, come with me, and I'll fix you a bite to eat," Anne-Marie said, stepping forward, taking my hand and leading me inside the house and towards the kitchen.

"Do you like milk?" Anne-Marie asked me. She had kind eyes, a nice, friendly voice and a comforting smile.

I nodded my head.

"Mumsie," Derrick said, trailing us as we arrived in their kitchen. "I need to get back to Stan."

Anne-Marie nodded, and then awkwardly squatted to speak to me. "You stay right here for me, sweetie-pie. I'll see Derrick off first, then I'll come straight back and get you that drink of milk and make you something to eat. Is that okay?"

I trembled as I replied, "Okay." and then watched the two of them walk the way we had come. I heard their footsteps leave the house. Heard the car door open and close again. Heard them having a hasty whispered conversation. Heard Anne-Marie gasp, and say, "Oh, no." And finally, a minute later, the 4WD backing out of the driveway, and Anne-Marie's rushed return inside the house and kitchen.

Anne-Marie's voice was even friendlier than before, and I guessed Anne-Marie was now in on the secret being denied passed on to me.

"Mum's hurt really bad, isn't she," I said to Anne-Marie to let her know I believed the adults were keeping something from me.

"Yes, sweetie-pie, I think that might be the case." But she hastily added, "But, I - I can't tell you any more than that."

I couldn't help myself. All the stress and strain of the evening, worrying about Mum; of being hungry and tired. I burst into tears. Just how hurt was Mum they were acting like this? Not telling me anything, instead of saying things like, "It'll be okay. Your Mum simply needs to get a cast on her broken leg," or something reassuring like that.

Anne-Marie comforted me, holding me close, letting me cry, and once I couldn't cry any longer quite some time later, and had hiccupped my way to calm, she asked kindly, "Would you like that glass of milk, now? And tell me, what would you like to eat for a late night snack to make up for you missing your dinner?"

Anne-Marie made me a toasted Vegemite and cheese sandwich and chocolate milk. It was the only food she had which I liked and was quick and easy to cook. Once I had finished, she said, "Let's get you set up for bed, shall we? You can sleep in the spare bed in the room next to me; it was where my daughter used to sleep before she grew up and moved out of home." She showed me where the bathroom and toilet was, and rummaged for ages in her wardrobe and drawers trying to find something suitable for me to sleep in - I was still in only my pink bikini, with a damp bottom from sitting in the sand.

"I'm so sorry I don't have anything else for you to sleep in, sweetie-pie; I cleared out all Sonya's clothes and gave them to charity months ago." I hadn't realised until Anne-Marie asked me, but yes, I was a little bit cold. In the end, everything was far too big, so she gave me the smallest t-shirt she owned, and it still swam on me like an over-sized nightie.

Anne-Marie tucked me into bed, asked me if I wanted her to keep the hallway light on so I could find my way to their bathroom in the middle of the night (I did), and if I wanted her to close the door or keep it open (I asked her to close it so the light didn't stay in my eyes but not close it fully).

"Okay, good night, precious," she said, and half closed the door.

I woke a few times during the night, I guess because I was in a strange bed with people who were kind but I did not know. So I heard when Derrick came home. He didn't make much noise, taking light slow steps in failing effort not to wake Anne-Marie or myself up, but it was soon clear she had stayed awake waiting for him to return, and find out more details about what was going on.

Derrick spoke at a low volume to Anne-Marie, but their voices carried clearly to me due to how quiet the neighbourhood was compared to home, where we always had cars and trucks and emergency vehicles with their lights and sirens on passing by out front. They obviously both thought I was asleep, or they might have spoken even quieter.

"She was raped and brutally murdered. Stan thinks she might have picked up a surfer or fisherman or hitchhiker as she was driving into town possibly offering the person a lift because of how far it'd take for him to walk. Looks like he might have tricked her to only take him to Wombat Beach or something, we don't know, but if she had any misgivings about driving to that isolated area with her hitchhiker on her own, we won't ever know that either. But it's clear once the perpetrator had her cornered and showed his true intentions, no one would've heard her cries for help. Her husband, Murk, is naturally distraught. They only got married last weekend; this was the last night of their honeymoon."

"They've been illegally camping in the dunes all week, they didn't have the money to go anywhere special and they needed to bring Amber along. Apparently, the wife didn't have any other family. Murk doesn't know who Amber's biological father is; said Marilyn had fallen out with her family when she first discovered she was pregnant. He asked Stan a couple of times, crying, what will happen to Amber? What will happen to my step daughter? Said it would break Marilyn's heart if Amber ended up in foster care because of this. Stan sent him to hospital to get him sedated, and is arranging for a counsellor to help him deal with his loss. But it looks like Stan should be able to arrange for Murk to gain temporary legal custody until the matter can go to Court, which was at least of some comfort to the poor bloke."

"Oh, Derrick, that poor woman, that poor child and husband. Outside our quiet little town. That sort of stuff only happens in cities. Not in beautiful, peaceful little beach-side suburbs like ours. Who'd have done such a thing? This is horrible."

"I know." Derrick sounded really sad about that. He broke the silence by adding, "I can only imagine an outsider. I can't imagine any of the locals doing anything as horrible as this. The media's already picked up on it... anyway, Stan wants me to deliver Amber to the hospital in the morning; they're going to get a counsellor to break the news her mother is dead to her." Derrick broke, unexpectedly sounding choked with tears. "It was absolutely heartbreaking witnessing that poor man have to identify his badly battered and beaten wife at the scene, Mumsie. He crumpled onto the ground and was sobbing to his wife's corpse, "I should never have let you go off to buy our dinner. I should have stopped fishing and gone instead. I'm so sorry, my darling. This should never have happened to you... Mumsie Hon, that man's distress - and the woman - is going to haunt me for the rest of my life."

I didn't understand what the words *raped* and *brutally murdered* meant when I first heard Derrick say them, I guess I was too young and hadn't been exposed to what such words meant, so I didn't really understand Anne-Marie's horrified gasp over them either. Only that it sounded serious. But I understood the word dead perfectly. That was when a person or animal died and their spirit left their body and you never got to see or talk to them again, ever.

In my strange room, I started crying again. Quietly to begin with, gradually worsening. I didn't want my Mum to be dead. Not my beautiful Mum, no. I wanted her alive and continuing being my Mum. And I especially didn't want to live the rest of my life with only Murk.

I overwhelmingly experienced the heaviest weight of sadness I had ever known in my life descend upon me, and didn't think I'd ever recover.

Before I knew it, I was sobbing uncontrollably into Anne-Marie's comforting hug.

$\mathscr{C}$HAPTER 7

I only have vague memories of the following week, and months come to think of it. I cried a lot, and was plagued with unending hollowness. I didn't want to talk to anyone; I didn't ever feel like playing.

Anne-Marie, having heard me crying had come into my room and hugged me for a long time, and although it was nice having an adult woman hugging me, it wasn't my Mum. And I realised if Mum had died, it meant she would never hug me ever again, which made me cry worse. I was too upset to even answer Anne-Marie asking if I'd had a bad dream.

Once the sun had risen, breakfast had been eaten and Anne-Marie had tied a craft ribbon around my waist to prettify her second t-shirt so it appeared more like I was wearing a dress and be "just as pretty as you are." Derrick drove me to the hospital, where I met the policeman named Stan, as well as plenty of other adults.

And finally I was taken into a room filled with toys which had a large glass window, where Stan the police officer and a few other adults and an anxious looking Murk all stood looking into the room with me and the lady, as the lady instructed me to take a seat on one of the small children's chair, grabbed one for herself and sat facing me, and then started a conversation with me until finally she told me Mum had died. By the end of the very long chat after that, I had a clearer idea what raped and murdered meant. My poor Mum had had a bad man touch her in her private places when Mum didn't want them to do so, and

38

then made Mum die from punching her many many times. She had tried fighting him and had many broken bones in her ribs, arms, legs, fingers and neck.

The lady reassured me Stan would help Murk, who was extremely worried about what would happen to me, gain temporary legal custody of me so I could have someone familiar and who loved me, and Mum would want me to live with, in place of me being sent to live with strangers or in a children's home while the Courts decided on a permanent arrangement.

I'd already sobbed in Anne-Marie's arms, without telling her why I was crying as much as I was; so when the lady told me Mum had died, although my sadness was squashing me painfully, only tears flooded my face. I was all sobbed out temporarily.

The lady told me she'd take me to go and play with the sick kids over in the children's ward "because you'll like that, it will help you not to feel so sad," while Murk went with Stan to attend the police station to write a formal statement and to get the legal paperwork started; someone had already been sent out to pack up and get all our camping things for us.

I was looking through a window in the children's play area gazing towards the cars parked outside in deep thought, when I saw Stan and Murk walking towards Stan's police car, and a group of people rushed forward and started taking photos of Murk and were all talking at once at him and pointing microphones and other devices at him. The lady who had explained Mum's death to me had come over to try to encourage me to play with the other kids. When she saw what I was looking at, she told me the people were from the TV stations and newspapers from the city, they were very interested in what had happened to Mum. I hoped those people wouldn't take photos of me like that once I was being taken to a car. I didn't like having my photo taken. Mum had found that strange, and used to laugh and say, "You're exactly like me." But she took plenty of photos of me and her anyway, to fill her albums. I found the whole scenario below quite frightening and glad I was here on the second floor, safe and away from it; relieved I wasn't an adult.

I was escorted to a small lounge room and left on my own, given a tray of hospital food when all the sick kids I hadn't been playing with returned to their beds to have their lunches. I spent the afternoon sitting quietly, ignoring the other kids and the lady who didn't give up trying to get me to, too sad to want to play with them and not interested in doing anything or talking with anyone, and returned again to the small lounge room again for early dinner time.

Learning how Mum had died, which I was sure had been sugar-coated and simpled down to me due to my young age, plagued me with horrible mental visions of Mum trying to fight off her attacker, or, more likely, attackers, plural, the lady had clarified. My beautiful, pretty, kind and loving Mum, who every one commented had the makings to have been a model. This horrific death wasn't the way she deserved to die. She must have been very scared. I know she'd have been very worried about me once she suspected she was going to die. And this made me even sadder, not being able to tell her I acknowledged her last thoughts must have been about me.

I was reconnected with Murk much later the same day, once it had gone dark. And Stan drove us to a motel room, where we stayed for the next few nights. Those people who had taken photos of Murk once again took photos which now included me. The lights from the cameras blinded me, and I walked numbly to where the crowd pushed me. Someone heavy stepped on my foot more than once, which had caused my tears to leak from my eyes again.

Back in the hotel room, Murk insisted I have a shower before getting into my nightie. And Murk was the one who washed, dried and dressed me despite me telling him I was capable of doing it all myself. But showering me made him happy.

I noticed this wasn't the only time he became happy while other people weren't around.

Murk watched the late night news, and although I was supposed to be asleep, once again the tears started moistening my pillow as I watched the news coverage of the story from a gap in my blankets so Murk didn't catch me out. Murk punched the air, pleased, when the reporter said things like, "the emotionally devastated new husband was too distraught to speak to reporters" and "in a statement by police, the victim, Marilyn Walters, who was on the last day of her honeymoon at the time she was brutally raped and murdered, all while her new husband and daughter from a previous relationship were beach-fishing, blissfully unaware of what was happening while they waited for her to return to their camp site with their evening dinner." and "police believe Mrs Walters may have stopped to give someone a ride back to town, before her attacker zapped her with a stun gun rendering her temporarily unconscious and drove her in her car to the remote bush location, where new evidence suggests as many as three others may have been waiting to carry out their crime on this unfortunate, innocent mother, who appears to have bravely defended herself against her multiple rapist attackers and made numerous bids for freedom before eventually being beaten so violently to death." and "police still don't know the identity of the person who made the hysterical Triple Zero call saying they stumbled upon a woman's dead and naked body in the middle of Wombat Trail where she was found and are still requesting this person to come forward."

And, then, after a week of living in the hotel room, Murk hired a car (the police were keeping his car as evidence) and we returned home.

Mrs Ryleland was the first to knock at our door, barely seconds after we had walked in. She threw her arms around Murk and sobbed, "I'm so sorry this has happened to you, and what those monsters did to Marilyn. I hope when the police catch them they string them up by their balls and they die an agonising death. To think they stole her life right while she had finally found happiness. She never said a word to us about she had been gang raped, which resulted in her having Amber."

Then Mrs Ryleland had seen me, and she sobbed even harder, "And poor Amber, what a horrible thing to happen to your mother, and to know you're the result of such a horrific act. Oh, Murk, I'm so glad Amber has you to take care of her … god knows what would've happened to poor Amber if she didn't have you, and this still ended up Marilyn's fate - she so loved that holiday spot, but look how dangerous a place it turned out to be. Took Amber there every summer, though of course, none of us had any idea she had been camping in the sand dunes *illegally*, but I guess that's the only way she was able to give Amber a seaside holiday."

Murk cried what I thought were fake tears for Mrs Ryleland's benefit, and Mrs Ryleland comforted Murk and told him if he ever needed anything to simply ask, and she walked to the little notepad and pencil Mum kept on the telephone stand in the hallway, and wrote her name and phone number, despite it already being in Mum's telephone address book. "Remember, you can call me, any time, alright. And I'll be right over to help you." I think Mrs Ryleland secretly hoped Murk might one day be so glad she had supported him in his time of great need, imagined she might replace Mum for his romantic intentions - once a suitable period had gone by.

(I want to clarify: according to later news reports Mum was already about a month pregnant with me when she was raped. An old close friend of Mum's from school came forward and told the media, after she had seen what they had reported, Mum had not long found out when she was grabbed off the street, and had feared throughout her ordeal she'd lose the baby; and Mum and my dad had only broken up because he couldn't deal with what had happened to her. And he wasn't even sure the baby was his because she hadn't told him before her attack.)

For the next few months, Murk played the role of grieving new husband. The day after Mum's funeral (which was the most distressing day I'd ever had - until an event I'll write about later), I returned to school. At Murk's request to the school Principal, I had to start seeing the School Councillor each week to talk about my feelings about Mum's death, to help me deal with my loss and grief and 'worrying' social withdrawal. I don't know why people wanted me to act happy and laughing when it was still so painful losing Mum? No one was trying to tell Murk his crying was wrong, or worrying. I missed Mum and was also sad about now having to live with Murk. I'd have preferred anyone else if it meant not him. Even to live with the Ryleland's!

Out in public, Murk was the quietly grieving husband; in the privacy of Mum's townhouse, Murk was cheerful and regularly spoke to and joked around with some mates of his on his other mobile phone. And every night, Murk took great pleasure soaping and rinsing me as I bathed, despite my continued annoyed and frustrated protests I was capable of doing this myself, and towelling me dry. He took much longer to bathe me than Mum ever had and although he never did anything he wasn't supposed to, as far as what my Mum had taught me was not allowed, he still derived a lot of pleasure when he washed my chest and panty area. And once, whispered absently to himself, "Not long left until the Court date. Everything's looking good I'll be awarded permanent custody - especially with that Principal Affidavit, so be patient, Murk." He got angry or frustrated with me sometimes, but he didn't punish me, saying I had a lot to deal with so he'd forgive me this time.

The midyear holidays arrived and Murk surprised me, the neighbours and Mrs Ryleland, who lived only a few streets away, when he arrived home the week after he had been granted permanent custody with a motorhome, and told people he can't bear living in Marilyn's rented townhouse any longer, it merely brought up too many painful memories, and now he had been named permanent legal guardian (not the temporary guardian Stan the policeman had arranged), and because staying there wasn't good for me, he was moving us to live in the country, on his parents farm, so they'd help him raise me, where he'd do his best to help me get through what we've been through. I'd live inside their house, but he'd be outside in the motorhome because they didn't have an additional spare room for him.

Mrs Ryleland sobbed and gave Murk the longest hug and kiss on his cheek, and told him Marilyn'd be so grateful about how he has taken on the burden of raising her child as a single dad, despite not being my biological father, and begged him to stay in touch. Oh, and she also asked him, "What about your photography career?" which Murk said, "My career will need to take a back seat so I can concentrate on raising Amber. She's the most important thing right now," which once again had Mrs Ryleland gushing with tears rolling down her cheek how wonderful a person Murk is.

While I'd been at school that week, Murk had been busy packing some of Mum's valuables (though, none of them were worth very much money) and my belongings ready to transport (into the motorhome he hadn't told anyone he was getting), and on the last day put the rest out on the kerb to await council collection (which was raided by locals and culled to junk before we even departed). He'd even sold Mum's car.

Murk left one box, the one with all Mum's photographs and scrapbook albums, inside the townhouse, which I pointed out he'd forgotten to load into the motorhome when he told me to go and hop in it and he'd follow on in a second after he'd locked up the townhouse, but he stared at me coldly and said, "I haven't forgotten that box at all. We have no need for it."

He then reordered me to do as I was told and go and hop into the motorhome, which I did so Murk wouldn't punish me, which I thought he was itching to do. I left him to close and lock the front door behind him, sad because Mum dearly loved her photographs, and regretting I hadn't grabbed at least one photo of Mum so I'd carry it with me wherever I was.

I didn't realise it at the time, but Murk was deliberately trying to erase my memories of Mum and my former happy life.

All I understood at the time was I didn't want to leave. This was the only home I had ever known. By leaving it, it felt like we were expelling Mum completely from our lives, and I wanted to stay where I could remember her easily. I was nearing ten years old now (only two months until my birthday), but I had grown much older. I guessed the next tenant would discover the photographs and albums box and people would automatically assume the box had been left behind accidentally. As Murk hadn't given Mrs Ryleland our new address, and had given her the number of a new mobile phone he also had, keying it into her phone himself (after he had smashed and disposed of the second one while in a car park one day - the one he'd sent and received messages on at the beach that night), it was clear to me if Murk didn't answer her calls or reply to her messages, no one would ever know where Murk had taken me to. I didn't even know where his parents lived. All Murk had said to Mrs Ryleland, which I had overheard, was they lived in country Victoria, and he warned her reception was bad but he'd be able to return any missed calls whenever he headed in to town. He'd get great reception there.

But we didn't even head in a southern direction.

Rather, we went inland and north, and after driving through the night, and all the next day and night again, with Murk only taking a few rest breaks, until we left tarred road to travel through bushland along a rough, dirt track, and eventually came, at around eleven a.m. the following morning again, to a compound consisting of small number of cars and caravans detached from each other in the middle of nowhere, all circled around in front of a large metal shed. Murk found a position for the motorhome he liked under the shade of a cluster of trees, and then said to me, "Come on, let's introduce you to everybody."

He got out of the motorhome, came around to my side, clamped his hand firmly at the base of my neck and pushed me the short distance towards the shed, never easing up on his firm grip as though he was affirming I should be scared of whatever was inside. I don't think I'd ever been as scared in my life as I was at that moment.

Inside the shed, which was a sort of made up lounge room, kitchen and dining room, that was it, there was no Murk's mother and father to meet. Only seven of Murk's mates, who once my eyes adjusted to the darkness after the intense brightness outside, all sat up and didn't stop staring at me from the moment Murk guided me in.

"See, I told you she is the prettiest little thing!" bragged the one man I recognised.

"Everyone," Murk announced to his friends with a big grin, not letting go of his hurting grip on my neck, "This is our little prize, Amber. Amber, I want you to meet your new uncles."

He pointed to each man in turn, and named them. It was a lot to take in at the time, but they were uncles Alister (the man I'd met at Mum and Murk's wedding), Ben, Spud, Bruno, Luke, Glen and Jack. I didn't like the look of any of them. They looked like the villainous characters in movies.

If only I had known how right my first impression of them had been.

Each of my new 'uncles' rose from their chairs to their feet, and suddenly I was circled. I had hands touch my chest, my panty area and my bum. And suddenly they were all talking at once, appreciating what a prize they had gained. They'd never had one as pretty as me before; and they still couldn't believe I was all theirs. I didn't know what they meant by me being a prize, but I learned the first of what this meant minutes later.

Murk gave me a nudge making me walk and he steered me to a chair and told me to take a seat. "We need to go over the rules, so everyone is clear." My 'uncles' groaned, but returned to their chairs and they kept staring at me, making me more nervous.

Murk started by telling me this was my permanent home now. It was half an hour's drive to reach the nearest neighbouring properties borders in all directions (which they also owned) and an hour and fifteen to town, and I was here to look after each of them.

"I'm the boss seeing as I put in the highest risk, so what I say goes." Murk said forcibly. "But I expect you to immediately obey any of your uncles too, so long as what they ask or tell you to do doesn't contradict with my rules - you do know what the word contradicts means, don't you Amber?"

I nodded my head so Murk understood my answer, too frightened to speak.

"Good," Murk said, obviously pleased he didn't have to try explain that to me. "You are to do as you are told, without back chat or argument, do I make myself clear? Or I will punish you, and I can tell you right now, it won't be any of that talking to you like an adult bullshit like your Mum did with you. No … if I don't like your attitude or behaviour, you'll cop a spanking like I've already given you once. Only this time, I won't trouble myself to smack you gently."

A ripple of fear shot through my body as I remembered how much his 'gentle' smacking had hurt me.

"During the day time, you'll perform some household chores. Mainly to keep our caravans and the shed tidied and clean. At night, you'll also perform some chores for us …" each of the uncles all chuckled and nudged each other excitedly at this point. "… but, I'll show you myself what's expected first. If any of your uncles want you to do some extra, special chores for them while it's your house cleaning time, you need to come and get my permission and approval first, do I make myself clear to everyone?"

My new uncles and I all agreed, though I had no idea what I was agreeing to. All I knew was Murk was no longer pretending to be my sweet and loving step dad. He acted and sounded like my owner or jailer or something - which I soon learned was exactly what he was. In this moment though, I simply found him scary, and myself keen as ever to avoid making him angry, fearing how strict a disciplinarian he'd get, and how quick and easy tiny things might set him off.

Murk told my uncles to clear off to their 'camps' now they had all met me. They all groaned about not getting to start the party straight away, but Murk insisted he needed a catnap and the deal was him first. And once they had all left the shed, Murk told me to get cleaning up the mess and warned me I had better work quietly so he could sleep and I had better do a good job or I'll receive my "first of many spankings to come". It was as I feared: Murk punished me physically for any little thing, just so he'd have the pleasure of causing me pain and letting his hand or his belt connect with my naked bottom.

I tentatively rose my hand in the air like I had to do at school when I wanted to ask a question. Murk replied with, "What?"

I informed him I needed toilet-time, and he pointed out a window towards a tiny little outdoor shed near our motorhome. Murk settled himself onto the three seater lounge, and said, sleepily, "Use the outdoor dunny. Check there's no Redback spiders on the seat before you sit. If you feel a sharp pain, then you've probably been bitten and will need to tell me so you don't die an agonising death like your mother." He spoke of my Mum dying without sadness, without caring, like he was glad she was no longer around to give him any trouble.

"Now, don't dawdle. You've got work to finish before I wake up. And mind the brown snakes, too. They're deadlier."

CHAPTER 8

The outdoor dunny was a sort of thick metal circle with a toilet seat over a deep hole. The moment I stepped inside the wooden shack I was overwhelmed by the stench of long rotting poo, and I noticed heaps of flies buzzed around inside the outhouse. I was so overwhelmed by the odour, I came close to vomiting. I did my business as quickly as I could, holding my breath, trying to avoid breathing any of it in, looking everywhere to check for deadly spiders.

I'd seen Mum clean on weekends, so I did my best to imitate what she had used to do. She kept her cleaning products under the kitchen sink, so that's where I checked in the shed. I worked as silently as the tasks permitted so I didn't disturb the snoring Murk. I found a roll of garbage bags, so I walked around the room picking up all the empty beer cans and bottles, the empty packs of snack foods, and gathered the plates with sickly-smelly uneaten food still on them and carried them into the kitchen.

It was hot and sticky work in a hot and sticky room. It wasn't even summer yet, but already every day was akin to living in an oven. And I craved going outside and sitting under the shade of a tree. But, I remained and scraped the wasted food into the garbage bag, half filled the sink with a mix of hot water I poured from the kettle (I didn't know how else to get hot water) and cold water I found in a bucket, located the washing detergent and squeezed a small dose into the water, and found a sponge to begin washing up once the water wasn't too hot for me to put my hands in. Of course, my eyes filled with tears again, as I endeavoured to stave them off. I guessed if Murk caught me crying, he'd use this as an excuse to punish me, so I did my best to keep my control and get on with doing the work I was now expected to do.

By the time Murk woke and I had finished, I was exhausted and wanted nothing more than to have a small nap myself. But Murk ordered me to go to our motorhome, which was where we both now slept each night, and to change the sheets on his double bed. And to bring them into the shed without dallying. I did that, and Murk pointed to a manually operated bush washing machine. Murk gave me the bucket I had emptied earlier (and another one) and pointed to a pump in the middle of all the caravans, "That's where you get water from. If you need it hot, you have to boil the kettles." (There were five of them next to each other on the kitchen bench). So, over multiple trips back and forth between the shed and manual water pump, and lining the buckets up so I didn't have to work harder than necessary, I filled the washing machine with enough cold water to wash the sheets and pillow cases, and then set about manually agitating the washing machine drum by the handle I had to constantly crank, and draining the machine by connecting an outlet to a hose pipe and turning a valve which allowed the water to escape outside to a vegetable patch behind the shed, and then was re-getting buckets of water so I could rinse the sheets of their suds and then 'spin' the sheets dry enough to hang out, which was achieved by more manual cranking.

I was still new and a novelty to my uncles, who watched me from inside their caravans and annexes every time I exited the shed. My basic instincts screamed internal warnings, as though they were hungry wolves eyeing me as if I was precious prey to eat but they were biding their time until they pounced.

I was sort of right about that, as I'd find out a few hours later.

After I had washed and hung the sheets, now more tired and exhausted than ever, Murk thrust a set of clean sheets into my arms and ordered me to now go and make his bed. On this day, I only had to do Murk's bed, but after this day I had to do each of my uncles' beds as well.

And then I had to help with dinner preparations. I guess I was lucky Murk didn't expect me to cook the meal; I guess there were some aspects to me only being roughly ten years old made him think it was best if himself or one of my uncles completed the task rather than me.

Dinner was steak, mashed potato, boiled peas and carrots with gravy (like it was most nights after that). Everyone ate in the shed at their favourite lounge chair. Murk and my uncles merely left their plates and cutlery on the floor or on the little side tables and I surmised it'd be my job the following day to have to gather them all and wash, dry and put them away so they were available for reuse again for tomorrow night's dinner. I was starting to see the scope of how much housework I was going to have to do each day. And I suddenly likened myself to Cinderella; except, instead of one wicked step mother and two ugly step sisters, I had one severely-mean step dad and seven ugly uncles. Cinderella lived an easier life with what she had to endure before Prince Charming rescued her! Somehow, I knew, I wasn't going to have a fairy tale ending the way Cinderella had. If anything, as far as I could see, mine was destined to be a happy never after.

After dinner, Murk joked we'd have dessert later. And my uncles, who were still constantly watching me, all roared with laughter. I didn't understand the joke; and wasn't in any mood to laugh anyway.

But I was pleased when Murk told me I could now go over to our motorhome, and have a catnap. "I'll come and get you when we are ready to have our party to welcome you to our family, and get started on our dessert."

I was so relieved to be allowed to go and sleep, I didn't really absorb anything Murk had said, except to understand I was being given permission to go and get some sleep. I fell asleep in an instant.

It was dark outside when Murk came into the motorhome, and roughly shook me awake. It took me a bit to wake up.

But rather than telling me to follow him out of the motorhome and across to the shed, Murk sat on his bed and instructed. "Come here, Amber."

I walked over to him filled with apprehension.

"Remember earlier I said in the evenings you perform some chores for us too?" Murk asked.

I nodded my head.

"Well, I'm going to teach you what those chores are, and how to do them properly. And we're going to practice every single day, sometimes again the following morning too, until you do these ones right. Because these are the important ones."

Moments later I learned what sex was.

Murk ordered me to undress, and get into bed with him. Whatever came next was what bad men did; I had no hesitation in believing that. I had done as I was told scared of Murk hurting me if I didn't and removed all my clothes, and once again he stared, then he told me I needed to undo the zipper of *his* jeans, and help him remove his clothing. I was so scared he'd suddenly get angry and start spanking me I did everything he told me to do even though I was embarrassed. I think Murk basked in scaring me into instant cooperation. And this made him very mighty, and happy.

Five minutes later, I was lying on my back on the bed with his heavy body pinning me below him, absolutely bawling uncontrollably as Murk showed me 'how a man loves their prizes.' Everything he did caused me pain, and even though he acknowledged he was causing me to hurt, he told me I'd get used to it the more I let him and my uncles love me like this until eventually it won't hurt me when they do this anymore, and I should be pleased I had so many men who loved me; that I didn't ever want to get to Sarah Ryleland's age and be a fat, middle-aged cow with no man who'd ever find her sexually attractive. He told me what he was doing that caused me to cry in so much pain right now was *why* I was dessert; their prize. They'd all waited very patiently indeed for Murk to bring me to their home so they could start loving me. And I was a "sweeter treat" than they ever have hoped to bring here to love.

Once Murk had finished assaulting my body, and told me he was happy I had been a "good girl despite all that wailing", and he was glad he didn't have to now punish me for having fought him. He told me my Mum would be proud I loved him better than she had tried. And, he told me I now needed to go and visit each of my uncles so they also taught me how to do more things which make men very happy and satisfied during my time here with them.

Murk grabbed his camera and escorted me, still naked, across the grass to the closest caravan to our left. When Murk knocked on their doors in turn, each of my uncles were so excited to see me, as Murk had been. Murk either waited outside while the uncle did the same thing Murk had done to me, or Murk was invited to come into the caravan too, and he took photographs or videos, careful to not get my uncles face or any 'give away body markings' into the frame. The first night it was all over and done with quite quickly - they were so ecstatic I had arrived and didn't waste time getting all of them to have their turn, and were so looking forward to it, so it was over very quickly. Murk didn't like me crying, but some of my uncles did and whined for Murk to let me continue, citing it turned them on, so he let me cry as much as I wanted to. And boy did I cry.

Once I'd been with each of my uncles the first night, we returned to Murk's motorhome. And that's where I learned I wouldn't be sleeping on the bed made up by lowering the dining table and then pulling together the padded pillowing of the dining chairs bottom and backing from both sides of the table to join them in the middle. The spare bed was still ready for use 'just in case' but, no, from now on; I was to sleep in bed with Murk. And I must willing to let Murk and my uncles touch, kiss and own my body whenever he and they were in the mood for that, which was every night and morning before I had my horribly cold water bucket bath and then started my housework duties.

If only Mum hadn't been tricked the night she had caught him staring at my naked body while she bathed me. Murk had wanted to do this to me all along, but had successfully convinced Mum he had been absently looking through me and was horrified she thought he had done what she thought. But, this was another perfect example of how good at lying Murk was. And if only some of the adults who had 'helped' me, after Mum was murdered, had bother to ask me if I wanted to live with Murk and for me to tell them what I had seen and known. I grew to hate the parents who'd given birth to my Mum for their unfair hatred towards me. And I resented every person I'd ever met for their small ways in which now allowed this to be happening to me.

And so you now have a fairly good idea of what my life looked like for the rest of my time there.

❧✧❧

$\mathcal{C}$HAPTER 9

Each morning Murk woke me up by 'loving the prize' again, and then headed for the shed to have breakfast (unless an uncle poked their head out their caravan door and I had to visit them first). My uncles, mostly, had all headed off to go to their various jobs on the weekdays or only the weekends, so often it was Murk and only one or two uncles and me most days. If my uncles, staying in, wanted a 'morning delight' also (which they always did) I had to go with them before allowed to have breakfast, my bucket bath and then start my labour-intensive housework chores.

When I eventually walked into the shed, I'd find the place messier and dirtier with even more plates and cups for me to have to later clean up.

The first morning only Murk showed me how to pour him coffee, how to reheat the sausages and bacon one of the uncles had cooked while we were still sleeping or before I arrived inside the already stifling shed, and how I needed to toast slices of bread and fry eggs and serve his breakfast with a dollop of barbecue sauce on the plate not the food. I got in trouble if I made his coffee too hot or too cold, burnt the toast and took too long to bring him his meal.

I had been used to eating muesli with milk for breakfast, or Vegemite, peanut butter or lemon spread on toast, with a glass of juice, all of which Mum had made for me. I couldn't stomach having sausages and bacon for breakfast, even though I liked both, so I made myself fried egg on toast each day.

Murk spent his days processing and editing the photographs he'd taken the night before, and doing things on a laptop. We didn't get mobile phone reception, but he had a device he plugged into his laptop which gave him internet access and he was able to have what he called 'Skype-calls'. When he wasn't using them, Murk hid his laptop, camera and memory cards somewhere, so if the police ever raided the property they'd never get hold of the 'evidence' to 'pin anything on us'. I figured out the hiding spot was somewhere in the scrub some distance behind the shed beyond the vegetable patch (not that I was ever supposed to know). I heard his footsteps always going and returning from that direction.

The day after I had arrived, Murk also showed me three places I had to hide in if we ever had visitors to the property, especially the police. The rough track in the distant hillside bend was visible from the motorhome, outhouse and shed, to know ahead of time if someone we weren't expecting was approaching. The property was generally quiet, except when the cockatoo's were loudly squawking their upset or delight about something, to hear motors before they came into view. It gave me time to hide. If I was in the shed I had to go and hide in the empty kitchen cupboard - the one next to where all the cleaning products were kept. And I had to stay in there being completely silent until Murk or one of my uncles came and told me it was okay to come out. If I was in the motorhome (or an uncle's caravan) then I had to go and lie inside the left hand dining chair, which is normally the built-in storage box where travellers keep their spare blankets, linen and towels and other items, because this was the same spot for each of them.

Murk warned me I had to be very careful about the cushioning on top of the chairs, so it wouldn't look out of place, and he made me practice lifting the cushions up, then the lid, then hopping in and lying flat without letting the lid slam down after me; and I had to keep practising until he was happy the cushioning fell into place properly - so it still looked like it was a bed not yet slept in. Again, Murk told me I had to stay in there, being as quiet as a mouse for as long as it took for him or one of my uncles to tell me it was okay for me to come out now. If I was outside, like at the water pump or in the outhouse, I was to proceed past the first row of trees and hide behind the second cluster if I couldn't make it into the shed or one of the caravans (but mostly always try to get to Uncle Jack's), and stay hidden behind the largest trees trunk until Murk or one of my uncles came and got me. But, Murk said, I was to always try to reach the shed or Uncle Jack's caravans hiding spot foremost as these were the more secure hiding places right now - until he was able to build another one, a wooden box he intended to bury in the ground past the trees, which when finished would serve as a third secure hiding place, the safest one of all.

Every week, Murk made me practice hiding in one of the hiding spots.

I only attempted to run away once, during the first week also. While I thought Murk was asleep.

He had spanked me hard twice for no reason to show me he is boss and to remind me to never ever forget it. I hadn't even done anything wrong. And I knew Mum wouldn't want me to live my life like this. So I made the decision to flee during the middle of the night. I didn't know where I was going to go, and I knew I could get bitten by a snake, but I was desperate. I wanted and needed to put as much distance between me and Murk before anyone at camp realised I was gone. I figured it'd probably take them ages to find me if they wouldn't know what direction I had taken off in. And I'd do my best to reach town through the bush rather than the track leading on and off the property, despite the long distance, where I'd go straight to the police station. But I hadn't even got as far as the outside toilet when his voice broke in the still night air. "Think you'd run away, Amber?"

I stammered, "No ... I - I was just going to the toilet."

"Liar." Murk stated simply. "Get back here, now."

I nervously did as I was told. And I got the hiding of my life, twofold. One for trying to escape. The other for lying about it.

Murk didn't use his hands. No, he used his belt. I cried and screamed so loud birds sleeping in nearby trees all took flight despite it being night time, and my uncles all poked their heads out of their caravan's to see what the ruckus was about. My bottom stayed red and tender for a week. I never even thought about trying to escape again after that. I got on with 'how life now was like' he ordered me I had to do, and striving to never think about what life used to be like, as this only made me sad until I reached wanting to cry and it made me miss Mum beyond any speakable words; and if Murk was around, meant more punishment with that belt.

Twice I had to hide, for real, not practice.

The first time I was in the shed washing up and I heard a car I soon worked out wasn't one of my uncles approaching. It was after I had turned ten. So even without Murk in the shed to instruct me to hide in the cupboard, I'd quickly comprehended if I didn't want punishment later by Murk and his belt I had to follow his rule to hide. I opened the kitchen cupboard, and used the small piece of rope Murk had installed for me to close the cupboard door properly behind me. I had to tuck my knees up to my chest and sit with my spine against the side. I found it more comfortable to hug my knees with my arms and rest my chin in the valley between my legs. And no matter how uncomfortable I was or how much I wanted or needed toilet-time, I did my best to keep silent.

Even though no one came inside the shed, which equated to the possibilities of hiding behind the lounge or something to not have been so uncomfortable, I heard a man talking loudly. He stayed only for about twenty minutes, but Murk didn't come in to give me the okay to exit the cupboard until the car had long left. I learned that night at dinner it had been a real estate agent, who had come to see if Murk was interested in selling the property.

"Told him the property isn't mine, it's yours, Spud, but I know for fact you aren't interested in selling; if anything, you wanted to know about any neighbouring properties coming onto the market, so you'd try and rummage the money together to increase the size of the land you own."

My uncles were concerned about whether the agent had spotted me, but Murk reassured them. "Nope, he didn't have a clue; our little prize was in the shed already and did exactly what she's been told and hid in the cupboard like a good little girl."

He announced to them all I should be rewarded for my good behaviour and they all enthusiastically agreed; but I wasn't given a break from any chores, and didn't receive any treats like ice-cream for sweets. I merely had Murk and my uncles each tell me what they were doing to me that particular night was I'd been a good little girl, and they did the same things to me as what they had been doing every other night and morning, perhaps a bit gentler (for me) than previously.

The second time, Murk and I were still in bed in his motorhome one morning, Murk had just started on loving me, when a mechanic arrived earlier than expected to take a look at the engine to see why the motor wasn't starting. Murk quickly got me to put my panties on and get into the hiding spot cursing with swear words there wouldn't be enough time for me to get to Uncle Jack's, the shed or the trees, so it would have to be his, and I stayed hidden inside for roughly the bulk of the day.

I'm not trying to lighten how bad the situation was living there, but I nearly laughed aloud at Murk trying to squash himself back into his pants. He pinched his dick on the zip in his haste and started cursing. I'm glad he didn't see me come close to laughing maliciously about it as I closed the lid to hide me, happy I had witnessed him getting hurt on his precious boy part.

Tools clinked, clangoured, and tinged; attempts at starting the engine occasionally were made, and the muffled voices of the two men talking while the mechanic worked at figuring out what the problem was, all the while unaware of me hiding so close by - especially when he jumped into the cabin to try starting her up where I was a mere metre and a half away.

Inside my hiding spot, I was able to lie on my back, stomach or my sides against the hard floor. No light drifted in, so I couldn't even see my hands in front of my eyes or where the edges of the coffin-wide walls were. I had no idea how much time was passing. Even one second clicked past as though a second was eternity. I was hungry: I'd missed breakfast, and lunch. I peed in my pants a little, unable to hold it in any longer. Thereafter, I had the horrible staling urine smell and the wetness of my pants to deal with on top of my other discomforts. And I kept leaking, making it worse.

To try and take my mind off how uncomfortable I was lying on the hard floor and urgently I wanted to let all of my full bladder out, not only the bits which determinedly escaped, and how hungry I was, I drifted in and out of sleep, trying to trick myself it was night time rather than me being holed inside the storage box so a stranger wouldn't think it weird a solitary child was living with eight men so they might talk about it in their community, which was sure to raise alarms with authority figures, as Murk called them.

"You are a convicted paedophile; it wouldn't take much to raise suspicion with you being part of our crowd." Murk joked with Uncle Jack.

Uncle Jack replied, equally jovially, "Yeah, that's why my van's the go to spot, and you guys better look after me as promised if I ever end up back in the slammer, and I'll keep my word none of you had any idea what was happenin' right under your innocent blokey noses."

The rest of the time I appreciated at least I was getting a day off from my backbreaking chores, and Murk wouldn't have *legitimate* reason to punish me again for not having completed them.

But I hated even practising hiding in the motorhome hiding spot after that. It was like I had to be in the coffin same as what we buried Mum in. Murk didn't care about how distressing I found it, and told me I had to keep practising - he'd heard me twice while the mechanic had been there, which meant the mechanic might have asked what was inside the motorhome. In other words, the two times I had accidentally knocked my knees against the wall of my hiding spot meant I had 'fucked up' and needed to practice regularly until I got it right. Murk had yanked me by the hair and threatened to install a lock so I couldn't open the lid to get out again and he'd leave me in for a couple of days or even a week if I kept arguing, so I instantly ceased protesting after that threat, scared he'd carry it out as promised. He'd carried out every other one.

My uncles all voiced feeling bad whenever I had to be or was punished, and told me, "But it's the only way to teach you how to be a good little prize, Amber honey." and invariably added at some point, "But come here, so I can kiss your gorgeous bot-bot all better."

A year or so into my living this new life in the middle of nowhere with only Murk and my uncles as my only source of human contact, Bruno complained I was starting to go through body changes. I was worried I'd get in trouble for that, but Murk said, "Yeah, well, we've all known she'd grow up eventually." and Bruno whined something like, "Yeah, but I prefer them when their younger."

It came as a surprise to me, but not to Murk when one night as we stood at the door waiting for Bruno to take me in, when he said, "Look, I'll pass tonight, mate."

Over the next eighteen months (I think), Darren, Luke, Ben and Jack followed Bruno's lead. They never stopped loving me completely, but the frequency became less and less over time, until eventually it had stopped with that particular uncle altogether, and the remaining uncles were each starting to beg off some nights too.

My breasts had started growing, and I now had some hair on my privates; and these two things became the apparent cause of them losing complete interest in wanting to love me, unless they watched footage of me when I first came to them to help them still love the real deal. They started talking about how they should try to replace me with a younger replacement, and move me on. Murk told them he will get a secure, encrypted connection and have a chat to some of his online buddies he sold many of the pictures he had taken of me with my uncles to.

So I started having a secret fear I'd have to move on, placed in the care of faceless strangers.

$\mathscr{C}$HAPTER 10

Then when I started getting my periods when I was thirteen and a half years old, the only person left still happy to keep loving me was Murk. All the others had lost all interest in me (even with the footage), and they were getting antsy about hurrying to get a replacement prize, so each of them got a slice of the fun again.

Three months later, Murk managed to find a seven year old from one of his online contacts, and my uncles all gave Murk a wad of money each, so he was able to set off to go and complete the transaction. Days later, I was left to stay in the shed under the care of Uncle Alister, while Murk took the motorhome and disappeared for two weeks, and my other uncles continued going to work on the weekdays like usual.

Now I was even more worried about being passed to strangers. And Uncle Alister confirmed 'despite how pretty you are' it was taking Murk a bit of time to find the right buyer for me; most people in the online group where he had been able to enter into negotiations to buy the seven year old he'd left to go and collect, were like them and only wanted pre-pubescent girls. Me, I was too old for the online group members, but too young for a different group Murk had been chatting with and it became too risky keeping both me and the new prize considering Jack was still always on the cop's radar.

When Murk returned, he introduced Daisy the same way he had introduced me to his ped-group. Daisy and I were forbidden from ever talking to each other. And that night, I was made to sleep on the lounge chair in the shed (for the first time ever, Murk locked me in).

Murk taught Daisy how to hide in the cupboard under the kitchen sink while I was made to sit on the lounge facing the door as instructed. And Daisy was given the chores I had had to do. Now, I had to do some temporary different ones until Murk worked out how to dispose of me for the highest price someone was willing to pay.

We watched television reports covering the abduction in the Australian Capital Territory of Daisy Mecklestein. Murk and the uncles were eager to know what the police and media knew. Did they have any suspects? Had cameras captured footage of them? But, it appeared the police didn't find any vehicle or person matching the description by the one eye-witness - Daisy's father - of the snatching.

A week later, during dinner, Murk announced excitedly to everyone in the room, "Good news. I've found Amber a new home. In America. Fifteen US, we'll get."

"Great, this means we're making a nice little profit," said Ben, punching the air victoriously.

"Yeah. So, I'm going to have to organise for her passport and visa, which I can only do by taking her into town. But the money for our flights will have to get deducted from that fifteen grand."

"Won't it put us at risk of attracting the cop's attention? Taking her into town, when you're known to live on the property with us?"

Murk reassured them, "Not if I start heading to Sydney and do it along the journey. I'll put a rush on the passport; I can have her on the plane in four weeks. We'll get her on a student exchange program visa; and she can become a missing kid a few months in or something. That'll be the new owner's problem to deal with."

"So, when'll you leave?"

"First thing tomorrow. No use delaying things, is there?"

I was instantly highly scared about what the future held for me. As much as I was scared of Murk, and didn't like being loved, I had sort of gotten used to my daily routine, and what was expected of me. And my uncles, although they did things they shouldn't be, were always nice to me. I was even tempted to talk when I wasn't allowed to, to beg Murk not to sell me and let me stay here with everybody. But I didn't find the courage to do that.

Again I had to sleep in the shed. Murk wanted to have a bit more time with Daisy before he'd be away for four or five long weeks. The uncles didn't begrudge him this; they truly appreciated how Murk kept them in good supply and away from police suspicion. Daisy stayed in my mind that night - I hated the times when Murk 'binge-fucked' me; poor Daisy was sure to feel the same way. One night he had loved me eleven times, and I hadn't been able to get more than four hours sleep.

I was again woken earlier than usual by my uncles coming in to have their breakfast before heading off to work, but this time, they each came and gave me a kiss and cuddle and wished me luck with my new owner.

"I look forward to watching the video's you'll star in, precious prize." Uncle Alister said with a tear in his eye. "I won't get turned on by them; but I'll be able to brag I used to know you and played a huge part in your training."

"Remember us when you become rich and famous," said Uncle Ben.

Uncle Jack patted me on my backside, and gave me a quick wink. "Just remember to suck dick exactly like I taught you, and you'll do fine Amber baby."

"Yeah," Uncle Alister agreed. "Yeah, oh your doing it that way was the best! Can't wait for Daisy to do it that way, too."

Despite hating what they'd been doing to me, I found myself wishing they weren't leaving; that the day wouldn't progress. I never thought I'd ever want to stay right where I was. I'd happily continue loving them if it meant I could stay. It was only really Murk who still scared and hurt me; but I was even used to him.

Uncle Bruno didn't go to work this day. He was the one in charge while Murk was away, and was therefore in charge of taking care of Daisy.

Murk exited the motorhome with a huge smile on his face, and walked the down-faced and silently crying Daisy to Bruno's caravan, and then came and got me.

Murk ordered me to wash, and then put on a pair of nice trendy looking shorts and a t-shirt I'd never seen before.

So after three and a half years living on a remote property, where at any moment a deadly brown snake or Redback spiders could've bitten me if I wasn't careful about where I put my feet and bottom, I was now strapped into the front passenger seat of Murk's motorhome, and was jostled about as the vehicle slowly climbed the bumpy dirt track once more. It was terrifying knowing in about four week's time, I was to fly on a plane to start a new phase of life in a different country.

Murk made me bend forward and stay looking at the floor, so I was lower than the dashboard, from the moment we neared town until we were well and truly past it. That was a very uncomfortable hour or so.

"Can't have you being seen, and ruining things for us now. Not when we're so close to finishing up with you." Murk had chirped.

We drove all day, only stopping in a truck stop for Murk to buy us lunch. I didn't much feel like eating, but did my best to not waste the burger and fries Murk had bought for me. I didn't want him to use his belt on my bottom once we arrived at wherever he had decided we'd camp overnight.

To my surprise, Murk pulled into a caravan park at around four p.m. After he had gone in and paid for the overnight site, and Murk had backed the motorhome in under the supervision of the site manager, who then waved and returned to his office once Murk was done, turned to me and said in a warning tone, "Don't say or do anything stupid or contradictory while we're here, or I'll use my belt on your skinny little backside the first chance I get, and you'll scream for your dead Mum for a week."

I nodded.

"Right. This is the story you have to go along with. You're my daughter, I'm a single dad - a widow, and we're on one week's holidays, alright."

"Yes, Murk," I replied softly.

"If anyone invites you to come and play, or anything like that, you need to decline. I don't care what bullshit reason you give, but you're not to leave my sight or earshot or the belt it will be. Actually, I think it would be best if I did the talking, if that's possible, so you're to step away from anyone who tries talking to you, and snuggle into my stomach like a scared child. This way I can tell people you haven't been yourself since your mum died eight months ago; which is why I've brought you on the holiday, to try and get you to break out of your shell."

"Okay, Murk."

"Right. First thing we need to do is to head back towards the Pharmacy I saw as we were coming in. We need to get your passport photo taken. We've only got forty five mins until the post office closes. I want your application in the mail box so it is collected and sent to the city today. This way it'll arrive early next week. Here, brush your hair, again."

Like was now my strong habit, I did as I was told without arguing, and then we headed for the pharmacy. Two boys, probably a year or so older than me whistled as I walked past despite me being with Murk. Once we were out of earshot, Murk smiled and then said, "I reckon they'd love it if I let them fuck you for a few bucks. Oh well, not enough time. Besides, I'll make more money with our current plan; between you and me now you can't tell the boys, I've negotiated I receive royalties if your films start grossing profits. This means, if you do well, I might end up rich, kid. I'm glad I picked you as our prize - I reckon you're gonna grow up a stunner, so guys with different tastes to us are gonna cream themselves over, like those little dickwads back there."

I had my passport photo taken, with the lady who took the photograph jokingly telling Murk to watch out for me, with my 'model looks' he'll be busy beating back the boys once I start my new high school, to which Murk played the role of loving dad already stressing over how he'll handle it once I start dating, he was very much aware of what hell he was in for to beat back 'all the horny little turds who'll try getting to her'.

Outside the pharmacy, Murk attached one of the four images onto the application form he'd already filled out, and then popped the application, a certified photocopy of my birth certificate and a couple of other documents, including a bank cheque, into an express envelope and rushed away from me when he noticed the postal worker was already outside the post office clearing the two mail boxes half an hour earlier than he expected.

"Thanks buddy," Murk said, before returning to me slightly

breathless. He was happy he'd made the day's post. It meant the passport office received my application early next week. Everything was on schedule for my transport and sale to my soon-to-be new owner in Murk's desired time frame.

We had four weeks to kill before our flight to America; Murk was in no rush for us to get to Sydney. Sometimes we stayed overnight in other caravan parks, other times we parked in free camping spots. And we only did an hour or two's travelling before calling it done for the day. Murk did his best to stay in places so the sleeping arrangement was me in bed with him and therefore snuck in yet another session of loving me in the evenings and first thing in the morning. On the nights where we were near other travellers, I slept on the converted dining table bed but had to give Murk a blow job (me kneeling on the floor, him at the edge of his bed, him controlling my head to take him in at the ever-fastening pace he liked) only after he closed all the curtains so there were no gaps and got the TV or radio working, so others wouldn't hear what we were really doing and with the lights off, so no one spied our telltale silhouettes. He came quickly on those occasions, knowing we were metres away from our closest motorhome neighbours still awake, and he was getting away with making me do this without anyone becoming wise to our actions.

We spent the last week in a hotel. Murk parked his motorhome at Sydney airport, had a mini freak out about how much the parking was going to cost him for the two week period he needed to park there, and then we had caught a train into the city, gone and collected my new passport and visa in person, and then after collecting some other documents, caught another train and walked through the city streets until we reached the hotel.

During the day, Murk didn't want to hang around stuck in the small but nice hotel room, saying he'd end up with claustrophobia if he had to hole up in it for a week, so we did what normal tourists did. We visited the Sydney Opera House, wandered around the Botanical Gardens, visited sites which didn't cost money, ate lunch at Circular Quay or The Rocks, and returned to our hotel room only once evening had come, after having eaten in different restaurants in Chinatown. Another father and daughter going about their normal existence.

At night, Murk made me briefly hop into the bed which if I was his real daughter I'd have slept in, so when hotel cleaners came they didn't think it strange my bed was untouched. But of course, Murk wanted to do it with me as many times as he could make the most of before we parted ways.

"I still get turned on because I know you're underage." he said by way of explaining why he hadn't lost interest in loving me like my uncles. I think he also got off by the control he had over me too. He had only to click his finger a certain way and I had to get busy servicing him immediately. Obey or be punished; this was my life.

And then came the day where Murk woke me and we did it twice, stating he thought this was probably the last time he'd ever get to do me again, and then I showered and dressed ready to catch the city to airport train with a suitcase of luggage Murk handed me after we stopped by the airport car park so he could retrieve it from his motorhome. Only this time, it was for real, we were checking in at Departures.

I'd never flown in an aeroplane before. But once again, Murk had given me the story I had to strictly play along with. He was my dad, and I had won some great opportunity and was participating in an exchange student program for six months. Yes, I was a bit scared, but I was also really looking forward to meeting and staying with my host family. Dad was staying with me for the first week, to check everything was as he'd been told it was due to "you can't be too careful these days, especially with a daughter as attractive as mine" - I was all Dad had now Mum had died. He was going to miss me terribly, but it was the right thing to support me in my dancing ambition. And of course, he intended coming to visit me in three months time for a week, so I didn't get too home sick, and we'd Skype each other every week.

If anyone bothered to look into the organisation and scholarship, they'd find the organisation was real; same with the scholarship. Murk was trusting the fact they wouldn't actually contact the organisation to verify my participation; the falsified documents Murk had somehow managed to get looked authentic enough to get us to pass through Customs.

Before we left the hotel room, Murk had also warned me in case the Australian or American customs officials *did* think something fishy was going on, I was to keep with the story, no matter how much they might pressure me, and I was strictly forbidden from ever telling anyone anything about my life he didn't want them to know.

"If you take the opportunity to tell them you're being sold, or have been our prize and how we've loved you, then I promise you, the men we hired to kill your mother, will come after you. They won't give up until they find you. Only, they'll take you some place secret and make you suffer much worse than they ever made your mother. You'll be punished for weeks, not hours like dear Mummy went through. Do we have complete understanding, Amber-sweetie?"

Once again, my only choice was to nod my head in agreement. Murdering my Mum, or rather having arranged it, had long ago proved to me Murk was serious about and carried out his threats. He wasn't filled 'with hot air' like my Mum used to call people who threatened but never carried it through - though she was referring to some of the mothers disciplining their children (like Mrs Ryleland), not bad men who had self-appointed themselves as my owner and conducted their dealings in secret and on the wrong side of the law.

The beautiful flight attendant told me its normal for first time passengers to feel scared when it's the first time they've ever flown in a plane, after I had suddenly started vomiting as a result of my worrying about who I was being sold to, and said, "But, if you're like me, you'll learn to love it."

We didn't have any trouble getting through customs on the American side either.

We caught a taxi to some motel Murk had pre-organised for us to stay in overnight; and then another one the following morning to enable us to get to our midday appointment. Murk made me leave the suitcase of clothes I'd never seen or worn which I'd brought with me on the airplane in the hotel room.

"You won't need them. You're new owner will get you whatever you need from now on. I'll dispose of these in a charity bin before I head back to Aus. They only cost me five bucks from the charity shop back home."

$\mathscr{C}$HAPTER 11

As we approached an unremarkable modern industrial building some twenty minutes later, Murk unexpectedly stopped me mere metres or two from the door.

"Look, this isn't the completely done deal I told the boys it is." Murk said, for the first time ever astounding me. He looked and sounded more nervous than what raged inside me, if that was even possible. "The buyer agreed you are prettier than most in the pics, and photogenic, but he has to like you in the flesh for him to decide to proceed with the transaction; he said he has an abundant pool of pretty girls he can choose from, so it's not only looks that makes him buy. His starlets all have to have a unique something so he can develop a marketing angle for the starlet. So you need to impress him."

I looked at Murk, not understanding what he meant.

"Oh, for fuck's sake, are you *stupid* or just *retarded*? You need to demonstrate your skills, Amber. You're a slut now, or about to become one if he buys you. You're probably gonna be one for the rest of your life whether it's him or someone else I can offload you too anyway. So you have to embrace and bring out that side of you. I don't know if he wants you to demo on him, on me, or some other bloke he brings in for the occasion; but if this buyer says to you to suck dick, you suck fucking dick. If he says, show me how you fuck, you goddamn show him how you fuck. You make sure you make whoever the bloke who does you cum and cum good - that's the goal you've got to meet. And you damn well convince this buyer you *love* sucking dick and *love* being fucked, up the fanny, up the arse, I don't give a shit, you suck and fuck and win me this sale. *Got it?*"

Yeah, I knew what was expected of me now. I had to convince the buyer to buy me. If the deal fell through, I'd seriously piss Murk off and suffer the consequence. And Murk intended teaching me my previous punishments had been child's play compared to what he'd do to me if I didn't make him want to purchase me at the price Murk was hoping for, or close enough to it.

"If you win him over, it means he'll be open to doing future business with me. He's never traded with me before, and he's worried I'm law enforcement with a dummy deal before my cop mates bust in to shut down their operation - well, I reckon he is, I know, that's always in the back of my mind when I meet with a buyer or seller the very first time. I know *he's* a legit buyer. And, he'll soon realise you are a genuine sale. That'll give me additional avenues for what to do with Daisy and our future ped-prizes once the boys are no longer interested in them too. Oh, but he thinks you're already sixteen, Amber. So go along with that. I had to lie about your age to get him to agree to auditioning you, which is why he probably got suss on the deal. Hopefully he won't figure out how old you really are until after it's a closed sale, but I'll confess to him about your real age when I think it's the right time so he'll buy from me again. He'll learn soon enough I'm a legit seller, that he's got nothin' to worry about with me."

If I ever thought I had been nervous about anything before this moment, I had been kidding myself what nervousness is. As Murk lost all signs of worry now he had shared with me his deception to my uncles and burdening me with what was really at stake, my hands were now shaking, and my legs became weakly unreliable and I needed to pee where seconds before I hadn't needed to. I now wore the full encumbrance of whatever happened next. Good or bad result. Regardless. And although I didn't like Murk for what he had done to me and Mum, I'll admit: at that moment I actually wanted to stay with him. So I pleaded and begged him not to sell me on, promising I'd keep doing him whenever however he wanted if he please didn't sell me. I'd have given him a blow job right there on the outdoor porch if it meant he'd agree.

"Aww, babes. As much as I could live a happy life fucking your little puss morning and night despite generally preferring the young chicklets every bit as your uncles, you *are* being sold and no amount of asking not to is gonna change that." He grabbed my face and kissed me on the lips. "It's not personal, Amber sweetie; this is all about the dosh... or I'd never have listed you. We never intended keeping you forever. Besides, this buyer's got a fab reputation, I'm sure you'll be fine."

Murk pressed the buzzer. It took a few moments before a male voice spoke to us from a speaker. "State your business."

"Ah, yes. The name's Murk Walters. Here to have an appointment with Mr J ... so Amber here can audition." he had said the last words quietly. "He's expecting us."

There was a pause, and then the door buzzed. Murk pushed the door and then me through it. Two big, and I mean big and bulky-muscled men, came towards us in the dark corridor. They looked like they'd crush me to death with only one hand. One of them pushed Murk to face the wall with his hands up high, and his legs spread apart, and then took his time patting him down, thoroughly.

"He's clean." One big bloke finally told his mate.

Then it was my turn.

Except, the big bloke took a moment to also give both my small breasts a squeeze, and rub my crotch when he got to that, because he could; there was no way Murk dared taking him on to insist the big bloke get his paws off the merchandise. My guess was the big guys were letting Murk wordlessly know they were boss without having to say so, and I was the means of conveying that information. But not for the first time in my life, I was struck at how entitled men believed themselves when it came to touching my body. I seriously hoped I wouldn't have to do it with one of either men who I was sure to have to do something to or with; these particular men possessed the capability to crush my petite frame and I'd likely find the experience extremely painful. They were that massive.

One big bloke led the way, and the other trailed us, as we next went along the hall and then turned into another. I wondered if I was a prisoner being led by prison guards to my death row execution. At the end of the second corridor, straight ahead, the first guy tapped on the door, and we waited barely a second when a voice commanded, "Bring them straight in."

An older man with peppered hair, wearing an expensive dark navy-blue business suit gestured for us to fully enter the room. He came round from behind the big desk he had been sitting at; Murk stepped forward and the two men shook hands. But the man was only interested in me.

"She doesn't look sixteen." He said, not asked. His next words were sharply businesslike. "Don't lie to me, girl, how old are you?"

I cast a nervous look at Murk, who grimaced but nodded his head to indicate I should tell him how old I really am.

"Almost fourteen, sir," I replied, not knowing what else to call the man.

"Alright, remove your clothes and show me what you look like."

Murk flashed me a warning look which said without speaking words, "Do as the man says or else." A fact the businessman didn't escape noticing, for he smiled for a moment, and relaxed.

Trying not to feel too self conscious of the fact three male strangers were about to see me naked, I nervously fumbled with removing my t-shirt and bra, and then with a piercing look from the man and another threatening one from Murk, I undid my shorts and slipped them off along with my panties and sandals.

I was made to open my mouth for the boss man to check inside, and to lie belly-up on a padded table one of the big men had gone and got and wheeled into position behind me. It reminded me of a baby's change table. I was ordered to lie back, and to spread my legs wide apart so the business man had an easy time of it checking my private parts. I wanted to cry and disappear into nothingness from the humiliation and embarrassment; but was strict and reminded myself things were sure to be completely different regardless of whether the man purchased me or not. Murk intended on keeping trying until someone eventually bought me, so I had better toughen up and simply deal with whatever comes next. I had no power or influence to change Murk's mind. To do so only incurred his wrath.

And then the man had his fingers inside me, feeling around. He took his sweet-arse time, too. Even Murk looked like he was starting to get pissed.

"Okay." he said, withdrawing his fingers and taking a hand towel the big man handed him, while looking at Murk. "She passes my preliminary examination. Sebastian, get the Med team in so we can have the full work up."

And another, even more expensive looking man, slimmer, more important looking, entered the room, and said, "And call off the starlet relocations. If our friend Mr Walters here was a cop or wired, the girl'd never have been allowed to undress, let alone be physically examined. Get the Roy's back too. I'll want her to do a screen test next, all going well."

He introduced himself to Murk as Mr J. as the two new, lab-coated men appeared and approached the padded table I was still lying on. One swabbed the inside of my cheeks, another put my feet into 'stirrups' and then pushed a metal contraption inside me and did something that must have made me wider and was so uncomfortable I couldn't help but let tears run down my face, and did a thorough close up of my insides, before taking another swab using a gigantic cotton bud, and then finally closing the metal thing and removing it.

"Sorry for not being here right from the start of the meeting, Mr Walters, but as you can appreciate, we needed to check you weren't a set up, and we wouldn't now currently be raided, and this facility soon shut down as a result."

"Yeah, look, I totally understand. It's the first time we're doing business, and you can never be too careful."

"My sentiments exactly. That's why Mr. D., here, fills in for me when it's a high risk. He knows he'll have to serve jail time for me, but he'd be well taken care of and handsomely compensated for his sacrifice and loyalty if such a situation were to happen. But I do order thorough background checks before either of us ever agree to meet with anyone. Including our regulars."

My pubic hair (and the hair on my head) was combed, I think they were checking I didn't have something, lice maybe; my nipples were iced so they could measure them. And blood was drawn from the veins on the inside bend of my left arm. (All while my legs were spread wide and strapped in, as Mr J. and Murk stood past my legs looking on as they chatted).

One the Med team turned to Mr J. and said, "Everything looks clean so far; only the tests can prove this for certain. We'll go get started on them right away, sir."

Mr J. clicked his fingers, and a Sebastian stepped forward. "Yeah, boss?"

"Get a Pete prepped - one we want to get off our books, you know the one I'm referring to, so it doesn't matter in case she has picked up something while she was gaining experience."

"Rightio, boss." And the big bloke left the room.

Mr J. gestured for someone out of my line of sight to next come forward. "Sebastian, unlock the leg restraints, and escort Amber to Room Two, please."

I hadn't even realised my feet had been locked in until he said that.

"I'm pleasantly surprised how well trained your merchandise is, Mr Walters. Normally we have to forcibly remove the clothes from the girl, have a Sebastian slap her into compliance, and restrain their arms and legs, and enforce their silence so we can do our work. So far, Amber is looking good for purchase; but, she still has to pass the screen testing before I make a final decision. I give fair warning, not all girls brought before me to audition pass the final screen testing stage of consideration. How well they do in this last part is what helps me determine the price I'm willing to pay, if I am indeed willing to pay anything at all. I'm always happy to take over ownership of the girl if the seller is desperate to dispose of their property though. But, let's see how Amber does onscreen before we think about sale and negotiating prices."

"How many girls do you generally get auditioning," Murk asked, nodding but looking disappointed over the detail my purchase might not be a done deal yet.

The big bloke unlocked the straps, removed my feet from the stirrups, folded the contraptions so they disappeared inside slots on both sides of the table so you'd never even guess they existed if you weren't aware of the fact they did. And then he pulled me into a sitting position and pulled me off the table and onto my feet.

"I personally see about ten girls a week. But, the gentleman you thought was me when you first arrived, he sees anywhere up to one hundred girls per week for me - though not at this location. We reject seventy to eighty percent of them. Mostly those who have been snatched off the streets from whatever country they lived in, so they haven't yet had their first forced experience, and are frightened cuffed young things still madly wondering what's going to happen to them and hoping the police might find them. Their constant crying and begging I find tedious, so I only personally oversee *special* transactions, usually meaning they are a resale or experienced first time sale, like your little puss here."

Another big bloke arrived, and Mr J. simply nodded at him, before turning to Murk. "Come. Let's progress downstairs; you can you can watch Amber's screen test with me from the control room."

He gestured for Murk to follow one of the big guys, and Mr J. waited for Murk to pass.

My clothes were no longer on the floor. I couldn't see where they were. But the businessman strode from the office behind Murk, and the remaining big man, who had wheeled away the table, clamped his large hand around the base of my neck, exactly like Murk had done the first day I arrived at the property all that time ago, only firmer, and moved me along the hall and then through a wall after an inconspicuous wall panel opened to reveal a hidden door, and we each made our way, single file down the steps of the narrow passageway, coming out into a long and wide basement corridor lined with lots of doors, and then finally into one of those side rooms, all the while following the others, with my big bloke making up the rear.

First, was an outer chamber with computers and a big glass window, which reminded me of the room I had been taken to at the hospital the day I was told by the lady how my Mum had died, like police office Stan was able to look on, not knowing Murk standing next to him had arranged for her attack and resulting in her planned death. Then was the door through to the room not much larger than Mum's old bedroom which was watched, and which smelled strongly like sex the moment I walked in, which had a large double or queen sized bed in the middle on the far wall, and was surrounded by a lot of electronic equipment: Lights, video cameras, funny looking pieces of metal and other accessories.

Murk whistled in admiration, and lovingly stroked one of the video cameras.

"Ah, yes, you're a photographer and videographer. Naturally, you'll appreciate the setup." the businessman, Mr J. said, smiling.

There were two doors at the room's side, one on each side.

"What are those for?" Murk asked with a sort of professional interest.

"One's the male dressing room, and the other is our starlet's quarters. I'll show you them, after we've done the screen test."

Behind me (still with the big man's hand clamped on my neck), in the computer room, lights had come on, and a team of about eight or nine men who had arrived en masse were settling into chairs, firing up computers and remotely switching on the lights and cameras in the room all pointed at the bed.

I was instructed by Mr J. to go and sit on the bed, face the 'control room' and to follow instructions given to me by 'Roy' through the speaker system.

Everyone else cleared the room, and took a seat in the row of chairs in front of the technicians' computers in rows behind that, all facing the window looking into the room I was in. Television screens pointed towards me from different positions high and low on the surrounding walls, but they only had the words 'standby' showing. A naked man with an already erect penis larger than Murk's and my uncles came from the side door on my left, and then a male voice with a strong American accent was issuing instructions. I was ordered to get on my knees on the bed and suck the man's dick, and every few minutes, the same voice barked into the room telling us to freeze and hold the position so the camera had time to zoom in and get close ups of the different things they told us to do from different angles.

"Okay, Pete. Slide your cock in and out real slow. Slower. Yes, that's right. Yes, keep going, no *don't* get faster yet, we need a bit more slow-mo action. Amber, try to act like you really, really like having Pete's dick in your mouth. That his dick is the only thing in the whole world you like sucking on. Yes, that's nearly it, smile a bit wider. If it helps, think of it like you're a little kid sucking your favourite lollipop."

From my angle half facing the starlet room door, half facing the watching window, I saw Mr J. occasionally twist his head to give instructions to a technician behind him.

And finally, Pete was allowed to 'finish off until you cum. Make sure you spray it all over her. Amber, honey, I want you to move your head around when he pulls out like you are desperate to swallow his spurt but he's denying you the treat and you're trying to get the treat anyway, okay starlet."

I didn't know what he meant by that, but I did my best to follow all instructions, knowing how much my getting this screen test right it was in Murk's view.

"Alright. That's a wrap for the screen test. You did great Pete."

Pete got off the bed and walked through the door he came from.

I saw Mr J. and Murk rise from their seats and then exited the door we came in from. I had no idea if either of them were happy or upset; I wasn't told I had done a great job, but then again I hadn't been ticked off for not doing it the way they wanted either.

The big man came into the room as Murk disappeared from my sight. He picked up a towel, wiped the man's stuff off my face and chest and then opened the other side door the businessman had earlier said was the starlet's quarters, and told me to wait in there. I heard him lock the door after he had closed it once I was in. It was only one of two entry and exits to this long but still small room; the other exited into the main corridor. I didn't bother testing the handle; it would without doubt also be locked. Mr J., the less pepper-haired, more silver at the temples, more smartly attired boss, ran a well controlled operation, so I would never get an opportunity to try to escape.

If he decided to purchase me, that is.

<h1>𝒞HAPTER 12</h1>

If Murk wasn't going to get the fifteen thousand American dollars he'd been counting on, would he 'offload me' for no or lesser cost simply so he no longer had to worry about trying to find a buyer for me? Every communication he had put him at risk of getting caught and jailed.

I was counting on Murk holding out to get the price he wanted. If not this first buyer, maybe the next. I was hoping I'd get a different buyer, even though this result meant I'd be in trouble with Murk.

I must have waited for about forty five minutes twiddling my thumbs wondering whether this was going to be my new home or I'd have to face Murk's fury before the corridor door clicking unlocked made me look up to see Mr J. and Murk as they walked in. They were already in relaxed conversation with each other, so I guessed negotiations must have gone well (in Murk's view).

Which meant only one thing: I'd been sold. At, or close to, Murk's asking price.

"…so every night from ten p.m. to about three a.m. we broadcast live action, but the real action only starts and is visible to those who pay, and the footage we capture during the day is used as supplementary cross-over's to help entice people in to watch the live action feed, and is ready to play if we experience technical difficulties, so our customers don't ask for refunds. Our customers know recycled footage if they see it; so we make sure they get what they pay for. It's why we're one of the more popular channels."

"So, pretty much, the actual action which takes place depends on what the customers' type in what they want to see?"

"Yes."

"Neat set up," Murk said, nodding appreciatively. "I sort of wish I didn't have to return to Australia so soon. I can see myself happily working in your computer room for a bit."

"Ah, yes, well, you're always welcome to come and work for us whenever you're in the States. We always need good videographers - we cycle through a pool of them so we can avoid them coming under the attention of authorities. I have my legit agency across town which pays them for services rendered for the fake photo shoots we get them to invoice us for, so their accounts don't come under investigation. Each of my sites is fully monitored, so we get advanced warning of anyone who approaches our studios from any entry and exit point. And we have concealed tunnels so we can evacuate our starlets and criminal record-free staff, so they are relocated to a safe place before anyone even uses the intercoms and steps foot in the building. Now, this is the room where Amber will live. If she cooperates and does everything she's told to do, then once she's finished performing, she is left in peace to pretty much do what she pleases between her nightly performances and the next day's screen recordings."

"And if she doesn't cooperate?" Murk asked, turning to look at me.

"Oh, Amber's not going to be uncooperative; you've trained her well. But, in case she gets any ideas once you're gone and not here to discipline her, she'll start being scheduled on the more unpleasant performance jobs - be assigned for a full week in rooms she'll soon regret being sent to, as punishment for each and every incident she gives anyone trouble on."

Murk actually beamed; pleased to hear I'd still receive punishment if I didn't do exactly as I was told to do.

"But you don't beat them?"

"No, no, we prefer our starlets to look their absolute best on camera. So they are never drugged or given any enhancers. It's only our girls who give us trouble who receive physical punishment, but that's all done on camera, sometimes to within an inch of the girls losing their lives, which is why we hire hookers the rest of the time when the punishment room isn't occupied by a starlet, again all at the request of customers who are into that sort of rough stuff and pay us well for the privilege to jack off to it. No, Amber is too pretty and young right now, and hopefully smart, to want to be beaten as part of her performances, but maybe when she's older she might fancy getting into the rough sex and request it - it happens with some of the girls, especially the ones who arrive here without any previous experience in this line of work and are desperate to end it all. But if she doesn't go that way, Amber's attractive enough and has the quality I was looking for. We're likely to gain plenty of offers to purchase her once we list her for resale; once she's earned back the money we've spent on her, of course - not merely the price we're paying you, but also her wardrobe, meals, accommodation and any work she gets done."

"Work she gets done?" Murk asked, confused.

"Teeth straightening, breast enhancements, strict regime of monthly health checks, pregnancy terminations, personal grooming and, of course, all the special costuming, which is custom made for each starlet, that kind of thing. On paper, the starlet's earn one percent of what their room makes, though like I said, it's only on paper. If they start becoming a higher earner, then we drop their rate as far as point one percent in point one percent increments so we can spend the money on maintenance and upgrades of equipment. The Pete's services are paid for by the starlet, out of her earnings, but I cover the costs of the Roy's and Sebastian's. The Pete's who go on camera and cum get one rate, and those appearing on camera without cum get slightly less, and those remaining on standby receive a lesser rate still."

"We cover the actual payment so the Pete's are paid immediately, especially when the starlets are new; they don't generate sufficient income yet and already have a sizeable debt to start repaying, which is of course all added to her personal debt to me. But, as you can see, Murk, I look after my starlets and am happy to pay top dollar for everything regardless whether it is mine or the starlet's responsibility to cover, so they look great on camera at all times. It's why my channel often gets the highest viewership and my starlets bring in top dollar when they're sold on. They never look like they are participating under duress or against their will, or need to get through their session by using drugs."

"Our audience must believe our starlets have come to us as a result of their having applied, for whatever reason - usually, they are lured by the promise of big money or they've gone and got themselves into a bit of bother, financially, so this is a way they can resolve it quickly, and end up liking the job or the money so choose to stay on, until I decide to resell them, that is, though that's rarely the reason the subscribers get to know."

Both Mr J. and Murk laughed hard at that.

"Every cent I spend on them needs to be recovered before I do that, as I'm sure you can understand; it's the only way to run a successful business or this type of business operation. Let the general public have what they want in a way they find socially acceptable, and we all win."

"So how many girls do you have at any one time?"

"For the live action feeds? Only between fifteen to twenty five, across five locations at present, but I also own either fifty seven or fifty eight brothels and sex-houses - I've lost track as I'm still in the process of buying some more - so in total I currently have around four thousand girls in my employ. But I'm always looking to keep expanding. I have plans for opening a few sites like this one in Europe this coming year, I'm in the process of getting some investors in to help me get the projects started, as well as three more here in the States. Doesn't pay to have them all in one site, or even in the same country, in case the cops raid and discover the studios entrances and escape routes..."

"... sure, you'd lose your business overnight with that type of business model."

"Precisely. But, each live action feed premise is fitted out with the absolute best and latest in technology and the basements built and laid out to suit our functional needs, and has what looks like a poorly trading legit business upstairs, and the hidden and secure area beneath without any council approvals knowing about the modifications. I have multiple escape routes you'd never find at either end, so I can keep as many staff members as I can to minimise how many I need to sacrifice so the police never become aware of how large my operations really are."

"Impressive," Murk said, nodding appreciatively. "Really impressive. So ... if Amber's not sold once she's finished her minimum two years of performance and she's no longer in debt to you?"

"Then if she's still pulling in decent dollars, I keep her working here in the studio until she's bought, or I keep her working for me at my top brothels until her sales start to decline. If she's already no longer raking in the dollars at the level I want, then I pass her on to some people or place her into one of my other operations. If it's not one run by me it is, of course, at the discretion of the new management as to how well they treat the girls, screen the men and minimise the risk of the girls catching anything nasty. But most of my girls are snapped up from my A-level sites, I only keep girls who remain clean, as in drug and disease-free despite their never using condoms and only let Pete's who have been thoroughly tested and declared clean as well service them." Mr J. boasted.

"I have built an impeccable reputation, and I'm determined to keep it. The starlets develop a strong, loyal fan base; and there's usually a suitable buyer who can afford and is willing to pay my asking price. I'd rather sell them than transfer them, which I'm sure you'll understand why. And I like having fresh faces, to keep the customers returning and telling their friends about our channel and rooms. We cater to a variety of tastes, some of which are not socially acceptable for the majority of the general public - but no blatant paedophilia, that's too risky - it's always on the authority's radar."

"I'm confident Amber's going to bring quite a tidy sum tonight. She has the potential to succeed as a rising elite model over in my genuine modelling agency. Being the case it's the first time her pretty little photogenic face and body is going to appear on our channel, I have a feeling, her blonde hair and innocent look on top of that is going to cause her to bring in the highest views for at least her first month - my other girls will hardly get anybody watching their sessions by comparison, so I need to capitalise on Amber being the fresh face and choosing the porn side of life, so she'll start out performing for the full broadcast hours at least for her first month, even if that means she has to perform with multiple Pete's."

"Multiple Pete's?" Murk interrupted the thoughts in my mind I'd never have had the courage to ask.

"Oh, we always have at least five males - we call all of them Pete - in the means change room, per starlet, ready to take over once the previous Pete has cum - but they're all professional if they work for me, and they know they should aim to be on camera for at least one hour each, except the first Pete, and draw out the action so it brings in higher dollars, and like I said, they undergo strict screening to confirm they don't have anything nasty to pass on to my A- or B-level starlets. I don't care whatsoever about the happenings for starlets sent to work at my D-level sites. Those sites are rough and have high turnovers of girls because inevitably they pick up sexually transmitted nasties relatively quickly or die from physical abuse and drug overdoses. I've only ever sent two former A-level starlets to a D-level brothel; both didn't last more than two years employed there."

I guessed much of this conversation was intentionally being said in front of me so I learned some of the new rules and way things work I now had to follow rather than satisfying Murk's curiosity about how Mr J. ran the illegal side of his business operations.

"And so our A-level starlet's can never name real names if busted, every technician is named Roy, and each of the bouncers are named Sebastian, and any sales and marketing visitors are Darren's or Zack's depending on whether they know the girls true state for working here. Like you must now be referred to as Darren, if you ever visit our facilities or conduct work on our behalf, in particular our starlets. I find it easier if everyone gets into the habit right from the start. And of course, I am only ever to be referred to as Mr J. and my business associate is Mr D."

"Now, Amber." Mr J turned to speak directly to me. "Come with us, I want you to join us while I continue giving Darren a tour around our basement facilities - it's probably best for you to see your new home for the next two years or so."

I was still naked and remained naked and self conscious of this fact for the tour.

$\mathscr{C}$HAPTER 13

There were six rooms in total at this (number one top) site (which meant six starlets) all looking identical to the one I had come from. Each had an outer room so the technicians and others watched on, and each had a large bed surrounded by cameras and equipment, and a door leading left and right. The left (when looking into the room) was always the starlet's room, and the right where the Pete's assigned to the room prepared for their time with the starlet of that room in front of the cameras. I soon learned there were different props and sex toys according to client preferences of that room's main online customers - some of which looked quite scary to me. I was sure they'd cause me much pain or discomfort - so the customers watched whatever sexual act took their fancy and no time was wasted for Pete's to get the toy on screen and inevitably into the starlet's body once the tease to drive higher sales had gone on long enough.

The starlet in Room Six was the only one I was allowed to see.

The dark haired girl was still naked and asleep on the performance bed from the previous night. She looked very badly bruised and beaten, and groaned constantly in her sleep. She looked like she had been in a serious car accident or something and was in too bad a condition to attempt escape … or even move. So she had been left where she was rather than being made to return to her Room, and they hadn't even bothered to lock the computer room door. Mr J. didn't seem at all perturbed by the starlet's condition or about the potential security lapse (actually, the more I looked at the girl, I was sure the room had been left unlocked on purpose; positive they were aware yet unconcerned she was in no fit state to even attempt escaping).

Mr J. turned to me and said, "See, Amber. You don't ever want me to schedule you to perform here in Room Six, or you might find out firsthand, like Honey, here, close to what it was like for your mother the night she died. Would you like to be punched and beaten up like that, Amber? Like your Mum and Honey? I can schedule you to live in this room in three night's time after Honey's finished, if you like."

I couldn't help it. A tear instantly leaked down the sides of my nose at mention of my Mum and the casual manner he spoke about the way she had died - like she had deserved it or something. But I managed to stammer, "No, sir."

When it was time for Murk to leave, one of the Sebastian's arrived to escort his safe exit of the building, for the Sebastian to check the coast was clear before opening the hidden door again to let him out. Mr J., who was completely oblivious to my embarrassment at still being naked, asked me when my next period was due, in the same sort of voice someone might ask another how they'd like their coffee; and told me I wouldn't be required to perform during that time. He said he'd organise for me to have my tubes tied (I didn't know what this meant), "so we can avoid the problem" of me needing time off to go deal with terminating "such inconvenient and unwanted pregnancies". He'd probably organise for this to be completed within the next four weeks, and give me three days off for me to get over any pain from the procedure - I'm not a heartless monster, Amber. I look after my girls.

"Your teeth are already perfectly straight and beautifully white, so I won't need to organise straightening or whitening; but I'll wait and see what feedback we get after your first week's performance before I make a decision whether I'll organise for you to have breast implants. Yours are rather small, but your nips are perky; the audience can go either way. If I'm guessing correctly, I'll probably only have to start you on a course of treatment to stretch your nipples so they stand out more on camera - that will help make you look turned on which in turn will help your audience. Someone'll make sure your diet keeps you at your current size; I don't have an idea of how I want to market you as a starlet yet, so I don't want you to lose weight but I don't want you to get curved either unless that's what they want. I'll make some decisions once I've worked out how the audience responds to you. It's about what the public responds to best which will ultimately decide how best to attract them into viewing your room."

Mr J. clicked his fingers and one of the Sebastian's appeared virtually instantly. "Yeah, boss?"

"Take Amber E porn starlet - that's your new porn name, dear, so never use any of your former surnames anymore; you live, breathe and die by your porn name now even after you've been sold on. Amber Entacott no longer exists as of right this moment - take her to her quarters. Have puss rested and washed up, and moisten her puss so she's ready to go live at ten. Make sure she's given a leg wax - she doesn't need bikini wax yet, but we'll keep an eye on her growth and get that waxed if and when we need to."

"Right boss," Sebastian answered. "They might like her better kept untrimmed to begin with. She's not overly bushy."

"Yes, my thoughts exactly. They should like she's a natural silver blonde and has light pubes, which don't look like they'll get in the way of the audience seeing the close-up action. A bit of natural mess might be more attractive for them."

Sebastian escorted me to my room, again with the heavy hand gripping my neck, and gave me a buzzer to press if I needed to use the bathroom or anything else.

"Ya best eat your lunch over there ... " he pointed to a desk which had a sandwich pre-cut into triangles and a glass of water with ice "... and then get some sleep first up. Mr J. and Mr D. don't like sleepy starlets while their scheduled for duty. And it's going to be a long night until you get accustomed to the routine. I'll take you to get showered at eight thirty, and someone will help you with your hair and makeup, and do your legs and get you pussied up - but ya're not allowed to talk to them, okay."

With that, he locked me in.

It was a comfortable and pretty enough room despite its narrowness. A single bed tucked against the wall on one corner; a massive wardrobe filled with an array of sexy lingerie and silky throw-over robes in every imaginable colour and material; a dresser with a mirror and lights, and a chair to sit on, filled with makeup and delicious-smelling perfumes which reminded me of flowers. All, from the looks of it, brand new and luxury-priced. I wondered how many performances I had to give to repay how much it had all cost. I reckoned I owed a lot of money already from the dresser stuff alone.

I anxiously ate my sandwiches, still feeling hungry afterwards and then went and curled on the bed. I wasn't sure if I was allowed to put on any of the robes or lingerie, no one had said; and figured if I wanted to avoid being made to spend a week working in Room Six and ending up like that starlet, then it was probably best if I stayed naked. I was sure to learn what did and didn't get me into trouble to earn me punishment over the coming weeks. But I'd be wise to follow instructions and not assume what is and isn't permissible until I had learned those sorts of details. (That proved smart decision-making on my part).

I was required to perform seven days a week. I was the permanent starlet of Room Two for the time being (but they said I'd be reassigned to a different live action room, including to one of the other sites at Mr J.'s instructions - most starlets being shifted around every month), so long as I didn't get myself in trouble for whatever reason that's where I lived (for now). Rooms made anywhere from as little as one hundred dollars (usually a weeknight by a B-level starlet) to quite a few thousand dollars (the record for one evening for one room was eighty two thousand one hundred and fifty dollars - "all those one's, five's, ten's and twenty's, and occasional fifty's add up, you know").

Even though I hadn't finished my schooling, I had been in advanced classes, so I mentally calculated: if my room earned one hundred dollars, I'd make (on paper) one dollar, and out of that still had to pay all the Pete's (the standby Pete's were paid three hundred dollars for their trouble at keeping sexually clean and not getting onscreen for that particular session). I didn't know how I would ever make enough money for me to not have a debt to have to repay Mr J.

Everything was mathematically impossible.

CHAPTER 14

For the first few weeks, I was kept busy doing however many takes were needed enabling the Roy's to piece together a personal message from me for in case we were ever offline from technical difficulties, or in case us starlets were quickly smuggled from the building if police ever came raiding. The highest dollar earners (rarely Room Two) were evacuated first. Anyone not yet evacuated and thus caught and arrested had to confess to voluntary participation, and Mr J. guaranteed organising their legal representation (though no one outside the organisation would ever learn it was him). Mr J. only ever visited the site from one of the secret entries; this way if the cops ever had the place under surveillance they'd never get any evidence of who the 'power' running things were. And judging by how much all the Roy's and Sebastian's respected Mr J. (not his real surname, of course), not one of them intended ever passing on their bosses name or real identity even if they knew it.

"Earn well, and we'll make sure you get released on bail and get a good behaviour bond, and we'll organise your taken to another site until I can get another facility setup and operational; don't earn well, then be prepared to serve some prison time, and once out, likely be sold on to one of the many buyers of Mr J.'s starlets. But, if you ever give the authorities any information about what you do know of and learn about our operation (none of which they troubled them self from me learning), so much as a single detail, then you will be made to regret that poor decision or accidental indiscretion. The girl in Room Six is only the minimum of what will happen to any starlet - or any one in my employ, actually - who reveals a word."

The scripts and how they wanted me to deliver the lines made it seem like I had chosen this way of life, loved what I do and did it so men of all ages and sizes were able to 'whack off' with my blessing and I was their means to get them to their ejaculation however long or slow they wanted or needed for it to take for them to get there. But, the me loving it aspect was slowly being ramped up with each week. The Roy's wanted to create best use of my girlish voice, and nervous giggle, which came across even more girlish on playback and made me come across as 'sexily sweet and promiscuously playful'. And so, I had to giggle every time they gave me the gestured order, and it was my giggle which Mr J. said held the best promise to cause them all fall in love with me and return hungry for more me, Amber E porn starlet's live action.

I was moved from my room, and shifted to another one not off a performance room and adjacent control room - one with an ensuite, and was well stocked with sanitary pads and hot water bottles and anything else we might need, only while I had my periods. Someone, I didn't know who, lived in my room and performed in my Room whenever I wasn't 'in residence' there. I was never moved from there, but my room remained the main room aka least pervasive action of the channels rooms, the rules for room two were simple: the starlet only sucked and fucked men, and dildo sex toys. Any request outside of the room rules and the customer was politely directed by the chat room moderator to a different room matching the requested unaccepted action.

I never saw any of the other starlets over the years I've worked here (unless specifically detailed in this memoir or autobiography or whatever the notes I record all this is called). Just all the Pete's, Roy's (but only through the observation window) and Sebastian's, and sometimes I caught a glimpse of Mr J. or Mr D. if they visited the control room, and occasionally unnamed men, who, like Murk were given a tour and were addressed as Darren's or Zack's.

As soon as my periods were over, I was returned to my room, and starred as the main performance again. But my bedroom and performance 'bedroom' were all cleared out, and my beds re-freshened so it was all clean and ready for me and my assigned Pete's again.

Once a month, right before my periods were due, of which Mr J.'s team knew better than I did when they were due, I was given medical checkups. I'd pretty much been permanently naked in the panty area, except when Sebastian pointed to lingerie they wanted me to start my performances in lying on my bed since the day I arrived, but I quickly learned I needed to wear a bra whenever a Pete hadn't removed it during performance or while I was being examined or groomed and in my personal time, so I didn't start developing sagging breasts. I thought it strange I was only covering my top half but my bottom half was always on show. But, we existed to pleasure men, on and off camera, and any Sebastian, Roy, Darren or Zack was free to give my pubic hair a little rub as they passed me by, if he so desired (which they did whenever they wanted to). I soon stopped feeling so self conscious about always being on display and manhandled.

Each evening, I performed from ten p.m. until three a.m. If there weren't any or many customers after one a.m., the other starlets were allowed to wind up and call it a night. But not me. I remained a bigger than expected income earner from day one, and always had audience members even on a weekday so always had viewers to watch me even when the Roy's cut the live feed precisely at three a.m. whether the last Pete had cum or not.

My fans, which were growing in numbers every single day, and increasingly spending more money to watch me fulfil their requests, even started emailing the company delivering the live action feeds to the world asking, then demanding, my feed be extended to four and five a.m. But Mr J. issued a feed notice to let them know Amber E loves her fans support but is on a strict schedule and can't accommodate their requests at this time. Leaving them with the hope I'll try to schedule it happen as soon as my commitments allows; reinforcing the character they were slowly inventing for me, that I listen to what my customer wants and will do my absolute best to give them what pleases them.

I heard Mr J. telling one of the Roy's that keeping my supply limited was the best way to keeping demand growing otherwise he'd have made me work longer hours. And it seems he'd been right. Customers were abandoning his competitors channels also broadcast via the same hosting company and subscribing and tuning in near exclusively to my feed with every day that passed. Apparently, the channel was even getting requests from guys from all over the world asking how they can be one of the men on camera with me. If I loved to fuck all the time (which they were convinced I was, and more so), they'd be happy to do it with me, even for no fee. I smashed the previous highest earnings record in my fourth month - the new record was 'probably a never repeatable' hundred grand plus. Each month for the next thirty-seven months afterward I broke my own personal bests.

Special days of the year meant special themed performances.

On Valentine's Day, I had two Pete's in the room for the five hours, to give 'double the love' to my fans, the sessions started with a recorded message from me, wishing everyone who watches me tonight a happy valentine, thank them for the flowers, lingerie, sex toys and cards, and tell them I loved their kind generosity and was thinking of each and every one of them even more so than my usual performances, and then end by giggling my signature giggle and say, "I promise I'll get round to wearing each and every one of the bras and panties you've gifted me, onscreen, and make great use of the toys (which the studio then started receiving them also) so why don't I get started, right now." and the broadcast cut to the live action about to start as soon as they paid more (than their base channel subscription fee) to tell me what they wanted to see.

At Easter, I wore bunny ears and a pouffie ball of fluff sewn on the rear of my panties, and I giggled and told them I hope they had had an Eggcellent Easter, and I hope they take advantage of the Eggtra toys only here in the room with me as a treat for tonight's performance only. On fourth of July, I was patriotically wearing a bra and panties set with stars and stripes and in colours of red, white and blue of the American flag, and my Pete's were more bulky and massive in manly hood than usual; Halloween, I was a sexy witch, or mummy or other Halloween imagery which never detracted from my (alleged) natural sweet, girly but sexually hungry and playful image.

Thanksgiving, my sessions started with another recorded message, of me thanking every viewer for being with me tonight and always, and thanking everyone who had ever visited my room and paid to do what they'd like to see me do, always in my girlish voice and to give my signature giggle when cued to do so either by Roy's voice which they cut from the transmission or as written instructions on the television screens I had to keep my eye on without it being obvious. But, someone had always ran through what the recorded message was going to be, so I already comprehended exactly what words they wanted me to emphasise, when they wanted me to look shy and sweet or giggle. Amber E, porn starlet was more than thankful for every single cock she got to suck or fuck and always would be. That's how they were now heavily marketing me.

I understood fully althouth I hated it the character that was 'Amber E, porn starlet' was keen to suck and fuck her way to mega stardom; and my job was to give consistent performances so viewers never believed anything other than the story and personality they had made up for me; Black Friday's I teased them into paying more money and making them think they were getting a bargain while giving me what I want; Christmas I was Santa's helper, a "personal gift to all you guys and gals wanting to celebrate such a wonderful holidays season with me", and wink, wink, here were some wonderful little presents again I'd love them to give me, so please make sure to ask me or instruct Pete to use them; and New Year's Eve I was more excited than I've ever been, and 'let's get the party started and we'll countdown to midnight and celebrate the first few hours together,' "I'm so, excited, so let's get me fucking and have a jolly good time together, shall we?" Giggle, then cut to live feed, and at the stroke of midnight the Pete's each came over me as celebration of the New Year (to mimic popping a bottle of champagne).

I was never the sultry seductress, or merely another wannabe starlet or porn model or star who pushed her breasts forward and puff-lifted her hair trying to look seductive and make guys become interested in me; those weren't the poses for me.

I was 'just Amber E', sweet and innocent by nature despite her insatiable sexual appetite who loved every second of her promiscuous and titillating antics, and bounced around the bed excitedly (impatient when my audience wasn't getting me to suck or fuck fast enough). I was never 'hooker' or fake boob whore. I was fun, and refreshingly real; believable personality plus. My nipples made up for my lack of cup size. And my pussy and lips would love, love, love to experience every hard cock in the world at least once in my lifetime. And if you're lucky, you'll end up one of the lucky ones who get to do me for real, which I was always welcoming to offers of, and would be fulfilled if they can be fitted into my schedule. *And*, you'll leave the experience knowing you've had the best suck or fuck you'll ever receive in your lifetime, because I aim to please and guarantee, so you'll receive one hundred percent satisfaction and effort to get you there from me, Amber E, porn starlet.

It was never about me orgasming, only my Pete's. That was the 'Amber E starlet' way. I was all about the positions they'd like to try (so long as it was only suck or fuck and not something which tarnished the image Mr J. was cultivating).

Once I had finished my performances, a Sebastian stood waiting to escort me to the bathroom to have a shower and get all the dried cum off me. I'd then be given a meal in my bedroom, and get to sleep until twelve midday. That's when a Sebastian unlocked the door to my screen room, told me it was time for screen testing, where it was more promo video recording time and posing for the cameras so still shots and a small amount of action took place, but not the main thing (aka, the Pete didn't cum), it was all to capture the essence for the main event and given another meal.

Mr J. quickly had one of the Roy's to join in the room live feed chat screens, so the Roy drove up people sharing costs if they looked like they might leave without influencing what me and my Pete did next. This worked too, apparently; he was getting to start customers fighting over me and who's action would be done next, and having them agree on what they'd get me to do with the little time left, and what they agreed they'd have to wait to see me do on another night by paying more money so their request was what happened.

And then I'd wait my turn for a Sebastian to escort me for a shower again (depending on the other starlets if they wrapped up before me still in there, otherwise I was given priority), and then I'd be returned to my room, where I'd find another meal, and thereafter fell into bed exhausted on fresh linen sheets and a clean room until midday arrived and the day started all over again.

I was made priority for everything: promo, promo, promo, shower, afternoon rest, and I'd be the first to get my hair and makeup done, and waxing touch ups and then be returned to Room Two, where I'd wait in whatever costume they had picked for me on the clean performance bed, alone and locked in until nine thirty when the first of all the Roy's running the equipment for my room came in, until a minute to ten p.m. when the first Pete entered the room, and we'd be in position on the bed - him with a full erection bulging under his pants - so we commenced performing as all the customers started logging in, which they were now starting to arrive early so they were ready, waiting the moment the feed started at precisely ten p.m.

Usually by two minutes past ten, I had removed Pete's pants and was giving the first Pete a blow job, nice and slow, still in my outfit, so the cameras caught all the action, and switched to close-ups and full body shots as needed. But on rare occasions it started with Pete fingering me and then sucking his own finger and telling the audience, "Gawd she tastes as sweet as she looks."

The first Pete was allowed to blow from ten thirty p.m. (ten twenty p.m. if they really, really had to, but strictly no earlier than that or they'd never get to work for Mr J. again), but all the Pete's after that had to be with me on camera for at least an hour. It was usually the second Pete who removed my costume, either only the bra, and he mainly bit and sucked my nipples; and after a suitable time, away went my knickers, or, if I was wearing a crotch less style, Pete had me on my back or on my knees so viewers gleaned tantalising tiny glimpses encouraging them to request being shown more until it was time for the Pete to get them off me, and give them the unrestricted view they craved.

Due to performing for the full five hours though, I had additional Pete's in the waiting room on standby as backup in case I needed more than the five Pete's for the session (which I always needed when I was on my 'double duties' specials). Apparently they requested assigned to me rather than the other starlets, who I never saw. They all wanted to put they'd performed with Amber E, porn starlet in their professional portfolios and resumes.

In that first four year period, I couldn't tell you if I ever worked with the same Pete again or not. After that I know it was a different one every time. It was simply one hard penis after another I had to suck or fuck, and convince viewers I absolutely loved. I wasn't allowed to have a conversation with any of them, only say what popped up on the instruction prompt monitors and I stopped noticing what the man looked like within the first six months.

Sometimes the customers wanted Pete to 'give it to her hard and fast', other times it was things like 'give her three fingers' other times it was 'make her sit against the back wall and fuck her in the mouth but make sure I can see her pussy while you do that'. And whatever the customer told the particular Pete to do, I was 'thrilled' and we immediately got into position and started doing it the way paid for. With toys, without toys. Holding me by the hair so I might lightly choke on his cock. Whatever. Just fuck and suck, suck and fuck. That's what the customer wanted, so that's what we had to give them. And I had to look like I was having the time of my life and wanted more, more, more. Me being sexually satisfied wasn't the goal - it was to ensure my Pete's came, whatever my discomforts or distastes.

On my sixteenth birthday, Mr J. came in to see me in my room. He told me customers had been demanding since a month after I first started working for him that they'd also like to own a copy of my performances on DVD, so they can watch me at any time of the day or night, and watch re-runs of their favourite session for longer than the restricted to forty eight hours. (The hosting company somehow managed to block them being able to record their screens, which kept footage from being shared without all the financial stakeholders getting their full cut of the money the system and shows were generating. And the few poor quality phones recording computer or television screens posted to the internet were quickly corrupted by the tech-savvy Roy's).

"I've held off until now, to keep your audience hungry. But I'm worried if I don't get you starring in at least one or two porn films, they might start dropping off. So anyway, I signed - well, not me personally, but someone who does those things for me - well, they signed a release form today which says you understand you will be making a restricted category adult film, and you willingly consent to starring in the films and you declare that you are not a minor. So, next week, a Sebastian will drive you to the first filming location, both cheap productions until we can see what my return on secret investment will be, and, all going to plan, once it wraps, he'll take you to where the second will be filmed. The scripts have been written exclusively for you, so it's in keeping with the public porn starlet image we've been building for you. Then, we'll see how the sales of those two fuck flicks do before we decide if you'll do more or not, and if we will give any future films higher budgets to work with."

I didn't dare raise the point to Mr J. I was still a minor. They easily made me look older than my age so they didn't attract police interest having a minor stream live each night with my subtle (not tarty) make up. I was technically still a minor based on my date of birth; but I'd lost any sense of being a child long, long ago. I was a professional slut now, and as Murk had casually once said, the impression I was left with: this was indeed most likely how I was destined to spend the rest of my life. Apparently a market still existed, even once I was old, grey, and approaching my elderly natural death to have someone interested in paying for me to suck or be fucked. I had indeed been vastly unlucky Murk had targeted me.

But I was sort of looking forward to leaving the confines of Room Two for a while. I hated being imprisoned in my windowless basement home, it was stifling existing constantly in such as small space never getting to learn about what's happening in the outside world, never getting to experience being outdoors in the fresh air or have the company of people other than my male captors, which I lived for two years.

Mr J. via Mr D. arranged for another feed notice to precede me coming onto the screen that night, which said (I saw and heard it on the monitors facing me - text first, then clip of me, finishing with text):

Amber E wants her loving, admiring fans to know as a birthday treat to herself, she has decided to sign on to star in two porn films. [cut to recorded message of me] "I've wanted to give you this treat for a while now, and my agent wanted to keep this hush hush until they are released, but agrees it is time for me to give fans even more of what they want. So, now you know where I'll be disappearing too soon. [Giggle] But don't worry, I'll be back as soon as filming wraps, I promise. [Blow them a kiss]" [Cut to written details on screen] *So make sure you subscribe to Amber E special Porn Flicks Newsletter we've set up so you receive advanced notification of when filming commences, get some filming sneak peeks, and get details on how to get your hands on a copy of the DVD when it is released. Click the Subscribe button below - membership is limited to the first 10,000 subscribers only."*

That feed notice came close to crashing the host's server, apparently, before I appeared live - whatever crashing the server meant. But the slow moving Roy's were instantly full attention working hard at their computers, doing everything they could, shouting urgently to each other, 'we need more bandwidth! Come on, quick, we still need more than that even!" and "Shit! We're losing some!" (Pete and I weren't supposed to hear anything of what was happening in the observation room, the walls and glass were soundproofed, but we did this night - muffled as their words were to us.)

Mr J. was standing in the doorway behind them, smiling broadly. I heard him say, once the calamity was dying down, mere seconds before the prolonged message on the screen cut to Pete and me on the bed, "See, I told you making them think it was is strictly limited to a particular number of sign ups only equates to making them act straight away, and then phone their mates so they don't miss out either."

CHAPTER 15

A few weeks later, Sebastian escorted me to some warehouse where the inside had been made to look like the hall and boys locker room of a typical American high school. The film team were all aware I was one of Mr D.'s starlets (and therefore present non-voluntarily, as they downplayed the truth to) - my keepers didn't hide this from me; none of these new people were fazed in the slightest a Sebastian was to remain in the same room or location, out of the cameras range, and if need be, filming was to be postponed and I was collar-cuffed and chained to one of the stable anchor fixtures which had been drilled into the floor if there was ever a need for him to have to temporarily leave the shoot at the warehouse, or to a bracket securely anchored in the rear of the black van while on location, and I couldn't be pulled off set to accompany him.

The first day's filming was in a football stadium they had slipped someone who managed the grounds some money to let them come in and film the outdoor scenes even though they didn't have the proper filming permissions.

I had some guys and girls (I shocked myself when I realised this was the first close contact with females I'd had for around six years) I wasn't allowed to talk with (except to answer their hair and makeup questions, if they asked any, which they didn't unless absolutely necessary) help to get me dressed into a cheerleader outfit, and the first scene we filmed was me racing over to a male lead as he supposedly finished team practice after everyone else. And I had to gush about how great a player the lead male was. This was the cue for the male lead to ask me to sneak into the boys change room with him. But I had to say with a girly (upset) voice, "But, Steve, if coach finds us doing it again, he said he'd dump you from the team."

"Yeah, but I can't wait until the weekend to have my cock inside you." And this was when the script (and the director) told me I had to look at his pants, lick my lips and then say softly, "Neither can I."

"…And cut!" the director called. "That was great Amber E," (which he said my name as though it was one word, Amberee, and soon after others on the team followed suit.) You're a natural in front of the camera, and can actually act. Mr D. *will* be pleased."

Sebastian then returned me to the motel he and I stayed in while I was to complete shooting this low budget film (again, where they'd collar and cuff me if the Sebastian wanted or needed to leave me on my own, and we never shared the same bed; he didn't attempt to try to fuck me, but did get me to suck his cock, like I fully expected if he didn't want the first option. There must be a rule they can't do this at the basement).

Then, we returned to the warehouse, where we started filming the first of me and Steve making out. So Steve removed my cheerleader outfit and got me completely naked, and Steve removed his shirt and shoulder pads, and I pulled Steve upon me on a wooden change bench and helped him lower his pants and told him to hurry up and start fucking me in case Coach Rixon came along, and really wanted him inside me. (I figured out most of the industry language and what it meant now, I think). We had to do a number of takes so they could get all the shots they needed. The bench was really hard and uncomfortable, but that's what we had to use for him to hard-fuck me on. And I wasn't allowed to complain, or let the discomfort show on my face no matter how much it hurt. Any time it did, the director called out, "Cut!" and we'd have to do another take.

Anyway, I think all up it took two, or maybe it was three, weeks, I can't remember any more, life became a bit of a blur. Fuck and suck, suck and fuck. Make whoever's cock it was cum, make sure I looked like I loved every minute of it.

Mr J. learned about how the director had pronounced my porn

name, he loved it and decided he'd change the spelling to Amberee, and to reflect how the public viewed me, from porn *starlet* to porn *princess.*

Shooting went for twelve hours a day and Sebastian took me to start on the second film before the first one had even finished, in a high rise building. (The second crew were also aware of my not-here-by-choice circumstance and were equally unfazed by this fact), and I was back and forth between the two movies fucking and sucking with different male leads and their stand ins (or should I say backup hardened cocks?) playing the role of cheerleader and job seeker turned personal assistant.

The rest of the first story line went, Coach Rixon indeed walked in on us (of course, it's a fuck-flick so as much 'two or more' action they could write in added to my story of aiming to fuck as many and as often as I can), and he threatens Steve with he's off the team, and I beg the coach not to boot him off, and I suck the coach's cock to convince him on doing Steve and I this great favour, while Steve finished off cuming by doing me from behind.

(That killed my knees - and my puss! Especially as we had to do a few takes. They wanted Steve more aggressive in his fucking of me, and Steve wanted to do it slower so the viewers could appreciate how long his cock is which is best showed by him doing the movements slow, so he kept doing me his way until the frustrated director finally snapped and yelled, "Either fuck her like a teenage animal you're playing or I'll replace you in the role of Steve, and we'll re-shoot all previous scenes". And then Steve cooperated, and fucked me too aggressively until we had to do it again shouting furiously "Mr D. never said anything about injuring her. So do it properly or you're out!")

And once both partners are satisfied, I ask coach if he's keeping Steve on the team, and coach tells me he still needs to think about it and to come and see him again the following night, where he'll let me know his final decision.

The following night I go to coach's office, and he does me roughly on his desk (I was so sore I practically passed out trying not to cry) before I even realise what his intentions are and immediately get into it without protest (a girls got to do whatever it takes to help her man, right?). And he says he'll keep Steve on the team if I do the rest of

Steve's team mates at Friday night's team bonding party which Steve couldn't attend. I, of course, am more than happy to do this (why would I stop supporting my man now?), and so there's a party scene where each of the team mates do me one after another (and I'm often with more than one at the same time), and it's the team and coach's little secret for Steve to never know, but now they feel they could make the team win and support their best player. (Me personally, I had always believed people committed to just one person in a relationship, so I didn't understand my character's motive to sleep with whoever wanted their cock in me.)

Then there's a final scene where Steve and the boys have won their game the following day, and the coach tells me to come to his office, so he can personally thank me for my part at helping the school win - I had really helped them bond and be united. And the coach says (as he's fucking me), "Just so long as your principal daddy doesn't catch us in what our star cheerleader really does to spur the team on and support their star player."

And I say, "Oh, coach. Who do you think asked me to do this?" and then giggle my signature giggle.

End of movie.

Porn Flick entitled, '*Ride-Her High.*' (Such an imaginative title - not!)

The second movie was, '*The Millionaire's Best Asset*'.

My role was a young office assistant looking for a job. She'd been searching for some time and was starting to get desperate; we're in this high rise building and when he tells me I don't have the skills or qualifications he is after, I beg him to give me the job and I tell him I'll do anything to convince him I'm right for the job, and I tell him I know I have the skills to help grow the company by three hundred and sixty five million dollars in precisely twelve months.

He says, "You'll do anything to prove this to me?" and I respond, seductively, "Yes, I said and mean, *anything*."

He then responds, "I'll give you the job, if you give me one." And that's my cue to get off my chair, and sashay around to his side of the desk with a smile on my face and say, "Oh, I was hoping you'd say that. It'll be my pleasure, sir. I'm going to give you the best job you've ever had." Giggle, kneel on the floor, unzip his trousers and get the action going on. Lots and lots of sucking, swallow his cum and then stand up, remove my panties, hitch up my skirt and ask him how soon he will be ready for job two. I sit with my butt on his desk, then lift each stilettoed leg in turn to rest on the arms of his chair, giving him full view of my pussy, and tell him:

"Why don't you play with my clit for a bit, until your cock recovers"? Then it's straight into another round of hardcore fucking (actors secretly swapped out, because the male leads of this flick are identical twins, so they can take over from each other without the audience ever knowing). And in the background, you can see the office workers in the building opposite getting a free peep show; they're all males, and they're cheering my efforts to win the job. I blow them an Amberee, porn princess kiss and they all let me know how much they are loving my show by blowing kisses and making gestures for me to come over and interview for them next - and I return gestured, 'only if I don't get the job here'.

Then I am redressed, and walking towards the door to exit, and I say in my girlie voice, "So, what time would you like me to start tomorrow?"

The manager says trying to fob me off and keep to I didn't get the job despite the fun, "Oh, I have a meeting all morning until ten a.m., and then I have to meet with a very important investor."

And I giggle my signature giggle, and say, "Great, so I'll be here in the office by ten a.m. then, so I help you get the first million dollar check. Not a problem." Give him a wink. And giggle as I exit the office.

Jump cut to next day (me wearing a different too-revealing outfit), and I go and take a seat in a chair I place off to one side behind his side of the table, and pick up a notepad and pen ready to 'take dictation'. (Get it? Dick-tation; Dick Action). The crew found it amusing when they saw it in brackets in the script.

The manager walks in, is surprised, then smiles and winks, and sees his important investor into taking a seat. The manager takes his chair and the two men start talking business, not minding me. I put the notepad and pen onto the desk, and unbutton my blouse so the investor is momentarily distracted. I say, "Oh, don't let me stop your important negotiations."

I take my blouse off, and then wander casually over to the investor and ask, "Be a sweetie and unhook me. I need to let my little girls out of their cage for a bit." The investor unhooks my bra and I'm naked up top.

The manager resumes the conversation as I lean in and ask the investor if he likes my tits. He mutters, "Yes, very much. Especially your nipples," and then I tell him he can take a nibble on them to see what they taste like and if he can get them bigger, if he wants. Of course, he is able to suck and nibble and bite on my nipples as they continue business.

And then, I say, "Oh, Mr. You're getting me horny doing that. You should feel how big my clit is getting." And he slides my panties off, slips his finger between my legs, and then says, "Oh, yes. You are getting horny."

I then face the manager and ask, sweetly. "Boss, you don't need Mr [Whatever the Character's name was] to sign any documents right now, do you?"

The boss says, "No, we haven't agreed to all the terms and conditions, yet." and I say, "Oh, goodie" and refaced the investor and straddle his legs and say, "Carry on negotiating." and unzip his trousers and expose his cock, and make sure it is nice and hard, then lower my pussy on to him.

At this point, as I start sliding up and down his hard shaft, I push the investor to recline in the chair, making sure he doesn't slip from me, and the boss comes round from his side of the desk, as I get my legs into position, so the boss can lose his own trousers, spread my bum cheeks apart and then penetrate me from behind. While I have both men inside me, I say, "You're going to back my boss aren't you, sir?"

He moans, "I sure am" and we all go for it. Lots and lots of close up action until the boss and the investor both cum, which delights me.

Jump cut, both men are dressed but I'm still completely naked and Mr Investor signs the contract then finishes re-zipping his trousers, and says, "I'll transfer the funds into your account as soon as I get back to my office."

He tells the manager, "That's one hell of a million dollar asset, you got there." And my boss pats me, still standing next to him completely naked, on my bottom affectionately and says, "You've got that right."

A buzzer sounds and then a woman's voice says, Mr [Manager's Name], your next appointment has arrived." Manager tells secretary, won't be long. He's confused - he was only making one investor meeting per day.

The two men walk toward the door, as I go over and take a seat where I started, and they shake hands. "Now you know the secret to why I've been so successful all these years."

The investor leaves, and the manager walks to his desk. "Don't you want to get dressed, Amberee, love?" I say, "No, they're only going to come straight off again. May as well not waste precious fucking time."

"Oh, Amber, I'm so glad I hired you," he says. "You *are* the perfect replacement. I was foolish not to see this yesterday."

And once again, I giggle my signature giggle as the film starts fading to black. "Oh Mr [Manager's Name], I told you I had what it takes to help your business to grow by at least three hundred and sixty five million dollars over the next twelve months, if we schedule appointments every single day. Today's simply a little bonus, silly me forgot we're in a leap year. So, I'm aiming to reach three hundred and sixty six million dollars." And I giggle again.

And bravo, with the director calling, "That's a wrap." and the post production team piecing all the footage into order so as much of the action is shown from lots of different angles and the film is much longer to play out than the short story lines, and the audience gets value for their money.

The final product out-grossed the number one (off season) mainstream (non porn) movies takings by quadruple on the first day (someone claimed), and I'd go on to later win a porn industry award for this starring role, along with many, many other industry accolades (not that I attended the awards or was present to receive the accolade). The Millionaire's Best Asset was destined to become my most famous role ever. Well, it was the one which catapulted the starlet from a (not quite a) nobody to everyone came clamouring to offer me a contract (beyond *The Sexhouse Slave* which was an even bigger role which smashed out as a number one hit).

The Millionaire's Best Asset, this initial fuck flick caused businessmen all over the world to immediately want me to recreate scenes in their offices, with them playing the lead - which only happened at Amberee, headquarters purpose-built studio, if they paid the right price (I think it was a hundred thousand dollars) and only allowed to happen after they had gone through the full standard process of having their sexual health verified as clean with the doctor Mr J. said was the only one allowed to give that verification, so the original film set was rebuilt exactly as it had been, and propped right down to the last detail of notepad and pencil, so as these scenes could usually be filmed after hours (and paid highest) or during the day, I was taken off Room Two duty for those nights.

If you find it strange I don't remember the names of the two male characters for The Millionaire's Best Asset, it's due to how many recreations I had to do following release of this movie. Every replicated scene was identical to the movie, only swapping the two businessmen names with the names of the real wealthy businessmen fucking me. (I can't remember how many times I had to recreate this role, but it was well over a thousand. One night it was Mr Kosnikovski and Blatzanokov, the next might be Mr Wong and Xiao.)

In total, I was away from Room Two to film those two films for seven weeks. Then I was straight back on air from ten p.m. to three a.m., sucking and fucking Pete's and toys again. The movies were released simultaneously a month or so after. And Mr D. came in to tell me Mr J.'d been approached by some porn magazine which was only allowably sold in sealed packaging, and Mr J. was really pleased my fan base was growing in numbers even more rapidly, every single day since the DVDs went on sale. And I'd have the frequent nights away from Room Two to ride the wave of recreation offers - I had an abundance of high-wealth businessmen who could indulge their fantasies and were happy to pay the fee the moment the doctor gave Mr D. the go ahead, which were the more lucrative endeavours.

"They love you for loving dick so much, starlet! I'm so glad I trusted my gut to have you sparkle from the rest." Mr J. came and told me in person. "I had been prepared to pay twenty thousand dollars to buy you from Mr Walters - the highest amount I'd have ever paid for any girl. I saw you had the special something none of the other starlets have before I even arranged your priority audition. Oh, well, Mr Walter's financial loss was my huge gain. Though, I really should throw him a bone so I can purchase his next offerings for the same ridiculously low prices and he doesn't regret how poorly he negotiated the deal."

Once again I was struck over everyone buying into the made up story when the reality behind my doing every bit was so very different from the perception. Even the man who had came up with the idea was starting to believe his own fiction.

By the time I had my eighteenth birthday, I had made twelve more specially scripted for me as 'star in' movies, and done 'exclusive naughties' for three big name magazines, too.

But me now starring in my two porn flicks with intentions to do more brought interest from the police. One afternoon, I had come from my shower and a Sebastian was walking me to my starlet room when another Sebastian came rushing towards us and said urgently, "Cops are still staking out Starlet House, and the bosses have been warned her lack of coming and going from the house without a Sebastian is starting to cause them suspicion she's being held against her will. We've been tipped off the cops're considering busting in soon, to try catch an illegal film shack, so we're to be ready to transport Amberee to Starlet House at a moment's notice, even if she's on air. If they bust into the house and not find her in there, they'll start poking around more thoroughly to work out how she has left the house without them noticing."

I had barely fallen asleep, when a Sebastian busted into my room, and said, "Quick, the cops came knocking, and we're doing our best to refuse them entry, but they said they aren't going anywhere and a warrant for them to enter and search the place is on its way to them. We need to get you there, pronto."

Sebastian was telling me this, as he had lifted me up, thrown me over his shoulder and rushed me to the underground cart to whisk me over to starlet house where I supposedly lived in half a block away on street level. And we were speeding towards the house's underground entry. I was taken up the secret stairs, and arrived in my supposed second storey bedroom's walk in robe without being breathless; I hadn't needed to exert any energy getting myself there.

"The boss says say and do whatever it takes for you to convince them we're bodyguards you've personally hired to keep you safe, and to state your limited outside activities is personal choice not result of being imprisoned against your will."

I didn't need Sebastian to tell me I had to convince people the Amberee story is one hundred percent legit, and I appreciated the Sebastian not having time to threaten me yet again with physical violence long ago drilled into me would occur if I in any way fucked up.

I could hear the Sebastian downstairs arguing with the police officers, saying I have given him strict instructions not to disturb me. I liked to have a catnap before I went live each night. I knew hidden cameras where everywhere and Mr D. and maybe even a summoned Mr J., and the Sebastian's and Roy's would all be closely monitoring everything said and done. (I guess they figured I might try to mouth or otherwise gesture or indicate to the police officers contradicting whatever I said to alert them I really was being held against my will and wanted help. I understood the price of what would happen to me if I 'fucked' anything up on the whole operation.)

In the brief moment while I waited for the wardrobe shelves of shoes to close so the hidden passageway clicked silently closed, so I could then exit the walk in cupboard and then go downstairs to 'see what the commotion ruining my sleep is', I heard as clear as if he was right here next to me Murk's' voice whispering them, 'Pay attention to all the finer details." and his full philosophy was rolling around in my head. "It can make all the difference between getting away with things or being caught."

And there laid my dilemma, as I stepped out from the wardrobe.

Did I make sure, little details like ... like... the bed looking perfectly made up and un-slept in, and hope Mr J. and the Sebastian's and the Roy's didn't notice (and quickly remedy) this while they were concentrating so heavily on what I said and did in the hope the police *did* gain access inside the house, checked the bedroom, *and* noticed this small, inconsistent easily overlooked detail of the story they've disturbed me from my nap (which was true, by the way).

Or, did I play along, help the people who kept me imprisoned and doing the work I hated, to keep their lies a secret so they weren't exposed, just so I wouldn't receive the ever-promised being beaten to within an inch of my life, so they could keep me imprisoned and doing the work I hated, with *no one* in the outside world still suspicious and possibly investigating to hope one day the site I starred from was indeed raided before anyone had time to successfully orchestra my relocation to one of their 'safe houses'.

No Sebastian, Roy, fuck flick crew, Murk or even Mr J. himself, was ever going to conduct small (at first) and then increasing lacks in security when it comes to me, if they didn't believe I had fully accepted my fate to live the rest of my life as Amberee, mega porn princess, and was completely on board to help them make as much money from me as their Million Dollar Asset (as I overheard they'd dubbed me as). I'd never be able to erase what I had been through that got me here, but I could silently, smartly suck and fuck cock without them ever knowing I was slowly defiantly building my way forward to a one golden opportunity leading to my eventual escape.

Like Murk had had patience, for two years, until he was able to rob me of my childhood to satisfy his and my uncles sexual appetites, I had to have patience in getting them to start being lax in security around me. The singular core lesson I'd gleaned as a ped-prize was the art of patience; having to take my time and complete chores properly the first time to avoid Murk making me do them over from scratch.

And it all started right now: I was, from this moment forward until I achieved my secret goal, playing the most secretive bid for freedom against the world's most dangerous men.

$\mathscr{C}$HAPTER 16

I took a deep breath, realising what I hadn't consciously realised what I had subconsciously known for some time: I had already made up my mind. This short term loss (for me) was ultimately what might be my long term gain (a great opportunity to successfully make a run for it to regain my freedom), and to achieve that, I had to be every bit as smart and savvy when it came to *her* career as my very team of imprisoners had made the public believe was what got me to where I was behind the scenes.

I wrapped the sheer robe Sebastian had thrust into my arms before he closed the concealed door again, and stepped fully into the master bedroom. Scary as it was to do this, yes, I was committing to playing a long-game.

Rather than immediately heading from the bedroom directly to the landing like I suspected the bosses wanted and expected me to do, and knowing they'd be getting pissed off, yelling at the monitors and getting ready for the moment when they saw me in the flesh again to threaten me with Room Six (until they worked out what I was doing), I detoured to the queen-sized bed I had supposedly rested in. I tossed back the bed covers, and quickly started roughing the sheets so they looked like the ones of my performance-bed at three a.m. All the while Murk's words repeated, encouragingly, inside my head, "That's right, pay attention to as many of the finer details you can, and the plan will all come together one day. At the right moment".

I could practically hear my keepers all cheering, "Way to go, starlet." at their oversight.

And, switching into character, I calmly straightened my back, loosely tied the robe, and then marched to the bedroom door, flung it open like I was enraged, and then called in my angriest voice, "Sebastian! What's all the racket? You know I don't want anyone or anything disturbing me during my nap time!"

Now it was for me to put on the best performance of my life - to act assertively and as though I was, am, in command, despite all my lessons since my youth were to always act passively. Nope; nervousness meant I wasn't performing properly.

Standing the tallest I had done in a very long time, I strode purposefully towards the gorgeous marble staircase, and started descending. (The action would have made much more of a dramatic impact if I had of been wearing stilettos so they could have clattered as I descended the stairs for the benefit of those below. My quiet footsteps ruined the effect for me, but not so for the three men at the door below the sweeping semi-circular stairs).

"Sorry, boss," the Sebastian at the front door replied, looking at me. His size alone was preventing the two officers entering. "These policemen have been insisting I let them in, and I said not until they produce a warrant or something; I'm not going to disturb you from your sleep. I know my orders, and when you say, I don't want to be disturbed by anyone, I know that means every one."

For performance sake, I patted and thanked Sebastian on his bulky arms and told him I'd ensure he received a nice bonus next payday for trying to do his job properly (not that I wanted the Sebastian to be rewarded. More, that I suspected the only way to ever hurt Mr J. was financially) I turned my attention towards the two officers, who despite supposed to being professional while on official police business, were trying real hard not to notice I didn't have any bottom underwear on under my sheer robe, and trying harder not to keep glancing at my bush again and again.

Continuing my performance as 'boss lady' upset at being woken despite my orders, I turned and addressed the officers. "What's so important you're disturbing my beauty rests? There's no threat to those in the vicinity, or Sebastian would have stepped aside immediately and woken me despite his orders so we could evacuate. What's so important, gentlemen? I don't want bags under my eyes when I go on camera tonight. I'll blame you if I end up with them!"

One of the brave officers, apologised, and awkwardly admitted I'd come to their attention due to the nature of my work, and they have reason to believe I might work the job I do under threat.

I was ready for that.

I tossed my head back, and giggled a forced version of my signature giggle. "Oh, my goodness, don't be ridiculous. So, what, you're here to try and rescue me from some …' I waved my arms around as though trying to find the right words, 'imaginary *bad man* holding me in captivity?' I strung the last word longer than necessary to deride it as jokingly ludicrous.

I could tell by their confused looks they were taken by complete surprise by my slightly amused but also annoyed and fully accurate summarisation of why they were disturbing me, so I seized keeping up the charade for my captors benefit. "Okay, let me get it straight, you're not going to leave me alone to return to my beauty sleep until you've looked around to ascertain the bad people un-cuffed me or let me out of my basement prison or Rapunzel tower, am I right? Sebastian, be a dear and let them in. I don't have time to stand around waiting for them to get their little piece of warrant paper to enforce their way into intruding upon my privacy. Let them in so we can get this all over with - and maybe then I won't lose too much rest time."

Sebastian, unable to help himself smirking at me, stood aside to let the two officers in.

"Alright, officers. I'll give you a guided tour of the house, so can we get your inspection over with *quickly*. Follow me."

And now, my personality was again Amberee, porn princess, who loved sucking and fucking cock any chance she can get (as opposed to pissed off boss lady being denied her sleep). I made sure I sashayed my hips, like the character of Amberee, leading the way up the stairs for two police officers who'd have no doubt I wasn't wearing any underwear. I showed them the messy bed I had presumably minutes before gotten disrupted from. I showed them the guest bedrooms, "So you can see these imaginary captors of mine haven't supposedly imprisoned anyone else here in the house against their will either."

The guest bedrooms were perfectly un-lived in, ready and waiting for guests staying overnight. And, well, I wasn't shy about men looking at my naked bottom half any more; I didn't bother trying to keep the robe closed when I turned to ask them, "Would you like to look under the beds and in the mattresses to check no one is hiding in them?"

They stammered, their eyes trying to look everywhere except my puss, that wouldn't be necessary. I responded with touch of a bite to my voice, "Good, well then, I'll now take you downstairs."

One of the officers awkwardly asked me to close my robes, and I snapped, "No! You don't have jurisdiction in my home. I'll dress as what makes me comfortable, and if you don't like it, we can end the tour right now."

And added flirtily, "You get used to it, don't you Sebastian, sweetie," and gave him a wink.

"Yeah, boss. I've never had reason to complain."

Amberee touched his arm and told him he's such a sweetie and compliments like that earn him another bonus in his next pay check. (Seriously, I remembered the payments for Sebastian's were not my responsibility; and this was my small way of punishing Mr J. for keeping me prisoner, in the serious hopes the Sebastian received those bonuses. Again, not for the Sebastian's benefit, but as secretly hurting Mr J.'s sore point).

The lounge room was perfectly clean and tidy, but the kitchen had coffee cups and plates and cutlery on the sink waiting for someone to wash them (I'd known these were permanently staged there, like the rest of the things I intended showing the two officers).

And I said, "Okay, now down here, I'll show you where I broadcast each night."

And I lead them down the stairs from the kitchen leading to the basement. I pointed-out the door on the left at the bottom. "I assume you already know what my garage and car looks from when I come and go from the house?" but I opened the door, turned the lights on, and gestured for them to enter the garage without me, if they wanted to check people weren't hiding in the garage or in the car itself. They looked in, trying not to have to physically touch my body to do so, but didn't enter.

It was at this point I realised I had a potential big problem: the door to replica Room Two would be locked - and I didn't have keys. My mind encouraged me to see how suspicious not having them might appear.

I looked at Sebastian to try to let him know without the two officers noticing, but he was too busy watching them, ready to spring into action until other Sebastian's arrived to whisk me off to safety, while the one's prepared to go to jail did what they could to stop the two officers if the situation unexpectedly turned to shit. I looked towards a hidden camera disguised as a light, in the hope one of my watchers, too, cottoned on, and quickly sent a Sebastian to exit from the other side. But the door remained resolutely locked, and it seemed I was the only one to foresee the problem.

I was relieved when the resolution came to me.

"Sebastian, be a dear and open my studio for me, hon. I wasn't expecting to come here so I didn't bring my set of keys to open it up."

"Oh, sure boss," Sebastian said, cottoning on very quickly. I saw the alarm flash in his eyes, as he realised how suss it would have been. He came forward, making the two police officers have to step closer to me - still with my full lower half on show only wearing my lacey bra and the robe.

"Now, boys, you're going to see where and how I make my *magic*, and why I've come to your notice." I giggled again. Sebastian stepped aside so the boss lady could lead the party in.

There on the other side of the room, looking exactly what Room Two back in the real location looked like, was the bed I supposedly performed on, lighting and cameras (though I could tell they were probably older models no longer in use, but still set up to look like they were), and a small but comfortable area for my Pete's to get dressed and wait in the wings, and a small (sound proof?) room which comfortably fit three technicians. The equipment looked expensive; it made sense the room would be locked as additional security in case the place was ever robbed. What the two police officers couldn't see, even though it was in this very room, was another hidden entry to the secret passageway I'd shortly been brought through; but it was well disguised and blended in as being a decorative feature wall..

I walked over to and ran my hand lightly on the bed, and then faced the two awestruck officers, and asked teasingly. "Do you need me to show you what I do in here, so you can write your reports *accurately?*" I sat on the bed, eyed both their trousers while moving my tongue and lips around as though I seriously wanted to get their trousers off, giggled, and said, "I won't tell your bosses, will I Sebastian?"

"No ma'am."

I went all coy and encouraging, "You can store your clothes and gear over there in my Pete's change area. We can have fun separately or together; whatever you prefer."

The main officer coughed uncomfortably, and started saying something about they're on duty, so I said what Amberee realistically would sweetly whine, and stared constantly at their trousers, "Aww, don't be party-poopers. You've both got delicious erections, and I can tell already you both have the types of cocks Amberee really, really loves playing with, so come on, let's play. *Go on.*"

'Ma'am, we're sorry to have disturbed you—"

"Aww," I pouted like I was being denied fun (and well, I really was enjoying how uncomfortable I was making these two men. It wasn't every day I got to have or do anything fun). "Can I at least give you both a blow job each, if you really don't have time to fuck me? Come on, you got me down here, now I want to play. *Pretty please?*" and another perfectly timed giggle.

I don't think Mr J., Mr D. or the Roy's watching would've ever seen two tough cops kerscuffle from the building before they gave in to how hot and bothered I had made them both, especially after I got off the bed, went over and picked up one of the live feed promo cards with a discount voucher I had seen on a table near the door and tucked two of them in to one of the officers top pocket as I backed him against the wall with nowhere to escape my naked puss, and said with a wink, "Maybe when you're off duty then boys, cause I really, *really* want to do the both of you."

If they were married or had girlfriends, I guessed who both of them might fantasise about tonight. Pity for them if they were single. Either a cold shower or risking their jobs to tune in for them.

We never had the police come raiding 'my house' again.

But one of Mr J.'s contacts let him know three or so months later they had learned moments earlier the police were still investigating to see if there's anything they could arrest me, my body guards, the Pete's or my technicians with.

I misjudged Mr J. would worry about that.

He laughed and said, "Well, what they'll find is you don't accept payment for any of what you do, your husband does, and—"

"—my what?"

"Your husband - so you having sex, even if it is a hundred guy's a night isn't breaking any law anywhere in the world. The Pete's aren't paid by you; again, everyone is paid by your husband, who lives overseas, where it is not illegal for him to receive the payments for your feeds, films and everything else you want to do. And, is also not illegal for him to pay all the people who you hire. They're all to 'treat you as boss lady' but it's really your husband who is; he's the one who hires and pays for their services in helping you achieve your goals and dreams.'

"But, won't they question why a husband would—"

"—question why you have sex with everyone but him?"

"Well, yes."

"Amberee, puss, my best-ever little porn princess, the poor non-existent man is aged and impotent and is ecstatic his beautiful young wife is enjoying her youth, so who is he to stand in her way? If you want to fuck a hundred men a night, he is happy to support you do that. He's the one you wanted to marry. That's why he setup his business overseas, and he controls and manages all the financial side of you doing what you love. He is proud of how well you are doing, and happy to help you become the porn mega star you want to become. He visits you often, and the public don't know for fact, only what's rumoured, you've done a few sneaky recordings which can be played while you take the night off to spend with your husband when one of you visits the other, which you do at least once a month. And you both signed all the paperwork, so when he dies, a manager will be appointed to take over his business for him, so you can continue to do what you love doing for as long as you love doing it, and it is never a crime for you to have cock in your sweet little mouth or pussy. But don't worry; he'll live to an old age."

I was dumbfounded, and it certainly nearly made me forget to ask what I had been determined to ask Mr J. "How long have I been married? And, don't you have to have a ceremony or something?"

"The day you turned eighteen and became legal. It's all legal and properly filed."

I was starting to see how deeply trapped I was - they had lied about my age so no one ever figured out I had only been fourteen when I first started doing my live feeds - and how I'd never gain a chance to escape. I was too valuable; Amberee too loved - she *wants* to do this and loves every second of it. This made me realise my long game could take longer than I imagined.

"Now, don't you worry about all the efforts I've gone to, to ensure you can't be arrested. You've got a photo shoot for a triple X magazine to get to tomorrow, early morning. So, make sure you get a good night's sleep, Amberee. They've paid me eight million to get you to star in their girlie sealed section - well, they don't realise it's me or my company, but that's what I personally will profit from the deal. The rate you're going, I'm on track to become a billionaire in a couple of years. Maybe even before you really turn twenty one, if I'm lucky."

Mr J. gave me a peck on the cheek as he prepared to leave, saying, "Good luck with the shoot tomorrow." He'd never done this before, so again, another thing came close to causing me to forget making my request.

The door had practically closed, when I called, "Mr J."

"Yes, puss?"

"I - I'd really like, if it is alright with you, of course, to … to personally reply to some of my fans?"

I don't know what Mr J. had thought I might ask him, but he certainly hadn't been expecting me to ask that. First, was a betraying flicker of genuine surprise; second, was the shrewd businessman certain he knew I was up to some kind of trick.

"You want to personally respond to your fans," he said, not asked. He stopped to think for a moment, then said barely hiding a smirk, "I think a small portion could be arranged."

I giggled (Amberee's first ever unprompted giggle) and thanked Mr J. and told him I appreciated him allowing me to do that. Again he looked at me intensely, and I guessed he thought I was playing games. He didn't buy into me giggling the Amberee giggle without being told she had to one little iota. Oh, I'm sure he thought the real Amber, Amber Entacott, human being (not Amberee, porn princess) had decided she was skilled enough as an actress to try and fool her captors. And he suspected exactly why the little 'idiot' was asking, too - I saw the smile behind the smile which could only mean he thought he was smarter than me and he'd play along and I'd soon find out how quickly he'd catch me trying to send secret pleas for help to fans, trying to get the truth out into the world I am being held prisoner against my will and in desperate need of help.

"I'll get it organised, you can receive up to twenty fan letters a day starting tomorrow afternoon."

With that, he closed the door.

$\mathcal{C}$HAPTER 17

To seal the deal Mr J. may soon catch me mid-defiance, I smiled like I was pleased, so when he re-watched the footage of me in the moments after he left the room, he'd further take the bait I was trying to get one over them now they all thought I had long since accepted my captivity.

I had no doubt in my mind, Mr J. was fully expecting I'd 'play it smart to begin with' by not saying or doing anything not strictly Amberee in the first day or two's batches, but I'd inevitably be the foolish girl falling for his trap - they wouldn't be fooled by my silly-girl charade. Every sealed letter destined for reopening and checking and thus they'd be prepared for my immediate relocation to Room Six or other punishment the moment they caught me in the act.

But more fool them. It was the closest thing to fun amid no drama for me at this point. I had no intentions of giving them the satisfaction of learning the truth. I was more than aware I was going to need to do this for months, maybe a few years (though I silently prayed not) before I could ever risk doing such a thing.

The next morning, I got the surprise of my life for the first photo-shoot, when Murk entered the room and rushed up to me and gave me a brief hug, before standing back to take me in.

"Amberee, love. The uncles send you their love, and wanted me to pass on how thrilled they are you're starting to become a right little mega-star. Our little Amber. Look how experienced you are now, compared to when I introduced you to this career. And to think at one stage we were worried you were going to end up in one of the drugged-up sex-houses until you wouldn't be able to work anymore from whatever nasty you picked up. You're too pretty and fuckable to have taken that path." And he kissed me on the lips, and ran his hand over my panties, "for old times' sake".

"Okay, but enough reminiscing for now, we have a very busy day ahead of us, and I want to go over the plans: the bulk of this photo-shoot will be you in various lingerie. I'll get you to do some poses - but don't worry, nothing which doesn't go with the Amberee image - with you minus your panties, but leave the suspenders and stockings on, I'll decide on bra once you are in position, and you'll suck on your finger, finger your clit, that sort of stuff, before we move on to getting a lot of you with Pete's - well, you know what to do. And then we'll finish off the add-pics: you with a vibrator or two, and then we'll do the feature shots, you side on, one in your puss and you blowing the other, so the two Pete's ripped bod's are barely visible in and framing the shot so you're all a letter H, which the XXXX-Hotstuff Mag4Men - that's who we're shooting for - executives thought was genius on my part, but don't worry, babe, it's you doing and receiving the action which will fully remain the focus, alright."

"You're the photographer?"

"Sure am, starlet. Mr J. thought it would be a great opportunity to get me to fly in and do a few professional shoots for him once or twice a year. And to give you a little reward after your outstanding performance getting the cops radar off you're the other month."

I had known Murk sometimes did porn photo-shoots in Australia when he was low on child porn images to sell (there's only so many he can sell of the same ped-prize before no one's interested in buying, as they crave a new ped-prize to replace the old), so he always had money to live on and enough to purchase his controlling share of their private little ped-group prizes. But my maturer body wasn't what he was after any more - unless it was part of control, which is what got him there to spurt. I had close to four years experience with Murk taking photos of me. He demanded pics at precisely the right angle so the viewer could 'feel' and 'live' the action which had taken place, and could look at the image and imagine it was their dick, and they were the one conquering me (or whichever other ped-prize he was snapping pics of).

You see, for Murk, it had always been the men who fucked or got sucked by a woman, whatever her age, shape and willingness levels were, made the man a Hero, a star who triumphed every time they spurted, in whatever way got him there. He got me to "hold that pose" while he came in and shifted the male (back then, my uncles) or my flaps or lips, maybe one-thousandth of a millimetre, for one reason: this could make all the difference to him between an okay versus a perfect fuck or suck shot. When it came to his form of photography, he gave and demanded perfectionism. He excelled in his art.

And my memory hadn't failed me. This shoot, surely, required the same attention to specifics.

"Nope! Nope, remove the bra. Leave the suspenders on but up top I only want her in a sheer, see-through robe. White! The one with the magenta flowerettes to match the suspenders. Make sure it is both obvious she is robed, but she's still fully naked with all the good bits on show. Amberee, babes, close your legs tight together for this next bit so your puss parts aren't revealed yet for this shot, but don't squeeze them legs together so tight it ends up making you look constipated like the first time I ever told you to do this pose for me back in Spud's van, okay starlet." and he laughed briefly at his recalled memory before adding, "Someone get a fucking air con pointed down on her too - I want those little titties fully erect the highest they go - I *know* for fact they can double the current height! Come on people give me your A-game! This is for XXXX-Hotstuff Mag4Men for fuck's sake. Porn mag royalty!"

Lots of poses. Hours on the job. Me sucking cock; me fucking a variety of cocks, in the puss and arse. Me with 'my favourite toys', and even giving a raspberry ice-block shaped into a huge cock a blow job (I went through the full tray. The studio lighting made them melt too quickly.)

The 'feature shot', the one of me with two male partners, was actually more than the one shooting of me with two partners as presumed. XXXX-Hotstuff Mag4Men was distributed in a number of countries around the world. I was the Miss Whatever of the Month for this special Amberee edition, but the readers of specific countries preferred any shots of men in the photos to be of their own race.

So, I had two of a couple of races - two 'virile-n-sweetfatsticks', two 'chocolate long-johns', and two 'cream- sweeteners' (well, that's how Murk referred to them affectionately and everyone went along with that, including the men who loved those titles given to their cocks), so most of the various countries were satisfied from those three pairings.

Murk snapped readers expected to see a lot 'more shaft visible' in pussy or anus fuck shots "so only head in please, long-john, maybe a little bit not yet made it in - perfect!", and the exact opposite, deeper penetration of the shaft on the suck shots with the long-john photos but not so much 'Amberee puss' gagged on. "That's not the makings of good still-pornography!" A hint of "give it to her rough" top and tail with the sweeteners, "So Amberee puss, I want you to look a little uncomfortable, yes, like that, hold it!" and a more submissive and obedient me for the n-sweetfatsticks, "So Amberee, puss, I want you to really look into blow-hunks eyes while you blow him. And blow-hunk, give it a little sterner look, suggestive you'll punish her if she doesn't satisfy, but only mild with the sternness, Amberee loves sucking cocks so you don't need to force her into doing any of this." Murk took hundreds, maybe thousands of shots with each pair and for each pose, although he kept snapping off a round of autos, then coming out from behind the cameras, and repositioning us trying to get everything perfect, and never seeming satisfied we'd got the ideal, flawless shot in his view yet, until we actually did.

As Murk had once told me and I was now using as the basis of my long-plan, 'the difference between his group getting away with their illegal activities and going to jail all condensed to planning and executing all the tiny nit-picky details'.

I was using this precise strategy to slowly build their trust in me, to convince them contrary to their fears I was looking for an opportunity to escape I was genuinely embracing my life as Amberee so one day, when the right moment came along, they wouldn't expect it, suspicion long ago fallen off their radar. As much as I hated the idea, I couldn't see an opportunity ever occurring before I turned twenty one. I needed to have patience, and do everything I could along the journey until the eventual moment of freedom came. (I had to think of it in terms of it will happen rather than hope it would happen, to buoy my strength to keep secretly resisting.)

Murk on the other hand applied the same principle of sorts to getting the shot the magazine execs wanted for the magazine, and particular starlet. And his little former ped-prize, and him being the first fuck she had ever had, had driven him to new levels of wanting absolute perfection - so he could continue to do his part to enable my stardom to even higher rise, and do his part to get me more movies and still photo shoots in addition to my nightly live or private action gigs.

It wasn't me who frustrated Murk because they had moved a millimetre, it was the ones who had their cock in my puss or I had in my mouth. My solo shots had all been taken in the amount of time Murk had estimated. Over my roughly four years as the ped-group prize, I had learned to listen to instructions and had had to obey them precisely, or suffer the punishment for not following all the tiniest details. And I fell easily into doing this again now. But, not so the cock's I had to pose with.

Twice a frustrated Murk threw his arms in the air and stormed, "Is Amberee the only one here who knows how to work like a professional? For fuck's sake!"

Coming from Murk, this was nearly a compliment - except for the circumstance I was receiving it. NOT enjoying a single act or day of doing what I had to do, despite what came across on camera. Below the surface, I was always on the edge of having an emotional meltdown over how hopeless my situation was - with no possible ending in sight for at least two years, and still having no guarantee my long-plan would even work. I worried I had made the wrong call and doomed myself to remain a porn star for the rest of my life.

And regularly, "Hey, cock in starlet's puss. Give it a couple of thrusts to get yourself hard again. Amberee, hon, while he's doing that you may as well help re-harden blow cock too, so we don't waste time having to stop for *him* to re-swell next."

All up, even though the shoot was only suppose to have taken twelve hours, we were holed-up in the basement studio for fifty something, with a high percent of that time me with a cock to give love and me only allowed to take a catnap when the lack of sleep started showing on my face, and touch-up makeup wasn't going to hide it. I was the star, required in every pic. The cocks could be switched out and were done so frequently, but I had to be present for it all.

Nobody whinged and bitched about how difficult Murk was to work with again when the magazine was published. Mr J. was so pleased, he had the feature photo of me with the cream-sweeteners of the American cover blown up and added to my starlet living quarters - we made a great, subtle letter H - and a copy of the magazine and the interview they fabricated with one of their 'leading reporters' in on all the latest porn gossip, so I could view the final product. I think it was a tiny reward never afforded to any of the other starlets - I was key performer making Mr J. rise in the dollar amount of being a multi millionnaire with the prospect of becoming a billionaire too due to him always getting a high-cut of all earnings from all starlets, and of course the cops radar deactivating - I was still receiving small rewards for that performance months and months later.

And Mr J. personally risked coming to our site and having direct conversations with me.

Mr J. joked he thinks *The Millionaire's Best Asset* script writer must have had some psychic intuition or something. His personal worth from owning me as an asset had grown from the Amberee sales generation (across all hundred or more streams) alone was into the three hundred and sixty six million mark, 'with some extra loose change' to date, so it was ironic this was the figure used in the fuck flick.

I still couldn't believe it when I read the interview I never gave summarising how I ended up where I am today though: I had supposedly run away from home in country Victoria where I was being raised by my loving single father following my mother dying in a car accident, and ...

"After I had sex with a boy from my school (we were caught mid act by my dad), something had switched on inside me, I wanted to do more of that, and my horrible dad tried to go stricter and threatened to lock me up or send me to a nunnery to try and not let me do that, so I got out of that place as soon as I could and hitched a ride to Sydney - yes, the truckie ended up being my first paying customer, thanks Joe, you were awesome, I've never forgotten! - and I went to work at the Cross for a while so I could save the money to get a passport and head over to sight-see America. It's my absolute favourite country.

Okay, yes, I did lie about my age: I found out men could get in trouble for fucking earlier than a girl being eighteen years old. So, I lied so it wasn't their fault, and I didn't have to wait forever for me to become legal. Lying about my age was the only way I could look after them and me.

Everyone had been telling me I was really pretty and could be an actress, and although my intention was exclusively to fuck those willing to pay me, to enable me to tour the country (which I never had trouble finding a willing sweetie), I was staying in LA, and after I visited Hollywood with some new friends, one day we all went to see a porn movie, you know, I thought it might help me to learn some new tricks so I could make sure I was satisfying my delicious treats, I suddenly realised I should try to get a job in a porn movie myself. And I never wanted to return home. I already was where I needed to be to pursue this aspiration.

But, it's really hard, there's plenty of girls like me trying to break in, so I figured I needed to do something to make myself shine better than the other wannabe starlets. Me being Aussie wasn't unique enough; I ran into a few wannabes like me and recognised their Aussie accent immediately. Anyway, I heard about this party, where it was rumoured three great porn directors were all going to be; so I snuck in without the bouncers seeing me, and blended in, waiting for an opportunity, though I didn't know what that might be. I guess I was trusting my gut I'd be able to talk to a director or something when the right moment came along.

I was talking to some guy who was instantly in to me like most of the guys at school and in the Cross and I'd met while new here, and he was kind of hinting he'd like to take me back to his place, and we could do it for fun or for payment, whatever suited me - he had a wealthy dad - and I suddenly thought, "Bingo!" I could make myself stand out by performing with this guy right in front of them - you know, let them audition me without them even realising it. So I told the guy I wanted to blow him right here in front of everyone if he was game, and then we could go to his place to fuck but if he wasn't, then I wasn't going to bother and I'd circle the party until I found a guy who was up for letting me provide the unexpected party entertainment.

And, well, you guys all know the rest. I had to wait a few days and continue on at my live action gig I'd already secured, I never wanted to let that audience down while I embarked on my other porn aspirations. After the directors saw how good I was, and I was willing to commit fully to working like a professional porn princess, they had scripts written specifically for me in mind.

And those first two films sold really well, and I started getting fan mail straightaway - thank you guys! - so I started getting more and more film offers and ended up having to get an agent to help me stay on top of it all - I didn't want the hassle of having to schedule what days I was required where, so my agent got me a personal assistant to manage those types of things, so all I had to do was get my hair and makeup done, and get in front of the camera and give it my best performance for you guys. I never dreamed for a moment I'd ever reach this level of fanship. They tell me I'm eighty seven percent of most guys favourite; that's never been achieved by any other starlet or mega pornstar before, so I'm really proud of this unexpected achievement, but personally, I want to reach one hundred percent."

Our conversation turned to how long Amberee thinks she'll keep making films and working her live action gig.

"Oh, I'm never leaving my live action gig, if I can help it, well, not my weekend live actions, no matter how well my movies and other gigs do, I love it too much. I love how I can engage with my fans and do it the way which gets them off. But, I get too busy to do the live actions every weeknight, too. Honestly, I'm hoping I keep my looks for as long as I can, and I do what I can to keep my body in good shape, so I don't see any reason why I can't work until I'm into my thirties or longer so long as I have fans who like seeing me perform. I do it for you, guys. (At this point, Amber blew kisses 'for every person who buys my DVDS, subscribes to my live broadcast room, and buys the magazines I get featured in'.)

Actually, do you want me to share with you a little secret? She asks, as she leans forwards and places a hand gently on my inner upper thigh as though itching to touch my junk. I distractedly agree. She giggles the way only Amberee giggles, though a lot of other wannabes are now trying to imitate her style, and sits straight delighted.

From the moment I arrived here I always hoped I'd one day appear in XXXX-Hotstuff Mag4Men. I never thought I'd ever become the featured starlet, but I hoped to get a topless on one of the other pages. But look what happened! My DVDs did really well, and my live broadcast subscribers wrote to the magazine to ask if they planned to feature me any time soon - they had already approached my agents guys quite a few times, but for a while I couldn't fit into my schedule no matter how hard I tried, and then when we finally were able to start setting it all up, we had a teeny weeny problem with one of my other gigs the delay of which prevented me from being able to do the shoot for them for a while again. I had so many other already confirmed and contracted commitments - so they kindly worked around my schedule so we all could give you what you want guys, and well, here I am, finally.

Would you like to grace the cover and be the featured starlet in future editions?

Oh for sure!

I've never heard anyone so keen to do more. Even though Amberee was more than happy to keep sharing with me what it is about being a starlet that lights her up and keeps her happy, it was at this point Amberee's personal assistant interrupted us to say the starlet really had to leave as she had a meeting with another film director to ask if filming can be brought forward a few weeks and was now going to run late, which isn't likely to get them to agree - Yay, that'll mean an earlier release of another, what's sure to impress as another great, Amberee flick, if they agree, so I was more than happy to let her leave so she could make that happen for us - and so she had to leave.

But let me tell you folks, Amberee is as sweet, and funny and sexy in person as she appears on camera, film and live TV. There's no secret diva behind the scenes, and one very enthusiastic to participate and aim to satisfy above and beyond all other starlets young woman, who is every bit as true as what we see on screen. And her giggle is truly infectious. She certainly won this reporter over with her passion for and dedication to her craft (not merely owing to the fact she offered to give me a personal demo on why she's the best in the industry before she had to race off, and an invitation to set a date whenever I want.) Amberee is genuinely an absolute knockout, with and without makeup.

On behalf of the magazine and all your raving fans, we wish you continued ongoing success, Amberee!

I wanted to gag on the bullshit.

Were men (and the lesbian and straight women who had also fallen in love with me) really that gullible to believe this shit? I flicked through the images. The magazine had included over fifty of them. Sucking my finger, fingering my clit, and all the other poses which gave people full view of every part of me, but supposedly more tastefully done than most other starlets - what my puss and anus looked like, how high my nipples could poke up after all that agonising deliberate nip-stretching treatments Mr J. had ordered rather than going the traditional breast enhancement route of other starlets, during my first two years.

And still they wanted more, more and more of me. But, you only had to look at the quality of each image to see Murk's perfectionism had resulted in still-porn perfection. Murk might be able to command higher fees next time he got asked to do another porn shoot. And the poor little ped-prizes most likely, definitely, be purchased by Mr J. due to we were already trained as thoroughly compliant, and he didn't have any of the problems with me he had with every other starlet in his employ who (apparently, and I have no reason to doubt) cried frequently and uncontrollably at the drop of a hat.

Like when they had their first fuck, their first rough fuck, their first back passage fuck and or came to really realise the life, family and friendships they had once known and taken for granted they'd never be returned to, and what they were being forced to do was the only future they could foresee. Which had them bursting into tears uncontrollably, resulting in a hasty cut of the feed, with a pre-programmed and ready to instantly fire up continuous streamed message, "We're experiencing technical difficulties for this room, but here's an access code to gain free access to one of our other full live action rooms not experiencing the same technical problems, which we assure you we are hastening to fix" to take over the live action's placement.

Until the offending starlet was 'sorted out' and learned the hard way to become compliant, and obey instructions instantly. The usual threats: "fucking pull a stunt like that ever again on camera" promises of painful punishment.

The usual last stated point: she should be *thankful* Mr J. treated her the best of all others in the same industry.

Mr J. was impressed Murk only got a hold of girls who could be easily forgotten about, and were well passed the emotionally unstable phase of their transition. He liked the starlets only when they were perfectly accepting this was their life now (no matter how reluctant or resentful), and did as instructed regardless. And he loved he had made great decisions about how to build the most money he could out of me.

It was clear me ever being sold on had long ago gone off his agenda. I had no idea whether I still 'owed him money' or was in the black. The rules still applying to other starlets may have no longer been relevant for me. I may have been elevated to special case level, so the usual cycle wasn't followed with me. I was a money making machine and they were going to keep using it until they got every cent they could from it. I brought in from my live feeds over two hundred thousand on a weeknight (when I did a full week), half a million on weekends. Why wouldn't they keep milking the cash cow?

As I closed the magazine, and went to lie down for my afternoon rest, my mind drifted to young Daisy, the girl who had replaced me. I was now eighteen and a half; what did that make her? Eleven, twelve? It wouldn't be long, if it hadn't already happened, until she too became the property of Mr J.

For some bizarre reason I actually considered myself partly responsible for Daisy ending up at the uncles property. If I hadn't matured when I did, she might have never been snatched off the streets, sold to a ped-buyer group and now live her life the horrible way I did, servant and sex-toy, all over my uncles losing interest in screwing me, making it my fault she was in the same position as me - wondering how to end it all.

$\mathcal{C}$HAPTER 18

Days after the XXXX Hotstuff Mag4Men shoot, I got my first ever bundle of selected fan mail.

They were from men writing to tell me I was really hot, they loved how I sucked cock and enjoyed fucking more than most women. And what I chose to do brought them great pleasure. If they had paid for me to do something in the room once, twice or even multiple times, they were quick to let me know they had done this and idealised they 'fully supported' me.

So, my replies thanked them for doing that, for saying such nice things, and I'm really glad they enjoyed my performances, and I'd very much like it if next time they visited my room and paid to get me to do something, they know it is their cock I wish I was doing. And to give it a little love from me.

I have another unfortunate confession: I thought reading the fan mail would make me feel sick and I'd find it hard to compose replies I was going to have to force myself to do as part of my long-term freedom plan, so was glad I was being restricted to twenty only per day to begin with; but actually, it weirdly helped me to cope with what I had to do, right from the very first letter. I think it was the contact with any outsider aspect, and I was comforted - like I was being hugged by people who truly loved me - and so I found the words of Amberee quite easy to write. She was a character to play for me. These were some very lonely men I - she - was bringing joy to (sexually and emotionally);

and their words, were unexpectedly bringing some joy to me, because I was acutely as lonely. Maybe more so.

The people holding me captive had trained me from a young age to lie. To lie convincingly. It was why I was able to act for the cameras. Inventing experiences I'd never had now also came easily to me. Trips I'd never taken; people, celebrities, I had not met. Items I hadn't bought. All lies. All things I wished I had the freedom to say, go, do and spend on. Those things were denied to me, so I imagined and invented enjoying what life freely gave to others.

Each afternoon, after I had answered the mail, sometimes taking a few hours giving lengthy replies, enjoying my own escapism storytelling, I inserted a full colour photograph of me (tastefully posed) but fully naked from the previous day's screen tests which had been stamped with an official Amberee endorsement.

Sometimes I wrote on the back of the photograph, too. "That kiss I'm giving goes to *your* cock, Ben, or Dave, or whatever the fan's name was. I then licked the envelope shut, and placed the little stack in a neat pile, and then went for my required afternoon catnap so I wouldn't look or be tired during the live feed. The letters were always gone by the time I returned to my room after the live performance and post performance routine. And the next day's selected fan mail was ready and waiting for me.

After a week of this, I basked in feeling I must have been frustrating Mr J., (which was genuinely fun for me to think about; sure my words were forced as some sort of secret plan he'd catch me out on) so I think he gave the order to 'make it happen' to 'get our gorgeous little starlet to reveal her real intentions'.

As a Sebastian escorted me to my starlet room after my post live-feed shower, I noticed the door always kept shut and locked was open, revealing the staircase for the floor above - a major security oversight by a Sebastian or Mr D. or Mr J. (All the Darren's and Zack's, and anyone else had to arrive by one of the secret accesses, to make it seem to any watching outsiders that they worked in Starlet House, never by that staircase which was for the Sebastian's who monitored the above floor visitors).

Just as my Sebastian opened my bedroom door, another Sebastian came running, yelling at my Sebastian to help, saying, "A starlet is making an escape and has fled the building," and my Sebastian streaked off up the stairs and raced off to deal with (what resonated as a phony emergency to me), conveniently forgetting to close and lock the door behind me. And leaving the hidden passageway to the outside world above open behind them.

They were really too obvious about wanting me to believe all the on duty Sebastian's were in pursuit of another starlet and I'd think all the Roy's monitoring the cameras would focus all their time and attention on the pursuit and making sure the fleeing starlet didn't escape their clutches, so I could do so unnoticed. But I refused to give Mr J. the confirmation he wanted.

The whole thing screamed blatant trap to me (men, I noticed weren't subtle like females). I simply closed the door myself for a change, sat at my table to eat the delicious looking chicken and avocado salad evidently on my night's menu, and then feeling honestly tired after my long evening of sucking and fucking, settled myself into bed and fell asleep quickly, like I had done every other night since I had come to live here and gotten used to our daily routine I lived and breathed by when I wasn't off doing all *The Millionaire's Best Asset* re-enactments (which I was still doing at least twice a weeknight).

Mr J. must have decided to keep getting my keepers to try tempt me, perhaps suspecting I had suspected it had all been an entrapment; I started witnessing other minor progressing to major security fuck ups over the next three months which had never occurred before (and surely never occurred around any of the other starlets). I didn't take a bite of any one of them. They still all screamed 'trap' to me (though I always stressed about them afterwards, worried I'd lost a genuine chance to flee).

So, at the next porn film set, when I accidentally on purpose wasn't properly anchored in a collar cuff so I normally couldn't move more than a few metres away from the anchor point, but on this day could make a serious run for it to try and escape the building (but far too many people were around to notice if I attempted leaving and I'd be captured in seconds.)

I mean, seriously, how dumb were they? I was fully naked, and had a lot of the film crew unable to help looking, even though I wasn't the first porn princess they'd ever seen), so I appreciated sitting and 'basking in' the freedom the not collar cuffed properly gave me my full range of neck movements (obviously the cuff was custom designed to keep a starlet's head always tilted upwards at an angle, which made it very difficult for any girl to see where she was going if she was ever foolish enough to try escaping while wearing it. Running? Near impossible to carry out successfully.)

But, I did make sure I took a 'sneaky advantage' of discovering I wasn't properly restrained. It may have looked too suspicious if I didn't. So my shifty-eyes were all about committing the 'crime' of stealing two strawberries off the crews food table - which was about a metre from my reach if I had of been really restrained. So I looked constantly around making sure they noticed I was ready to run for it, but instead only inched my way forward to their food table, 'sneakily' grabbed the two strawberries all the while making sure no one caught me in the act, and then made my way back against the wall, where I slid to sit and only took small nibbles every time I supposedly thought no one was watching (but at least someone was), and ate the two strawberries which were not approved for as part of my diet, trying really hard not to look too guilty at eating the unapproved fruit, but only after I secretly practised blow job moves, as though I was testing a new way to do them on the only thing I could get my hands on.

I sometimes did things like this to amuse myself. I missed being able to laugh and have fun like how I used to when Mum was alive. My unprompted giggling helped me release how bleak my inside nature had become coloured. But like I said, I was fully committed to convincing everyone I had accepted my life as Amberee porn princess; and was on-board with their goal for me to seen as a sex-loving starlet. So to help me do that, I mentally painted my inside nature silver. I should have tried a different colour, like, green, or pink or sunshine yellow. Silver sometimes changed of its own accord to grey, and persisted in reaching its darkest tint.

It was worth the small punishment I received when Mr D. arrived when I was in my basement bedroom when he marched in and backhanded me across the face and yelled at me I had been caught and one of the film crew had been quick to report me, and I had better never pull a 'stunt like that again'. I was on a *strictly* controlled diet to ensure my weight was kept the same.

And then him stepping forward, closer, and saying with a nasty edge, that, "Mr J. will be informed about this, so this might not be the last of your punishment, starlet. It might mean Room Six for you." I of course begged him to please don't do that, and promised 'very frightened' I will never do anything like that again.

Mr D. left my room looking very satisfied. (He appeared to like the idea of hurting me far more than Murk had ever done, which was saying something. *He* gave me that belt at least three times a week). I stayed 'looking slightly anxious' he'd return, and my eyes flicked towards the corridor door whenever I heard steps outside for at least the next hour, to keep up the charade.

Men - they weren't anywhere near as smart as they gave them self credit as.

It must have been a believable performance - well, they *did* praise me for having a natural talent for acting - I didn't receive any further punishments for my criminal two-strawberry stealing. As I had long now suspected, if I was making them as much money as I was, unless I seriously fucked up, they wouldn't dare damage me with a week assigned to Room Six - a day maybe - but not the full seven days. And nothing too visible, due to how much they stood to lose financially for every day I was left recovering. Bruises weren't in keeping with what the public thought about Amberee were they?

After that, I think they were finally convinced I was genuinely embracing becoming *Amberee porn princess*, on and off camera, in and out of my rare public appearances. And my best hopes may ultimately earn me increasingly relaxed security soon started becoming un-staged reality.

I wasn't fool enough to misuse *small* opportunities for escape. I was willing to wait for a big one. Off site.

I was allowed to return to my bedroom from the showers only being watched by a Sebastian rather than having one escort me at my side or rear like had been the routine since I had first got here.

Slowly, slowly, I was becoming more trusted, with every subtly placed non-instructed Amberee giggle. I still had a lot more trust building to do so those security relaxations occurred more when I left the building too - I was certain: the only time I'd make my proper attempt to run for it was while I was in public and away from their cameras which made it easy for them to corner and recapture me, hopefully close to a police station. (Remember, I'd known about the cameras right from day one, and although I could tell many of the other staff forgot about them, I never did), thus ruining any chance of a second attempt. They'd *never* trust me ever again - and definitely earning me time to really serve in Room Six.

"Pay attention to finer details, Amberee."

And think smartly.

Never forget the cameras watched my every move.

The real problem I faced was to not ever start believing in myself as *Amberee porn princess* while fully living and breathing and adopting the porn-and-cock-loving personality to convince them. To remain mindful it was *all an act*, and I wouldn't ever abandon my secret goal.

You'd think that would be a cinch to do, but I can tell you with the honesty I promised: at times it became much harder than I thought.

PART 3
THE LONG-GAME PLAN

@HAPTER 19

Remember I told you in my earlier letters (well, I think I did, I don't have the pages any more to check) I only ever saw another starlet twice the complete period I worked there? The first, if you recall, was the starlet in Room Six, who I believe it was an intentional part of my orientation tour of the basement facilities the day Mr J. purchased me from Murk to see, to keep me compliant. I suspect all new recruits get the same orientation.

The other starlet was Daisy, the ped-prize who replaced me on the property. The meeting of which nearly caused me to abandon my long-play escape plan - I saw with my own eyes how extremely dangerous my trying to escape would undoubtedly be. (Up until that meeting, I had only imagined the level of danger; after the meeting, now I realised the fully entirety).

A Sebastian came to get me one day - it was not long before my twentieth birthday - and said Mr J. had ordered each of the starlet bedrooms and performance areas to have the beds and carpets replaced with newer ones, and our rooms, and every surface, thoroughly professionally cleaned, walls and ceilings included. (This had happened once previously, but I'd been sent into the period bedroom alone).

So Sebastian had arrived to escort me to (what I thought was all)

135

the starlets period bedroom until all the work had been completed. My identity had been thrown into the darkly strange familiar zone, escorted to do things like this again; I'd become accustomed to my small freedoms, but never forgotten my internal compressing walls.

As we walked along the corridor towards the room, Mr J. was walking towards us with a Darren on one of his infrequent visits. Sebastian made me stop walking, and Mr J. told the Darren with a wink, "Ahhh, this is our darling starlet, Amberee now. It's okay, you're allowed to do a little touchy-feel of her pubes and clit. Our little star puss just *loves* it."

A delighted Darren immediately stepped forward, slipped a finger straight into my puss, and gushed like an overwhelmed fan," It's a thrill to meet you in person, Amberee. I've watched your live shows and own every DVD of course, but you're even more beautiful in person."

It frustrated me they were encouraged to do that, but of course I couldn't say or do anything except to pretend it was my pleasure and they were welcome to do this every time they saw me. That the 'honour' was all mine. Mr J. had told me that first day (and meant every word), "Your sole existence is to pleasure men; and that is precisely what you will do for the rest of your life."

And once he'd removed his finger again, Sebastian nudged me to continue in the direction we were heading, so Mr J. could finish giving the wide-eyed, can't believe his luck to secure this gig and meet-and-finger-Amberee Darren instructions. When I entered the room, I saw another starlet was sitting upon a hard wooden chair (that wasn't normally in there).

I was horrified by the starlet's appearance and fully comprehended why she didn't look up to greet or even look at me: I had never seen anyone in my life before with such a sorrow-filled, broken demeanour. And I could tell exactly why she was the way she was.

Sebastian told me, "You and Daisy will share this room together. Mr J. wants both of you still aired tonight. Amberee, as Mr J.'s favourite and biggest money earner, you get to sleep in the bed, Daisy already knows she has to find herself a spot on the floor. Cameras will still watch you in here, starlets."

I wondered if this was the same Daisy as from back home in

Australia.

"Are - are we allowed to talk - to - to each other?" I asked Sebastian curiously, aware I was still not allowed to talk to my Pete's or film crews and wondering how I wouldn't break the no-talking rule being holed up with another starlet for so many hours. I didn't want to undo any of the privilege's I had carefully built up to receiving through the making of one mistake.

"Oh, yeah, I almost forgot … big boss says you'll both be here for a few hours and have already met previously, so it's okay for you both to not only talk to each other but fully share details with each other about your lives here, as our two favourite, highest earning Aussie starlets. Actually, Mr J. said to encourage it, so go ahead, starlets, happy chatting."

With that he closed and locked the door.

I had my confirmation it was the same Daisy though.

Whereas I always wore a bra but no panties, and sometimes a sheer or silky robe and soft slippers (and still no panties), and lived in my starlet room amongst comfortable and luxurious items I was freely allowed to use, Daisy was completely naked, and clearly did not. Her too thin body was heavily pierced, and most of her arms and torso were covered in tattoos, some of them raw as they were new.

As I looked closer at the poor, miserable starlet still not even having looked up to see me, I was horrified to realise the tattoo on both sides of her face were of a large penis disappearing inside her mouth; her eyelids, most likely from always looking towards the ground avoiding eye contact, had been inked with "I love," on the left side eyelid, and "cock" on the right side. The remaining tattoos covering her body were names of men, and right above her pubic hair were the words 'Ram one in here. The bigger the better', with an arrow underneath pointing towards her puss. The same message and arrow was inked into her lower back. My best guess was the grotesque face tattoo was to cover-up how underage she still looked if you took the time to look beyond the tattoos to see her face, like I had.

I was instantly sickened as I finally comprehended these were probably the names of men who visited her room and paid to get their name tattooed on her. For the right price, their first-name only added to her skin; and she'd had plenty of males pay whatever price was charged to see their name permanently inked for all other subscribers who visited her room to admire, as enticement for them to do the same.

Probably the marketing brainchild of Mr J.'s; and if not, it was Mr D.'s but definitely done on Mr J.'s approval.

But even more shocking to me than two colour-filled realistic-looking penises on her face disappearing into her mouth, and the too many to count names of men, was she had both her nipples and clit pierced with bull-rings (well, that's what she said they were when we eventually started talking to each other), with shiny metal chains, connected by a ring at her belly button, forming the chains into the shape of a capital letter 'Y', which her Pete could pull on to stretch her nipples and clit for viewers (I imagined at considerable pain and discomfort to Daisy). And she wore collars around her skinny neck, wrists and ankles, which each had a thick and secure U-ring sticking out of, I guessed so the chains could be attached to restrain her as part of whatever she had to do during her live feeds.

The first thing I gushed was my genuinely sympathetic offer - what I was living through was in no way near as bad as what Daisy lived and I was more than happy to give up any comforts so she could temporarily have some, even if it was only for the limited few hours. "You can sleep in the bed, if you want. I'll take the floor." which is what finally made the despondent Daisy look up.

(I couldn't think of a suitable word to describe her to myself at the time I met Daisy, but, now I know what I saw when I spent those eight hours in her company - it was like she had died inside. She'd lost all hope. She no longer cared to live, she wanted to die and perhaps prayed for it to happen, which was sad; she was about six or seven years younger than myself.)

"Can't." She spoke with the morose voice I've ever heard. "On strict orders of Mr D. I'm not allowed. Even though I bring in a lot of money for them, you're their favourite and best asset - they're always calling you their Millionaire's Best Asset or the best non-kink suck and fuck porn princess they've ever seen or had work for them - so you're not to experience what it's like for the rest of us."

I honestly didn't know what to say to Daisy, my heart bled so painfully in sympathy at her circumstance.

"What they do to me each night is already painful enough without me doing something that will get me sent to Room Six for a week." Not once did Daisy sound bitter towards me; simply overwhelmingly sad, as she looked longingly at the bed she was declining to accept.

I couldn't help myself. I cried at what these monsters were doing to this poor girl. And it was ironic, really, Daisy was the one who needed to walk over and comfort me before she returned to her chair worried she'd gotten too close to my comforts and she'd later get punished for that.

Perhaps my behaviour not mimicking that of some high and mighty diva porn princess the other starlets might have imagined me to be, Daisy told me in her lifeless voice her and I were the only starlet's who hadn't been taken temporarily off to one of the other sites Mr J. owned. "Probably wants me to see how beautiful you are, and how that means you're being treated better than us so I can pass the information on to all the other starlets. So we'll know he won't put you in one of our rooms unless you do something to seriously fuck up, or no longer bring in the megabucks."

I don't think we were made to share the room for a few hours exclusively for Daisy to see how differently we are treated. I think Mr J. wanted us to both see how the other Aussie ped-prize now lived.

I learned all the other starlets got to see each other all the time, and were allowed to talk to each other too - mostly in the showers, while they had their hair and makeup done, in a meal room I'd never been to where they always got to share all their meals together, and when they travelled together to attend their monthly health check appointments. And it was the same at the other site she had started out at some four or five months ago.

I have to admit, I found myself more than a little envious they were getting to socialise with the other starlets, even have times when they could find something to laugh and joke around with each other over before one of them inevitably broke down in tears and then were hugged and comforted by their similarly imprisoned friends. I even had thoughts it may be worth having to work in some of the other rooms, obviously which could be more unpleasant than what I experience, for me to have the same type of contact - until I learned more about the other rooms which made me stop having any more thoughts like that completely.

The sex I had with my ever changing Pete's, was all about having their long or thick cocks sliding in and out of my mouth or puss (and occasionally back passage, like this was a normal rarely permitted no-no unless it was looking after two men simultaneously); I was the fantasy men had which they wanted their wives and girlfriends and dates to behave like; but Daisy and the other starlets were 'the more hardcore acts'. I didn't know what this meant (I hadn't experienced it, though my guess was fairly accurate), but I was rather horrified at some of the descriptions of what Daisy had had to do before they decided her marketing angle was tattooed while restrained and someone did her as the tattooing took place, until the day every inch of her body was covered.

Daisy reluctantly told me, "When Mr J. is ready for me to leave, not that it will be for a few years yet, as you can see, I'm still relatively new here and they have a long way to go before they start tattooing my back and legs during the performance, but Mr D. said Mr J.'s not going to put me up for resale like he does with all the others."

"He's not?" I asked surprised, though I reminded myself I shouldn't find anything surprising any more. "Why's—"

She sounded on the verge of tears when she said, "Nope. He's going to give me five grand whether I've paid off my debt or not and release me and send me on my 'merry way'; guaranteed, I don't have to do men anymore if I don't want to."

But rather than sounding elated, or she couldn't wait for that day of guaranteed freedom to arrive, an unknown date to cling on to hope it will all one day in the foreseeable future all this to come to end, tears really started rolling down the poor girls face, and I rushed the few steps to comfort her, and brought her to sit on my bed, which she also caught me unprepared as she urgently shook her head and told me she wasn't allowed to even sit on.

I asked Daisy why the thought of freedom was so terrifying to her. Told her I got through each and every day due to that one small hope I'd be rewarded with being allowed to leave once they no longer wanted me, "Don't you *want* to return home and see your family and friends again—" But I cut myself off as I saw the tattoo cock move as her jawbone did.

She nodded; I'm positive she concluded I instantly finally understood exactly her reasons why.

"Mr D. showed me a skimpy outfit he's already picked for me to wear on my release date - it has cut outs in the t-shirt and I won't wear any underwear under the mini skirt so my nipples and puss ring and chains will be on show. My feet will be in a leg spreader so everyone who first comes across me gets a 'good free show' as my final performance, he said."

"And he's going to organise for my drop off to occur in a large crowd - most likely they'll quickly dump me outside the front entrance of a shopping mall on pay day, or airport or train station during peak period - he hasn't decided that part yet. He's promised the cops will have a hard time removing any of my equipment, because, well my body chains and piercings will be welded so they can't come off easily, and so will the leg spreader be - so I have to remain on show - while it's difficult for the cops to remove. But even when they do, I'll still have all the tattoos on my face and body as 'permanent reminders' whenever I see my reflection. They're in a really good quality ink, and they've been done making them next to impossible to remove without me undergoing a lot more pain. So it will be live with the tattoos or suffer getting them removed, and here's five grand to do so."

"Oh, Daisy," I said, bawling like I hadn't cried since that day the first time Murk fucked me when it hurt so badly. "I'm so sorry this has happened to you."

"Yeah, well, the worst of it is, I'll be taken across the country, so there's no proof you and I ever worked in the same building, which makes it look only coincidental we ended up working for the same live action channel."

"Why did he do this to you?" I asked myself repeatedly. I thought I was only asking myself. But I must have said it aloud, for Daisy unexpectedly answered me.

"No matter how hard I genuinely tried, I couldn't smile and fake loving any of it. They said my smile came across on camera as if I was in agony even without a cock inside me. Mr J. paid three grand to purchase me from the uncles; he was happy about how I also came already fully trained as docilely compliant - the only reason I wasn't made to star in Room Six was they knew I wasn't trying to not cooperate. Said it's how my eyes and mouth 'drooped' which made me look always miserable. So, he trialled me in the different rooms until Mr D. worked out how to market me. Mr J.'d been considering making me have work done to my face to get rid of the droop until they came up with this idea. And now they make sure I have mirrors wherever I look so I always have to see what my face and body looks like while I'm performing."

A face lift, at her young age? Mirrors? To rub their disfiguring her in? With difficulty I encouraged Daisy to look at the positives, "But I guess, even with all that, it'll still be good you'll get to see your mother and father again. They *killed* my Mum, so I don't have any other family, well, I don't count my grandparents, they never even wanted to know me; and, I don't have any friends who might remember me, either." (I barely kept the bitterness out of my voice, mentioning the grandparents who condemned me to the life I now lived. What type of arsehole people were they to be unable to have any room in their hearts to love an innocent young child?)

But Daisy, for the first time, sounded bitter. "Why would I want to see or be handed over to my Dad again? He'd been fucking me for three years before he sold me to the uncles. I don't think my mother ever learned about it, but I don't know, maybe she had, maybe she was in on it with my dad, sometimes I thought she knew, other times not, I guess I'll never know for sure."

"But, I saw on the news … you were snatched while you and your Dad were shopping—" Once again I cut myself off. "Oh, that was merely the set-up, to help Murk, whoever he hired to do the actual snatch and your Dad all get away with it."

I learned I was the only starlet always getting different Pete's; they all mostly reused the same ones over and over again. And the male cocks that so willingly serviced them often had a Porn Name, like the starlets. And they each had their 'specialty kinky shit' and it wasn't always male-on-starlet action either, a lot of the times the starlets had to perform with each other, "but they hire female porn leads to do all the domination stuff to us. They are seriously bad-arse women who chose to work in the porn industry, and they love to cause you to hurt - worse than the men."

"Nancy-No-Nice, that's a starlet who lives at the other site I first started at, she now has the 'castle dungeon cell', rather than a bed like you and me now, she took over the room from me, even though we're supposed to only be in each room for one week per round. What happens in that room is the starlet is always restrained on either what's called 'the block' or else the 'fuckstation' table, which are what they restrain you on (she lifted her arms to show her wrist cuffs), which keeps the starlet's mouth, puss and arse in specific positions. It prevents them from moving their arms and legs, even a fraction. So these two guys, ChocCockHammer and RanchoRamO mostly, who both have the longest and fattest cocks in the whole porn industry and are in high demand, give it to you as a tag team."

"What's that?" I asked, feeling stupid and ignorant compared to the younger Daisy's worldliness.

"That's where they try to either coordinate their moves so they are both ramming their cocks in at the same time as each other to see how much pain you can take or one rams it in while the other's slides out and vice versa - you know, so the little bit of our body movement caused by the rammer makes you go that tiny extra bit deeper on the other."

"Oh my!" I was horrified by the very thought of this surely painful and frightful performance.

"Before you go in each night, you get given real heavy cheap eye makeup, so it all runs down the starlets face as she cries. Their goal is to get the starlet to beg them to stop or to slow down or do it slower, or more gently, which if you do means they go a bit easier until they blow, but as punishment you have to have a go in another position or station before the live feed session can end. There's eight stations in total, and they get worse as you go along. Mr D. loves being present to watch when he can; he came up with the idea for that room, and the two cocks get sizeable bonus payments if they can keep us on air for the full five hour broadcast, and the more they make the starlet beg, the higher the bonus for that station.

"Unless you're forewarned by another starlet, which they try to avoid, you don't learn for a day or two through experience if you beg it means you have to have another station, until you eventually figure it out. They actively taunt and encourage you to beg to get them to stop, slow down and go gentler while your spluttering to swallow the cum or trying not to gag on how far down your throat his cock is and are finding it too hard to get some breath from ChocCockHammer's cock - he's the one who prefers deepthroating more than fucking starlets, though he does that too, and takes ages to cum - blocks your airway his cock's that big, and he blows way more cum than the average guy too, so you're struggling not to drown in his juice."

I couldn't even imagine a cock that big, and trust me I'd seen plenty of them at this point.

"But RanchoRamO, he's only a little bit smaller than ChocCockHammer, he loves the rear end, and once he cums he's ready to go again before they even finish forcing you into the next position and he can blow multiple times each station. But, they have these mechanical cocks on standby, that ram it to you too, to help make the sessions go as long as they're supposed to from either feed cut off time or the starlet never begged, for if either of them tire out due to how much energy it takes for them to keep doing it like that. Because, Amberee you'll only ever know it if you work in the room, trust me, you're *always* begging them to stop or slow down and give you a moments break, even without their encouragement. And it is so hard not to even once you figure it out. They're really powerful, and both have great stamina and love the roughhousing you. I hated being sent to The Dungeon, even though they then give you three weeks off to recover from how bruised and tender you end up."

I didn't doubt her word even for a second.

I had always thought Room Six was the only punishment girls received; but now I realised, they were punished daily for the privilege of having had their lives stolen from them; as far as Daisy could tell, we were the only two that hadn't been snatched straight off the streets, or somehow tricked into going to a party or other place with some bloke only to arrive and learn it had been a mistake to come without telling anyone, from whatever country they had been born in.

"It's hardest for the starlets who don't speak English. They don't get given any leniency for not understanding what they've been ordered to do. One of the starlet's, a Russian girl, who's in her thirties and can speak English now, but arrived when she was fifteen and didn't speak a word, she told us one of the original starlets was Mr J.'s own step-daughter, before she was sent to a sex-house for not making enough money. But, she's always banging on about stuff that's not true, like she was the favourite, living it up and getting special privileges before you, prior to Mr J. losing interest in her around the time when you came along, so she was supposedly down-levelled to C-level and might be down-levelled again to a D-level Sexhouse any day now, so I don't believe her, and neither do many of the other girls, except Honey, probably 'cause she's Russian, too. I've noticed the foreign girls all become closest to each other with someone from their own country. I'm the only other Aussie, except for you."

"We'd probably have become friends, if we were allowed to see each other," I agreed. I did feel close to Daisy even though this was the first time I had ever been allowed to talk to her.

As I laid in my comfy bed to get some rest after a Sebastian came in to order us we both had to now, I had difficulty switching off my brain, aware the young girl lying on the floor was as much uncomfortable as I was every bit comfortable. The guilt that by some weird stroke of good fortune I was pretty and naturally 'sexy hot' being the reason I had been spared the same fate as Daisy divided me.

On the one hand, after the stories, I was so glad I was the beautiful face and desirable body they all said I was; on the other hand, I was scared now to ever have my good looks fade so that wouldn't be where I was eventually sent to work as well - and then I'd straightaway feel guilty and horrible as a person for even thinking I was glad I wasn't one of the other starlets and I didn't want my 'star' appeal to ever diminish so I only had to do what I already did for the remaining duration of my captivity, not something worse.

I also got to thinking about why Mr J. had kept me isolated from the other starlets since the day I arrived. And I concluded, which I think I am right on, it was so I didn't see or hear about anything which might cause me to deliver an inconsistent performance while they were building up my character and story: Amberee striving to become world famous and every man's fantasy happy megastar porn princess. Now I had long ago convinced the public, and my continuing rise to new levels of stardom was snowballing in with ever increasing offers, it no longer mattered to Mr J. if I had an 'off' day or fuck session. Even the most famous celebrities had the occasional 'bad hair day', and my captors could now fob a one-off bad performance as such.

It went to show me, Mr J. understood although I was perfectly compliant as expected to be, to avoid physical punishment aimed at causing much pain and agony, and genuinely believed I was embracing my character, he suspected something might arise one day which might well break me, like it did other starlets too.

And this made me realise precisely how important it was for me to try to gain the perfect opportunity to escape and regain my freedom more so than ever. The only thing I couldn't figure out was how to get an opportunity to do so. And if it was worth taking the risk to run, because of the horrors I'd face experiencing if I was ever re-caught.

Yes, can you believe it: he had me second-guessing whether or not I had made the right decision to try and one day regain my freedom?

$\mathscr{C}$HAPTER 20

On my twenty-first birthday, a Sebastian, a new one not quite as hulking as many of the others but still muscular and strong in appearance who was always nice and friendly towards me rather than gruff like many of the others, came and woke me early, and said Mr J. had phoned to say he wanted me in attendance at today's Starlet marketing meeting, because it was only about myself. He went to my wardrobe and eventually retrieved a pretty white flowy mini-dress. And once I was ready, he escorted me through the secret tunnels. I came out in Starlet House replica basement recording studio, and then was whisked across into the garage, then the car like so many times before.

The solo Sebastian drove me across town (the rear door's could not be opened from the inside, so I had zero chance to run for it while stopped at a set of traffic lights) to an industrial building with signage saying Amberee Headquarters. He was a happy, friendly Sebastian, and rather talkative when it was him and I alone, but silent the rest of the time. He tried multiple attempts to get me to talk to him, but, I wasn't interested in becoming friends with one of my jailers now I had my fan mail to keep me company. I answered his questions, of course; I simply didn't volunteer any more than my short responses, and didn't ask him any in return. Though, I appreciated the effort he made towards trying to engage me. I think he worked out why I didn't respond as he hoped.

He then guided me through the building into the large meeting room, which was full of Darren's and Zack's, a handful of Sebastian's and Mr D. (Mr J. 'attended' via a secure-line video call (but his face was blurred out, and voice distorted from the complicated encryption, and the fact they'd invited some Ted's to attend - whatever role Ted's played.))

As soon as I took my seat, they were ready to get started. They had a number of items on the agenda.

Mr J. told everyone present his legit agency had been approached by a film production house eight months earlier with the script for a full length movie dealing with the topic of sex trafficking.

"Of course, they approached me in the hopes I might have an actress on our books who might agree to star in their movie. Now, they knew whatever my answer was, it'd be echoed, same moral line taken with all the other agencies, and of course, I declined. But, I organised one of my staff, to secretly agree to meet with the producer off-record and for me 'to never find out'. What this staffer suggested on my behalf was the only way to get the project into production might be for them to hire a porn princess, telling them, "You'll never get people to start making changes if the sex scenes are staged, it'll ruin the ring of authenticity, which will lower the impact such an important film needs to leave."

"I had that staff member not only convince them hiring a porn star would be the right way to proceed for the main character - despite the conflict in messaging - but once the producers agreed they'd find it too hard to get a named and credentialed actress to star in the role, to draw in the audience - the staffer hinted they should consider our little starlet, and gorgeous puss, Amberee."

"They were against the idea to begin with - the expected arguments, she's too pretty, she's likes being with lots of men, has too much of a girl-next-door vibe about her with the exception of an insatiable sexual appetite, they don't think she'd be able to pull it off despite her decent acting abilities, due to the serious nature of the film. A few other porn star names were tossed about, and in the end, none of the others had the appeal Amberee had. So, they've finally approached Amberee's agent, and they're now in talks negotiating Amberee starring in the role."

I couldn't believe it, Mr J. was manipulating things so I gained the offer for the lead role in a *non-porn* movie? Was this part of some secret plan to move me on, maybe? Were my sales dropping? Dare I hope I might one day within the foreseeable future be released from captivity?

But I didn't get to ponder this much further - the first order of business arose, and I abandoned my thoughts to pay attention. (It was in my own best interest to know what they had in store for me).

"Of course, Amberee will sign the contract having agreed to star in the film. We'll have her quoted as saying although she entered the porn industry of her own free choice, she fully understands so many girls enter the industry against their will, and are threatened, beaten and punished, and forced to do untold horrors so she wanted to do this film to support them."

"The reason for this meeting, gentlemen, is I want a brainstorming of ideas. Amberee will insist on having real sex scenes (of course, that's the only way to keep in with my public image, isn't it?). So, you've all read the film script, you know the montage of the character being forced to have sex with her captor's rough clientele. The production team don't want to hire any additional people who work in the porn industry. They don't want to *dilute* the message they're trying to sell. Be accused of hypocrisy more than they will over hiring Amberee. So, we need to come up with ideas for how to work around hiring professional Pete's."

What Mr J. was telling them, Mr D. explained after Mr J. signed off, was he wanted the movie to go ahead, and was going to increase their production budget, but he wanted real men in all shapes and sizes, akin to those who pay to have sex with enslaved trafficked girls as the men to appear on camera having realistic sex with Amberee. So, do they know of any suitable male actors, "We'll need at least twenty five of them."

So Mr D. pulled a whiteboard over from the side of the room, picked up a black marker and called for ideas he could present to Mr J.

"A set will be built to replica one of our D-level sex-houses, but apart from hiring the men who really visit them, we're at a loss for what to do, as most of them wouldn't pass the required medical testing for us to approve them to really fuck Amberee" He pointed me out sitting quietly wondering why I was required to attend. Were they expecting *me* to come up with ideas for how to get shady looking men to fuck me? Thankfully, no, it didn't seem so. My presence was to help spark ideas for the twenty-seven strong group of men in the room. I soon realised, the Ted's were men who worked at some of the other facilities, and my best guess was they weren't privy to Mr J.'s real identity.

With regular looking at me for long periods by all those seated around the room (except the Sebastian who had brought me), ideas started being thrown onto the whiteboard, the first being, "use some of Amberee's real fans instead of actors".

Mr D. got excited by that and said this was precisely the type of ideas Mr J and himself were hoping for.

Two hours later, with many who had come up with ideas being promised nice bonus payments in their next pay checks (with their real name and the amount recorded in a little black notebook Mr D. kept in his breast pocket - I had partial view of what he was writing), the proposal they had settled on presenting to Mr J. being they'd run a competition in men's magazines scouting for Amberee's fans to work with her on a super secret project. They agreed one hundred of those who pass the required health checks to guarantee having Amberee give their cock a little love. (Oh, yeah, sure, why not make sure I do as many as possible?)

"Real fans, fucking Amberee in the manner they'd genuinely fuck her if they had the opportunity." That's what they were pitching to Mr J. when they got him on the line in again an hour's time.

A Darren added, "And, not that we really want to see them, but we get them to send us in a photo of their stiffs as part of the application process. We say Amberee herself will be personally choosing the top one hundred dicks she wants to work with."

"Brilliant, Darren!" Mr D. shouted excitedly, taking the notebook from his pocket again and writing plus five thousand behind the Darren's name. "I'm positive Mr J. will love these unique ideas. They'll help us keep starlet's popularity at Number One. But we'll get the contestant to send three photo's, a close up of their hard cock Amberee will supposedly use to choose her favourite's from, a full body and a face shot her management team use to determine if their face and body type matches the criteria we're looking for."

"So in the ads we'll say Amberee's scouting for real fans, with real bodies, faces and delicious disease-free cocks to suck and fuck."

"Oh, oh, and we should get them to tell us in one page, what's their favourite way of fucking a chick. So we can look for the ones who will be happy to appear on film giving it to her while she's chained to the bed." And out whipped the little notebook again, with the Ted's name having his details added.

Mr D. dialled Mr J. while we were all still gathered, and he loved the ideas they had conjured. While they had Mr J. still on the line, another Darren blurted unexpectedly, "Oh, I've had another idea. Maybe, in keeping with the Amberee brand, she declines accepting payment for her part in the movie."

For the first time during the meeting I spoke up, "If she believes it is such an important message to give to the public, which she does, then she personally should contribute money towards the project."

No one except myself realised I was being sarcastic, except perhaps for the new Sebastian, who hadn't offered up a single idea and was now, I thought, doing a terrible job at hiding how impressed he was over me saying that and poorly trying to disguise a smirk - if he wasn't careful would be noticed by Mr D sitting next to him.

Luckily for him, he wasn't - they had all turned to look at me.

That Darren was personally to receive a bonus ten thousand dollars in next week's pay check. Me, not a cent. Mr J. loved all the ideas (including, no, especially, mine), agreed Amberee contribute to the amount of five million for the project, and now it was time to start working behind the scenes to get all those things into action. "I want filming to begin as soon as possible."

I was nicer to my new Sebastian on the drive home. I even asked him what his real name was, and he looked in the rear view mirror and said, "It's Adrian. But, you best not let anyone know I told you that, or we'll both be in trouble."

I promised him I wouldn't tell on him if he didn't tell on me.

I even pushed my luck by asking him if he could let the window open by an inch or so, so I could feel the breeze on my face. He looked genuinely upset he couldn't do this one small request, "That would get us both into a lot of trouble, Miss."

(I found it strange he didn't call me puss like the rest of them, who only called me 'puss' as an affectionate, shortened version of 'pussy' which is what I always had to have on show and how they all saw me and the other starlets).

"You're originally from Australia, aren't you?"

"My accent that much of a giveaway?" He asked, as he navigated a left hand turn. "And here was me thinking I sounded all Yank now."

"It stands out against all the heavy American ones, yes," I answered him. "You're the first other Aussie accent, apart from Murk and another starlet, I've come across since I got here."

I didn't feel up to sharing with him his accent made me homesick, and therefore harder to fight down my past life memories.

My last teacher at school. Mr Barryson. Talking to my Mum seated beside me. Parent teacher interview. Saying to Mum, "Amber is a model student, and quite advanced for her age group. I'm always mindful that she could become easily bored, so I set challenges for her alone, to help keep her interested and motivated."

I had to force myself to think of other things, or else I would start crying.

Roughly six months after that meeting, Mr J. came to visit me.

"To the outside world, Amberee I am seen as an important, influential man now owning a number of multi-million dollar business enterprises, including the prestigious Models & Actors Management Agency, or M.A.M.A for short, where, ironically, my wife and I am well-known for donating to sex trafficked victim causes, and a leading, strong voice fiercely protecting the girls and women on the agency's books from perversive sexual exploitation my real starlets live each and every day. My wife's daughter was stolen off the streets, you see, before she died from the line of work she was forced to do. So the community expects this from us. My wife, well, it has become a strong passion for her, after what happened to her daughter and all. But, I digress…"

"It was only natural I was the first agency approached for this movie. Naturally, M.A.M.A never agrees to allow any of their actors and actresses to appear in such films, despite the importance and timeliness of delivering the message to the public for this one. Your smart little head has probably already worked out I'm secretly backing the movie's production, at my wife's insistence, but of course, that idea of yours gives me a way to do so now. As planned, your name is now on top of everyone's lips as the perfect star for the lead character, so the agency that manages your little porn-loving puss has finalised your taking on the role."

"So, my dear, dear little puss, you're going to star in a mainstream movie. And, if you stay a good little puss that does as she's told, you'll be afforded some, shall we call it, leniency - permitted to go out in public with a small team of Sebastian's. I'm sinking a lot of money into this project, so naturally I want you to give your best possible performance in the film so I not only recuperate my investment but receive a sizeable chunk of the expected profits, which will only happen if you deliver an exceptional performance. Therefore, my dear, I am arranging a little treat for you. Mr D. will take you to a real Sexhouse for a day or two - no, no, puss, not to work, only to observe for now so you know what it is really like for those girls who aren't as pretty as you and those fallen out of my grace."

I noted his words 'for now'; I feared this could still be my fate one day once I stopped being such a money earner to him. I was positive the day would come when some other girl might overtake me as 'the star', relegating me to descend the star-levels until I was on par with the other starlets, the older I got. I intensely hoped my looks never faded completely or I'd be relegated to D-level status and suffer the worst conditions imaginable.

"I don't need to warn you about what will happen to you, if you say or do anything you're not supposed to while I loosen the noose for you for a bit, do I?"

"No, sir," I replied.

"Excellent. Mr D. will take you to one of the facilities some time before filming commences."

A month later, I was taken to one of the real D-level facilities owned by Mr J. but managed by Mr D., who was disappointed I was dressed in proper clothes for the visitation, a nice pale-mint sun-dress with bra *and* panties. (Can you believe it? Panties! I was excited at first, until I found them uncomfortable from not being used to wearing them.) I think he had envisioned being able to play with my puss while I was there.

"Mr J. wants you delivering a realistic, believable portrayal of what happens to girls sent to sex-houses like this, Amberee" He told me, not realising Mr J. had told me this himself, personally. "So, I've set up an observation room, and you'll get to see a real girl, a new arrival, about to get her first experience. A good, local find, so I must say, I'm a bit disappointed to only observe on this occasion. But, sometimes you have to let your second in command have some of the fun."

I was made to watch on a monitor as a young woman of about twenty years of age was dragged into the room by two ordinary men who you could tell merely by looking at them lived and operated on the wrong side of the law. One ordered the girl to remove her panties, and when she pleaded no, he backhanded her, causing the edge of her mouth to bleed, and he gave her 'one last chance' to remove her panties herself, 'or we'll do it the hard way.' The girl started crying, and made no move to remove her underwear herself, and the man said spitefully, 'Alright, the hard way it is. My personal favourite."

Mr D. leant towards me, "I'm usually the one doing all this, but, Jaso—Sebastian is my choice to take over from me when I am off doing other things. The next bit is my favourite part too."

It was difficult to watch, but every time I turned my head away to not look, Mr D. grabbed me, hard, and said meanly, "No, Amberee. The boss wants you to see what happens to most girls. It's the only way you'll be able to deliver a good performance. I'll restrain your head to force you, if you keep turning away. The equipment to do so is all here."

He sounded like he'd do that happily, that he wished it was me in the room in place of the girl, so I had to watch in horror as it unfolded before my eyes, helpless to do anything to help the poor girl, or my own self.

The second man grabbed the girl, pinning her arms behind her back, and she used her legs to try kick the main man in desperate attempt to prevent him from tearing them off her. Another backhand, and then a forceful punch in her stomach, and while she was doubled over gasping for air, he ripped her panties apart, grabbed a plastic zip-tie from his pocket and got the first of her ankles strapped to a corner of the bed.

"No, please, don't, please, let me go," the girl begged and sobbed futilely between hard breaths, as the man behind her kept her from being able to fight, and the other man got her second ankle restrained, and then the rest of her was thrown roughly on the bed, and both arms were tied above her head on the metal bed-head. And then the main man, wearing a nasty smile and making eye contact with the terrified girl, was undoing his pants, as the other man placed a hand over her mouth, and she struggled about, her eyes bulging with fear, trying to shake her head, unable to plead, 'no.'

"Oh, yeah, baby, it's happening. I'm the only one who gets to break girls in when my boss is off doing other things."

The first man rough-fucked her until he came; she stopped fighting half way through, when the pain from her bleeding wrists and ankles may have become too much, and she came to know she couldn't say or do anything further to stop him giving it to her. She'd surrendered to minimise her pain and discomfort, like I had done myself rather early as Murk and the uncle's ped-prize. That's all you could do when you were powerless to assert yourself.

Then, he undid her legs; they flipped her body over, twisting her arms into what had to be agony. And then the second man had his turn, doing it up her rear. Again, while one of them (the main man this time) covered her mouth to muffle her agonised wails and screams, so people on the streets nearby wouldn't call the police to investigate why a girl was screaming as though her life depended on it.

"That's what you do from now on," the first man whispered nastily, once the second had finished too. "You cooperate; you give the customers what they want, or that pretty little daughter of yours, we go and get her, and we do this to her, too. Only, we get you to watch her first time. We have an observation room now, all set up."

The girl lay tied up on the bed in her awkward and surely painful position, and the two men left. Only then did she struggle to roll back onto her back, sobbing. And moments later, the bedroom door opened again. This time the main man had brought in another man, and was carrying a needle.

She immediately started pleading, "Please, no, not again."

"Here," he told her, as he stabbed the needle into her arm. "A little something to help you until you get used to it."

Within minutes the girl had relaxed, and her head and eyes were uncoordinated. They uncut the cable ties and then put a metal collar around her neck, and a length of chain was hooked around a bedpost, and the other side to her collar. And then the main guy pocketed the key, lifted her into sitting position roughly by the hair, as the new second man unzipped his jeans, and the main man said, "You give my mate here a decent blow job, and you don't get beaten up. Don't make him satisfied, and we do beat you while someone goes get your little girl, and we'll make her show you how it's done."

"No," the girl said, swaying heavily, "Please, leave my daughter alone."

"Well, then, Mummy. Start proving to me why I shouldn't go get her."

And then the girl, woozily opened her mouth and took the cock without further protest, and did the best she could at sucking him until he came. I could tell she'd never really given a man a blow job before. I'd seen enough of how I did it on the screen test playbacks to tell the difference between her newness and my unfortunate extensive experience.

The main man, backhanded her for no reason, bent forward and said nastily, "Alright, Mummy. I'll leave your daughter alone for now, but if you give me any more trouble, if you try to escape, if you scream for help like that again, then you know it's your own fault when I get a five year old to come work next to her mum." He straightened again. "Alright, your shift is about to start. Remember, you suck and fuck every client I send in here. Cry all you want about your being here in your own time. While you're on duty, you keep those tears in your fucking head. Stupid slut." He backhanded her for no reason again, and they left the room.

And solo man after man after man came into the room. Some started by getting her to suck his cock, which she did docilely enforcing the man do all the work, others walked in, pushed her to lie back, spread her legs apart and mounted her. She was too spaced, she didn't resist. One man dragged her half off the bed, flipped her to lie on her stomach and then rough-fucked her up the rear, while pulling her head by the hair as far as it would physically bend back. The more she groaned in pain, the harder and faster he rode her. I was worried he was going to break her neck and paralyse her. I only realised she was bleeding once he was done, and the main man and a partner entered the room, threw her back onto the bed, and then let the next customer in.

"She has another five hours to go before her shift ends," Mr D. said beaming, after we had been observing for close to three hours. "I don't think you need to stay to watch all of who visits her room - unless you want to. I think you get the point by now."

I was so glad when I was allowed to leave. I couldn't shake off what I had seen for months.

On the drive returning to Starlet House, Mr D. patted me on the leg, "See how lucky you were Mr J. and I decided to buy you, Amberee? Mr J. nearly didn't agree to you auditioning. I hope you appreciate I talked him into it - you auditioning was the luckiest day in each of our lives."

I didn't say anything, but I could feel my eyebrow raise as the words rolled around my head, desiring letting be voiced aloud in challenge: luckiest? I didn't believe for a second Mr J. hadn't taken one look at the photo Murk had posted of me and decided instantly he wanted to audition me.

Mr D. rubbed his hand along my inner leg again.

"Yes, Amberee luckiest. You saw with your own eyes what it is like for other starlets. Not many get to do live feeds the way you and your other little ped-prize are set to work in. When you start filming, many of your scenes will have you doing it with men who are similar in appearance and nature to the types of men you witnessed. You'll act on a set made to look like a grungy Sexhouse; the difference is, the men you fuck will have all passed health checks to ensure you don't catch something nasty and they won't be allowed to hurt you, unlike the poor girl you watched who will probably end up catching something within the next few months, and then we'll toss her, depending on what that nasty is. You should consider yourself lucky: we can't have our keen, clean, condom-free little fucking machine having one of her fans ruining the party for everyone, can we?"

And with that, he slipped his finger inside me despite my clothing, smiling in a horrible, mean way at my not being able to tell him I didn't want him touching me like that.

I don't know why, but his doing this made me feel the most violated I'd ever been violated.

𝒞HAPTER 21

I had not long turned twenty-two before filming actually started, and my one hundred real fans (of which they only really needed about twenty five, but were going to let all have a turn so they could choose the best ones to appear in the montage) were all set and ready to work with me on my super secret project.

The porn industry was rife with speculation I was going to do a fuck-film with real fans not male porn stars this time.

There had been over three hundred and fifty thousand entries from men all over the world, who had plucked the courage to send in the pictures and commit to undertaking the full health checks to receive the opportunity to have me pick them (which I didn't really do).

So, my team had decided to turn it into an event, too.

I was unshakably certain Mr D. might have sneakily entered the competition if he had had the opportunity. Luckily, I think him entering was against Mr J.'s policy. Mr D. was always looking at me lately, the way Murk had before he revealed his true nature to me, and I had no doubts that before long, Mr D. will have found or created an opportunity so he could make me suck or fuck his cock. I didn't know what was holding him back; it was clear he was determined to have his moment with me though. Was I off-limits to staff?

At Amberee Headquarters, a top five hundred, who had all passed and contractually agreed to abstain from sex with anyone else until after they had been ruled out of contention (or had their shining moment with Amberee on screen), had been picked. They'd been grilled about their sex life with things like, "Have you ever visited a sex-house?" or "Have you ever been with a hooker?" And they were described a few different scenarios and asked to pick their favourite fantasy of the handful described. And the top one hundred were picked from the ones who revealed they had been a customer of a sex-house, and had picked the scene where they said enthusiastically they'd do Amberee even if she was chained to a bed, naked and asleep or unconscious so they could feel what it's like to fuck her.

For the winners and losers ceremony, I was dressed in sheer, revealing clothing. In batches of one hundred, fully naked men were lined in rows, and with a camera man or two, like a squadron leader walking the row inspecting his troops, I, with the aid of helper-captors, walked the line inspecting cocks in my sexy outfit and camera makeup.

If the candidate had progressed to last stage of elimination, I simply smiled at his cock (sometimes licking my lips) and moved on passed him without saying anything (and thus he gained confirmation he had made the cut). If the man was earmarked as eliminated, I stepped up to him, took his cock and balls into my hands, gave a gentle squeeze and held on, playing with it, while I said a few kind words to him. I had to say a range of things to sound like I was regretful on this occasion he wasn't progressing to final stage, but to seem like I hadn't wanted to make that hard decision, or now on meeting in person was regretting it. Every single eliminated contestant had to welcome a little bit of Amberee love, so they went away completely happy even though they had missed out. And my assistants told me whether I had to walk past or approach the next man in line.

Only three of the contestants being eliminated came on me while I was saying those things. I'd been pre-warned that could be a possibility, so I was to giggle and say how I'm glad me holding him gave him pleasure.

So words came from my mouth, "Oh, I'm so sorry, not for this secret project, sweetie; but maybe next time, okay?" or "Oh, gorgeous, you have no idea how much I'm regretting having decided to cut you from contention. I think I made a mistake, which I can't change now." and "Oh, sweet cock, you only missed out by a fraction; hope I get to do something like this again in the future. You'll be the first one I insist make it to final stage next time."

Four hundred times.

Pretty much, if the guy was good looking and had nice bodies, they mostly were sent home. And all the uglier and meaner faces, bodies and cocks were the ones making it through and were going to get to do me. Most of those guys couldn't believe their luck I had chosen them.

It was too much for me to constantly have to giggle, my key-captors understood - so I only had to Amberee giggle when I first entered the massive function room and saw all the naked men, and again when I thanked all those remaining how I couldn't wait to get to do them as soon as the filming started next week, and tell them how much I was looking forward to it, to getting to do it with them, so keep their promise to not do it with anyone else so they don't ruin things for everyone. Blow them a kiss, giggle, and leave the auditorium. And, even though they threatened me if I wasn't believable, I had already decided to do this to ensure they never learned I was building my way to one day freedom. Amberee porn star, and Amber, me, were two completely different people in my mind: an actress playing a part and a real being. I knew when I had to play the role using the best of my ability.

I waved a 'sad farewell' to those leaving the competition, and reminded them the video of today's proceedings, with proof I had touched their cock, would be available for them to receive in two week's time, so make sure they pre-ordered a copy today: "the video isn't going to be released to the public to purchase".

Mr D. had told us later Mr J. was hopeful at least one broke the rules of their contract to rip and then illegally post it to one of their social media pages so all others who had entered the competition saw the competition had been genuine - which, of course, more than one someone did, and so the event was secretly circulated on the internet and watched by an estimated two million plus viewers.

$\mathcal{C}$HAPTER 22

The following week, I started the first few weeks filming, of me doing it with the competition winners. "We'll get the montage scene filming over with, and then we can film the storyline." Five men a day to get the montage footage appearing towards the end of the movie; shot by porn film makers not the makers of the movie. The latter, naturally, didn't want to tarnish their careers.

First thing in the morning, I'd meet with that day's five men. They'd be given a rundown of the scene we were filming; it was explained to them (sometimes by me or with me present and 'eagerly' nodding my head in support) the Amberee character would be chained to the bed, looking and acting drugged, and she'd say things like, "please, no," but they were to ignore this no matter how realistic I sounded and do me for however long it took them to cum (that's what I was supposedly really most looking forward to). They were told it'd mostly be a camera pointed towards the bed which was primary filming, but another in the wall could be adjusted to capture their face when they came. And once they were done, they were to put (fake) money (given to them for the purpose) into the glass jar on a bedside table before they leave the room, same as if they had paid a prostitute. (With the exception of my jar wouldn't be emptied after each 'john'.)

Then, they'd each have their turn at having ChocCockHammer, RanchoRamO (both of who had gained non-porn support acting roles playing 'the bad guys') or another male character unlock and open the fake bedroom door for them. They'd see me drugged, naked and anchored, unable to escape (real chains but not drugged, and in makeup to give me the appearance of not well taken care of, which the winners had seen me get done to know it was make-believe), and they'd undo their pants (without taking them off), and he'd start fucking me. (The set was so realistic, I think most of them forgot they were doing Amberee and were ecstatic to fuck the scared and mildly protesting young thing that couldn't fight them and they had full permission to fuck for free.)

At the end of that day's filming, I'd see them one last time (restored to my usual looking self) to give them a kiss on the cheek and thank them for helping me with the scene, and I hoped they were the one's chosen to appear on film (all this being filmed too). Each of them told me I was one of the best fucks they'd ever had, and thanked me for choosing their cock and glad they could help. Even though they hadn't been told what movie the filming was for.

Those twenty days went by like a blur, nothing really much different to how I was forced to live my life. What I didn't expect, and neither did those male fans, was for them to get invited to also do a blow job scene before their contract guaranteeing abstaining from sexual interaction with anyone other than me, and filming ended; so another twenty days, in the same bedroom, still chained (real), and the fan came in, unzipped his pants, and stood in front of me while I had to suck him until he came. And then, once again, right before he left the room, he had to put money in the glass jar.

None of the fans begged off going a second round with Amberee.

But eventually, the fun and real part-freedom of being in a real, non porn movie moment arrived. (With the one more exception of fucking.)

Five months I spent filming the real movie. The experience was so different to other porn films I had filmed so far to date. For one thing, I had a character to play which wasn't based on me being Amberee so for the first time in years, I wasn't sucking and fucking cocks every day - you have no idea how happy this made me (or maybe you do by now). For another, we had to do many takes for the same scene. And even more happily, I wasn't collar cuffed and anchored somewhere to prevent me trying to escape.

I'd been warned about the unprecedented freedoms being afforded to me so I could star in this real movie, and any attempt to escape or tell people I was Amberee by force instantly resulted in me "seriously regretting your foolishness". If asked why I always had a Sebastian with me, I had to tell the person quietly, and ask them not to repeat, "I received death threats, so I hired body guards to keep me safe."

As far as I knew, it was another lie I had to tell to disguise the truth. I don't know if I had genuinely received death threats or not.

At night I was living in a temporary small apartment, with four Sebastian's taking shifts at being my 'body guard'. During the day, one of the Sebastian's brought me to set, and stayed to ensure I was okay. Not one of the film crew were in on the fact I was Amberee by force, and would indeed be very much concerned and do what they can to help me achieve my freedom had they known. These were moral men, making a movie to make the issue more widely known, after all.

But, they didn't socialise with me much. They were all aware I was a porn star, and the only reason I was in the movie was they needed an actress who'd suck and fuck for real, to give the film more credibility, so none of them were interested in becoming my friend (except a couple of the male actors who hinted if I had the time, they wouldn't mind me sucking or fucking their cock. I had to tell them to speak to one of my Sebastian's who'd pass the message on to my agent to see if it could be arranged. They had the same rules of sexual health to meet like all approved to do me.)

The first time my favourite Sebastian was rostered to mind me, he said, jokingly (leaving me unsure if he was serious or not) as he drove me to set, "If you do have any plans of trying to escape at any point over the next few months, could you do me a great favour and not make your break for it while I'm on shift? I'd rather not cop a bullet for failing my duties, if you don't mind. Thanks Miss."

During the complete filming, I never got a single opportunity to run for it any way, or to tell one of the film crew my real circumstance, even on the few times when my Sebastian and I were temporarily separated, like when I went into the makeup trailer and he was made to wait outside. I was still intent on waiting for the right moment for my bid to escape (now with the added burden of not doing so while

Adrian-Sebastian was on duty in case there was any truth to the threat to his safety too if I did so); that would only come when I had plenty of time to run and bolt to safety before my absence became noticed. It wasn't worth trying to seize a small moment which failed in seconds to ruin everything.

Much of the filming took place in a vacant warehouse set up with 'bedrooms' for each of the captive girls to work and other needed sets. Other times, we filmed on locations: a suburban street where my character rushed along the road at night time, looking over her shoulder, then jumped into a car, kissed the guy behind the wheel, and said, sneaking out of the house had gone far better than she had thought, and her parents had gone to bed, so no one would ever know she'd gone unless we didn't arrive back before my dad woke early to go to work and I delivered the line, "My heart's pounding, I've never done anything like this before!" To arriving outside a nightclub, me being nervous they'd work out I was underage, being reassured by the new boyfriend; where bouncers let us both in no problems, and we descended a flight of stairs rather than into the main nightclub area, where the character's gorgeous new boyfriend told her was where the better nightclub party happened.

And my character didn't think it was at all strange (or suspect something was amiss) to consider she was walking into a trap over the underground bouncers having to unlock the door for us to enter; and then me walking into a scene, where a whole lot of girls were only in bras and panties (and two men) and chained together in different groups, and I turned to my boyfriend and asked, "What's going on?" as some other man (ChocCockHammer) comes up and grabs me roughly by the base of the neck (aka Murk-style) and takes me further into the room, easily controlling me despite my trying to resist and where I am forcibly stripped (by RanchoRamO and another man) to only my bra and panties, my hands are tied behind my back and I'm chained to other actresses, all the while dumbfounded and watching as my new boyfriend still at the door is paid and then leaves and the door is then relocked (which is when the reality this is real and not some sort of joke kicks in for me). And shortly after, another guy and girl arrive and the same thing happens to her what happened to my character.

There's a heart-wrenching moment when twins are brought in and then separated, one to my group of six girls, and the other in a different group. And then five of us plus me and a solitary chained up male are shunted via a rear access into a van, and driven for a long time, and backhanded and yelled at to 'shut up' if we spoke. We all look frightened and wondering what's going to happen to us, including the male victim, a boy my character knows from school.

We arrive at a rundown old two-storey house, in a rundown part of town, and shuffled inside the building (really a set in the warehouse), where we are taken upstairs, and only unshackled from the others once outside a bedroom. Two of our captors take us into our bedrooms, and the rest of us are shunted forward by others towards the next bedroom.

And then, me being the main character was the last girl put into a room, and the man who now owns me, a horrible-looking, nasty character, is the first of many to fuck me. I'm pinned by his minders, and I struggle and are slapped. And then I'm crying as I lose my virginity to a 'beast of a man'. This actor really did fuck me as part of the action. (But unlike porn movies, no close ups of the action were included, cameras simply capturing me lying with him on top pumping his cock into me while his fellow actor mates held my arms and legs to (realistically) simulate stopping me fighting.)

Then I'm put to work in one of the bedrooms, where I'm often drugged and abused for months.

My character, despite her resolve to try to escape the first chance she got - and her two daring and dramatic solo unsuccessful attempts, plus trying to help the twin make an escape too (resulting in the twin being the first of our group to die) - was another of the 'unlucky' ones who died - except mine as a result of overdose as it is the only way to keep her subdued to do the work they insisted she do.

The final scenes are me, dead, in the back of a van being driven to a remote state forest, where my lifeless body is dragged and dumped in a shallow grave, presumably where the twin had been buried - and the audience can tell, I'm not the first or the last sex trafficked girl to end up in this isolated burial place where we might not be found for years, or ever.

Right while at the sex-house, police bust in and raid the place, thus rescuing the remaining girls, making it clear I was the last death for this particular enterprise, and the male prisoner would be able to let the police and parents know I should be present (and when found not to be, he says it means that I must have died. With the film closing with the police officer telling my parents they won't give up until my body is found.)

I'd had to lose some weight - just six kilos - to further look realistic my character wasn't fed properly during her captivity. I wasn't used to seeing myself this horribly underweight.

Throughout the filming, Mr D. often poked his head on set, and one day, I saw him talking to the two men known as ChocCockHammer and RanchoRamO, both playing roles as sex traffickers imprisoning and beating the girls working for their boss of the Sexhouse I'm taken to. Personally, I thought they suited the parts they were playing perfectly - something deviant radiated from them both (which is why they were great for the roles they were playing).

And one day, ChocCockHammer came up to me, while I watched filming, not required to act on camera until the scene being filmed was finished, and said in a voice much softer and quieter than his outward appearance, "Amberee, I do wish you'd agree to a Tag Team session. Seeing you perform some of the scenes … well, I'd really love to have my cock down your delish little throat. Let our agency know if you ever change your mind and want to experience The Dungeon, babes."

All I could do was smile politely, and then move to go stand a bit closer to my favourite Sebastian. But I wanted to punch Mr D. who had been listening in and was licking his lips as though he'd love nothing better than to have me visit their Dungeon, too. At the mere recall of what Daisy had once told me, I took another step closer to Sebastian, where I felt somewhat safer.

Unbeknown to me for the full duration of filming, the necklace, a treasured possession my character is allowed to keep wearing after she pleads with the captors to not take from her and was still being worn as I was dumped in the shallow grave (signalling, my body would become identifiable if the site was one day ever discovered), was a real tracking device; so that if I made any real attempt to escape, my real captors effortlessly would track me down and find me with ease. (So I was glad no opportunity had come up to encourage me to decide to run.) It was the only part of the script Mr J. (via his 'people') had insisted on for my character.

But me making a run for it wasn't because Mr J. or the Sebastian's truly thought I'd try to escape working as Amberee. No, they had a different reason for believing I might need to run.

I don't think Mr J. ever honestly imagined they'd need to use the tracking equipment to safeguard me; the reason they made me ignorantly wear it was precautionary.

And you have no idea how grateful I was they had planted the secret tracker on me once I later found out about it as being the only reason they were able to find me as quickly as they did.

$\mathscr{C}$HAPTER 23

Mr D. was always visiting on set and sending my Sebastian's off to do something, leaving only Mr D. as my secret minder.

On the last day of filming, we were wrapping early, so the filming crew could go and celebrate a long weekend same as every other industry. And I'd be returning to my starlet basement bedroom to begin the next day doing live action feeds and private recreations again, after these blissful months not doing that.

Mr D. yet again sent my Sebastian off on assignments, and told Adrian-Sebastian if filming wrapped before he got back, he'd take me himself.

Filming wrapped an hour earlier than expected. And Mr D. drove me and gave ChocCockHammer and RanchoRamO a lift. Mr D. told me he'd drop off the two porn stars along the way as they had a Dungeon gig first. My mind was a million miles away, disappointed I was returning to my imprisoned life again. (It was beyond cruel having been given this freedom and then taking it away again.)

Of course, when we got there, Mr D., unusually parking up the road so no one would notice the car, needed to go into the building for something he'd forgotten, so I had to accompany them all inside.

Like the building I lived most of my life in, a secret panel in the wall lead to a hidden basement provided access. The softly swooshing doors automatically closed and relocked themselves behind us as soon as the last person stepped through to the stairwell, like the ones at my facility. And Mr D. had to unlock the door at the bottom of the stairs for us to enter the secure area.

The basement looked the same as the one I lived in too, only the corridor was longer and it had more doors.

"I have some business to do before I can take you back to the other facility, Amberee so follow me, I'll take you to a secure area for you to wait." I followed along obediently, and then, Mr D. told me, "Wait here with Hammer and Rancho while I get a room cleared for you. Don't let her go anywhere."

There was nowhere for me to escape anyway. He disappeared inside a room, and the two porn stars barely said a word to each other, and neither engaged in or attempted conversation with me.

We waited five minutes before Mr D.'s voice called, "Okay, we're ready. You can bring her in now."

And with no hint of what they were about to do, RanchoRamO and ChocCockHammer had seized me by the hair and arms, and were dragging me into the room, down some steps to a centre area, all lit up with a wooden post in the middle, and in the darker, off stage areas below was a film crew, already recording.

At the bottom of the steps, I was struggling to free myself from the porn stars, but they easily over powered me, and my left wrist was forced into a tight leather cuff, from a nearby bench, as my clothes were ripped off me, not bothering to remove my clothes, bra and panties carefully so they could ever be washed and re-worn.

"What's going on?" I demanded, and protested, scared, but mainly confused. But nobody answered me.

My right wrist and both ankles both got tightly strapped leather cuffs on too, despite my desperate resistance. It was only as I was being forcibly dragged by both men towards the wooden post in the middle of the spotlighted stage area I comprehended where I was and what was about to happen.

What had I done to deserve this as punishment?

"Please, no, please, don't do this," I begged.

The next hour and fifteen minutes of my life was the worst that had ever happened to me. Nothing Murk, my uncles, and my Pete's - even my fans for the filming and private clients - did to me would ever be as terrifying as this ordeal.

I could only imagine this must have been similar to what my Mum had experienced the night she had died.

I was picked up, stood on my feet and forcefully bent over the post and held in position by RanchoRamO. ChocCockHammer easily pulled my struggling arms into position and locked them in place at the side of the post, then my other hand, and my ankles. I had virtually no 'give' to move any part of my body, and I was uncomfortable as hell.

And I was begging them to stop and not do this with as much force as they used against me.

I was frightened more than anything now. A smaller than usual team were filming me and none of them were a Sebastian or a Roy I recognised which sent internal alarms in me screaming. ChocCockHammer stood directly in front of me removing his clothes. I was already crying, sobbing, and begging them to please stop, telling them I didn't want to do this filming, begging to know what I had done wrong to get punished like I was about to be. And I saw the biggest, fattest cock I'd ever seen in my life, and was terrified of the damage it would do if inserted into me, even gently.

Still no one answered me. They were indifferent to my pleas.

And then ChocCockHammer stepped forward, looked to his partner who was in position behind me. I couldn't keep my eyes off the size of his cock.

"Ready?" ChocCockHammer said to his partner, and before I had prepared myself for what was to come, he had roughly grabbed me by the hair, lifted my head and was shoving his massive cock inside my mouth, as someone else, RanchoRamO, was pushing himself into my puss. Rancho was going to split me apart. "So, the famous Amberee, porn princess has decided she wants to try being tag-teamed by us after all, and wanted the full taken by surprise, not expecting it scenario. Well, beautiful lady, we aim to please. But remember, we don't go easy for *any one*," he rubbed cock around in my forced-open mouth, "you get the full Ribald Dungeon experience as promised, like every other slut who pays us to give it to them like this."

And then they started for real. My mouth was too blocked to let him know I hadn't asked for this as he apparently believed.

I honestly don't think I've ever known fear and pain like this. But one thing registered in my mind, someone had tricked these two brutal monsters into doing me. And Mr D. had sent my Sebastian's away to cause no one put a stop to it … until the two rough fucking human machines were done.

I endured the most painful, torturous, scary sex imaginable. I learned the hard way what 'deep throating' and 'deep ramming' is. I was powerless to try stopping them. RanchoRamO was doing me from behind, but apart from crying in pain whenever he rammed himself in and knew my puss was burning with the pain of it all. My watering eyes and attention were on ChocCockHammer, whose fearsome cock was already massive but was getting larger and harder the more he pushed himself as far down my burning throat as possible; all the while I choked and gagged, and desperately pleaded for them to stop in between gasping for air, wondering just how much bigger his cock would get.

Only vaguely aware my voice was becoming hoarser the more I begged (when I could speak), the wooden post dug into my stomach, that I might be bleeding from its now razor sharp corner, that RanchoRamO had already cum, while ChocCockHammer's cock was still only getting more and more swollen and harder, making everything increasingly harder for me, and he was sliding it in and down my burning throat only slowly, basking in how long, and snakelike it looked as it came all the way out, and then rushed towards me, as I was crying in desperation with a voice which no longer sounded like my own, "Please, no more," which only made ChocCockHammer smile and RanchoRamO to fasten his speed.

I became lightheaded, woozy, and blacked out multiple times, probably from the lack of air reaching my on fire lungs. But ChocCockHammer slapped my face (like Daisy had once told me) a few times to revive me and said, "Oh, no, princess, no starlet gets let off *that* easily. Passing out is for the wimps."

And still he kept shoving his fat and long cock in my mouth blocking my throat, picking up the pace himself now, keeping it driven in as far as it would go, before pulling out quickly and ramming it in fast again.

And then, finally, I had a new struggle on top of what I was already going through. I was now drowning in cum. His cock still fully down my throat, and him holding the base of my head ensuring it went the deepest it could go, plus a little bit more, my face buried into his bush, still only giving me the smallest amounts of relief before pushing his cock in again, and again and again. I was drooling and coughing, spluttering and gagging, and close to throwing up, between passing's out and being slapped to consciousness once more. I became so out of it, so disoriented, I didn't always remember what was happening to me until the pain and action happening behind me returned, as ChocCockHammer was going for a second cum; and RanchoRamO was going for cum number three or four, or maybe more, and had switched from ramming my puss to ramming my back passage. Both of which were bruised and tender beyond belief.

My body head to feet was screaming in pain, I was still fighting in my restraints, was being gripped by the head, still begging, even more urgently in an ever croakening and diminishing voice, still trying not to choke or drown, or both simultaneously. And eventually, ChocCockHammer came a second time, and I was a complete and utter mess. Pools of black tinted tears fell by the droplet onto the granite tiles. I could feel the mascara stinging my eyes, and streaking my face. And the clock on the wall behind him, told me they'd been doing me like this for nearing one hellish hour straight.

I didn't know how long I was going to have to keep doing this. Daisy had said they had multiple stations and could usually work for the full five hours. I didn't think I'd survive another four hours of this. I didn't want to go through another four hours of this. At some point, if ChocCockHammer lost concentration, I was going to die because a cock, an unnaturally fat and long cock, asphyxiated me. My life depended on him not 'disappearing' into his orgasmic feelings; of him staying fully aware of how long his cock was denying me oxygen to withdraw before I croaked it.

My wrists and ankles were bleeding, every part of my body, including internally, throbbed bruised and swollen from how much I had struggled in my restraints as part of my natural survival instinct and the beating I was enduring. My arms and legs were weakening from the nonstop effort of trying to break free, yet I still kept trying to get free though it was futile and my mind acknowledged this last fact.

And, then ChocCockHammer came a third time, and I thought for sure that time is when I really would die as I struggled not to drown in his cum more so then before; until he blessedly removed his cock from my mouth, bent forward, kissed my forehead and whispered while I sucked in as much air as I could, "You did great Amberee, love. Thanks for letting us play with you on The Post. Now how's about we move on to doing you at the Fuckstation, seeing as you begged and all."

My arms and legs were released, and I collapsed onto the floor unable to support my own body weight, still gasping for every precious breath, as I laid there trying to recover from the ordeal, thankful beyond words it was over. I'd only endured the tag-teaming for one hour and fifteen minutes, not a moment longer.

But then, they were picking me up, and had dragged me over to a solid wooden table, and I was already begging for them not to do this with the last of my voice, but they wrenched me off the tiles, easily tossed laying me backward, with my head falling over the edge at one end, my puss over the edge at the other, and I was being refastened to not be able to move in this new already uncomfortable position of me lying body-up this time.

Even with my head fallen right back, straining to hold it in a position that maximised my taking in air, I could tell upside down, Mr D. looked as though he had watched the best treat he'd ever been given in his life; he was absently massaging a hard on.

He gestured for the two male porn stars to approach him, and he handed them a fat wad of fifty dollar notes, which they tossed onto their discarded clothes still on the floor and then positioned themselves ready to start act two. My heart thumped so hard, I felt the pounding echo in my ears.

I was about to suffer a whole new level of hell.

Although never raised in any religion, I prayed for someone to come rescue me, like I did the night Murk had fucked me the first time. Once again, I soulfully cried over having no one in the world except for Mr D. and the others present knowing what was happening to me. Prayed that I would be rescued, and wouldn't have to endure whatever other sexual torture these sick men would torture me with.

Mr D. then walked to me, and crouched to my eye level, swiped a finger under my eye which blacked his finger padding with mascara. "How do you like the experience so far, Amberee? Did you cum as often as they did? Yes? No? Don't worry; the *real* party hasn't even started yet. Wait until you get to station four; that's my most favourite of all."

I couldn't muster the energy to reply, Mr D. returned to watch as the skeleton crew prepared to get the filming recommenced, and I knew, same as the night my innocence had been stolen from me, I had no one to rescue me now, either, and I was scared about what was going to happen to me, remembering Daisy had said there were eight stations in total, and they all got progressively worse: - her words, "They shouldn't call it The Dungeon; they should call it The Torture Room." My experience so far demonstrated she was absolutely right.

RanchoRamO was clipping some metal clamps to my nipples and clit, a new type of pain, when the Dungeon door was kicked open, and two Sebastian's burst into the room. Mr D. said, "Oh, fuck" and next minute, the two porn stars had been pushed aside and held their hands up to suggest they were no threat. The clamps were off. I'd been unrestrained. A robe or other cloth had been thrown over me. I was in the arms of one Sebastian. Before I was raced from the room, as other Sebastian's rushed in, I caught glimpse of the other original Sebastian beating up Mr D. The film crew and two porn stars stood looking confused about what was going on, all looking like they had made the decision to stay out of whatever dispute had put an end to the rest of the gig procedures.

Rushed along the underground tunnel to a waiting van, the Sebastian carrying me muttered, "Thank god we had the tracker on you, so we learned the location he'd taken you to." Then the car I had been placed in was speeding, as one Sebastian drove and the other one held me and spoke comfortingly in his reduced Aussie accent, "Mr J. is furious; heads are going to roll if you've been seriously hurt, Miss."

I think I must have passed out again during the trip, maybe my body had been so ill-equipped to deal with being so brutally assaulted it shut down as a self-preservation mechanism. All I remember is the trip didn't take anywhere near as long as it usually took to get from one side of the city to the other. Throughout the journey, Adrian-Sebastian lovingly stroked my hair back, telling me I was safe now, in a soft voice I found pleasantly reassuring. He looked like he was on the verge of tears, and that he wanted to kill, or at least smash something. And for a brief moment, I wondered, did this Sebastian love me or something?

I wasn't returned to my basement starlet bedroom; the car swept into the garage of Starlet House at speed, and as soon as the roller doors had closed, Sebastian carefully pulled me from the car and said, "Don't try to walk, Miss, I'll carry you," and swept me into his strong arms, and he carried me up the stairs, hasting through the kitchen then lounge room and up the marble stairs into the main bedroom, where he lowered me gently onto the bed, covered my aching and grunged body over with a sheet and said, "The doctor will be here any minute to check you over, Miss, to ensure you're alright."

I was to spend the next three to six weeks living in Starlet House for real.

A Sebastian was stationed in the hidden stairwell behind my walk in wardrobe's shoe shelving-come-secret-door, and another one outside my bedroom door inside the house. And I knew, they were not there as my captors for the time being, they were there, on duty, making sure no one unauthorised gained access to me. As protection.

The doctor arrived swiftly within minutes of my arrival, and thoroughly, attentively examined my condition. He declared to Mr J. who had entered the Starlet House main bedroom but for self-protection against being identified by any police surveillance remained hidden inside the walk in wardrobe, "Very bruised, some abrasions, sir. Will need a few weeks or a bit more to recover, but at best guess there'll be no permanent damage. She shouldn't develop any scarring from the cuts to her wrists and ankles. She will find it painful to speak for a bit but she's one very lucky young lady, Mr J. She could have ended up much, much worse. If they had of started on the fourth station, she could easily have become one of the ones to have permanently damaged vocal cords. Amberee's got a lot of splinters in her stomach I'll have to remove."

"Okay, afterwards, get a nurse to shower and tend to her wounds, and then give her a sedative to help her rest comfortably and whatever non-addictive medications you think she needs for a quick, full recovery. Don't speak of this to anyone. I need to go deal with those about to regret making decisions about my little asset *without my approval*."

I heard him leave. He sounded dangerously furious.

After my shower with the help of a female nurse who was told I'd been tied up and raped multiple times by a crazed fan (after she had recognised who I was as she walked in), I had dressings wrapped around my wrists and ankles, was injected in the arm, and soon slept for hours. When I woke up, the nurse was told to leave the room and I was questioned by the Sebastian who had carried me in.

"Amberee, Miss," he said gently, "Mr J. wants full details from you what happened before you were taken to that Dungeon room."

I wasn't privy to information they already knew, but I guessed my answers were to help establish the guilty due punishment for what giving the defiant approval to send me for that nightmarish treatment. And I had no reservations: I pointed the finger at Mr D. without any hesitation. It was all him, I blamed no one else. I was honest and croaked with great difficulty telling them in as little words as I could use, often having to let Adrian-Sebastian make suggestions which I only needed to nod or shake my head no to, to pass on the message: I don't think the two male porn stars had any idea I was there under duress, or even had the remotest suspicion they had been set up to take the blame if it all went wrong and the act was discovered. (Which luckily it had.)

"Yeah, that's what they claimed. They were beaten for a bit ... the other Sebastian's all reported ... the film crew all claimed the same thing... but Mr J wanted your version, in case you believed contrary..."

It was clear from how hoarse my voice was, it'd be impossible for me to giggle the Amberee signature giggle, or speak in her (or my) girlish voice - the two essentials that made Amberee's desire for porn princess mega stardom work and come across as believable. If I had been damaged, the loss of income to Mr J. ran into the millions.

No wonder he was pissed.

The next day, I was introduced to Mr B. who was taking over from Mr D.

At first, I didn't know why the man looked familiar to me; but then I remembered where I had seen him. He was the main man who had 'broken in' the new Sexhouse girl. He had been Mr D.'s 'second in command'. It appeared he'd received a promotion to running the show. I hadn't recognised him at first; he was now wearing a business suit not the t-shirt and jeans I'd first seen him in. He no longer looked like he existed on the wrong side of the law; he almost looked credible.

Two weeks later - when I wasn't so tender, when moving and my hoarse voice was starting to return to normal with hopes of full recovery, and I started feeling a bit better and didn't need to stay confined to bed-only and the lovely nurse now only had to visit twice a day no longer needing to keep a round-the-clock bedside vigil tending to my every need, making sure I was made as comfortable as possible - I made my way tentatively downstairs to get a cup of coffee, I found the courage to ask the Sebastian on duty, who helped me as I shakily took each step, "What happened with Mr D.?"

The Sebastian eyed me first, and then said, "Do you really want to know?"

I did. I wanted to know he'd been made to suffer physically as he'd made me suffer. I wanted to know the finer details, to learn he was in as much pain as he'd caused me to now be in. To put my mind at ease that he'd been appropriately punished. When I saw him next, I wanted to see him bruised and sorry he'd ever put me through that. More than that, I wanted him to seriously regret having messed me up.

I wasn't expecting the massive Sebastian to reply, bluntly unconcerned, "Big Boss was furious, so he copped a bullet right in the forehead. Dirty fucking pervert he was. Good riddance to him. We suspected he'd been planning something like this for a while."

I went instantly weak in the legs, and the hulking Sebastian caught me, stopping me from tumbling the remainder of the marble stairs.

"Don't worry, Amberee puss, you won't ever be made to appear in unauthorised filming like *that* ever again. And Mr D. won't be making secret money behind Mr J.'s back ever again."

The horrible, overstepping the boundaries by another person meant I would no longer ever get a chance to escape. I started having nightmare's in my sleep, reliving the horrible brutal ramming and the desperation to get breath again night after night and catnaps, imagining my Mum desperately trying to escape the people who had murdered her and Mr J. standing there, furious, calmly pulling a trigger on a begging Mr D. for the damage he had caused his 'property', his merchandise, his millionaire's best asset.

And I was right. I *would* no longer be able to escape; I no longer had to return to my starlet Room Two bedroom. No, during week four of recovery, I had a small modern microchip inserted under my skin near my collarbone, so I could be *permanently* tracked. Because of that, I was allowed to live in Starlet House, to come and go as I pleased, so long as I kept my various porn, diet and sleep schedules. Mr J. wanted me to regain my weight to my former petite but healthy weight size.

I now had what I call 'captive freedom'.

During the day, I was okay, and had most of the freedom I craved; at night, I once again became burdened by the full weight of the horror I had gone through, and the devastation knowing I was now stuck being Amberee porn princess, sex-hungry starlet who loves sucking and fucking cock for as long as the men who made money from my doing this decided to keep me. Judging by the strong reaction to my being brutally tag-teamed, I was still making them plenty of money; my star wasn't yet diminishing. But with girls entering the industry every day, I sometimes wondered, 'but for how much longer?'

A Sebastian drove me to and accompanied me wherever I wanted to go. And, everything was paid for. (Yes, I know it was me who the items were charged to, but I was confident I was racking in more profit than they could fairly charge me; besides, I didn't care. I defiantly decided I *deserved* a few of life's treats, so enjoyed them while I had the opportunity - you never could tell when such things might be taken away from you again). I could eat lunch in a restaurant and go shopping in shopping malls, but I didn't care; I was no longer trapped inside my claustrophobic basement bedroom, and even though I was discouraged from speaking to anyone, except a fan wanting my autograph, in which case I had to act fully Amberee, I loved this side of my new arrangement very much, and so from week six went to restaurants' and visited lingerie, clothes, shoe shops and occasionally to a bookstore, for the first time ever feeling somewhat free, and genuinely happy during those outings, now I had no external signs of what I had gone through.

The only part of my life I was still a prisoner was still being forced to suck and fuck cocks for a living which I resumed after an eight week recuperation break, I was encouraged not to speak to or socialise with people who weren't 'in the know' and I still had to ask permission to do things - if a Sebastian was available, it wasn't a problem (within reason). If not, the answer was no.

It was only once I had been living at Starlet House for five months I realised the daily fan mail was no longer being checked by one particular Sebastian; it was scooped up and added to other mail they wanted or needed to send out, without any letter being checked. The rest of the Sebastian's still checked, but not this particular one. And I realised: I could now, finally, have been able to reach out to the world beyond my containment and tell someone I was being held prisoner, but I not only didn't have anyone I could trust to tell, it was pointless even making an attempt. I could no longer escape like I wanted to, regardless.

The desire to scream in frustration nearly overwhelmed me.

You have no idea how much I cried each night, first while I was recovering when my mind kept recalling the horrific details against my desire; and then after the tracker was inserted.

I'd failed my long-term escape plan.

Failed.

Through no fault of my own.

I was now permanently stuck with the life I didn't want to live like.

Mr J. and team simply thought my nightmares and crying were only due to my Dungeon experience. I was still genuinely traumatised by that experience. I only got through it after buying a book on how to cope after a traumatic experience; and learned I had the power to view myself as a victim or to put the experience behind me and move on with my life, and to see I was loved and safe. The power was always inside me, ready and waiting for me to embrace.

But, I really *had* built up the trust in me I had worked so hard and carefully at building.

And I couldn't do anything with that any more.

Through no fault or misdeed of my own.

I had been robbed and cheated in life all over again - despite what the book taught.

The reason the team had planted the tracking-necklace on me was a result of more than one Sebastian becoming suss about Mr D.

Their suspicions had been reported, and they had grounds to become suss at what he might be planning; so much so, they implemented secret measures that only a small handful of Sebastian's that Mr J. could trust became privileged to know they had to keep a close watch on him, and be ready to spring into action.

Adrian-Sebastian was to receive a bonus in his pay for taking his initial concerns directly to Mr J. It was the reason he had been scheduled to participate on my filming guard team.

I was *always* friendly and responsive to him after finding this out. He had save me from a further four or more hours on the remaining fuckstations.

CHAPTER 24

The film was released and did really well.

Actually, it did better than the critics expected.

When news of my involvement in the production eventually broke out, ahead of its release, the movie critics were rather vocal about me having been cast as the lead character. Why had the producers hired a porn star not a proper actress to deliver such an important movie and message? Wasn't this more than a little hypocritical? And okay, if they had to create realistic sex scenes which was likely, and the only way to achieve this was using a porn actress, why on earth did they headhunt the world's most famous slut, who at best estimates has slept with about ten thousand men and seems determined to suck or fuck every male in the whole world before she retires and simply doesn't fit the character of an *innocent* young girl tricked by a new boyfriend none of her friends or family had yet met?

As to me being capable of pulling off being a virgin. *Impossible!* My fame had spread beyond the customers who paid to watch me in live action feeds and porn films; my management team had created social media accounts, and regularly updated, posing as me. I had developed a huge following, not only a fan base. I also had 'trolls' (though I didn't know what this terminology meant either). So, my reputation as the cheapest and easiest slut in the world was common knowledge to within general public worldwide, who'd be the audience of this movie.

It was hard hearing about those harsh criticisms about me. Especially as none of them ever would say this about me if my life hadn't ever come into contact with Murk, which had started this whole nightmare called my life.

There were a few critics who said I was attractive enough and might realistically be the type of target sex traffickers would love to get hold of. The few (male) critics who bothered to watch any of my porn films (not many were prepared to publicly admit it) commented that unlike many male and female porn stars, I was amongst those thought to have the better, maybe even best, acting skills, and it was a shame I was so slutty: I could have made it as a non porn actress, so they guessed we'll all have to wait it out for the film's release before making final judgement as to whether it was right or wrong choice for the producers having cast me.

Mr B. told me he had been nominated to accompany me as my date for the premiere; we were to look like we are dating. I didn't much like Mr B. (probably after what I had seen him do). I'd have rather gone with a Sebastian, or a Darren, or even Murk. Adrian-Sebastian would have been perfect.

I went shopping to buy a nice gown.

I discerned I had to become a toned-down version of Amberee porn princess as I walked the red carpet and up the steps for the premiere, but I still had to play Amberee. So rather than have someone else choose my gown for me and make me look like the slut they encouraged me to be, I chose a beautiful long, royal-purple, sheer-material dress, which had an off-centre split virtually all the way to visible crotch, which would show off my leg with each step. The split should keep the captors and fans happy; it was fully a slinky dress that Amberee porn princess would choose to wear, because it would occasionally flash my underwear.

But apart from having the revealing side to it, was otherwise elegant (and more me, Amber Entacott. Though I personally would've asked for part of the split to get restitched first, about two inches worth, so I didn't have to risk or worry about exposing my underwear). It was the first and probably only time I was being allowed to dress in a way where I wasn't trying to show the world I was a porn star, a cheap slut, and I was looking forward to this night very much, for a few hours of feeling admired and glamorous rather than lusted over. I wanted to feel Cinderella-ish; to look and feel as though I fit in with the other actors and celebrities invited to attend, though I had no delusions about any Prince Charming rescuing me from my life.

I spent the morning sleeping in after a late night filming as usual, then going off mid afternoon to have my hair and makeup done, and then get ready for the limousine Mr B. and I were to travel in. The full length mirror showed a glamorous movie star I wished my cheap slutty self could otherwise have been, as I looked before I was due any moment to leave. I couldn't be happier, pretending in the make-believe of the mirror - actually, this was the first time I had to live this tiny dream and genuinely let myself bask in the little happiness that entered my life since the day I discovered I had to fuck men all the time. Except at night when I still woke up gasping for breath.

Then Mr B. said something which made me remember I was merely the cheap slut they'd turned me into, and I couldn't see my treasured idyllic vision a moment longer.

"Why are you wearing underwear, Amberee?" he said, looking at my leg through the split.

"They're only g-strings," I said, confused. "So I don't have a visible panty line."

Mr B. stepped close to me and said, "Remove them this instant."

"But sir," I started arguing, but he slapped me across the face so quickly I was stunned, and didn't say anything more.

"You are Amberee, *porn princess*," he said firmly. "Remove your panties *immediately*. The famous little bush is what your fans will be hoping to see - so you're going to give them that sneaky-peek."

I had so been looking forward to do this one exciting thing and not being an attention seeking slut at every opportunity I got, to look beautiful and elegant; to fit in with the other actors and actresses. And instead, I was fighting tears from rising and flowing, so I wouldn't ruin my makeup, my face stinging, angry and frustrated over once again I was expected to cheapen myself, in the hopes one of the paparazzi in attendance scooped themselves a priceless 'wardrobe fail' shot, unable to voice what I really screamed unacknowledged in my mind.

Tomorrow's headlines were not allowed to become about the

movie and whether I could act or not; the newspapers and gossip columns were all being cluelessly influenced to gossip about me as porn princess all over again, to have haters and supporters arguing about me, about my desire to suck and fuck and to cast their judgements on me for that, all to keep me in the spotlight for all the wrong, scandalous reasons to send even more traffic to my live feeds (now being genuinely recorded in the refitted with better equipment basement studio of Starlet House).

This was so unfair. Why couldn't I have one night to enjoy myself without being a slut?

With a heavy heart, I obediently removed my panties before Mr B. either back-slapped me harder a second time, or worse, called off me even attending the event. I had worked too hard on the movie to not be able to go and see the finished version now.

"And if you're lucky, which you will be," Mr B. said, watching my every movement and then holding out his hand for me to give him the offending g-strings, "Someone might be able to sneak you into the men's bathroom and slip the skirt part of your dress apart so they can fuck you without spoiling it, once we're mingling afterwards. I'll let you know which of the men who ask you have the approval for you to go off to do that with. But, don't get any foolish ideas, puss. I'll be outside the men's room the entire time."

Right, luck. I'd never had any of that.

Misfortune. Plenty.

The limousine arrived, and I self consciously walked towards the car holding on to Mr B.'s arm as directed (there were a few cameramen stationed outside my 'home' on the other side of the road). He opened the door for me, and I found it extremely difficult not to flash as I got in (but luckily, it wasn't caught on camera. They were on the other side of the road, on the opposite to my getting in); I could only imagine the difficulty in swinging out again, with all the cameras snapping pictures or recording footage as we arrived on the same side this time and we walked the red carpet.

It was all timed to minute detail. Our limousine parked further along the road until we were cued to arrive. Some of the lesser known actors arrived first, and the main cast arrived after them. I was second-last. The main bad boy star drew arriving after me.

Everyone was waiting for Amberee porn princess, as a result of how rare an occurrence it was for her to attend events like these.

"Smile, Amberee" Mr B. snapped seconds before the limousine came to a stop.

With difficulty, I hitched a smile onto my face.

"And don't start walking the carpet until our Sebastian's are in position."

Apart from our limousine driver, we had no other Sebastian's in the vehicle with us. I guessed they had already arrived there, waiting for us to pull up.

Someone opened the door, and Mr B. had hopped out the other side and came round to help me, as my date, to get out of the car. I was to call him Brendon all night; though I'd learned for a fact this wasn't his real name (it was Jason Stefanto).

There were plenty of people, a heavy crowd, gathered behind each of the waist height barriers making a walkway between the road and the steps up to the theatre. Red carpet had been rolled all the way from the theatre entrance, down the steps to kerbside. On either side of the carpet was a wide concrete area before the barriers, where the different television networks, newspapers and magazine staff were waiting to talk to, if not already doing so, the movie's stars as they made their way inside. The male lead (the one who had really fucked me) was a well-followed 'bad boy' celebrity. I knew one of the questions they would all ask him is if he fucked me for real, and if so, how many times he 'landed' Amberee.

I was proud of myself: I somehow managed to swing my legs out without flashing.

People everywhere were calling my name: Amberee! Amberee! They all wanted my attention, all at the same time. Most people were cheering; but I did notice some signs being waved in the rear which read: 'Amberee, porn slut, you will go to hell for your sins.' And, 'Sluts Must Die'. And similar signage.

Now the part I feared most was over, much to Mr B.'s disappointment, I was ready to enjoy the most of being here, getting to go on a night out to do something most people took for granted: going to watch a movie. I waved to fans, not only because I had been pre-told I had to, as we headed the few metres before the steps until the theatre began, but I wanted to take pleasure in and create the most of this part of my night out while I could. Me and Mr B., flanked by four Sebastian's who appeared from who knows where, two in front of us, two behind, unless they needed to break formation for some reason. Mainly to block specific reporters and cameramen if Mr B. wasn't happy with the questioning.

"Amberee" a reporter called, as we approached, "Is it true five months ago you were kidnapped off the street and brutally raped by a crazed fan, which is why you disappeared off air for eight weeks, and cancelled all your engagements?"

"Just smile and don't answer," Mr B. muttered underneath his breath.

I waved to people in the crowd on the opposite side to the reporter, genuinely smiling at them as the best way to pretend I hadn't heard his question.

"Amberee" another called, "How did you like your Ribald Dungeon experience? Did you agree to ChocCockHammer and RanchoRamO doing it from being colleagues on this movie project? You didn't do the usual after session recording sharing how you enjoyed the experience? Did you enjoy it, or do you regret doing it? Is that why it hasn't been released?"

I thought Mr J. had successfully prevented all the footage from being distributed? And had silenced anyone knowing about it? And I thought the two male porn stars were to deny ever having me in their dungeon? So how had reporters got hold of this information? I looked to Mr B. for silent answers, but got none. He was looking in the opposite direction.

"Amberee" yet another thrust his microphone in front of Mr B. towards me. "How many men do you think you have been with since you started in the porn industry? Do you think it is over ten thousand yet? Do you keep tally?"

"Just keep smiling. Keep waving," Mr B. leant in and muttered in my ear. And that's what I did.

My favourite Sebastian conveniently coming to a stop in front of the reporter asking, so I could walk by holding Mr B.'s hand as we made our way ever closer to taking the first step.

"Amberee!" shouted more than one fan as we progressed, "Marry me!"

"Amberee," shouted others, "When can we fuck?"

Or, "Give me a blow job, Amberee!"

"Blow him a kiss," Mr B. muttered.

I blew the fan a kiss, and said, "Maybe another time, sweetie. As you can see, you know who I'm going to do tonight."

Mr B. smiled, and hammed it up for the camera, and then fans.

I worked out if I twisted my body towards the leg with the high split as I stepped up on that leg, the split didn't open as much as when I didn't do the waist twisting action. I was still focused on trying to get from the car to the safety of inside the theatre without exposing my naked part, without having the 'wardrobe fail' Mr B. was so hoping for.

So I was completely caught by surprise when a handsome slightly older journalist came from nowhere and started firing questions at me as I took my fourth of about twenty steps.

"Amberee, Philip Dweitt from The Night Life," he was ducking and weaving around other journalists and cameramen climbing the steps as Mr B. and I did. He half-shouted his questions at me, to ensure I'd hear him over the crowd still whistling, or calling to me. "The story we've been fed about you, Amberee, where you make your films and live action feeds willingly and it is something you've always aspired to do, is that *really* your own free will, or what some sleaze of a boss is forcing you to say and do under threat of physical punishment from his henchmen if you don't cooperate?"

I couldn't help myself, I turned to look at the man more closely, and then quickly, looked at Mr B. alarmed, and then back to face the journalist fearful of what other questions he intended asking which could easily give me away while I still had so many more steps left to climb.

"Tell us, Amberee. Tell us you've never been bought and sold in an underground sex trafficking deal, like many other girls working in your industry. Can you confirm for us you aren't one of those innocent girls who've had their lives stolen away from them?"

I wanted to faint mid-step.

There's no way I could answer truthfully, like I desperately wanted to. The man beside me, holding my hand, undoubted ready to have me bundled out a back door of the theatre and returned to a basement site, beaten and bruised and begging for mercy and them to stop before the rest of those in attendance had finished watching the screening. And I couldn't bring myself to lie either. But in all these years, it was the first time anyone had asked me these questions, as though they had delved deeply into my horrible secret, and I didn't know what to do.

I started feeling panicky the truth might already be revealed; I was the sole individual who would suffer if *that* truth came to light, no one else. This man was going to get me in trouble - again, through no fault of my own!

"Just keep walking, don't say a word," Mr B. snapped, aggressively under his breath, and I shook myself and continued to walk up the steps with a renewed hitched smile, though I increased my pace trying to flee in the fastest time possible without it being obvious to all those still waiting for me to answer those questions, forgetting all about trying to prevent flashing myself at everyone.

I was scared for my life now. If any part of my reaction to those unexpected questions upset Mr B., or worse, Mr J., then I was in serious trouble anyway. I couldn't say or do anything to stop the man as he continued dodging and weaving other people, firing the same question at me. "Are you sex trafficked, Amberee?"

But Mr B. gestured to the Sebastian's on our left, to cut across to the right and put a stop to this line of questioning.

"Amberee, are you *sex trafficked*?"

"Amberee, are you not answering because I've struck the *truth* and you're *scared* for your life? Amberee, *are you sex trafficked?*"

I only looked over my shoulder once more, so desperate was I to reach the top step and disappear inside the door. But that last look, only a few steps left, meant I caught sight of two Sebastian's - the two who had been present the first day I had been bought by Mr J - arriving next to that reporter, and one started punching into him with those massive bulky arms, in the stomach, in the face; and when the reporter keeled over, laying the boot in repeatedly with his equally powerful legs.

Mr B. and I were able to continue ascending the stairs quickly, without further hassle, as the crowd's attention and all the paparazzi cameras turned towards the massive bearlike Sebastian still beating up that poor man.

As soon as we were inside the building, I urgently rounded on Mr B. desperate for answers.

"Why did he ask me that? What's going on? Why did he ask such a thing? Have I done something to give myself away? I-I don't think I did, so why did he ask me that?" My voice was almost screeching.

I was desperate. I really wanted to know why. I wasn't faking what I asked. Had I done something for someone to work out my situation? Mr J. was not going to remain a very happy man if the public started believing I might be. He might get so furious I copped a bullet to my head next. I mean, I probably should have instantly lied and refuted the question right without delay; tried laughing it off as being ridiculous. To do so later wouldn't be believed, would it? So, had I fucked up for *not* answering? Was I destined for Room Six as punishment for not having handled the situation better than I did? But I was only *obeying* Mr B.'s instruction to ignore him and keep walking! Obey commands like I always had to do!

"No, I don't think so," Mr B. snapped at me, pulling a phone from his breast pocket and dialling. He didn't seem the slight bit concerned about my distress. "Are you watching? Yeah, boss, Sebastian's making a scene for us, beating the reporter up, doing as much damage as he can - he'll be arrested, of course."

I could hardly breathe trying to work out how much trouble I was going to get into as a result of the journalist and his damn questions.

Mr B. did more listening than talking after that... just agreeing, and, "Yeah, she's as confused and wasn't expecting it as much as I wasn't... well, do you know why he asked her that? ... no, no, I told her not to answer and to keep walking and ignore him ... oh shit ... yes, sir ... no, I don't think so ... okay, right boss."

He ended the call. "We're to continue on as though nothing

happened. Okay, compose yourself, *and* wipe that look of terror off your face! Are you as brainless as you look? There's still fucking reporters and cameras everywhere for fuck's sake."

I'm sure I'd have received another backhand if we weren't currently in public. His hand had nearly automatically raised - it had certainly travelled a few degrees before it stopped.

I breathed a sigh of relief though, and took a few moments to regain composure. I wasn't being blamed for my lack of answering, from what I could tell. Mr J. was aware I had been obeying Mr B.'s instructions. If anyone were in trouble now, it was him.

And together, Mr B. and I continued from the foyer, into the theatre, and found our seats.

Waiting for the lights to go down, took ages. I only calmed properly once the movie started playing.

This wasn't over yet.

<h1>ℂHAPTER 25</h1>

Two-ish hours later, everyone in the audience was on their feet clapping.

But this was now the part of my evening I was dreading. At some point from here on, I'd receive the order to go be the slut they believed me to be with which ever cock had the approval.

People came over to me in my seat and congratulated me on my fantastic performance. The sex scenes were all tastefully shown; I was fully naked as the first man entered the room (so men were going to love the movie), and then a series of progressive montages: of different men forward thrusting, one after another, until the next montage, of different men cuming, followed by a further montage of them getting back up once done, getting redressed, satisfied, and the glass jar becoming fuller.

And in a later scene, being told to give men a blow job, and again a 'progressive' montage showing the passing of time and number of men, suggestive of the action realistically, without any of the offensive real bits too overtly taking over. (The cameras had been angled so viewers could tell I was really sucking a cock, but not much of the penis was revealed at all. The makeup and the weary look on my face made me look forced into blowing each of them, too. Like I was doing it against my will.)

They were right. It could never have come across as realistic if it had of been a real actress and the sex only simulated. It was the realness which made the movie as impactful as it was.

Rightly so, I was proud of my performance: those horrible blow job and fuck scenes (because it really made a strong impact the horror girls in that situation go through) just as much as the rest of the movie. I had to wipe away my tears; I had really bought into the whole storyline and believed I was a young, innocent girl, taken to one of those horror houses, and how heartbreaking it was she didn't survive the ordeal, made worse by police raiding mere hours after my character died, while two of the key captors were burying me and therefore escaped being arrested for their role in imprisoning the sex slaves.

But I didn't see the memories of having to suck and fuck those hundred fans, those days were condensed to less than five minutes screen time. I was too used to sucking and fucking by now to remember those specific incidents. I did all that on auto-pilot; my mind off in other places. So I could die tomorrow, now, and I'd feel I had at least *accomplished* something worthwhile and meaningful in my life. It was an important message to raise general public awareness.

And yes, it *was* ironic a girl who only a handful of people knew was indeed a sex slave was chosen to raise that awareness powerfully advocating against sexual slavery.

Maybe, maybe, the movie might help even one girl not to have to go through what Daisy, the other starlets and myself were going through. And now knowing my own Mum had once been gang raped, I intuited without doubt she'd be proud of me too.

I don't know why I thought of her again seeing as I had long since trained myself to not look backwards to how things used to be, maybe it was over the depiction of my character's parents desperately searching for their daughter which triggered it. I hadn't allowed myself to think about Mum for a very long time. It was too hard to cope looking on those lovely memories of my life, love and fun times. It was far easier to deal with what I was currently confronted with, and stubbornly hold slight hope for the future one day they might release me, alive. Looking back is when the darkness overpowered me, making it hard to keep up appearances. I didn't re-hear her laughter today; just a small snippet of her lying in bed with me, as I read to her. Then kissing me on the tip of my nose once I'd finished that night's chapter.

"That was better than I hoped for," I told Mr B. as we stood meeting and greeting people who came to us.

He nodded and said, "It certainly took me by surprise how talented you are. I think you're going to have the critics raving. All positively. Mr J. will be happy; the movie will be profitable. His gamble, I think, will pay off."

I asked Mr B. if I could be allowed to see some of what the critics say, and he replied, "Maybe. That'll be up to Mr J."

The rest of the cast in turn came to me and congratulated me, sounding surprised as they all said or implied the same thing, "You were much better than I thought you'd be."

I was told I had 'presence' and 'screen charisma' and other nice things, like 'you've got great acting talent'.

And I had more than one person tell me they wouldn't be surprised if the film won an award; but then had equal amount of people with them then say, "Don't be silly, they'll never give the film an award because … well, they won't. It probably won't even get nominated," and they'd break off after glancing quickly at me, and I was left to fill in what wasn't said: the film would never win any prestigious award due to the lead character played by a porn star. Not of the right calibre' as non-slut actresses with real careers, so not worthy of real merit - such merits were deserved to only those *real* actors, not sluts, tarts and whores. Like me.

As the gathered crowd started thinning out, as many spread out to talk in groups while others started heading off to their various after parties, Mr B. talked to a husband and wife, I heard one small group of people standing some distance away, say, "Can you imagine it? And the award for best actress goes to porn star, oh sorry, I mean to porn *princess*, Amberee? Slut either way," and everyone in the group laughed raucously, and someone added, "who fucked and gave blow jobs to a hundred men so she could make her performance seem 'realistic'. What a tart." and someone else added, "The world's biggest whore." making them laugh even harder. And one of the women even mimed (I presumed me) giving a blow job, which made the group laugh even harder.

And it wasn't only the one group of three or four people saying similar things. At least three more groups, each thinking they were well out of my earshot were all saying the same type of nasty things about me. Including they'd kill themselves rather than so actively strive to gain the reputation as the world's biggest slut, having the loosest morals. And wondering why I hadn't already run off to either men's room to try and fuck as many men that entered, "All she'd have to do is lift the skirt part up to give them easy access." which then had the group laughing, "Yeah, but she'd beg to let them fuck her puss or wanting them to do it up her arse - or get two men to do her at the same time." which had them all clutching at their sides. "She's come prepared not wearing any underwear."

"I mean, seriously? Who arrives for an event like this not wearing underwear when the dress has a split that high?"

I was wounded when I realised I was the butt of so many people's jokes in the still rather packed theatre, all off chatting in small groups. The longer we stayed here, the more I'd receive the instruction to go and fuck someone; and those same groups of horrible snobbish people destined to soon laugh and gossip I must have heard them, "Well, we all agreed she was too much of a slut and we didn't even want her on our project. We must have given her the idea."

I turned to Mr B. who was chatting with the couple still, and asked with an uncharacteristic flatness, "When can we leave?"

I'd had enough, my evening ruined. My delight at having done a great job now tarred. I didn't want anyone to see how upset their words had made me. And I wasn't at all sure I could keep my feelings to myself, that I wouldn't breakdown and start crying, or worse, scream my truth to everyone present if I didn't leave, quickly. Mr B. was surprised by my request, but accommodating. Apparently Mr J. had instructed him that we could stay until everyone left, or either of us had had enough and wanted to leave. He may have seen how close I was to having a meltdown in public; so he simply excused himself from the couple, and got me out of there.

Only one person in the whole wide world, from my position, saw through the act to bother to ask if my situation was identical to the character I had played. Well, yes. I was. I *am*. That's *why* I was able to look as haunted as I did, so scared, humiliated, embarrassed, emotionally wounded. I used my memories, direct experience, not only what I'd had done to me, but also what I'd seen. When the director had wanted me to cry my 'first time' it was no effort at all to become emotional over the memory of Murk fucking me the first time had me 'pretend' crying for the camera. The one scene in the filming of the movie we got right in a single take (much to the chagrin of the male lead, who had wanted to brag about how many times he got to do 'the slut' and was unimpressed he could only honest-brag was the once).

One person, in a world with *how many?*

No one person inside the theatre had any idea what it was *really* like. Except me, and perhaps the people that kept me in captivity. Oh, they all *thought* they did; that's why they'd made the movie. But, their arrogant interpretation of the truth was only a *small* fraction of the reality - they thought they'd depicted the depths of it. But that was their ignorance. The *real* truth was way darker and nasty and dangerous and scarier than anything compared to what they'd shown.

And all those 'do-gooders', who had made this film alongside me, who looked at me with disgust, made me the butt of their jokes and called me mean names, had no idea of the hell I had been living through for a little over thirteen long years. *No idea.*

They'd go home to their happy trouble-free lives and families, and they'd resent me for being a cheap slut as the cause of them missing out on getting industry accolades they desperately wanted recognition for. None of them desired to acknowledge my performance is what made the storyline work as well as it did (that's what even the toughest critics in the industry said in their reviews). They only wanted to vilify my life choices, as they saw them. To blame me for what *they'd* miss out on. I was *their* easy target.

But what about me? I'd had my whole life stolen away from me. I wouldn't receive a pretty prestigious award even if I fully deserved one.

I had not even a glimmer of hope this enslaved life might come to an end anywhere within the foreseeable future. And *they* felt they had the right to consider life was unfair?

I'd had enough. I couldn't pretend any more.

Those people had just broken me.

On the journey 'home' I considered killing myself for the very first time, not sure I could continue to cope having to suck and fuck cock for a living; and to pretend to love every minute.

It was the pretending which was the *hardest* part.

What I'd done on screen, the misery, the heartbreak, the emotions had been *easy*.

It'd be a blessing if I was allowed to cry every time I had to do or be or pose with each hard on. It had been *especially* hard since my hour and fifteen minutes in The Dungeon. I cried myself to sleep again each night, something until that night in The Dungeon; I hadn't done for a very long time. Years.

I contemplated over and over in my mind as I sat silently looking out the window to the lit streets we travelled back to my prison: how I could go about ending my life without my captors ever finding me before I succeeded.

Escape or die: those were my only two choices.

If I had to put my options in statistic form, I'd say the ratio was one to ninety nine, escape to die. The one, probably due to, my heart intuited, I'd never be able to escape; and ninety nine, despite not knowing how to kill myself, because I assumed it was the only real alternative available to me.

I didn't want my death drawn out or painful, like being sent to Room Six. I'd be okay with a bullet to my head, like Mr D. - as long as it was done swiftly, and I didn't have prior warning it was going to happen.

And I mostly didn't want to kill myself in a manner which was too painful or too difficult for me to carry out.

I'd had more than my share of physical pain being inflicted upon me!

Escape, or die? Which one should I *really* choose?

My heart said escape, and my mind screamed, 'die, Amber, just die; it's the only way'.

I'd have to wait to see which ending it was fated for me, though. Now, I was pursuing whichever came first: silently, privately.

And same as my wait for an opportunistic escape previously, the troubling part was I might never get the right moment *for years*. How did I cope and live in the meantime?

I think Mr J. realised I had returned broken. I got up in the middle of the night to go to the ensuite, and seconds later a Sebastian opened the bedroom door and asked, "Everything okay, puss?"

They wouldn't even let me go to the medicine cabinet in the kitchen myself; and returned to dole out two paracetamol tablets rather than risk me swallowing the entire packet.

𝒞HAPTER 26

The days after the movie premiere was a flurry of media attention, so the television in the lounge room in Starlet House was now permanently on. I could hear it even when I wasn't allowed to watch or was doing other things. Both the Sebastian beating up on Philip Dweitt, and my not answering the questions caused a lot of 'social chatter'; oh, and to a much lesser degree how 'brilliant' I was in the movie. (And how they can't imagine any other actress could have pulled off the performance as brilliantly as I had).

At first I was still struggling I was so down, so dead inside, I just stayed in bed, but slowly, my immediate pain eased slightly, and inevitably I started 'living' again and I paid more attention to what was happening in the world beyond my self-imprisonment within my prison walls.

Philip Dweitt led a lot of the *sex slave or nymphomaniac* arguing. Firstly, and bravo to him, he didn't bother to have his bruises covered with makeup as he hosted his evening television show, to 'milk' as much mileage as he could over having been beaten up by my 'goon' (as Mr B. complained and Mr Dweitt name-called); and secondly, he had invited a range of experts to analyse and comment on the various footage of the premiere night while it was the hottest topic worldwide.

The footage of me exiting the limousine, and making the journey along the red carpet was constantly paused, zoomed in on, and heavily debated. Although it was occasionally mentioned it was clear I wasn't wearing any underwear, and was at risk of exposing myself with every step I took and they were amazed I hadn't, that wasn't the aspect focused on - that part was minor side talk while a heated 'is she or isn't she' debate raged on.

Those in favour of me being held captive as a sex slave all focused their attention on my realistic performance, "could only come from someone who has experienced the situation"; and, more so, the moments when Philip Dweitt first asked his questions to me. In slow motion, the experts in human behaviour claimed I became fearful, and turned my head to seek instructions on what they believe was not an escort, but a captor giving me instructions on how to behave and react. A captor who gave one of the bodyguards the order via a gesture to beat Philip Dweitt as a diversionary tactic, "which worked perfectly to plan". With many of the experts pausing the abundance of footage from different angles at precise moments, and saying excitedly, passionately, "Right there! See that? This is the *typical* reaction of someone who is fearful. See how she looks to her date for instructions?" And they even had a string of popular 'A-list' actresses all saying they could never have given such a strong, realistic performance like I had, despite their being some of the best in their craft and the industry.

Those taking the 'they're delusional' side (on other day and evening programs), equally showed footage, and paused in spots, with them refuting, "Someone fearing for their life, wouldn't smile. No, this is *undeniable proof* Miss Amberee was having the time of her life at the event. She knew, and was fully aware, at any moment she could give the paparazzi and fans a fleeting glimpse of her famous puss, and with every step she is hoping to give them that treat. You have to remember, Amberee is an attention seeker; she'd do anything to steal the limelight all on to herself - and all this ongoing argument must thrill her." This was often then accompanied by some men being interviewed, and I realised, they were many from top five hundred's four hundred eliminated contestants, who spoke with absolute conviction Amberee had personally held their cock in her hand, and told them she wished she hadn't eliminated him as a contestant, and she was fully 'the real deal' and 'no way she's doing any of it against her will'.

"She *loved* my cock, man. *No one* could fake holding me like that.

She wanted to do me, *bad*."

And then footage of the Elimination Event was shown, with the men's private parts pixellated out, which was followed by more experts, who declared equally as strongly, "See, Amberee is happy, and calm. There's no sign - not one - of her being under duress at any time throughout the whole day-long proceedings. Listen to what she says to this particular eliminated contestant." And the footage rolled again, and my strangely echoey-for impact voice was telling the naked man, "Oh, sorry, sweetie. Not this time, but if I ever run another competition like this, don't worry, I'll make sure it happens, make sure you enter again, okay?"

And footage resumed playing of me, winking at him, as though suggesting I'd make sure he got through the stages next time.

(Did they not hear the slight flatness, and lifelessness my voice sounded? Oh, yes, they did. They had the audacity to blame it on me being tired after a very long day. There could be no other possible, legitimate reason.)

So the Philip Dweitt camp stepped up their arguments and evidence, and presented more for the public to consider.

They pieced together footage from different networks, showing the Sebastian who had beaten him up, had first looked to Mr B., who had nodded, before the Sebastian started beating him up. "If Amberee was really dating this bloke, then why is *he* giving silent instructions to beat up a reporter? Was it to ensure Amberee couldn't answer the question at all rather than let her deny or lie with an unscripted answer? Why wouldn't the goons have turned to *her*? Isn't she supposedly their boss? I repeat: Why wasn't it *Amberee* giving the nod?"

Mr J. was becoming annoyed. He was instrumental in getting people to continually dispute and try to counteract the talk Philip Dweitt's was unrelenting in.

Practically every guest on his show was asked their opinion, and he had a lot of people on his side either fully agreed or were being swayed towards his claims, and he persisted in claiming, "Amberee needs help, whether she does this by choice or not. If, and I strongly emphasis the word if here, Amberee is a simply a nymphomaniac as some people claim, then why is she being encouraged to continue when she should receive counselling or psychiatric help."

"But you don't believe Amberee is a nymphomaniac. You believe she is a sex slave?" his guest inevitably asked. (I thought it strange; the little I knew of late night talk shows were the host interviewed the guest, not the other way round.)

"Yes. You only have to look at the evidence. I believe Amberee is Amber Entacott, even though no one ever admits or refutes that. Let's say she is Amber Entacott: discrepancies between how old she really is, her mother being murdered not dying in a car accident as claimed in the XXXX Hotstuff Mag4Men interview, and when she started. Do you honestly believe a girl not quite fourteen could mastermind her own way into getting a passport and visa and travel to America, and decide to work as a porn star?"

"No, records show Amber Entacott's step father, Murk Walters, accompanied her on the flight. A man, who lives on a rural property… with a convicted paedophile, I might add. That's a classic sign of a girl being trafficked. And that's why Amberee couldn't deny it when I asked if she had ever been bought or sold; it was safer for her to not say anything than to give away she is lying by saying no, or risking her life to answer a truthful yes. And it's why they won't confirm or deny if she is really Amber Entacott or not, despite the photographs which recently resurfaced. And I remind you Murk Walters was the photographer of the XXXX Hotstuff Mag4Men photo shoot; he was married to Amber Entacott's mother, and the photograph of which Amberee has a strong resemblance to murdered Marilyn Entacott, and the young girl in Marilyn's photo albums."

I couldn't believe someone had kept Mum's photographs all this time. Though I never learned how they ended up in possession of the American media. If only I could have even one of them to treasure as my own. Why hadn't they been returned to me? Didn't anyone think if they believed they were mine that I would want them returned?

Poor quality, un-doctored footage also surfaced of me and Mr B. inside the theatre foyer, too; me looking very scared indeed. Mr B. on the phone, listening not talking, which Philip Dweitt said was my minder being given instructions from someone higher in my captivity chain. (He was right; Mr B. was on the phone to Mr J.)

Mr J. played dirty.

He had the money to do so. In secret.

He immediately initiated (or ordered) a campaign to defame Philip Dweitt's good character and impeccable industry reputation, first with a sex scandal, then with a financial one. But Mr Dweitt bravely fought back and openly stated all these accusations, which would come to light as being false "in good time" (which they were), was simply a nasty smear campaign all being driven by the people holding me captive; they're not happy with him saying the truth. (It was true, but he didn't have any one to confirm its true publicly.)

I heard Mr J. rage at Mr B. - they were in the secret tunnels, I was in the basement recording studio. Everyone in the basement could hear them. "That bastard is ruining my efforts to discredit him! I want *different* social commentary happening! Do something, ASAP! Do more to end this son of a bitch's credibility and strength of conviction, he's costing me fucking money, both in lost income *and* in increased expenditure!"

Hundreds of offers came in to Amberee Headquarters from the different television networks, with increasing offers to gain an exclusive interview. Amberee finally 'agreed' to a rare face to face interview (for a massive sum of money). A night off from sucking and fucking so I could be interviewed by a rival late night talk show host to Philip Dweitt, who Mr J. assured us, will help us convincingly deliver Amberee's side of the story in exchange for a private audience with her, and finally get the commentary on to other topics so she can start earning money again.

The film was doing really well, and Mr J. was getting a large slice of the profits it made; the 'naughty toys' and other products I apparently endorsed on my official social media accounts (I'd never even seen) hadn't dropped in sales or profits (actually, they had risen in direct correlation from so much talk in the media about me), so I didn't really understand why he was so upset about the amount lost from live feeds. Which was now the lowest revenue generator, and I only still did as it kept all the other income streams selling high. But I found out weeks later, it was the private Millionaire's Best Asset recreations being cancelled were behind Mr J.'s frustration. None of the wealthy businessmen were prepared to go ahead with their pre-booked sessions if there was any possibility I was sex trafficked; they didn't need or want their good name to get caught up in amongst *that* type of sex scandal. (Notice none of them were saying they didn't want to still do it with me even if I was a sex slave.)

And we'd found the huge loss of money for Mr J.

The recreation sessions were pure profit direct to Mr J. exclusively; he didn't have to split the costs in any ratio with other businesses for this one gig-type, like he had to do with all the others. At one hundred thousand dollars per session, and me doing at least one or two recreations a week, yes, he was losing a lot of money.

But, what did it matter? He was already a multi-millionaire, always getting closer and closer to becoming a billionaire. Why did he have to reach billionaire status? He was already quietly influential within the wider community and could have secret conversations with politicians, judges, law enforcement, media executives and personalities he could bribe to help him get his own way for almost everything. Why was it so important for him to become even richer?

I was nervous going on camera; I understood this footage was likely to become just as scrutinised and heavily nitpicked as the rest, and it was more important than it ever had been for me to convince them if I didn't want Mr J.'s fury being turned into physical punishment for me.

Emililian Greinhouser was somehow related to RanchoRamO, though hardly anyone in the industry had made this connection. And Emililian was in the 'know' from his close relationship to RanchoRamO and was being paid handsomely to slant things in Mr J.'s favour. (He was happy to do that anyway. It meant he got to do me afterwards as part of the deal. He wanted having fucked me on his resume as much as the next guy. And his studio executives were mighty impressed he was the person I'd chosen to go exclusive with. They were more than happy to pay the fees. They suspected it to skyrocket their shows ratings. Which it did.)

I waited in the wings with people from the studio in my sexy little pink, black and white baby-doll dress and matching stilettos, ready to walk on stage for the live filming as soon as the stagehand gave me the go-ahead. I was dreading what I had to do at the end of the interview; actually, I was dreading the whole thing, scared I'd mess up one of my responses.

I walked from the side area into the set under a spotlight and to tremendous studio applause, and the tall Emililian greeted me, bending down to give me a kiss on my cheeks, and then gestured for me to take a seat before returning to his own behind a desk.

"Thank you for giving us this exclusive interview, Amberee. I believe you have come forward to stop the controversy about your role as a porn star which has blown up in the media of late as a result of you starring in the lead role in *The Sexhouse Slave*, when you attended the movie's premiere, the movie which was released in cinemas three weeks ago and is being hailed a masterpiece. And you, a great talent."

"Thank you, Emililian. Yes, that's right. I feel the need to speak up and put a stop to all these wild accusations and woefully wrong opinions about me."

Emililian started by saying I have a big following of both lovers and haters. And he mentioned people from religious organisations had been protesting at every porn film release since the day I started in my line of work. (I had never realised I had haters before this, this caught me by surprise when they were earlier coaching me on how to answer, multiple times until I was answering the way they wanted me to.)

Emililian had been given specific questions: asked in the rehearsed set order and he had to commit to memorising them so they didn't look planned.

I leant forward, touched Emililian on the arm, giggled, and then said, "Well, those people were never going to become my target audience, were they?" And then I re-erected myself in the chair and became 'all serious'. "Look, what I'm doing isn't harming anyone else. So they can have their personal beliefs, and I can have mine. It's been clear all the way along we will never agree on whose viewpoint is the right one."

"Some people, led by Philip Dweitt, have recently suggested you are either an out of control nymphomaniac or an enslaved young woman forced to work in the porn industry, baring all in the raunchiest live feeds, movies and men's magazines, and therefore, a young woman in desperate need of society's help, not encouragement to do more of what you're doing."

I turned to face the camera and audience. "Aww, that's so sweet of him. He is that reporter who upset my body guard, isn't he?"

I mean, really, as if I wouldn't have known his name after all the after-coverage? Could my captors not be consistent themselves in how they wanted me portrayed to the public? One minute I'm labelled 'smart and business-savvy, than then they follow with this with me being a bimbo-dope?

"Philip, honey, you don't need to worry about Amberee. I'm not some little damsel in distress, needing a hero like you to come along and rescue me. I get plenty of delicious heroes rescuing my insatiable desire to fuck men's cocks who come into my life everyday; so unless *that's* the type of hero you want to become in my life, sorry, you need to find someone else to try and rescue from your moral judgements. Though, I do apologise my body guard took it upon himself to beat up on you like he did. He never had my permission to do that, and he has been fired for crossing that line of authority."

"So, Amberee let's be absolutely clear here, you want Mr Dweitt and the public to know, you are not a sex slave, you have never been bought or sold, you are completely doing what you do of your own free will."

"That is absolutely right, Emililian. As I've said this to people so many times before: they don't have to *like* my way of life or choose to do what I love doing; but they don't have the right to try to inflict their personal beliefs and how they choose to live their lives onto me. I am my own person, and I'm fully comfortable and happy with the decisions I make for myself. I'm not doing anything illegal, so end of story, leave me be. I don't care about the people who dislike and hate me, so they should stop caring about me. But I *do* care very much about the people who do like and love me, my true fans. And that's why I'm here: to reassure them."

I waved at the audience again, and blew a kiss directed at the camera.

"Has anyone ever suggested getting you, umm, help, Amberee?"

"Yes, Emililian, yes they have." This was the moment I had to frown and seem very upset. "The first person was my wonderful surrogate dad, Murk, who, for the record, I am very close to and love very dearly like a real father; and—"

"So, does that mean you are confirming you *are* Amber Entacott,

Amberee?"

"No, I am, or rather, was, Amber *Ebony*. I've met his step-daughter Amber Entacott, when I visited him in Australia. We are definitely two separate people. I'm two years older than her. Now, as I was saying, I have had many of the people I work closely with, at some point become worried when they think I'm being too outrageous or too controversial and suggest I tone myself back a bit, and maybe seek some help."

Again, I turned to face the audience again. "And I'll tell you what I told each of them: I do not have a problem. I don't want or need to become anyone except *who I am*. Nobody ever tells a person with the passion to play a musical instrument, for example, not to spend their time doing what they love - that they shouldn't practice and perfect their craft or aspire to become the best at it as they could possibly be, do they? So why do so many people feel entitled to criticise me? People, sex is a *natural* part of life, not something to ever be ashamed of. And it certainly isn't all about doing it in the boring missionary position, either. You never tell the couple who make love every single night they have a problem. So, please, if you don't like what I do, stick your nose out of my bedroom. It's really that simple to me. The only difference between me and the in love couple is I choose to do it in front of the cameras, for the enjoyment of more than merely me and who I do it with."

"So, Amberee you have absolutely no plans to seek—"

"Absolutely not. I will be in my live action feed at precisely ten p.m. tomorrow night - I'd have been tonight too, except, well, I felt the need to come here. And I will be there every other night I'm not away on location filming, because … I … LOVE … IT." Pause for a long moment. "I… choose… to do this… I can't make myself any clearer than that."

"And one last thing, Amberee The footage of you inside the theatre, you look scared about something."

"Oh, yes. I *was* scared, Emililian. I had moments earlier witnessed one of my body guards beating up on a reporter. I was worried about the legal ramifications for me. I had Brendon, my date, phone my agent for me, who phoned their legal team. I was very stressed waiting to learn what they said."

"Well, there you have it, folks. Amberee can't reiterate it strongly enough she is a porn princess through personal choice, she's a law abiding citizen, and Murk has two young Aussie females named Amber in his life. So, can we finally close the debate once and for all?"

"*Thank you, Emililian, thank you.*" I threw my hands up to suggest relief. "It's so great to have someone who isn't simply a paying fan supporting me in my life choices. We do, after all, live in the Land of the Free, and I am a girl born and originally raised in The Lucky Country. And I can tell you, I am not only lucky but I am *perfectly free.*"

Emililian turned to a camera and told the audience after the break, they'd return with some famous rap singer I'd never heard of, and unfortunately, Amberee won't stay for the rest of the show as she has another engagement to get to.

And then it was time for an advertisement, I farewell-waved the audience, teased them when I got to my feet with a little lifting my skirt higher so they may or may not see my famous puss (as instructed, and what I had been dreading to have to do), and then blew them a kiss and walked off stage to loud cheers from the male dominated audience.

All as instructed. Another perfectly delivered performance.

Maybe my wish should be adjusted to losing my *acting* talent.

I was then taken to Amberee headquarters, where I usually did *The Millionaire's Best Asset* recreations, waited an hour or so until Emililian arrived, and then had to give him a blow job, and then let him fuck me as part of the deal. (I was so relieved when I saw his cock; I had been worried I was going to face dealing with a cock as large as RanchoRamO's again, too. But I had no cause for alarm when I saw it; it was no bigger than Uncle Spud's, the smallest one I'd ever had to deal with.)

But, far from quietening the social chatter, Philip Dweitt, who live on his show had my exclusive interview playing, persisted; insisting the questions and my answers were staged, telling people, "Oh, what a load of poppycock! If you see Amberee in *The Sexhouse Slave*, you'll see how magnificent an actress Amberee is. That interview doesn't change anything for me. Actually, it only *supports* my claim Amberee is being forced to play the character of a free and easy porn princess, really. I'll certainly check into the birth records for a Miss Amber Ebony.

I am willing to bet we'll find no such birth record or person anywhere."

And Mr J. was getting more pissed off than ever before.

"I want this fucking social chatter ended! Do your fucking jobs and get them off Amberee's radar!" He raged over his secure and encrypted phone call while myself, some Sebastian's and Mr B sat in the conference room at Starlet Headquarters the next afternoon.

Secretly, I was rather impressed with Mr Dweitt, in how persistent he was being. I loved his tenacious spirit; I was silently cheering how much he was pissing Mr J. off, and hoped he found ways to keep it going.

I have to clarify of course; the Sebastian wasn't fired in the slightest. He went to court, had a great lawyer recommended by Mr J. and was let off by Mr J.'s country club mate judge on a good behaviour bond as agreed long before the Sebastian ever appeared in the judge's courtroom. The Sebastian still worked for Mr J. only now at a different facility, and sometimes at Starlet House (but only from one of the secret entrances so he wasn't ever seen).

But, someone on Mr J.'s payroll did figure out how to change the social chatter. And they did so spectacularly days later.

Daisy was given her freedom.

Released from sex slavery earlier than they originally planned. In the exact manner she had a few years earlier described to me. Her being dumped outside a major sporting stadium right before a one hundred thousand plus fan base came pouring out from a baseball grand final, as good as naked and with all that vulgarity inked into her skin, and no one having witnessed her drop off (the team had earlier disabled or rendered inoperable some of the security cameras for that specific area the day before the game and drop off).

She became exciting instant headline news the media dumped the Amberee story to pursue in place of the boring old recycled arguments.

Day by day, the evening and late night news added more details as they had come to light. Daisy was refusing to tell the police details, repeatedly quoting, "I can't, they said they will kill me if I tell you anything. And I believe that's exactly what they will do."

I assumed Daisy was sure to have received instructions about what she could and couldn't say about her captivity and release.

Despite the police's frustration, the connection was inevitably made she was abducted as a child, and her parents were being flown from Australia to the States to reunite with their missing daughter. And then her mother and father were interviewed as they arrived in the country, saying "We've never given up hope of one day finding her," and after they had seen their daughter, where they both cried, and Daisy's visibly upset father is quoted as saying in a media address, "What sort of monsters tattoo a penis on a young girl's face, as well as all the names of the men she was forced to have sex with? Who does this sick type of thing?"

Keeping the Amberee is a sex slave story alive ended the moment when Daisy, with pillow-slip (or similar) covering her face as she was ushered by police rushing her to a nearby car, trying to protect her against the media as she left hospital, her piercings and chains removed, said, "No, Amberee wasn't one of us - only me and seven other girls, and we all had showers and meals together, all chained to each other each day, so I'd have known and met her if she had been a sex slave like me." and "I was released because there's no room left anywhere on my body to tattoo any more names."

Which wasn't true, pictures the hospital or police had taken had been leaked to the media. It was clear room existed towards the bottom of her left leg, and a small patch remained on her back. But no one performed the same 'put two plus two together' calculations as I had, sadly not even Philip Dweitt; to come to the conclusion: Daisy was the deliberate distraction to end the Amberee debate.

And it worked.

Or maybe he did, but was pointless voicing that.

The sadness inside me over Daisy indeed having been returned to her father's care and to lie about not ever having met me caused my tears to flow once again. If I hadn't known the truth, that he was the first person to sexually assault her, I'd have been convinced by his tears and grief over what had been done to his daughter. I hoped Daisy might one day, with counselling, find some peace, and perhaps, in the future, be able to put what had happened to her, well into the past and move on in her life as a rare, freed starlet. I held no grudge about her denial over knowing me; she still feared for her life. And was still obeying her orders.

It was not surprising the media followed every step of the case until she had been returned home, where she self imprisoned herself over her appearance, and to force the media to give up on trying to snap pictures of her, and to stop people staring at the famous penises tattooed onto her face if they had been following the coverage (or even if they hadn't).

She was still having her life stolen away from her, only in a different manner now.

Chapter 27

That first live feed session I had to perform after Daisy's release was probably my hardest to act happy and thrilled about. My thoughts of ending my life as my only alternative to escaping plagued me.

And it was on one afternoon a week or so after Daisy had returned to Australia, after I had completed that day's screen testing, when I just couldn't take my own situation anymore and decided I no longer cared if I was sent to Room Six for a week, or even if they scheduled me for the Dungeon to go a full five hours with ChocCockHammer rammed down my throat (in the hope I'd die of asphyxiation with certainty this time), I contemplated telling one of the fans it was all a big lie, and Philip Dweitt was spot on with what he'd been forced to stop claiming (nobody believed or cared about that old topic anymore and cited 'he should stop flogging a dead horse'), as a means to help me die.

But, seated at my writing desk, I couldn't bring myself to write the message I wanted to and earlier decided upon committing to. I think the small part of me which still stubbornly hoped I'd one day be able to escape, or be released, so I too might be able to put the past and present behind me, stopped me from taking the risk of getting caught, or suffering the consequence of my forbidden actions I was tricking myself into I could handle if it ultimately led to my death.

A few days later, I came from my Starlet House bedroom to ground level, in my bikini to take a refreshing swim in the beautiful pool, considering maybe today I'd go towards the deep end, in the middle and let myself drown. As I reached the kitchen, I saw paperwork on the kitchen bench, and being curious but mindful of the every watching cameras, I took subtle peeks under the ruse of doing other things, without touching the papers, at the top page lying on the envelope. It was court paperwork; something to do with the Sebastian bashing Mr Dweitt case.

I learned the real name of the Sebastian, (Kelvin Grenville), and both his and Mr Dweitt's home addresses. I don't know what prompted me to do it, but I hastily committed Mr Dweitt's address to memory as I retrieved a clean glass, then grabbed a cold drink of bottled water from the fridge (the only thing I didn't have to obtain permission first to consume). I'd heard heavy footsteps coming, and offered one to Sebastian as he came into the kitchen. I shrugged when he declined, and then said, "I'm going to have a quick dip to cool off … oh, or are you doing something important for me to have to wait?"

"No, go ahead, starlet," he said. "I'll get another Sebastian to swap places with me."

He couldn't be seen being anywhere near me or Starlet House, so no one thought it odd he wasn't as fired as I'd declared him to be; so he couldn't sit in the backyard's sunshine to keep an eye on me himself. He grabbed his paperwork, went downstairs and swapped positions with the Sebastian manning the secret tunnel system.

Repeating Mr Dweitt's home address over and over silently in my mind, I got in the shallow end of the pool, and sat on the steps or carefully walked around not getting my face or hair wet (not because I was being a diva or princess, but I was truly scared to go underwater, not knowing how to swim and all). It had struck me maybe I might drown if I went into the deep section the day after Daisy had been returned home. But, rather than venturing to the seven foot portion as intended today, I stayed at the shallow end as I silently recited the address to myself, embedding it permanently into my memory.

Once refreshed on this horribly hot day, I then got out of the pool, went upstairs to my main bedroom, and sat at the beautiful writing desk to start on the day's fan mail replies before I had my required afternoon nap.

And it was at that moment when I concluded, they had no intention of ever releasing me, and even more unlikely I could successfully escape due to that damn tracker; so, if my only choice to end my enslavement was to die, then I wanted someone to first know the truth before I died - I had been involved with enough lies. I didn't want them continuing about me specifically after my death. At some point in the future, I wanted the truth to become known to at least one person, but preferably the world.

And I knew instinctively the one person I could now trust to tell my secret to.

Mr Philip Dweitt.

It was a gamble, a huge risk. My captors could still be randomly checking what I wrote. But if I was right, and that wasn't happening with this one particular Sebastian who never openly checked anymore (my personal favourite of all the Sebastian's), I still ran the risk Mr Dweitt might not believe the letters I wrote really came from me, or he might release details for Mr J. to end up knowing could only have come from an insider, of which I became an immediate natural suspect. But I was adamant like I had never been prior to this moment - my version of the truth would one day be given to people. Today was the day my favourite Sebastian was on duty; today was the day I could risk sending a letter.

So, I wrote my very first secret letter to Philip Dweitt.

I told him I'd only be able to infrequently give him my side of the story, and he needed to promise me our correspondence remained an absolute secret until I either died or could successfully escape to personally give him the go ahead. And he should give me a secret clue he understood and agreed, by saying on air he was starting to change his mind and no longer believed Amberee was in any way forced against her will, merely a nymphomaniac he still believed needing proper psychiatric help, as his way of letting me know he'd received my note and understood how dangerous it was if any of my captors discovered what I was doing. I believed Philip Dweitt was never going to believe or ever say that without my asking him to.

My heart was pounding as I slipped the letter to being third from the top. I self reasoned, the top letter couldn't escape being looked at, and a random letter likely drawn from the middle to bottom of the bundle if they were checking the odd letter. I was a goner if they checked all. And I addressed the letter to Peter Dwyer - both close enough Mr

Dweitt might realise the letter was indeed meant for him, but different enough it wouldn't be obvious if the Sebastian saw the envelope (but didn't open it). I realised right before I sealed the envelope it wasn't as stiff as the real fan mail, so hastily added a photograph of me to correct the problem.

I was on tenterhooks until I learned whether I had successfully gotten away with sending that first letter or not.

A week or so later, Mr B., working in the lounge room of Starlet House, said loudly, "Finally!"

I asked him what he was talking about as he had startled me as I was walking by, and he told me Philip Dweitt was "changing his tune". I asked what that meant (it wasn't an expression I had come across before) and he said, "He finally believes you're a nymphomaniac rather than sex slave. This is great news. Great, great news."

I played ignorant, but my heart was pounding in my chest. "What - what made him 'change his tune' I wonder?" I asked as innocently as my guilty self could.

Mr B. said, "I don't know, and don't care, something about evidence he'd uncovered while researching your background. I think it means he's found an Amber Ebony. What a lucky coincidence for us. Excuse me; I need to phone Mr J. to let him know the good news."

And like that, I had gotten away with it.

Maybe, Mr Dweitt and I could conjure a means for me to escape. But, my main reason for risking writing to him was so someone learned my full, honest story. I had made a promise, which I fully intended on keeping: not a single word penned by me would be untruthful, nor an exaggeration. I have not knowingly broken this promise.

I decided to tell Mr Dweitt my story, starting at the beginning of it all and writing it chronologically, as opposed to where I am at life in the present. I thought it might make it easier for me to tell my story that way. I was only doing nightly live action feeds again due to the drop off in recreation gigs. After he heard the great news, Mr J. wanted me to keep a low profile for a little bit longer to help keep Philip Dweitt off my back, in case he changed tunes again, and to give time for the millionaire's to stop being scared and start re-booking gigs.

I didn't have any more TMBA recreations currently scheduled, so

I was able to write as much as I could each replying-to-fans session; I had long ago started writing fat, decent replies to a few, rather than short notes to many as part of my original plan and which became a habit, so it didn't look at all strange to any Roy if they were monitoring me on their screens writing a longer than usual one. I aimed to tell as much of my story and give as much detail as I clearly remembered as if it were only the previous day, with each secret extra reply I wrote and mailed.

Mr Dweitt must have understood the danger I was in if my captors ever caught me; nothing of what I told him appeared in the media. Thank goodness.

It's funny, because when I first started writing my replies to fans, I found the writing part hard to do. I only attended school until I was ten years old; I never made it to high school. But luckily for me, even though I had been in Year 5 when I finished school, I was in the advanced classes, already doing Year 6 coursework. But I hadn't handwritten anything in the years between prematurely finishing school until I started doing the fan mail replies, so my handwriting was really rough when I first started out. I got better and better with each letter. From practice, and the dictionary they gave me after I asked to have one so I could write better replies to them. I loved flicking through it and learning new words, and its meaning. That little pocket dictionary, for a while, had been my only friend.

And I realised, if I hadn't ever become a sex slave, I'd probably have wanted to become a writer. It simply felt so perfectly me. Mr Dweitt and I had a love of writing in common. I hoped my spelling, punctuation and grammar wasn't too below standard for him. I think it was about my fifth or sixth letter I started providing as much detail about what I had learned outright or deduced into my manuscript pages rather than omitting them. Maybe Mr Dweitt might be able to at least look into those otherwise unknowable specifics I provided.

While we waited for *TMBA* recreations to pick up again, Mr J. arranged for me to do a nude photo shoot for some luxury car brand. I laid on the bonnet of the beautiful sleek, black vehicle, suggesting the naked older man (successful businessman) was about to fuck me (the car and me together supposedly represented they had achieved the ultimate success in their life). And I did other shoots for other products too.

Time swept by, next thing out of the mundane was my twenty-fifth birthday, and I'd been writing to Mr Dweitt, a single double-sided page at a time, always trying to keep in my mind where I had written to, for nearing nine months. Every letter sent had me on edge, wondering if today's letter was the one my captors caught me out on. I was always worried the Sebastian's would change their shifts around, and I'd slip my letter to Mr Dweitt in not knowing a different Sebastian on duty from the usual called to collect it.

And I realised, I hadn't thought about killing myself in a long while - but of course, I was only up to my trip to America and being sold, so I still had a long way to go before I caught up to my story's current day.

TMBA recreations did pick up again not too long after the Amberee is possibly sex trafficked story died away, and everything was going along 'great' in Mr J.'s view; the decline in income had been nothing more than a temporary blip and we were 'back on track' and sales were picking up - but never quite reached the financial former level. Other new starlets arrived on the porn scene all the time, some appearing fully of their own free will, many not; but I was still holding on as a perennial favourite despite my growing older.

But, I was getting close to my twenty-seventh birthday when something happened which I correctly guessed immediately was going to change everything about my life as Amberee mega porn princess.

Mr J. had come to Starlet House basement recording studio to talk to one of the Roy's about setting up some new equipment in his new facility opening in another part of the country (I think it was in Texas, or that could have been the previous one), while I was doing my afternoon screen testing.

(Actually, I don't know why they still called it screen testing. I mean, they already knew what I was like on film. It was more accurately, promo recordings).

One of the other Roy's interrupted my take, meaning I'd have to do it again, by yelling aloud, "Boss. You're gonna wanna see this."

"What is it?" Mr J. snapped. He didn't like it when perfectly good takes were ruined. That meant wasting time and resources to do another take. And Mr J. didn't like wasting money unnecessarily.

"New starlet's come on the market, ten minutes ago. Dark-haired, dark-skinned girl, with blue eyes. Fifteen years old, a resale, they're only asking five to eight thousand dollars, US. Says "trained since nine years old"... you gotta take a look at her pics, boss, I haven't seen one this stunning since we saw Amberee come on the market. I reckon she might have the extra quality to become the next big thing you're always after, boss."

Mr J. eyed the Roy for a moment. It was clear he didn't think he'd be likely to agree. Then he walked around the others towards the Roy to take a look at the computer monitor.

"Who's the seller?" Mr J. asked, all businesslike.

"GreekGoddessTrainer."

"Really? He hasn't listed any merchandise for a while. I was only looking at his file yesterday, thinking he might resurface over the next couple of months, and was getting my investigators to do an update into his background. Well spotted, Roy, another one who doesn't know how to negotiate himself a better deal," Mr J. said excitedly, straightening again and clapping the Roy on the back. "Oh, how I love these dumb paedophiles and their hastiness to offload their quality merchandise once he's finished with them, never seeing or appreciating their true worth. Someone get me Mr B. on the line. We need to secure getting her to audition for us before someone else tries to snap up this bargain."

The Roy at the computer said with a proud and flourished click on his keyboard, "Already tagged as first interest, boss."

Another Roy was already dialling Mr B. on his mobile phone.

"Boss for you," he said into the phone, and then passed the device to Mr J.

"New special-level merchandise just entered the market. Arrange for an audition, pronto. I don't want to miss out on this potential buy. They're asking five to eight, but all going well during audition, I'm prepared to negotiate up to twenty four thousand at this stage. More if the competition tries to compete heavily for her. Don't think they will though - they're idiots and not as cash-asseted as me. Here's Roy for the details."

Mr J. handed the phone to the Roy. And patted him on the shoulder again. "This'll be a huge bonus for you if I secure purchasing her. Alright everyone. Back to work.”

And as quickly as that, the room went straight to how it had been - efficiently businesslike. Mr J. approached me, looking the happiest I had ever seen him, and said, “Well, well, well, Amberee puss. I think it might soon be time to start thinking about retiring you from my employ instead of trying to rebuild your sales to their former level; but I’ll wait and see what happens with Candee’s audition first. All going well, I already know *exactly* how I want to market this little blue-eyed stunner.”

He didn’t give any more explanation than that, and I was left wondering what retirement meant for me.

What *did* this mean for me? Would I be resold, transferred to another facility, down-levelled, or dare I hope it, be released same as Daisy?

But I wasn’t able to dwell on what it meant; I had to do the retake, and then complete the rest of my afternoon’s screen testing before my required pre-performance nap.

Mr J. left via the hidden passage door before I even started the retake - he must have been in a really good mood over this find; it was the first time I heard him whistling.

$\mathscr{C}$HAPTER 28

Even though I wasn't one of the privileged told details directly (unless I was required to attend a meeting at Amberee headquarters), it was amazing how much you learned about the operations and what was happening when you lived in Starlet House and had multiple Sebastian's on duty, and a frequently visiting Mr B.

I learned: about two weeks later, Mr J. bought Candee for only thirteen thousand US dollars. And she had been given my old Room Two starlet bedroom, though hers was renamed Room Thirty Two. The girl was dark-skinned, spoke English well. Her former paedophile owner figured he'd get more money for an English speaker, so taught her to speak the language as part of her training.

And Room Thirty Two, on her first night, performed really well. The Sebastian's talked to each other about how Mr J. was thrilled her first night's takings were on par with what I had made my first night (though my sales had been fifteen hundred dollars higher). And once again, with the right marketing to suit the girl, she'd be a high income earner for at least the first month.

I concluded Mr J. was marketing her similarly but differently to me from the snippets I gleaned. Whereas the character of Amberee was all about wanting to do it with as many men as she could to please them; they were marketing Candee as men needing to please her. The 'sameness' was she was going to get continually different Pete's like I did; the difference was it was all about them giving her an orgasm. The more, the better.

It'd be fair to say I did feel a touch envious her experience was to be about her enjoyment of the act, whereas for me, I had been in service having sex now for seventeen years, and I had never once had a single orgasm. I had no idea if something was wrong with me (maybe as a result of me having sex younger than supposed to, or due to how many times I had fucked men), or simply as a result of not being the goal for my character so the sex ended before I might have orgasmed (perhaps in a different, loving circumstance I would have). But, in some way, I knew, it'd make Candee's situation harder to deal with compared to me, harder to remember this wasn't the life she had chosen for herself, so I wasn't outrightly jealous or too envious of the new competition, either. More sympathetic to her, an innocent only at the beginning of her new circumstance as a live porn actress, who would inevitably be marketed as big a slut as they'd marketed me.

Desperately wanting to know what retiring me entailed, still, I didn't have the confidence to directly ask it. I didn't have the courage to indirectly try to get the information either. I did the only thing I could do to reduce the stress and worry I was feeling over the unknown aspects: write as many letters as I could to Philip Dweitt so he'd get as much of the story while I was still forced to live and breathe it, in case retiring me meant my days of being able to write to him were coming to an end, which I greatly feared could happen.

I didn't know if it was 'intuition' or plain fear, but I kept thinking of the worst possible scenarios for myself. What if I was transferred to another facility? What if this Candee started making more money than me? How would that affect me? Would I be kept as an A-level earner? Be down-levelled to B, C or D? What sort of rooms did it make me due to be scheduled to perform in? I anxiously wished someone might tell me or let slip what I desperately wanted to know. It was this not knowing aspect which was worrying and stressing me.

With every day, some of my worst fears were starting to become realised, too: Candee was indeed starting to become the new favourite; and this indeed meant her sales started climbing to new heights very quickly. I still earned alright, for now, but from the day Candee was first broadcast, my sales started slowly slipping. (No one could beat mine yet, not even Candee, but if the trend continued, which it surely would, I'd soon be demoted and de-favoured in the operations eyes -

well, I was already second favourite now, not number one, despite the sales. But how long until I wasn't treated well as a direct consequence of those diminishing sales?)

On my twenty-seventh birthday, I was taken to Amberee Headquarters, and I finally learned what retiring me meant.

Over the next twelve months, I was to do six last low budget porn films, and one 'retirement' event, and in between, only TMBA recreations, and progressively lessened Room Two live action feeds. They hadn't yet decided what the retirement event entailed - only it definitely involved my doing it with my real fans again, as a 'finale'. On my twenty-eighth birthday, they expected Amberee Headquarters and each of the product streams to undergo re-branding to Candee Headquarters and Candee endorsements instead. They'd decide on what to do with me once I got closer to my retirement date; it all depended on how much money I was still raking in for Mr J. from the leftover few income streams.

I wasn't sure if it was my imagination or I had progressed to paranoia, but, after one of the starlet meetings I was invited to attend, they stopped having discussions around me. And, the one Sebastian who had never ever touched me, the one who had carried me to safety and stroked my hair and reassured me I was safe when I was bruised and battered, and continued to fail in his duty to check my mail, didn't seem happy any more (not that he ever did, but he never used to look so worried before, like something serious was on his mind).

Five of the six scripts were written, so once again I was taken off to porn sets to do filming. (And once again, the story lines were all about me getting into situations where I had to suck and fuck lots of cocks, more always being what they strove to achieve. And of course, I was unable to continue writing to Philip Dweitt due to the long day filming schedules. Luckily I didn't have much of my story left to go for him to know my story until the present date.)

Mr J. managed to increase the number of recreations I had to perform to twice a week, too. He couldn't command as much from the recreations any more. I had to perform a one-hour blow job marathon, all because Mr J. wanted to test how many men I could make cum in a one hour period; so I had a line-up of men, and I had to kneel on a cushion placed in the auditorium of Amberee Headquarters, and had to 'race the clock' to try and do as many as I could. No explanation why I had to do this test. (I honestly can't tell you how many I did, I was being yelled at to go faster, and it was one after another, so I lost count, and they didn't tell me. I think it was over twenty.) I suspected they were trialling ideas for my finale event.

So the year flew by.

With four months left to go before my twenty-eighth birthday, my impending retirement, Mr B. came in to my bedroom and dumped the final porn script for me to read.

"I wrote this script myself," Mr B. said grinning with pride. "I want you to retire with one last smash hit to have the public raving about you. And I'm sure this script will be the one to achieve that."

And he then told me my management team had decided on, some months ago, the retirement event would involve me trying to set a world record for how many blow jobs I could complete in twenty four hours.

I thought I must have misheard him. But no. They'd been planning all the details for the last eight months. Ads had been placed in men's magazines; I'd had eighty seven thousand diehard fans enter. They were going to have fifteen hundred men in attendance, they'd hired out a function place big enough to host it; I'd race against the clock to get through as many of the fifteen hundred men in that twenty four hour period, the men would already be partially erect, they'd step into position one after the other, while I had a quick rinse and spit of my mouth and start on the next one. The event would be filmed (of course).

"We have two thousand men currently undergoing a basic health declaration, and we have a further amount of applicants in reserve so we have sufficient supply of cocks for you to blow. When we tested you a few months ago, you got through twenty six in the hour. Mr J. wants you to fasten your pace and aim to do one thousand of the fifteen hundred, which means you'll need to try to average forty an hour."

Were they for real?

Yes, they were serious. It wasn't a prank or wacky joke. They seriously, outrageously expected me to try and give one thousand men a blow job in a twenty four hour period! I had no words. I wasn't being asked to do this; it was another order: do this or else.

"But don't worry about the retirement event yet, Amberee" He continued, oblivious to my being stunned beyond anything I've ever experienced before. "You still have to film your last fuck-flick first. You start filming in three days time. Sorry for the late script, but I only started writing it last week. So, you need to get learning your lines. Oh, and Candee has started her period, so you'll do the Room Two live action feed tonight."

And with that, he left.

I couldn't even think about reading the script my head was spinning so much with disbelief. They wanted me to give blow jobs to one thousand men. *One thousand.* Were they crazy? I could only imagine what the social commentary was saying. Of course, I had no doubt they intended presenting this insane idea as something I came up with. I had an instant headache even thinking about what they expected me to do. Had they ever done anything like this with other starlets? Or was this exclusively a 'treat send off' for me.

Alarmingly, I had noticed Mr B. had said the men were only having to *declare* themselves disease free; it didn't sound like they were making sure the men actually were, like in the past. It looked like my star was taking a fast nose dive. I was worried this might mean serious down-levelling for me, too.

To distract myself, I decided to try reading the script.

It worked.

At distracting me, that is.

If I thought their plan to have me give a thousand men a blow job was the makings of a nightmare, a new level of hell, it was nothing compared to the role they wanted me to play for this last fuck-flick.

And it hit me, powerfully, once I flicked through the manuscript. Yes, this was worse than I had ever imagined. My owners were setting out to *intentionally* destroy fans from continuing to follow me. I still wasn't sure if they planned on transferring me, down-levelling me or releasing me, but it was clear they had a strong plan to destroy my public image *permanently.* They wanted me remembered as a slutty trollop, which my public image would never, could never recover from.

I couldn't wait until I was able to sit at my writing desk so I could respond to my fan mail, I desperately needed to tell Philip Dweitt what they have in store for me: if I did this movie, they meant for me to become the most hated person in the world. If they released me back into the public after they released the film, my life would be in serious danger. I'd have to defend myself alone and without support.

Oh, who was I kidding, my life would be in serious danger whatever my next phase of life I had to live as a result of this last fuck flick.

And it struck me while I was writing.

If they didn't plan on releasing me, then I was being transferred *and* down-levelled.

In my churning, worrying mind, it instantly all made sense: they were sending me to a Sexhouse.

I hadn't want to accept this as my fate earlier.

The one I had visited for the role of *The Sexhouse Slave.*

Now my time as *The Millionaire's Best Asset* had come to an end, it was time for me to recreate my second most famous role: as a Sexhouse slave.

Only this time, for real.

There was no leaving a Sexhouse owned by Mr J. alive and untainted. They worked you impossibly long hours, didn't look after you, feeding and showering you poorly, without screening the men and without letting you use a condom, until you tested positive to or showed symptoms of a nasty - you either died, or was tossed penniless with a disease which slowly killed you soon thereafter anyway. Mr J. had said it front of me my very first day: he didn't care what happened to his D-level sex slaves and those who'd fallen out of his favour.

They were already *prepping* me for the worst of it, with my retirement event.

Did Mr J.'s cruelness not have an end?

He had given me the sweet taste of captive freedom. Had this been his plan all along? One day, when the timing was right, and some other girl came onto the scene and my income generation diminished, he'd punish me for those lessening returns by removing my freedom again?

For no longer being The Favourite.

This was all the harder to cope with. I was *meant* to die on the inside long before I physically ceased to exist.

Like Daisy, one way or another, Mr J. ensured his girls were left with a *permanent* reminder of their servitude to him. Permanent until the day they *physically* died. He didn't care if they died on the inside way before then.

He didn't care at all about me. He would not reward me with freedom.

And Mr J.'s arrogant words once snobbishly spoken to me, resounded in my head. "To the outside world I am seen as an important, influential man who owns a number of multi-million dollar business enterprises, including the prestigious Models & Actors Management Agency, where, ironically, I am well-known for fiercely protecting the girls and women from perversive sexual exploitation..."

Followed by words Daisy had once told me, "One of the starlet's, a Russian girl, who's in her thirties and can speak English now, but arrived when she was fifteen and didn't speak a word, she told us one of the original starlets was Mr J.'s own step-daughter who had supposedly been snatched off the streets, before she was sent to a sex-house for not making him enough money."

That Russian girl was right. Daisy and the non-believing starlets wrong.

Mr J. had arranged for his own step-daughter to become one of his first ever starlet's, I somehow knew this too now. She made money him and his wife (her mother) lived on, his wife never knowing part of the wealth they were gaining came from the very industry she fiercely campaign against, never knowing her own husband had secretly forced her daughter to work as a starlet that started their wealth as one of his first ever victims.

I think I might have replaced her as the new special-level favourite when I came onto the black-market for original sale. The only starlet, the Russian girl, remaining in service that remembered his step-daughter had also fallen out of favour like the step-daughter, like herself, and now me.

I needed to tell Philip Dweitt this piece of news. It might help him, once he's lost contact with me - I'd never get a chance to write again once I was 'retired' from the porn industry. I knew that with absolute certainty now. I was as good as disappeared and lost to Philip Dweitt the moment the event came to a close.

Retiring didn't mean mine or the others stop becoming a sex worker; it simply translated into becoming a piece of meat, no longer a 'glamour-puss' on screen. Someone Mr J. still made pocket money out of, but couldn't care less about. When she died, he'd just get another one.

Maybe Philip Dweitt could discover what happened to his step-daughter - if he could just work out what Mr J's real name might be. Surely not too many millionaire business men who run modelling agencies - especially M.A.M.A!

But I had no doubt now what *my* fate was: I was unlikely to survive living to reach my thirty-fifth birthday.

Maybe not even as old as that.

I was to become a victim of the lifestyle I had supposedly chosen, for anyone who bothered to find out what had happened to a once famous mega starlet who retired from her live action gig at the tender young age of twenty-eight after the outrage which ended her popularity and career.

I hastily wrote as much as I could, ignoring the pain and cramping in my hand when it flared in unswerving protest. I hadn't quite finished the five double-sided pages, when my favourite Sebastian appeared behind me. I'd been concentrating so much on writing I hadn't heard him enter the bedroom.

"Amberee, Miss. Did you hear me? I said it's time to have your afternoon nap." He took the pen from my hand.

I was instantly terrified.

I couldn't move.

He could read what I had written.

I expected at any moment for him to seize the forbidden correspondence and urgently shout for Mr B. working downstairs to come deal with me. Or roughly seize me.

What I wasn't expecting, was for the Sebastian to take the pages, insert them into the one envelope already addressed to Peter Dwyer. And then gather the rest of the day's mail, then bark annoyed, "Stop dilly dallying, Amberee. Get to bed this instant."

And he slapped me across the face; it made a lot of noise, but didn't hurt in the slightest.

Still trying to cover my confusion, and not give either of us away, I obeyed him. My mind speeding with thoughts.

The Sebastian bundled the mail in an elastic band, my letter being third from the top, and then left the bedroom.

How long had the Sebastian known I was sending secret messages to Philip Dweitt?

And more importantly, why hadn't he told the bosses anything? And, *why* had he staged punishing me for being too slow to obey him for the cameras benefit in case someone was watching?

Was he as mindful of them always watching as I was? If so, why?

CHAPTER 29

I hated every day of filming, *Absexlution*. Everything from being a church priestess wearing slutty, see-through robes while wearing no underwear as I gave sermons, to clerically 'forgiving' men of their sins when they came to purge their guilt, by sucking their cocks in the confessional; to my 'secret baptismal' late night outdoor ceremonies, where my arms and feet are ritualistically tied to stakes in the earth by the thirteen men forming a circle around the pentagram my naked body is lying spread-eagled on, and their each having to take turn at fucking my 'holy body' as a sign of their taking on and committing to their new faith.

Never had I found it so hard to fake being in love with what I was required to do.

I was completely dead inside myself now (and merely waiting to become as dead on the outside too), and my performances reflected that. I was forced to re-shoot many of my scenes, so they could try to cutting them into one.

I'd finally gotten my wish to lose my acting talent. But it was all too late.

Every single moment, I knew, was not only blatantly and horribly blasphemous, but intentionally designed to cause people to hate me, with strong passion. Each of the male porn stars wore hoods and masks while they fucked me. Their identities were being kept hidden, so none of the fall-out damaged *their* reputations or careers. They all knew this flick was a career killer as much as I knew it.

My captors deduced I had made the connection too; but they didn't care. I was soon to no longer be a problem for them. So what if my last fuck-flick I gave a terrible performance. The media would speculate. No one would be able to find me, to hear or learn my side of the story.

This filming was all supposedly Amberee's sick, perverted idea, naturally, according to their long term marketing plans; that the cocks hadn't wanted any part of, so I had got cocks by agreeing to let them keep their anonymity, to keep them safe and able to continue in the industry. Fake names in the credits.

Filming took the full four months, rather than couple of weeks, even though the script was short and fleshed out with plenty of the typical raunchy close-ups to give viewers the action they bought the movies to see. My performance was that miserable. As lifeless as I was.

I had one day and night off, and then the next day I was to star in my retirement blow job event. I had never been more scared - not even in The Dungeon. It was the worst birthday present imaginable. But, even the marathon blow job to so many men was sure to end up more pleasant than what was in store for me once the event was finished.

This was my last night ever in Starlet House. I dreaded every tick of the clock taking me closer and closer to my public demise.

Mr B. had told me, with a wickedness and spite to his words, what I had already guessed: after the marathon blow job event, I was being permanently transferred to a Sexhouse - the very Sexhouse I had been taken to once previously. For extra condemnation, required to work in the very room the girl I once was forced to watch worked. "She died a couple of years ago, but the girl who took over from her died last week, and we're missing out on a lot of pocket money keeping the room waiting for you."

I couldn't even cry any more tears over the new hell I was about to enter. And I slept restlessly, hardly getting any more than about an hour all up.

I was woken at eight a.m., given a large breakfast which I was forced to eat to keep my energy levels high so I got through the next twenty four hours; was sent to the basement recording studio, where

I had my hair and makeup done for me, and then given a bra and panty set, and a sheer robe; and was then bundled into the car, and driven to an auditorium a few suburbs over, so the marathon could begin at precisely midday. I wasn't anxious; simply numb and dead.

Not one person had even said, "Happy Birthday, starlet." I wasn't even worthy of being wished a good day - not that this birthday was going to ever be one. I was now that level of meaningless. To them, for now. Soon to the entire world.

They wouldn't even wind-down the window so I could enjoy the mild breeze on my face (one last moment of life's free pleasures). My captors didn't want me ruining my hair and makeup.

Normally I would have been dreading having to give so many men a blow job, but all I dreaded was the moment the event ended. When my new diminished life began. My real nightmare began.

What lower life form was there than slut?

Diseased and meaningless.

In need of discarding and secret burying, or unattended funeral.

The event was larger than I imagined the attendance level might be. Much larger. Well graced. The crowd outside the auditorium was mightier than the movie premiere I had been too, what, four or five years earlier. And that had been packed. Paparazzi and the media were in higher presence too. But this would be the last time they ever gave a damn about me.

The walk from the street towards the auditorium was the longest I'd ever seen. They couldn't have chosen a more dangerous, exposed facility. I was too dead internally to fake waving at or even smiling to people. Just lead me to my death.

I had people shouting and cheering as I headed towards the auditorium, in my bare minimum of clothing, supporting me.

I had far more booing and insults being thrown at me, too. Everywhere along the left hand side of the 'runway' were signs condemning me bobbing madly in the air.

If those people hated me now, I could only envision how much they'd hate me when the last fuck flick actually was released in a few weeks time - I was positive the porn industry had been informed about the basic storyline of what the last fuck flick entails (though, they wouldn't have been given this fact directly by Starlet Headquarters), which had sparked further controversy requiring social commentary, which is why so many people who were members of religious groups were in attendance today to protest my vulgar personality and existence.

I wasn't important to Mr J. any more, I had barely any favour left; so I didn't have four Sebastian's accompanying me, I only had the one.

And Mr B.

But he wasn't pretending to act as my boyfriend this time round.

And again, reporters were yelling questions at me, "Amberee, how did you come up with this idea?" and "How many do you think you'll be able to suck?"

Mr B. didn't even try making me answer the questions.

I had tears running down my face, which no one noticed.

The supportive crowd were yelling, "Amberee! Amberee! Marry me … fuck me … suck my cock, Amberee!"

And the haters were yelling even louder, "Slut … whore … devil-girl…"

My solitary Sebastian said with an urgency to his voice, "Just keep going until you both get inside." and then left me and Mr B. to rush towards a group of haters who had jumped the barriers intent on attacking me, as the first egg splattered on my back.

"Quick, this is turning to shit," Mr B. said. "Hurry, get inside."

I started walking at a very fast pace, as fast as my super-high heels allowed me, as tomatoes, faeces and goodness knows what else were being hurled in my direction. Some of it landing and splattering on the business-suited Mr B.

The supporters were protesting what the haters were doing; the haters were yelling even nastier things about me, and my loose morals. Fights were starting to break as the two opposing teams went into battle. As I drew nearer the doors for the auditorium, I came to a sudden stop, despite Mr B. at first attempting to push me to keep moving. Until he, too, must have seen what I already had, to cease trying to push me forward and stand there unmoving half behind me.

A single figure, a woman, perhaps in her forties was pointing a gun at me.

"Evil, slutty whores like yourself don't deserve to live." She said, staring at me eye to eye across the distance (roughly the width of a standard house) between us.

And she fired her gun.

No drama. No further pre-warning.

She fired. Not once … or twice … but three … four … five … six times.

Each time after the first two shots, pain ripped through my body somewhere around my chest.

The noise of the crowd had gone even louder. People were screaming. Some started running in sideway directions. Fleeing the scene. Scared this was a commonplace massacre rather than the assassination attempt by a single religious protester.

Absently, I looked towards my stomach and took my hand away from my body, my mind was trying to catch up to what everyone else present already knew, and saw the blood confirming I'd been hit; I was returning my shocked gaze to regain eye contact with the woman as the thought, "But the movie hasn't even been released yet, why are you doing this?" looped in my mind on continuous repeat. The woman left the impression in me that she was mentally-crazed; she was laughing maliciously, victoriously. She dropped the spent handgun onto the ground and pulled another from the bag hanging over her shoulder.

She took forever.

I didn't even think to try running.

The thought never occurred to me.

I kept watching what she was doing - mesmerised, captivated by her actions, not afraid. Just in disbelief.

She held it pointing directly at me and fired some more.

One bullet struck me in the side of my neck.

Blood was staining my outfit.

I had fallen.

Police were already arriving from different directions. I saw the red and blue flashing lights, heard the wailing of their many sirens, the urgent screeching of tires coming to a stop. Feet still running, fleeing. And coming.

Then Sebastian, my nicest Sebastian, real name Adrian, was at my side, risking being shot himself, pressing the shirt he ripped off his muscled and surprisingly hulking body against the wound at my neck, even as another bullet resounded amongst the yelling and screaming and ploughed into the flesh on my arm.

He lifted my head off the hard ground, to pillow me on his thick legs; my head tilted sideways, he grappled to keep pressure on my wound and I saw Mr B. lying on the ground, not moving.

I don't think he was breathing.

Sebastian said something, pressing against my neck more firmly, but I didn't hear what he said - that must have been when I slipped out of consciousness.

The blackness engulfed me very quickly.

I have vague, hazy recollections of hearing a man's voice say, as though from far, far away, and getting even further, "Stay with me, Miss Entacott. Don't die on us now, not when we're this close to…" as I was held in Sebastian's arms.

Later of bright lights overhead and people wearing face masks, talking to each other, beeps were sounding and then someone putting a black mask over my nose; and hearing lots and lots of machines bleeping.

Some rhythmically, others sounding sudden warning alarms, sometimes sounding urgent as it got louder and louder.

And then a woman, a nurse, not facing towards me, holding onto my wrist as she was watching the little watch she held in her other hand, and then dropping my hand carefully onto the bed again, unaware I had woken to see her doing that.

Eventually I realised I was in hospital, I'm not sure the exact point.

That I had had surgery. I had doctors and nurses talking to me, still far, far away, me not really connecting to their words, telling me I needed to have more. I'd been too unstable to remove all the bullets the first time, I had come close to dying multiple times on their operating table; but each time they had successfully been able to revive me, but I wasn't 'out of the woods' yet. There's still the one near my heart which was extremely dangerous to leave in and remove, but it needs to come out. Although currently well lodged and stable, if it moved of its own accord, I'd die before they could get me back into the operating theatre. Don't worry, they'll have me back in surgery as soon as they've stabilised me sufficiently.

My body was screaming in pain at even the slightest movement.

Hot, searing pain.

Like someone was poking me with a branding iron; or I'd placed my chest and back on an ironing board and had someone steam ironing me. But, I was hooked to a machine (actually, I was tethered to many machines, some feeding into the intravenous fluids tubing, others monitoring various bodily reactions clamped or adhered to various body parts) auto-administering morphine directly into my veins at regular intervals. Heart beat bleeping rhythmically. Blood pressure compression squeezing my lower legs infrequently. The pain relief why I had to leave the oxygen feeding into me, via my nostrils on, not try taking it off.

The tears which rolled down my cheeks though, they weren't from the pain.

They were from the frustration: couldn't *anything* go right in my life?

Why was life being so cruel towards me, forcing me to still be alive? Why couldn't I have *not* survived my injuries?

At least then I' be dead.

I'd not have the ever-looming threat of being sent to a D-level Sexhouse once I eventually recovered.

𝒞HAPTER 30

Unfortunately, my bad luck kept continuing.

I survived the surgery which removed the bullet lodged close to my heart, too. That miracle surgery they were worried I wouldn't survive, due to the terribly poor odds. Doctors were pleased I was out of immediate danger now; was going to attain *full* recovery status. I was told, multiple times, "You're one very *lucky* young woman."

I couldn't even laugh with derision.

I couldn't laugh or talk, period.

Too much pain to even attempt it.

Especially from the fragility of the wound in my neck.

Eventually, I was transferred from the Intensive Care ward after a week to a general ward for the remainder of my recuperation. I had no idea how much time had passed. My pain likely to be great for some time, the bullets which had broken many of my ribs meant to turn even a fraction sent searing pain throughout my whole torso. I was still weak from the heavy blood loss, but they assured me my strength would 'return in no time'.

My favourite Sebastian followed my bed as the Orderly wheeled me through the hospital. He looked like he hadn't left my side since I'd arrived, and had only been sleeping in waiting room chairs. He wore a worried expression, but when he noticed I was looking at him, he gave me a reassuring smile.

Something about his easy smile didn't add up to what Mr J. had in store for me. But I didn't get a chance to ask him. Was he relieved and merely happy I had lived? Or was something more going on I wasn't privy to? As much as I liked this Sebastian, I blamed him for saving my life. He'd have been kinder letting me be reunited with my Mum.

Once the ward staff had done their thing in accepting me as their patient, and done the first round of obs, which Sebastian was told he had to wait outside, one of the nurses, a skinny, mean-looking woman, who looked like she'd had a very tough life, asked, "Would you like to sit for a while?"

I shook my head millimetres in both directions, gingerly. Croaked with a dry and bruised throat. "No."

But she came and lifted the bed's backrest to close to ninety degree angle anyway. She only returned the backrest to horizontal position again when all the monitor alarms screamed all their warnings in clashing chorus. I was in too much agony, waiting for the next dose of morphine to kick in, unable to speak when another nurse rushed in and asked, "What happened?" and the first nurse replied dismissively, "The patient requested to sit up, so I was helping her."

"No, no," the second nurse scolded, "She's to remain lying flat for at least the next twenty-four hours. *Then* we can start trying to ambulate her. But only in very small increments - the Physio will oversee that. It'll be at least a week before we can have her sitting at more than a forty-five degree angle. We need careful handling, especially the wound on her neck, and one in her chest."

That wasn't the only time this nurse deliberately caused me further pain.

I soon learned she was of the same faith as the woman who had shot me, who, by the way, had dropped her weapon the moment she had been ordered to by police and had not resisted arrest, asking repeatedly, "Did I kill the slut?", and when asked by the reporters why she had shot me while being escorted away, had replied, "*Someone* had to stop the slut from her evil ways."

The religious nurse believed it her right, her duty, to punish me for my slutty ways too - I needed a moral lesson forcibly taught to me by the people of their faith. Every time this nurse came into take my blood pressure readings, once done she also 'Chinese-burned' my arms (I remembered this is what it had been called - it's what Chad Ryleland and his bully brothers did to kids at school). This was achieved from grabbing my arm with both hands and then twisting the skin in opposite directions - like trying to wring a towel dry. Only, I imagine she was attempting to split my skin open. Having bullet holes wasn't enough for her.

While she did that, she whispered nasty things into my ear.

Or she jabbed her little bandage scissors into one of my wounds, before slipping them into the pocket of her uniform apron, no one knowing what she'd done. Including my fragile neck wound.

Anyone looking into the room might reasonably assume she was taking good care of me. But the woman took every opportunity she could - she had self-appointed herself to being my only carer - to call me every name she could think of, and to cause me additional pain and discomfort to what I was already experiencing. I'm positive she reduced the flow of pain medication to ensure I suffered.

Is it any wonder I didn't like people anymore? Didn't even want to know anyone?

Men had stolen my life away from me, forced me to have sex with other men so they could selfishly get money; marketed me to the general public so they whole-heartedly embraced the belief I was a cheap slut who enjoyed an 'immoral' way of life; so other men desired sexually violating my body; so church-goers, dedicated to their faith, tried - and succeeded - in inflicting me with torturous physical pain. And sat in moral judgement of me. Tried and punished me via their vigilante-justice.

The world I lived in was - is - a horrible one. The number of decent people to horrible people who had no qualms in hurting me in whatever form they could, so they got what they wanted was approximately, in ratio, zero to all.

I could count on my one hand the people who looked after me: my deceased Mum, Philip Dweitt, and, to a lesser degree, my favourite Sebastian, Adrian. Three people in all of the thousands of people I had met in my life.

Three!

Mrs Ryleland and the Mum's group had failed me and Mum, with their pressuring her to go against her wishes to not date anyone. For not following up on where Murk was taking me to.

The police officers and media who never once asked me to recount to them the information I knew about the night Mum died. I could have told them about Murk's lies and the phone he sent and received text messages on. His phones could have been located. Evidence to prosecute retrieved.

The staff who worked on those porn film sets, who were aware with certainty I was being held and worked in the industry against my will, who did nothing, said nothing to make the statement: what they're doing to her is wrong. Because, it's how they made their living, so who were they to upset the apple-cart as my Mum's old expression went.

Even the damn book I had purchased to help me recover from my session in The Dungeon failed me - for only covering how to move on *after* a traumatic event. The author assumed the trauma and situation was ended - it failed to address what to do if you were still in an abusive situation and couldn't escape or 'just leave' that as advised. That's the help I'd wanted to know since the day I found myself in my situation.

Adrian-Sebastian, the paramedics, doctors and medical staff that had saved my life. When they should have let me die from my injuries.

Three people out of thousands who might have helped me if they hadn't chosen to overlook the voice, pain and concerns of a young child through to womanhood. And so many with a direct hand at keeping me in captivity. So ... make that *two and a half* people: Adrian Sebastian was both protector and jailer; he didn't deserve a full point value, despite having shown me some decency. Okay, make that *two and three quarters* then, I did have a soft-spot for him being a fellow-Aussie; this was the fairest amount - he'd never manhandled me like so many others. I liked his accent.

Settled then: *two and three quarter* people hadn't failed me.

Was my life really this meaningless? Me, that unlovable? Uncareable about. Whatever had I done to deserve this level of disregard? Yes, I had been mean at school calling the other class the dum-dum group.

But I had been a clueless child. And my life's punishment way beyond the level deserved of such a "crime".

Sebastian worked out what the nurse was doing after four days of her doing this uninterrupted when he came in to ask me if I wanted or needed anything before he stepped out for fifteen minutes. He was furious and in seconds had the woman pinned against the wall, and I could hear she was struggling to breath. "Do anything like this to Miss Entacott again, and you'll regret your action. I'm reporting you, you nasty, religious bitch. Get out of this room and don't let me catch you in here again!"

Sebastian grabbed a seat and dragged it toward the edge of my bed, sat and picked up one of my hands. "Amber, there's some things you need updating on—"

But whatever they were, I didn't get to learn them. Murk entered the two bedroom ward I was occupying on my own like a private suite.

Sebastian reluctantly got up, and left the room. Murk came and kissed me on the lips like a lover he was still hot for.

"The uncles all send you their love, and wish you a speedy recovery," he said, giving me another kiss on the lips. Then, he looked awkward and added, "Well, they would, if they weren't all currently under arrest to know what has happened to you."

Murk must have seen I didn't know what he was talking about. And he sighed heavily, and grabbed a remote for the ceiling mounted television. "Only now found out myself as I travelled here. You're gonna find out sooner or later, sweet-puss."

The television sprang to life, and Murk flicked through the channels. I didn't have to wait long for the evening news report to start.

First, the channel covered the information Murk wanted me to know about.

While he was on a flight here to do a photo shoot of Candee for XXXX Hotstuff Mag4Men, the Queensland property Uncle Spud owned had been raided by police. All seven uncles were at home at the time of the surprise raid. And a naked six year old girl was discovered hiding in the buried wooden box beyond the trees. I shivered as I remembered having to hide in that box. It was like you were in a coffin, buried. Just hearing mention of it brought me back to having to hide in there. All seven uncles were arrested and taken in for questioning, despite Uncle Jack coming forward and claiming the other men knew nothing about him having the little girl right under their noses on the compound.

But the next part of the coverage was a surprise to even Murk.

Two days later (Australia time, the next day American time), Police had gone to collect Daisy Mecklestein, so she could identify which of the men she had been forced to sleep with during her captivity. Unfortunately, she was shot in the forehead by a sniper as they arrived at the police station and was killed instantly, no longer able to testify in court about this suspected paedophile ring.

Poor Daisy.

Mr J. hadn't trusted she wouldn't speak, and had had time to act to ensure it.

I hoped she finally had peace now.

The peace I desperately craved.

And when the news reporter said that, "In the latest development of the case, police have found a secret hiding spot and retrieved professional cameras, a laptop computer and internet plug-in device, which allegedly establishes all the men living on the compound were involved, not just the convicted paedophile claiming the others had no knowledge."

Murk had gone very white all of a sudden.

"Well, Amber, sweet-puss," he said, raising the remote intending to switch off the television. "I think it's time for me to go and make myself scarce - go underground until I can get a new identity."

But before he could leave, two police officers entered the room.

Murk lost his smile.

He understood what was going to happen to him, as I did, before one officer spoke, "Murk Walters, we're placing you under arrest for the kidnap and sexual abuse and exploitation of minors."

They turned and pinned him against the wall in front of me, and secured handcuffs first to one wrist then the other behind his back. Murk looked resigned to spending a stint in jail as they patted him down checking for concealed weaponry.

"Bye, Amber, starlet-babes," Murk said, as the officers led him towards the door. "Hope you get well soon, sweetums."

One of the officers told me someone would return to talk to me at more convenient time for me and handed me the television's remote.

I was about to attempt slowly raising my arm to turn it off myself, but the news coverage was continuing, and then abruptly switched to 'Breaking News', and on camera, the news channel was capturing Murk being escorted under arrest from the hospital entrance towards the awaiting police vehicle.

Reporters rushed forward. Camera's flashbulbs momentarily lit Murk and all of the people swamped around him. Hands with phones or microphones were pointed at him, trying to get as close as they could, so they could capture every word he said. And they fired questions at him, all at once. An irritated Murk turned his head from left to right to get them out of his face, and snapped at questions he took offence to.

He intended sticking to his lies. It's what he did best - even better than his porn photography, which he had now earned a reputation for.

"Mr Walters, is it true the property you normally live at was raided by the Australian police, and a naked and traumatised six year old was discovered hiding in a wooden grave not far from where you parked your motorhome?"

I thought it was stupid asking a question they already knew the answer to.

"Yes," Murk grunted.

"And you still claim you had absolutely no knowledge —"

"I had no fucking idea the people I thought of as best buddies, were keeping that little girl prisoner, and secretly doing to her the disgusting and depraved acts you've been saying in your news reports these last few days. I'm as shocked as you are!"

"Mr Walters, so are you telling us the allegations you were involved in the little girl's abduction three months ago are false, and you never partook in being one of the 'uncles' who treated her as a prize?"

"Of course they're fucking false!" Murk shouted, shoving his chest into the blonde reporter in front of him, as the police officers were asking her to step from being in the way and hastened to renewed their grip on him. They were getting closer to the police vehicle, but the reporters were impeding a fast escape.

"What about your step daughter, Mr Walters? Now quite the famous porn star. Do you still think the public should buy your story Amberee was a girl called Amber Ebony, and not Amber Entacott, who you became official step father of, and who no one has seen or heard from since you uprooted her from the home she had been raised in, presumably to go and live on the same farm not long ago raided."

"Yes, they are two separate people!"

"There's renewed speculation Amberee might be a sex trafficked young woman being held against her will, not the promiscuous nymphomaniac she claimed to be. That her situation may well be identical to the little girl they found. If you have no direct family relationship to Amberee as you claim, then why is it you have visited her in hospital?"

"I've known Amberee for a few years now. I was the photographer on her XXXX Hotstuff Mag4Men shoot."

They had reached the police car now. An officer was opening the rear door.

"Did you sex traffic your own fourteen year old step daughter, Mr Walters? Did you sell her —?"

"You people are fucking sick in the head!" And with that he sat on the seat, swung his legs in and the officer closed the door.

"Okay, that's enough," one of the officers said, and he opened the front passenger seat, as his partner moved around towards the driver's side. The engine started, the lights but no sirens were turned on, and the police vehicle drove off.

With no desire to watch any more lies, I lifted my wrist and successfully switched the television off without causing myself any further physical pain.

I had no delusions I'd ever be able to testify myself in court for the case, which is what the returning police officers would request of me.

But I was comforted with the knowledge Philip Dweitt might be able to get the documents I had handwritten submitted as evidence against them - I needed to somehow get word to Philip to use the letters I have sent him these past three or more years, to release them into the public, regardless of me still being held prisoner. Let Mr J. send an assassin to shoot me dead when I least expected it like he'd ordered for Daisy. Maybe I was meant to learn about Murk and the uncle's arrest before I was permitted by the universe to die.

By the time the police returned to interview me, my gut feeling was telling me I'd have already disappeared from the hospital, and no one knowledgeable about who had taken me or where I had been taken to. And unknown to police, I'd already be in re-service making Mr J. money over at the Sexhouse, where mistreatment and physical abuse were already being re-inflicted on me.

Personally, I was surprised I hadn't already been relocated.

The only reason I wasn't being interviewed immediately, from the sounds of it, was from me being still in too much pain and heavily sedated for my word to reliably be held up in court. The police were prepared to wait until such time as I came off the addictive meds and able to have a conversation with me so it wouldn't end up getting thrown out by the rules governing the justice system, which seemed to favour the guilty, especially when they had money. Like Murk and I had once had to do, the police were now needing patience so they could gain the solid, reliable evidence to bring about prosecutions. Hopefully Mr J. decided it would be less hassle for all involved if he just had me killed instead.

But why then weren't other police officers guarding my door? Keeping me safe and protected from further harm. Or, maybe I was but didn't know it; perhaps they were outside in the hall?

One of the things about being in so much pain, and heavily medicated to keep it under control meant I slept a lot. As in, close to twenty-four hours a day, with hourly disruptions as doctors and nurses came in to do their work. So I stopped worrying about what would happen next and took advantage of getting the rest I needed now.

And I woke a few times to find Sebastian sitting beside my bed.

When he saw I had woken on this one occasion, he had put the writing pad and pen he'd been using into my bedside drawer, and had closed it and was pulling his seat closer to my bed, I think to have the discussion with me he had been trying to have for several days now, when the bitch nurse poked her head into the room ruining our privacy when she told him, "Mr Titsson, the doctor wants to have a word to you."

With a look of frustration, he rose from his chair again.

"Oh, no," he said firmly to her. "Out! You're not to enter this room without me being here, unless it's an emergency, remember?"

I had progressed to sitting at a forty-five degree angle at this stage, and was currently in this half-sitting, half-lying position supported by a mass of pillows. The wound in my neck was still fragilely holding together, so my head was kept still as possible. On 'auto-pilot' I made the mental note: my favourite captors name was Adrian Titsson. I now had his surname.

But would I dob him into the police via my manuscript notes so directly? I hadn't decided.

A young man, about the same age as me, took advantage of my room not being guarded by my Adrian-Sebastian - which I realised for the first time, was the only Sebastian on guard duty. Mr J. really had abandoned me from receiving star attention, hadn't he?

They had their tracker to know I couldn't make a run for it (not that I was in any way fit to doing that); so I guessed they only needed to keep a Sebastian close by, making sure I didn't try to alert anyone of my being a prisoner status.

And I was finally alone with a person I could possibly reach out to.

With the privacy to do so!

After all this time, and patience. Who'd have thought the perfect moment would finally have come?

$\mathscr{C}$HAPTER 31

"Oh, wow, it's really you," he said. I could tell he was Australian at once by the strength of his accent.

"Who are you?" I asked. He wasn't hospital staff I deduced over the way he had snuck into the room, kept glancing at the door, and was wearing a crushed shirt and pair of jeans and no identification badge.

"My name's Chad Ryleland. I entered the competition." He was a bit of a mumbler.

"Competition?"

"Yeah, you know. Your blow job marathon." It sounded strange hearing the accent again. But somewhere in my memory, his name stirred. I knew I had heard it before, but with all the drugs they had given me, my brain was slower than usual and I couldn't quite place it.

"Oh, right. Do I know you?"

"Is your real name Amber Entacott?"

Forgetting about how quick movements instantly caused me pain, I hastily lifted a finger to my mouth and shh'ed him. "I'm not allowed to ever use my real name. I have to go by my porn name only; please, don't tell anyone, you'll get me into a lot of trouble."

And still his name was close to coming to mind, but was stubbornly not revealing how and where I heard it before.

"Oh, right," Chad nodded his head and smirked widely at me. "You're under contract to only go by your porn name, aren't you?"

It was so much easier to simply play along with his mis-assumption than to try to explain the truth - which was forbidden anyway. I needed to test the waters carefully before I trusted him with my secret. But test quickly. I didn't have much time left.

Chad punched the air victoriously. "I *knew* it was you."

Instantly, I was mentally transported to a moment eighteen years previously, and the colour vision of a young dark haired boy of age ten, encouraging his older brother to steal fish fingers from me played like a micro-movie within my mind.

"You were the first live action show me and me brothers and mates ever whacked off to. And we said all along you looked like the Amber we went to school with. We took a screenshot of your face off the screen and all, and looked through Mum's photo album, and we all agreed we reckoned it really was you, not our imagination tricking us or somethin'. I told Micky, if only your step dad hadn't taken you away, it would've been us who got to root you and helped you realise you wanted to fuck guys for a livin'. Man, we were seriously ripped off by him takin' you away."

As great and all as it was that *Chad* was happy to 'catch up' with the girl who once was his school mate, his talkativeness was ruining my chance to try to get the help I needed. No wonder it had taken me a bit to recognise his name; when he had mumbled I had thought he said Chad *Rydeland*. It hadn't sounded right. But I knew exactly who he was now.

"Chad—"

"Like I said, I entered the competition and was finally gonna get a real blow job from ya. Boy was I pissed when they told us you'd been shot by a psycho religious nut. I wasn't the only one. We all felt like we were jipped."

"Chad—"

"Hey, Amberee" Chad said, turning to check the room door was still closed behind him. "Before your body guard protector guy comes back and gets me tossed outta the hospital, do you reckon you could suck my cock, now? And let me get a picture of you doing it, so I can show the guys back home?"

He made his request coincidentally as I quietly pleaded, "Chad, please, help me. Please, Chad. Before they come back."

So you can imagine my horror when I realised Chad had mistaken my plea for help as permission for me to give him a blow job, when he said with elation, "Okay!"

He whipped two slim phones from his jeans pocket.

"Lucky I still carry my Australian phone one wiv me too," He said, rushing over the window and set one camera to record video, and hastened to my bedside again, unzipped his jeans, and had a fully hard cock in one hand and the second phone in the other.

Another memory instantly played before my mind. I had seen this cock once before too. Only, it was merely a little dick on a little ten year old kid when I had seen it the first time. This kid had grown to have a member I was sure he might well be satisfied with - not quite in the league of what my Pete's had, he'd have had his application rejected if he had ever auditioned as a Pete, but certainly girthed enough to satisfy the experienced and frighten away the prudish at home in Australia.

I shook my head trying to let him know this wasn't what I meant; instantly rewarding myself with increased pain for the effort. So I re-tried again, pleading for him to listen to what I was saying (and why I was saying it), "Please, Chad, I desperately need your help. Quick, we don't have much time; my body guard will return any moment."

"Oh, right," Chad said nodding at me. "You're hooked up to all those machines. And the side rails of the bed are up."

He stepped forward and immediately found the release bar and lowered the side rail. "Here, let me lean you sideways, so your mouth's at the right height."

Before I could say anything, and not giving a damn moving me sent pain ripping through my body, so much so I came close to passing out again, he had put his second camera on the bed, grabbed me with both hands around my neck, leant me sideways, and mistook my opened mouth as me letting him know I was ready for him to shove his cock in, and he should quickly start taking the pictures he'd come for, so he could get the evidence he needed to reach legend status with his mates at home.

The stitches in my neck were straining; I wasn't sure if it was my imagination or not, but I thought I heard and sensed a small pop within.

Chad took quite a few pictures; making sure my agony-filled face and me hooked up to hospital machinery was fully captured along with his dick in my mouth, completely oblivious to my pain, discomfort and inability to move. Next he pulled his cock out, leant his head on the pillow next to mine, stuck his tongue towards mine and took several more shots so both our faces were in the frame at the same time. He was ensuring none of his mates could argue it wasn't Amberee's mouth wrapped around his dick, but some other starlet he'd shelled a few bucks on, to fake make it look like the real deal.

He re-pocketed his phone camera most likely to ensure he got carted off with his evidence if thrown out any second now, and then said, "Hey, seeing I'm still here in your room, and you're always wantin' it, can you give me a blow job for real. I feel kinda ripped off you got popped before you got to do me in your marathon record, especially after coming all the way over here and all." He didn't wait for an answer. He simply stood back up, dropped his dacks some more so I could try to take in his balls as well, and then started thrusting in and out, to help me.

I couldn't do anything except let his cock slide in and out.

With tears splashing onto my pillows, my only possible saviour alone in my company for the first time in eighteen years, fully immersed in only having me get him off, made me realise how I was going to keep having to suck men's dicks, swallow their cum, let them finger me, and fuck my fanny and arse - nothing was off limits to these sexually hungry men - for the rest of my life, something I had always known but never fully appreciated the magnitude to my problem until this very moment as my former friend was having the time of his life.

As Chad did all the work sliding his cock in and out of my mouth, still oblivious to anything except getting what he had come for, an excerpt from the recovering from trauma book I had once bought came to mind. *The power lies within you; you need to find the courage to not see yourself as the victim, to reclaim the power which is always inside you waiting discovery.*

I saw plainly the final detail clearest I had ever seen before: there was no off the mouse wheel Mr J. had set for me. Same as Daisy had never got one despite her release.

The monitors started beeping with my state of distress, and Chad groaned out his mounting pleasure, "I'm nearly there ... I'll cum in a second ... almost ..." and squirted his fluid into my mouth as the first nurse came rushing in.

Oh, great. It was the highly religious one who had Chinese burned my arm the previous day and whispered nastily in my ear God intended to cause me to suffer for my evil, evil ways, first on earth, then in hell.

"You ... slutty little ... good for nothing ... whore!" Her eyes were wide with fury.

Of course *she* had to witness me 'at it' again; and jump straight to a wrong conclusion I had initiated the lurid act.

But to my instant relief, Sebastian also burst into the room, and in seconds, had Chad in a headlock and was choking him, limped penis still exposed to everyone who saw, as Sebastian, my secret protector, dragged the beaming and shuffling in the jeans at his ankles jerk out the door.

If it wasn't so serious, I'd have laughed. If I could.

That left me at the mercy of the religious-bitch. Only, this time, I was ready for her opportunist taunt.

While she muttered words I wasn't even listening to in my ear, and was once again twisting the flesh on my arm in two different directions, practically splitting the skin apart, I miraculously found the strength inside me I'd never found before; to no longer see myself as a victim and was determined to reclaim my life, so was able to calmly not feel the pain, taste the cum or be wounded by her insults.

I took an opportunity of my own; I was taking decisive action, not reacting to life's circumstance as the book advocated. An opportunity I might never get a second chance of gaining, because this was the other finer little detail had I known but been too scared to take decisive action on for seven years: I had to try to rescue myself; it's what I'd been biding my time and quietly working towards (but really only hoping to) gain now also for seven years; though, I realised now my opportunity was not for me to run like I had once, long ago secretly hoped for all that time.

I had to go for a brave, bold move.

I had the perfectly clear, renewed echo of my Mum's beautiful infectious laughter dancing merrily in my head to keep me focused on what I needed to do. The laughter, I dearly missed, gave me strength. I aimed to return to being Amber Entacott, and with the encouragement of my Mum's long ago lost love, dammit, I was going to succeed.

I slipped my other hand into the nastiest bitch-nurse's uniform front pocket, and my fingers found and securely retrieved the tiny scissors she used for cutting dressing tape, and I slipped those little scissors under my hospital blankets, and under my leg. And my hand was returned above the covers before she jumped straight, as my protector Sebastian entered barking threateningly at the instantly fearful skinny cowardice retch.

"OUT, BITCH." Adrian Sebastian roared. I had never heard him as dangerous as he sounded in this moment. "And if Amber tells me you say one more nasty word to her, you better be scared you'll join your fucking God in heaven faster than you can say A-fucking-men."

Sebastian gently, carefully, tenderly helped straighten me, instantly providing glorious relief from the strain in my neck wound and then he thumped the Call for Assistance button and yelled, "A doctor better fucking get in here and tend to Miss Entacott in five seconds, or heads are going to fucking roll!"

And close to instantly every doctor and nurse in the hospital (not really) was running through the door asking how they can be of assistance.

They gave me another dose of pain relier to help take the edge off my flared pain straight into the muscle in my arm. Under the watchful eye of Sebastian, they anxiously checked I was comfortable.

Only once Sebastian was satisfied all my immediate needs and wants were fully attended were dismissed, ordered to leave the room - bar the supervisor doctor until Sebastian was a hundred percent sure. "Can they do anything else for you, Amber?"

I thanked Sebastian for always looking out for me - he appeared pleasantly surprised and swelled a little larger with pride. He had an amazingly beautiful smile. Yeah, I'd leave out his last name. Not make it too easy for him to be found and charged for his part in holding me undeserved prisoner.

But, I didn't want to delay; I wanted and needed to act the soonest I could. So I pleaded, "Do you think you could get them to let me try to get about 3 or 4 hours of sleep before I'm next disturbed by their doing obs and administering meds, *please*, Sebastian? Please, can I lie here and rest without all the constant interruptions. I just want to sleep."

"Rightio, Miss. I'll stay on guard outside your door so no more little whack-offs sneak into your room. And I'll make sure the noise level doesn't cause you any disruptions. And when you wake up, you and I'll have that little chat I've been trying to have with you, alright?"

I smiled as my way of acknowledging him. I wasn't going to tell him when he next saw me, I'd no longer be alive; I didn't want anyone, not even my favourite Sebastian knowing, or he'd try to stop me. I usually became drowsy after a dose of pain meds, so I fluttered my eyes so he'd think I was becoming sleepy.

"Okay, doc, you heard the pretty lady, fuck off outta her room."

I thanked Sebastian very much. I wanted him to know, I appreciated the risks he taken to keep me safe. I thought, apart from Philip, this Sebastian, might be the only ones who'd be (genuinely) sad over my passing. But I was careful not to give him any hint as to what I was next about to do.

With the room now all to myself, first, I wrote to you, Philip, this, what will be my last set of manuscript pages, using the pen and paper and stamped envelope Sebastian had stored in the bedside draw. I can't tell you how much I had to push through the pain to sit up, reach over and get them, and pull the little table on wheels over to me so I could write what I know will be my last ever letter without crying aloud in the agony I caused myself. And then to turn off the machines, the way I had seen the nurses do it, so the alarms wouldn't cause the hospital staff and Sebastian to race in here before I was unrevivably dead.

I'm sure people are likely to assume I must hate the woman who shot me; for her having such strong beliefs in her church and god she had become so compelled to take drastic action to force me to see the error of my ways.

But I don't.

Yes, her actions have caused me pain; and I think she is a hypocrite towards the very faith she claims to live and breathe by. But I truly hold no hate for her, and hope she one day understands why her actions were more *sinful* than any she misjudged me to ever have held. How could I possibly hate the woman who rescued me from the very event I did not want to participate in; and unintentionally gave me the renewed strength to try rescue myself. I should *thank* her for being so judgemental - it spurred her into hateful action.

You see, she got two things seriously wrong: she believed she knew the truth and full story better and more than those who actually knew, valuing her own fact-less beliefs to blame and punish the victim instead of the perpetrators, but even more importantly, she believed it only possible for me to *fear* death, believed I'd desperately want to escape that, to live at all costs; and therefore she was robbing me of that personal freedom to continuing my slutty living. But she unintentionally helped me comprehend death was *my only way out.*

I am not afraid of it; I am welcoming to death if it is at my own choosing.

Because death is the only way I finally *gain* the freedom I have wanted each day for the last eighteen years.

Her shooting me dead was acceptable to me.

She failed in her quest.

But the quest isn't over for me.

Philip, I've now given you each of the significant moments of my story right up to present date. It can't be any more complete than this.

As this is my last opportunity to end my life, that's what I'm about to do.

It's time for me to *save myself* from people who do this sort of thing to other people.

The biggest lesson I'd learned in life, you see, is: no one else can.

Unfortunately, saving myself equates to a death on this occasion.

And maybe, just maybe, I will meet up with Mum again if there is indeed an afterlife; and she can chase me around the house like she used to and we can both collapse on the floor with laughter when she catches me, and she can take me on a nice trip to the beach where we can camp out in the dunes again, only this time happy and secure in the knowledge that no-one can ever hurt either of us ever again.

PART 4

POST-SCANDAL WRAP-UP

$\mathscr{C}$HAPTER 32

UNDERCOVER OFFICER, ADRIAN TITSSON

Senior Sergeant Adrian Titsson - the Australian undercover officer who as part of a secret international cooperative task-force became a Sebastian to learn and pass on as much intelligence about the criminal organisation from within, so the activities could one day be completely dismantled - heard a thud and a 'ting' of something metal hitting the polished concrete ward floor. He jumped from his chair immediately, and rushed through the door to find Amber Entacott collapsed on the floor in a growing pool of blood.

He shouted for help, thumped the Call for Emergency Assistance button on the wall, and then rolled the deathly pale Amber onto her back. While he waited for help to arrive, he implemented his training, checking to see if Amber was breathing. When he found she wasn't, he checked to see if Amber still had a pulse and immediately alternated between one-handed chest compressions and mouth-to-mouth resuscitation, while keeping pressure against her reopened neck wound, until help arrived.

But Amberee, correction, Amber Entacott, never recovered from her jugular re-splitting open. She'd lost too much blood in too short a period.

The other officers who afterwards attended the scene to take official photographs came across the letter Amber had written, and discovered the mobile phone still recording the events registered to

Chad Ryleland.

Her letter to me (Philip Dweitt), passed on to Officer Titsson said she was going into the private bathroom to slice the veins in her arms open - in other words, to commit suicide. But the video evidence later clearly proved Amber had realised her wound had reopened as she was making her way to the bathroom, and had appeared to understand something just moments before as she made her way to it and immediately attempted to abandon her plan.

Sadly, she died while trying to reach across to press the Call for Emergency Assistance button, which she couldn't quite make it to. With a look of panic on her beautiful young face, she grappled to stem the flow of bleeding with her closest hand having earlier disabled all the equipment monitoring her state of health which would have alerted the Senior Sergeant and the medical team.

The devastated Senior Sergeant broke-down and cried over none of the staff or himself having noticed her reddening dressing (later confirmed by the coroner report): Chad Ryleland had caused the stitches in Amber's to pop and her wound to re-bleed, when he had repositioned her. This had to have been made worse through her movements to write the last pages of her auto-biography and personal note and then walking to the bathroom.

On his way leaving the hospital, her last letter securely in his pocket, in an emotional outburst, the officer punched his hand through a glass door, upset and blaming himself for Amber's death - he had never gotten to tell Amber he had successfully ordered her tracker removed, and she had finally been freed from her captivity, and was now officially deemed a sex traffic survivor. The hospital later dropped the charges they initiated against the officer for malicious damage to hospital property.

Thanks to her gutsy risk sending detailed letters, and his own reports, 'Mr J.', aka John Pembarlteen was soon arrested and a small known amount of his American underground facilities and sex-houses simultaneously raided, staff arrested and operations permanently ceased trading and profiteering, though they suspected they hadn't gained details of even half of them. The coordinated police raids in Australia, Europe and America were delayed for a few days before finally being executed due to the unexpected shooting of Amber

Entacott mere minutes before each site was intended for simultaneous raiding, with the exception of Australia which went ahead as planned due to time differences.

Senior Sergeant Adrian has since been a strong voice to have Amber's manuscript pages entered as evidence in John Pembarlteen's and Murk Walters criminal trials; and during his 'employment' was able to provide his real colleagues with a detailed list of the names of the Roy's, Sebastian's, and Darren's, some who, like, the girls being held against their will, were unable to leave the employment of Mr J. under threat of losing their life (compared to those known to be participating willingly) not knowing what they had got themselves into before it was too late to change their minds.

The Senior Sergeant suggested to Mr J. personally, there was one way the organisation could end the Is Amberee a Sex Slave social debate; that being, to release Daisy Mecklestein from her sex slavery ahead of schedule. This was the only idea he ever contributed to the organisations meetings as a means of helping Daisy to escape the abuse being inflicted on her daily.

He also confirmed (although Senior Sergeant had not started working undercover at the time) that the Sebastian's had been ordered to regularly stage security lapses to entice Amberee to reveal secret motive to flee, and he'd been impressed by her intelligence to not fall for any of the set ups the Sebastian's and Roys openly still bragged about. She'd have been caught if she'd taken what, on the surface, appeared as a golden escape opportunity - they had Sebastian's lying in wait.

CHAPTER 33

CHAD RYLELAND

Chad Ryleland was quick to post the pictures Amberee giving him a blow job to his social media accounts upon release outside of the hospital. Where, at first, his mates all congratulated and wrote comments expressing their envy of him for getting what he'd come for after all; many hastily deleted their comments following Chad being arrested after he had checked in for his flight home to Australia, held in relation to his involvement in causing Amber Entacott's death, pending possible charges.

The sequence of pictures clearly showed the progression of blood becoming larger on Amber's neck dressings, and the footage showed he indeed inadvertently tore back the dressing protecting the badly damaged area.

Chad remained adamant Amberee told him she was happy to give him a blow job, despite her being in hospital. He only truly realised he'd misinterpreted the situation after being shown the video footage from the camera he'd forgotten he'd left behind when he was seized, and its accompanying clear audio.

Charges were laid against him; he is still awaiting a hearing date.

CHAPTER 34

JOHN AND BEVERLEY PEMBARLTEEN

Mr John Pembarlteen was arrested at his Models & Actors Management Agency Board Meeting.

The Pembarlteen's property and financial assets were immediately seized under proceeds of crime.

Mrs Beverley Pembarlteen, who had no knowledge of her husband's criminal activity, was devastated when she learned her husband was the power and financial recipient for the J Organisation Sex Trafficking ring.

Mrs Pembarlteen, who has long been an active community campaigner in the fight against sex trafficking since her daughter from her first marriage was kidnapped off the streets and discovered five years later dead from a drug overdose, immediately filed for divorce.

She has since been instrumental in leading police to find the accounts and records which showed the full details of the portfolio of facilities he owns, the names of all the staff he has hired and the girls he kept imprisoned and enslaved against their will at those locations - including her own daughter.

Thanks to Beverley's determined efforts to see justice served on her former husband and her willingness to assist police, over two thousand young women, ranging in age from thirteen years to thirty-two years in six different countries, were freed and returned to their families.

Mrs Pembarlteen has pledged any further monies found to have been legally earned and therefore entitled to be returned to her, shall be divided equally amongst the young victims, 'to help them rebuild their lives, with my deepest and sincerest apologies for what that despicable man did.'

Other celebrities have since come forth and donated large amounts for the fund, including Eric Hub bins, 'ChocCockHammer' and 'RanchoRamO', the three leading co-stars of Amber's in The Sexhouse Slave.

As at publishing this second edition, so far an additional one hundred and fifty million has been raised or donated and distributed to those young women; the police are still trying to locate the rest of the locations and workers.

𝒞HAPTER 35

ABSEXLUTION

Police seized all copies of the porn film, and all computers involved in the editing of the footage of Amberee's last ever porn film, *Absexlution*. They went on to successfully gain court orders for the movie to never be released, on the grounds the main actress was forced to film while under enslavement and distribution therefore being unethical if not unlawful.

Police will be seeking further court orders to have all other of Amberee's porn films removed from distribution on those same grounds.

Many of the men who have been known to have had sex with Amber during her eighteen year enslavement, or with the other young starlets forced to air on *The Porn Shack*, including most of the businessmen who booked *The Millionaire's Best Asset* recreations, have since gone on to seek legal advice to protect themselves against potential criminal proceedings, claiming they had no knowledge whatsoever the acts they participated in weren't consentual.

There has also been a loud call from the public for *Irene Vaan Der Been*, the woman arrested for shooting Amber Entacott, along with her fellow church constituents to publicly apologise for their wrongful judgements and vigilantism against Miss Entacott. So far, the church have failed to retract any of their comments saying they, "highly doubt the blasphemous slut has done any of it by force", despite the overwhelming evidence, nor retract their funding of Mrs Vaan

Der Been's criminal defence and nurse *Agnes Carenmore's* claim for unfair dismissal from the hospital following her instant termination and having her nursing qualifications cancelled when the intentional inflicting pain on Amberee caught on camera, while under the nurses care, came to light.

CHAPTER 36

PHILIP DWEITT

Amber took a huge risk in trusting me with her secret and had given me her complete story. With thanks to her, I was able to take the truth to the public - confirming she had indeed been a victim of sex trafficking and enslavement, breaking the distressing news Amber had died, and quick publishing the first edition of her autobiography.

In the interest of being completely honest, to respect Amber Entacott's aims in writing this book, I confess when I received the first letter from the writer claiming they were Amberee, porn princess, I wasn't at all convinced I was dealing with the real person. On the contrary, I was positive someone not entirely of full mental health had written to me, so I was only prepared to keep the letter on file and not take the actions requested.

Almost a week after I had continued on not having fulfilled Miss Entacott's request (to publicly state I now believed the porn princess to only be a nymphomaniac in much need of help), I had a visit to my home from one Senior Sergeant Adrian Titsson of the Australian Federal Police International Organised Crime Division, who risked providing me with his real identity and police credentials and asked to have our subsequent highly confidential conversation.

Senior Sergeant Titsson *stated* I had received a letter from a girl claiming she was Amberee. He knew this, he said, because he was working undercover in a crime organisation and had personally slipped the envelope into my home postal box, and was here now paying me a personal visit to ask for my cooperation and assistance in helping her and the many other girls like her.

The officer explained he had successfully infiltrated the criminal organisation and was working in secret partnership with a small, dedicated team of law enforcement in both countries, and confirmed my researched guesses about Amberee being the victim of sex slavery were, sadly, indeed her reality; but until he'd procured sufficient information to end the criminal operation, his higher authorities weren't prepared to expose the truth to save the life of a solitary victim. Their aim was, and rightly so, to save many. One of his partners, a close personal Australian colleague and friend, also having gained a trusted role as a 'Sebastian' had already been killed six months earlier to Miss Entacott over his trying to leave the organisation (following his wife becoming pregnant and his subsequent request to superiors for transfer from active undercover operations to other, less dangerous, time-consuming policing duties, which had been approved by his department, but resulted in his being coldly shot in the head when he notified Mr B.)

"I can only do tiny things to help Amberee, and the other girls," the officer told me. "I've taken a huge risk to meet with you. And I take a huge risk every time I let her mail to you slip through."

I understood, and offered to fulfil Amberee's request without the officer needing to issue a direct request.

So, I made the on-air announcement and settled the bet the public assumed I'd lost and my opponents arrogantly gloated over.

Senior Sergeant promised to keep ensuring he'd do whatever he could to help Amber write her letter's to me, on the condition I do as she requested and not break the story until she was safe.

With each letter which made its way into my letterbox, I was able to pass on the information to his trusted contacts as well as conduct my own private research without raising any suspicion. Not even my executive producers were made aware of the fact I was working on this one day explosive story. And, via my contact with his confidantes, I learned the officer had a sub-mission to help get the tracker removed from Amberee so she could escape once it was safe for him to risk assisting her.

The authorities, I thereafter dealt through, warned me a lot was happening behind the scenes and his team were proceeding very cautiously as the department were motivated to avoid information leaks, which could easily filter their way across to anyone in or dealing with the ring, ultimately ruining their pending sting.

I'd like to thank those undercover agents for suppling me with the computer and software systems which enabled me to carry out the research, without leaving any trace for outsiders to find what I, too, was up to behind the scenes in my attempt to assist free Amber Entacott and the other imprisoned starlets.

I, personally, was devastated Amber mimicked the fate of her character in *The Sexhouse Slave*; but I take small comfort knowing she is properly laid to rest.

CHAPTER 37

AMBER ENTACOTT

Amber Entacott is now buried in a grave next to her mother's holding pictures of her Mum and herself from her childhood. Officer Titsson, myself and Amber's former best school friends, Katie Westmore (nee Pearson) and Sally Cooper and their mothers, were amongst those in attendance. Sarah Ryleland claimed her strong feelings of guilt at not seeing Murk as an unsavoury character and the humiliation over her son's actions as reason she didn't think her attendance was appropriate. Amber's grandparents, who came under enormous public attack, after the release of the first edition of this book, over their indifference to their granddaughter's care ultimately resulting in the crimes against her being able to continue as long as they had, were conspicuously absent from the well-attended funeral service also. Both headstones stated mother and daughter were twenty eight years old when they died.

Amber Entacott made more than just the single achievement she believed she'd gained of credit-worthy acting worth noting in her young life:

- To her credit, she was instrumental in the discovery of a worldwide paedophilia ring. Australian police were able to track the names and identities of the underground chat rooms Murk Walters had socialised in, and sold pictures and videos of their 'ped-group prizes'.

- She aided in the demise in one of the largest sex trafficking and enslavement organisation exposed (though only a fraction of the operation was found and shut down) and was instrumental in enabling so many young women regaining their freedom and being able to return home to their loved ones.

- And lastly, thanks to her bravely risking her life to document what she knew, specifically recounting Daisy Mecklestein's background prior to her coming into the ownership of Murk Walters and the Seven Uncles, and the later seizing of computers enabled the department to find evidence to substantiate these allegations, Daisy's father, Mr Eric Mecklestein was charged with sexual molestation of his now deceased daughter and his involvement which ultimately led to her being sold to the criminal organisation that carried out her assassination.

In special recognition to Amber, earlier this year the film industry awarded her with an honorary Best Actress Award for Outstanding Performance in a recreation docu-movie, which is what The Sexhouse Slave has now been uniquely re-categorised to. The credits have rightly been changed from Amberee, porn princess to Amber Entacott, because that was her true identity.

The End

$\mathscr{W}$HY I WROTE THIS $\mathscr{S}$TORY

First up, I want to say that although I'm not a prude, I never intentionally set out to write a sexually graphic story. But it sort of came to me one day, and I abandoned every other project I was working on and 'channelled' Amber's story immediately - and kept writing her story, learning along with readers all the events that occurred in her short life. I didn't know what purpose I had been chosen to write her words for her, but I've never been so certain that I had to help her get her story into the world.

It may have occurred as a result of me doing research on the internet one day, for a completely unrelated topic that I was writing a course on, when I clicked on one of the search result links but when I clicked on a button to read more, I had about 25 windows all pop up. Every one of them what I considered offensive, sexually explicit content that I was not interested in exploring.

I had to close each window, and that made me briefly see some of what was on the web pages. So many of the pages had videos of women having sex, a close up of a penis pumping the girls vagina or mouth, semen being spurted onto girls that came in different shapes, sizes, and ethnicities. Some of the girls looked like they loved every second of what they were doing, and wanted to star in the video or live stream action that you, the web browser, clicked on to see more than the short snippet to attract your attention and get your juices flowing.

One image upset me greatly.

Of a supposed 18+ year old, naturally skinny though severely underweight Asian girl lying on her back looking like she was failing in her fight, a natural reaction to cry and grimace over the dick being rammed aggressively into her fragile looking body by the massively muscled up male pumping himself into her.

It was the silent pleading in her eyes, the way she was gripping the bed sheets and trying to cope with the next forceful insertion that made her body slide up a few inches on the bed on the forward penetration and backward by the same amount of inches on the exits. I burst into tears from the little that I was forced to watch of that auto playing video. Nobody is ever going to convince me that she wanted what was happening to her. It was the haunting look in her eyes that spoke the truth. The thing that distressed me most about that particular page, though, was the large text of a dollar sign, with numbers that ticked over counting upwards, and next to that a button that I could "click to keep the rough pumping" going. $10 would keep the action going for another thirty seconds.

Someone in the world paid during the time it took for me to move my mouse to the close button.

That girl looked nothing like Amberee to me.

Having to close so many different web pages that all seemed to flash lights and videos and still images, is, I think, what made Amberee the next day tap on my writer's shoulder and beg me to write her version of her story. She must have known that she was about to end her life, because Amberee kept me awake day and night urgently telling me her story over the three week period - I struggled to keep up with her, and even had to plead with her to let me get some sleep some nights.

Amberee, The Millionaire's Best Asset is not trying to glorify suicide nor suggest that that is an action for people in similar situations to take; Amberee strongly believed she had no alternative available to her. She'd tried resisting and was abused; she'd tried cooperating and was abused. Mr J. was determined to keep using and abusing her, and putting her through the hell she had been living through. She knew it was only about to get inconceivably worse for her - after all the horrible things that had already happened to her. And she let me know her story was a tragedy, with no happy ending.

Amberee deeply feared what was to come once she recovered from the shooting, feared gaining discharge from hospital.

I came to know her ... as she walked towards the bathroom, moments before the blood started gushing from her neck at an alarming rate, Amber, a smart girl who did pay attention to small details (even if it took her a while because of the medication) made the mental connection that Adrian-Sebastian had, since arriving at hospital, been calling her Miss Entacott and Amber or Miss (not Amberee nor puss). She feverishly attempted to summon the medical assistance she needed to save her own life. She had worked out that he must work as an undercover police officer - the only thing that made sense to her smart and logical reasoning. Amber sensed it had been him that had pleaded with her to "hold on and not die". She correctly intuited with all her heart and mind that the words she had missed hearing him finish with were "not when we are so close to rescuing you."

The behaviours in this fictional story is how some people mistreat other people in the real world - and that occurs in many forms far more commonly than we care to ever acknowledge.

Thanks for reading her story.

Kaycee

Please Donate

Sex Trafficking is a worldwide social problem; the victim's are not just teenage girls.

Please consider making a donation to any reputable charitable or humanitarian organisation that specifically helps rescue and support sex trafficked survivors.

Please Leave a Review

If you enjoyed this fictional story, please help spread the word by telling your family and friends about it, and consider leaving a review on Good reads and or the bookstore you purchased the print or ebook through, as this can really help the author.